THE POETICS OF MURDER

THE POETICS OF MURDER

Detective Fiction and Literary Theory

EDITED WITH AN INTRODUCTION BY
GLENN W. MOST AND WILLIAM W. STOWE

HARCOURT BRACE JOVANOVICH, PUBLISHERS
SAN DIEGO   NEW YORK   LONDON

Copyright © 1983 by Glenn W. Most and William W. Stowe

All rights reserved. No part of this publication may be reproduced or transmitted in any form or by any means, electronic or mechanical, including photocopy, recording, or any information storage and retrieval system, without permission in writing from the publisher.

Requests for permission to make copies of any part of the work should be mailed to: Permissions, Harcourt Brace Jovanovich, Publishers, 757 Third Avenue, New York, NY 10017.

Grateful acknowledgement is hereby given for permission to reprint the following works:

Roger Callois, II "Le roman policier: jeu" of IV "Puissances du roman," reprinted from *Approches de l'Imaginaire* by permission of Editions Gallimard. © Editions Gallimard 1974.

Geraldine Pederson-Krag, "Detective Stories and the Primal Scene," reprinted from *The Psychoanalytic Quarterly* 18, 1949 by permission of *The Psychoanalytic Quarterly*.

Jacques Lacan, "Seminar on 'The Purloined Letter,'" translated with introductory notes by Jeffrey Mehlman, reprinted from *Yale French Studies* by permission of *Yale French Studies*. No. 48, 1973 © 1973 by *Yale French Studies*.

Ernst Kaemmel, "Literatur unterm Tisch. Der Detektivroman und sein gesellschaftlicher Auftrag," reprinted from *Neue Deutsche Literatur* 10, 1962 by permission of Büro für Urheberrechte, German Democratic Republic. © Hanna Kaemmel, DDR–Berlin, 1962.

Richard Alewyn, "Der Ursprung des Detektivromans," reprinted from *Probleme und Gestalten* by permission of Insel Verlag. © Insel Verlag Frankfurt am Main 1974.

Helmut Heissenbüttel, "Spielregeln des Kriminalromans," reprinted from *Aufsätze zur Literatur,* by permission of the author.

Umberto Eco, "Narrative Structures in Fleming," reprinted from *The Role of The Reader: Explorations in the Semiotics of Texts,* translated by R. A. Downie, by permission of Indiana University Press.

Roland Barthes, Section XXXII "Delay" and Section XXXVII "The Hermeneutic Sentence," reprinted from *S/Z,* translated by Richard Miller, by permission of Hill and Wang, a division of Farrar, Straus and Giroux, Inc. and by permission of Jonathan Cape Limited on behalf of the Estate of Roland Barthes. Translation copyright © 1974 by Farrar, Straus and Giroux, Inc.

F. R. Jameson, "On Raymond Chandler," reprinted from *Southern Review* 6 (1970) by permission of the author.

Michael Holquist, "Whodunit and Other Questions: Metaphysical Detective Stories in Post-War Fiction," reprinted from *New Literary History* 3 (1971–1972) by permission of Johns Hopkins University Press.

Frank Kermode, "Novel and Narrative," reprinted from *Theory of the Novel: New Essays*, edited by John Halperin, by permission of Oxford University Press. Copyright © 1974 by Oxford University Press, Inc.

Steven Marcus, "Introduction" to *The Continental Op* by Dashiell Hammett reprinted by permission of the author.

Geoffrey H. Hartman, "Literature High and Low: The Case of the Mystery Story," reprinted from *The Fate of Reading and Other Essays* by permission of The University of Chicago Press, Copyright © 1975 by the University of Chicago, and by permission of *The New York Review of Books*, Copyright © 1972 Nyrev, Inc.

Albert D. Hutter, "Dreams, Transformations and Literature: The Implications of Detective Fiction," reprinted from *Victorian Studies* 19 (1975) by permission of *Victorian Studies* and the Trustees of Indiana University.

Stephen Knight, "'... some men come up'—the Detective appears," reprinted from *Form and Ideology in Crime Fiction* by permission of Indiana University Press and by permission of Macmillan, London and Basingstoke.

Dennis Porter, "Backward Construction and the Art of Suspense," reprinted from *The Pursuit of Crime* by permission of Yale University Press. Copyright © 1981 by Yale University.

Library of Congress Cataloging in Publication Data
Main entry under title:
The Poetics of murder.
  Bibliography: p.
  Includes index.
  1. Detective and mystery stories—History and criticism—Addresses, essays, lectures. I. Most, Glenn W. II. Stowe, William W., 1946–
PN3448.D4P54   1983   809.3′872   82-23429
ISBN 0-15-172280-3
ISBN 0-15-672312-3 (A Harvest/HBJ book : pbk.)

Designed by Jacqueline Schuman
Printed in the United States of America

First edition

A B C D E

CONTENTS

Introduction xi

Roger Caillois, The Detective Novel as Game *1*

Geraldine Pederson-Krag, Detective Stories and the Primal Scene *13*

Jacques Lacan, Seminar on "The Purloined Letter" *21*

Ernst Kaemmel, Literature under the Table: The Detective Novel and its Social Mission *55*

Richard Alewyn, The Origin of the Detective Novel *62*

Helmut Heissenbüttel, Rules of the Game of the Crime Novel *79*

Umberto Eco, Narrative Structures in Fleming *93*

Roland Barthes, Delay and The Hermeneutic Sentence *118*

F. R. Jameson, On Raymond Chandler *122*

Michael Holquist, Whodunit and Other Questions: Metaphysical Detective Stories in Postwar Fiction *149*

Frank Kermode, Novel and Narrative *175*

Steven Marcus, Dashiell Hammett *197*

Geoffrey H. Hartman, Literature High and Low: The Case of the Mystery Story *210*

Albert D. Hutter, Dreams, Transformations, and Literature: The Implications of Detective Fiction *230*

David I. Grossvogel, Agatha Christie: Containment of the Unknown *252*

Stephen Knight, ". . . some men come up"—the Detective appears *266*

D. A. Miller, The Novel and the Police *299*

Dennis Porter, Backward Construction and the Art of Suspense *327*

Glenn W. Most, The Hippocratic Smile: John le Carré and the Traditions of the Detective Novel *341*

William W. Stowe, From Semiotics to Hermeneutics: Modes of Detection in Doyle and Chandler 366

Source References 385
Suggestions for Further Reading 387
Index 389

ACKNOWLEDGMENTS

This book would not exist without the help of a large number of individuals and institutions. Howard Sandum and his staff at Harcourt Brace Jovanovich have been most helpful, as have the staffs of the English Department at Wesleyan (especially Janice Guarino) and the Classics Department at Princeton. The resources of the Princeton, Wesleyan, and New York University libraries have been put variously at our disposal, as have those of the Research Division of the New York Public Library. Many of the writers here have contributed more to the project than the simple permission to reprint their work. And our friends and colleagues—Karin A. Trainer, Richard H. Brodhead, Khachig Tölölyan, Charles Larmore, and many others—have been generous with support and advice. Much of the cost of typing and photocopying, finally, has been borne by our respective universities.

INTRODUCTION

The Golden Age of the detective novel is over, we are told, and so is the Golden Age of detective criticism. Chandler and Hammett are dead, and Sayers and Christie, and both halves of Ellery Queen. Some forty years have passed since W. H. Auden made his celebrated pitch for detective novels as profane replays of the Christian drama of guilt, confession, and atonement and since Edmund Wilson likened reading them to unpacking "large crates by swallowing the excelsior in order to find at the bottom a few bent and rusty nails." Meanwhile, though a large number of detective titles continue to be published every year, the pre-TV days of the "whodunit" as mass entertainment and intellectual *cause célèbre* are dead and gone. Hercule Poirot, Lord Peter Wimsey, the Continental Op, Philip Marlowe, and even such latecomers as Inspector Maigret, have all taken their places with Strephon and Amaryllis as emblems of a golden time.

But myths require revisions, and new traditions arise from the ashes of the old. While scholars are most usefully engaged in preserving and anthologizing the past, novelists and critics—even novelists and critics of detective fiction—go on writing, making it new, as Pound counseled, and making it strange, as the Russian Formalists advised. Just as poetry and its criticism—and, incidentally, sheep raising—survived the Golden Age that was already long gone when Theocritus and Virgil sang, so, too, detective fiction and its criticism—and, incidentally, murder—are thriving today, when the slouch hat and the sleek roadster have gone the way of the shepherd's crook. When, in the title of a famous attack on the genre, Edmund Wilson asked, "Who Cares Who Killed Roger Ackroyd?" he thought the answer—"No one"—was self-evident. History has proved him wrong; millions of readers continue to care who killed whom in thousands of detective novels, both old and new.

Furthermore, the criticism of detective fiction has never been healthier or more wide ranging than it is today. Taking advantage of their popularity, their relative simplicity, and their clear position as a model for many other kinds of narrative, contemporary literary critics and theorists have used detective novels as test cases and examples for all sorts of literary speculation, from investigations of narrative techniques to discussions of the social function of literature, its psychological effects, and the philosophical systems it assumes or promotes. These novels have come to be seen as contemporary folktales, cultural documents par excellence, and prime illustrations of mental and social processes.

This book brings together some of the most important studies of detective fiction to have been published in the last forty years. Rather than reprint the classic essays of the prewar years, we have chosen to assume that these studies are well known to most readers and have provided a bibliography for those who need to search them out. Here we have reprinted only more recent work. Most of it has been published before, but none of it has been easily and affordably available to readers, scholars, and students in college courses.

The emphasis in these essays is different, too, from what would have been the emphasis in an anthology of classic pieces. The earlier studies often were essentially attacks on the detective novel's pretensions or defenses of its literary merit. The debate on these issues continues; questions about the genre's value persist despite any number of claims to have answered them once and for all. But for the most part the articles collected here tend to put such questions to one side. Instead, they start from the obvious and indisputable fact of the popularity of detective fiction and ask, "Why?" Depending on the kind of answers they give, they can be arranged roughly into three groups.

The first of these emphasizes the relation of detective fiction to the art of storytelling, to "narrativity" as it is called, the structure of stories and the nature of narration. In its essence, the detective novel is almost pure narrative. Niceties of setting and characterization add charm, it is true, but the real power of the genre derives from its manipulation of stories and of the ways they can be told. Some detective stories are all plot, intricately woven tissues of causes and effects, coincidences and missed chances, that challenge the reader by their complexity. Others focus more on the telling, teasing their readers out of thought and patience by limiting the narrative point of view and controlling the rhythm and tempo of the exposition. As a result, detective novels have provided ideal material for theorists of plot and of narration.

Introduction

The essay by Roger Caillois, for example, treats plot intuitively, attributing the genre's popularity to its gamelike qualities, the way it stakes out a special world for itself and follows its own self-imposed rules and restrictions. Umberto Eco combines the scientific rigor of a structuralist with Caillois' speculative imagination. His essay on Ian Fleming's James Bond novels explores the effects such plot manipulations can be expected to have on readers and speculates on the cultural forces that make particular plots popular at particular times. Such questions occupied Roland Barthes throughout his career, and although the selections from his book *S/Z* reprinted here do not specifically deal with the detective novel, they formulate his approach to the general problem of narrativity in a way that has influenced many later discussions of detective fiction. The recent articles by Kermode and Porter are good examples, the former drawing on Barthes' work to relate detective fiction to the French *nouveau roman* and the latter applying his ideas to the analysis of a novel by Raymond Chandler.

A second approach found here is that of the sociologist, the critic who sees in detective fictions clues, not only to the solution of a murder, but also to profounder truths about the societies in which such murders are performed or recounted. After all, the detective novel is a form of popular entertainment: it should be possible to learn from the novel something about the populace it entertains. What connection, if any, is there between the rise of detective fiction in Western Europe and the United States in the last 150 years and the basic political, economic, and social features of the modern industrial democracies? Do detective novels celebrate a rage for disorder, spattering their readers with gore and titillating them with sex, or do they instead strengthen the conservative, rational bonds of repression and cooperation by reminding us always that, in the end, crime doesn't pay? These are the kind of questions that interest critics for whom literature can be read as a sophisticated barometer of social pressures.

The sociologically oriented essays we have chosen all diagnose the detective novel as a symptom of a certain stage in the development of capitalism. Knight focuses on the beginnings of modern industrial society, examining how its view of the committing and solving of crimes changes when the predominantly rural communities of the eighteenth century yield to the large cities of the early nineteenth century. In Miller's analysis, an already established urban industrial society uses the form of the police story to reflect upon the mechanisms of power and repression. Marcus and Jameson examine twentieth-century developments from a viewpoint closer to orthodox Marxism; the former discusses Dashiell Hammett, the latter Raymond Chandler. Finally, Kaemmel, an East German critic, claims on the basis of the absence of detective fiction in the socialist countries that its popularity in the West depends upon an adversary relationship between the capitalist state and its oppressed citizens.

A different kind of diagnosis is performed by a third group of critics who account for the appeal of the detective mode by reference to psychoanalytic theory. Freud himself was a great fan of detective fiction, and his therapeutic practice casts the analyst in the role of a detective, interpreting clues, uncovering "crimes," revealing the truth. His case studies—the Rat Man, Dora, the Wolf Man—rank with the best of Poe and Doyle. The most interesting of his modern followers have avoided crudely applying his techniques to the analysis of literary characters as though they were patients to be cured. Instead, they have used his doctrines to explore the motivation for the production of literary texts and to analyze their effects on their readers' psychic lives.

In her classic article of 1949, Geraldine Pederson-Krag attributes the fascination detective novels exert upon their readers to the analogy between the crime to be uncovered and the primal scene, which plays a central role in the Freudian theory of neurosis. The article by Lacan—which has influenced European thinkers at least as much as Pederson-Krag's has influenced American ones—uses a sophisticated analysis of a story by Poe to demonstrate the role of language in the constitution of personal identity, whereas Hutter explores the relations between detective fiction and dream interpretation in Wilkie Collins's *The Moonstone*. Freudian doctrines are not foreign to Hartman's approach; but rather than using literary texts to illustrate the theories, he exploits the insights the theories suggest in order to account for the literary qualities of the texts he considers.

Not all the essays we have reprinted fit neatly into one or another of these categories. Alewyn and Holquist are interested primarily in literary history. The former explores the irrationalist elements of detective fiction and connects them to German Romanticism; the latter examines the ties between classic detective fiction and postmodernist writing. Grossvogel and Heissenbüttel are more concerned with the literary value of the detective novel and with its effect upon its readers. Grossvogel condemns the traditional detective novel for creating easily solvable pseudomysteries that distract their readers from the more serious mysteries of real life; Heissenbüttel praises the genre for its openness and universal appeal.

Our own contributions represent, or so it seems to us, a more philosophical approach to the genre, an attempt to relate fictional investigation of crimes to an understanding of the nature of knowing itself, which sees questions of epistemology in terms of theories of interpretation. This tradition, loosely known as hermeneutics, has been represented most forcefully in recent years in the work of Hans-Georg Gadamer, notably in his major book, *Truth and Method.* Our essays consider the detective as a figure for the reader and take every method of fictional detection as a model for a theory of reading.

These categories, it will be seen, are neither hidebound nor exhaustive. We have therefore chosen not to use them to organize the essays themselves but rather to print the articles in the order in which they were first published and to let our readers piece together the puzzle they present in whatever manner they choose. As it happens, this chronological order reveals interesting groupings and provides an exemplary history of the development of literary theory in the last forty years.

THE POETICS OF MURDER

ROGER CAILLOIS

The Detective Novel as Game

What follows is the central section of a three-part essay called "Le Roman policier," and subtitled, "How intelligence retires from the world in order to devote itself to its games, and how society introduces its problems into those games." The first section outlines a history of the roman policier *(a term that need not be but is in this essay synonymous with "detective novel," and always so translated). The section reprinted here demonstrates the progressive strictness of the rules of the genre and their tendency to widen the distance between detective fiction and real life. The third section shows how detective novels maintain their relation to life despite the rules, and indirectly reminds us of the concerns and ambitions of such writers as Raymond Chandler, Georges Simenon, and John Le Carré. Interested readers will find a translation of this section in the magazine* Chimera *(vol. 5, no. 4, Summer 1947).*

Roger Caillois (1913–1978) was a scholar, teacher, editor, and member of the French Academy. His ideas in this essay fruitfully foreshadow a great deal of formalist, structuralist, and even moralist(ic) criticism of the detective novel. Interesting parallels can be drawn between his work and the essays by Heissenbüttel, Eco, and Grossvogel reprinted here. This piece was first published in Caillois' Le Roman Policier, ou comment l'intelligence se retire du monde pour se consacrer à ses jeux et comment la société introduit ses problèmes dans ceux-ci *(Buenos Aires: Sur [Editions des lettres françaises], 1941).*

The intellectual character of the detective novel is well established: rigorous reasoning has replaced frantic pursuit; the detective no longer disguises himself, but thinks. His investigation consists of a discussion of possibilities. He triumphs by demonstrating that one person had both a motive and an opportunity to commit a crime. The investigation clears those who have alibis or who can prove that they had nothing to gain by the victim's death. But these alibis must, of course, be verified, and it is always possible to discover that a certain solid citizen was not quite so indifferent to the dead man's disappearance as had been supposed: perhaps they had an old score to settle, or the survivor had plans to marry the victim's heir. The process of identifying the criminal is full of pitfalls: one realizes early on that all the characters had equally good reasons and perfectly good opportunities for killing, so one must find another procedure for separating the guilty from the innocent. The conditions of the murder lead one to impute a certain psychological character to the murderer. If the detective is hesitating among several suspects, he subjects them to a test, thereby revealing their true characters. Philo Vance in *The "Canary" Murder Case,* by S. S. Van Dine, attains in the course of a poker game the moral certitude he had lacked; in *Trois crimes à Veules-les-Roses,* by Marcel Marc, the murderer gives himself away in a chess game.[1] Tell me how you play, and I'll tell you if you've murdered anyone: people play in the same way that they kill, prudently or boldly, risking little, or a great deal.

And there are other methods for fixing guilt in current use: the guilty party, for example, is the one who is lying. But everybody lies, because everybody has some peccadillo on his or her conscience, some minor offense to be hidden in order to avoid a husband's anger in the case of an unfaithful wife or a master's rage if the offender is an indiscreet servant. The detective attempts to discover the source of these various lies, and the person who has lied without having anything to hide but the crime is the murderer. This progression sketches out the usual structure of the detective story: a series of hypotheses is first laboriously constructed and then summarily rejected until one last theory is found to fit all the facts which have forced previous theories to be abandoned and demonstrated the innocence of previous

---

[1] In similar fashion, M. Crabtree, in Stanislas-André Steeman's *L'assassin habite au 21,* discovers the truth while playing bridge. The three other players automatically team up against him: if they make such a natural team in a game, this must be the result of habit, and so they must be accomplices in real life.

suspects. This architecture is so predictable that it can be parodied in a brief anecdote such as the following. In a club for detective novel buffs someone is poisoned by a chocolate candy; each member carries out his own investigation and each establishes beyond any doubt the guilt of a different suspect. One of them even proves his own guilt by the most convincing arguments, and since he does not remember committing the murder, concludes that he must have plotted the crime and carried it out in moments of absent-mindedness. At last, all the contradictory proofs are laid out on a comparative chart of motives and opportunities, and the truth leaps forth of its own accord.

A detective in a novel uses his ingenuity to answer the same traditional questions that an actual investigator puts to himself: who? when? where? how? why? These questions do not evoke equal interest, however: one of them—how?—usually constitutes the central problem. Rarely has the crime been committed in banal circumstances. It must be enigmatic, and seem to mock natural law, verisimilitude, and good sense. The ingenuity of the *author* is demonstrated in the preparation of such a situation and in its simple and surprising resolution. He triumphs by *explaining the impossible*. He first presents an event as inadmissible, and then accounts for it easily, elegantly, without forcing anything or using elaborate contrivances. The value of a detective novel can be quite neatly defined by the affront to reason and experience contained in its point of departure, and the more or less complete and believable way that both reason and experience are satisfied by its conclusion. At bottom, the unmasking of a criminal is less important than the reduction of the impossible to the possible, of the inexplicable to the explained, of the supernatural to the natural. Each enigma is subject to as many solutions as the imagination can invent for it: the goal is to produce successively more rigorous ones; the pleasure comes from toying with the difficulties, from enumerating the obstacles which one sets out to overcome. This is why we come again and again across the so-called closed-room problem: a murder was committed in a place where the victim was alone and which no one could either have entered or escaped. If the whole setting of a detective novel constitutes a closed world, the fateful chamber is a compartment doubly sealed, a citadel doubly inaccessible, the ultimate enclosure at the heart of the holy of holies. A preliminary screening cuts off from the outside world all those who could possibly have taken part in the drama: this second closure makes it impossible that any of them actually did take part and inconceivable that the drama actually took place. It goes without saying, of course, that secret passages and devices capable of striking through solid walls are strictly forbidden. Still, there is a body in there, and it outrages reason. Perhaps the room was closed for a man but not for an ape (Edgar Allan Poe, "The Murders in the Rue Morgue") or a snake (Arthur Conan Doyle, "The Adventure of the Speckled Band"). Or perhaps the murder took place elsewhere and the victim was locked in after being struck down (G. Leroux, *Le Mystère de la chambre jaune*). Or maybe the murder was done in the room, but before it was closed up, and some mechanical device, a phonograph and a system of clockwork, for example, was used to suggest that the victim was alive after the place was sealed off (S. S. Van Dine, *The "Canary" Murder Case*). Or again, the door may have been locked from the outside with a key which was then placed on a table in the middle of the room using a wire fastened to the table with a pin which was jerked out when the wire was withdrawn (Edgar Wallace, *The Clue of the New Pine*). Or, finally, perhaps the person who opens the room loudly announces a murder *which has not been committed,* but which he commits forthwith, or he removes the clue which would clear up the mystery, or replaces the key with which the victim is supposed to have locked himself in.

It is easy to see in how many ways one can account for the inconceivable even in a case where all the material conditions have been deliberately invented to make such an accounting difficult. But in order to answer the *How?* question any degree of ingenuity is permissible. One has an inexhaustible reservoir of concrete circumstances at one's disposal; all the riches of the world are reduced to elements which endlessly lend themselves to ever-new combinations. Here the imagination never comes up short: it can choose to set up some secret device, to astonish the public by an elaborately staged false miracle, and to reveal at last that this marvel was the product of nothing but skill and intelligence. The pleasure one gets from a detective novel is not that of listening to a story, but rather that of watching a "magic" trick which the magician immediately explains. The author has set everything up in advance. The story opens on a rigged set; we do not even see the main event, but only its disturbing consequences. Then, without delay, the detective comes on the scene and discovers bit by bit a pigeon feather in the magician's pocket, the deftly concealed mirrors, the false bottom in the trunk, the wire that held the egg to the hat's lining. He unmasks the impostor. He shows that nothing happened the way we thought, that the murder was not committed where they said it was, nor at the time they stated. He proves that we have been tricked about the time and the place, and after giving the real answers to the questions *When?* and *Where?* he explains the unlikely *How?*

In this area, where everything obeys him, the novelist invents and embellishes as many devices as he can. Human beings, however, are not quite so docile, nor is their nature so indefinitely variable. They will only kill for a very limited number of reasons; detective novelists are always proposing new, complex, and original ways of committing a murder—this is what makes reading them pleasurable—but they are also always in danger of spoiling our pleasure by the monotony and the simplicity of the motives that lead to the crime. In detective literature the murder is always the consequence of scheming in the service of an instinct. But if the scheming can be constantly renewed, the list of instincts is short. The reader is quickly shocked to see so much mental energy expended and such ingenious plots invented only to satisfy passions both elementary and regrettably predictable. We never get very far from vengeance, self-interest, or fear, from love of money or legitimate self-defense, and it seems that the time-honored commonplaces "Is fecit cui prodest" or "Cherchez la femme" can hardly be improved. This sad poverty of motive is so striking that M. Pierre Véry has written a detective novel, *M. Malbrough est mort*, with the sole intention of making some innovation in this area condemned to boring repetition: he devotes a sort of prologue to enumerating all the possible and imaginable motives for murder, from the most banal to the most *recherché,* and announces at the end that his assassin has killed for none of them. Nevertheless, he tells us, the crime had "the most natural cause in the world." At the end of the story we learn that it was a reflex, a quasi-automatic move to escape suffering, an uncontrollable reaction comparable to the need to make noises when the silence becomes unbearable. This is a desperate solution, which reveals both the extreme lengths to which detective authors have to go to get out of the old ruts, and the uneasiness they experience when forced to keep using the same old motivations. A spontaneous gesture eliminates the possibility of diabolical premeditation. The detective novel will collapse if it has to be built on such arbitrary foundations.

On the other hand, there is not much to be said for recounting a political crime or a tale of espionage: this sort of fiction works much better in the adventure novel, since it tempts the author to lead us into byways which are impenetrably mysterious by nature, and destined to remain in shadow; its strange and multiple complicities keep skewing the original version of the problem and make it possible to provide a magical solution at any moment. Finally, there is always the great temptation to appeal to causes outside the frame of the story or to introduce an irrational element which is by definition not subject to logical reasoning. These are the murders which appear to be the ultimate effects of causes obscured by time or distance, which the detective discovers by cabling suddenly to Valparaiso or Calcutta. These are the murders committed by an Oriental sent to Europe by his sect to punish a scholar for violating a sanctuary or profaning a tomb. These deviations make the discovery of motive impossible, and are clearly related to the procedure which lets the detective alone know certain clues so that the reader has no chance at all of discovering the guilty party.

Similarly, the use of scientific marvels which change material possibilities corresponds to the recourse to madness or error which destroys the conditions in which rigorous foresight and proper deduction can be expected to function. It is true, however, that madness can be used to mask shrewdness; an extremely sly murderer may find some advantage in suggesting that his crimes were the work of a maniac. In such a case the author gains all the fantasy and strangeness that madness brings with it without in any way giving up the privilege of reason when it comes time for a final explanation. In *The Bishop Murder Case,* by Van Dine, the circumstances of the murders mimic those in nursery rhymes: Cock Robin is killed with a bow and arrow like the robin in the song, a little man dies with a hole through his neck, like the hero of another couplet, a gentleman perched on a wall has a bad fall like Humpty Dumpty, and an aged lady who lives in a sordid garret is worried lest she be taken for the "old woman who lived in a shoe." Naturally, all these coincidences are premeditated.

In Ellery Queen's *The Chinese Orange Mystery*, it is essential that no one realize that the body is that of a clergyman. This body, however, is clearly labeled by its collar, worn as a clergyman would wear it, with the opening at the back, and without a tie, which makes it impossible to turn it around. In order to hide the victim's identity, then, it is necessary to reverse *all* his clothes. Furthermore, the murderer even turns over the pictures and upends the furniture in the room in order to make people think that the murder was the work of someone obsessed with a certain methodical kind of disorder. Other ruses, too, are imaginable: one of Agatha Christie's culprits (in *The ABC Murders*) tries to throw the investigators off the track by including his crime in a series of murders which seem to be automatically determined. First he kills someone whose name begins with A in a village which shares that initial; then he does the same thing for B and C and so on, leaving next to each body an English railway timetable with its title—*A.B.C.*—in large letters on the cover. He continues this way until he arrives at his intended victim's initial, which happens to coincide with the initial of the town in which he lives, a coincidence which gave the murderer the idea for the whole series.

It is interesting that in all these cases madness is never used to justify arbitrariness or a lapse in logic, but rather to give the murderer's actions a systematic character, the appearance of an absolutely imperious and externally determined necessity. It is the mechanical aspect of madness that comes into play, and it leads not to the possibility of anarchy but to an excess of rigor.

The last question remains to be resolved. We know how and why the murder was done. We still do not know who did it. Here a serious technical problem arises: in order to create difficulty, the writer must keep the killer's identity hidden; in order to give the reader some chance of identifying the killer, the writer must at least present him as a character. This double obligation is the origin of the writer's contradictory duties: he must provide the elements of a solution which he also renders difficult and surprising. Once more the detective novel is heading for combinations of elements which must be at the same time extraordinary and indispensable. The culprit's discovery must shock and satisfy simultaneously. Early writers led the reader astray with sentimental unlikelihoods: the murderer always turned out to be the victim's best friend or closest relative. But the public eventually began to suspect these characters first of all, so the stakes had to be raised: the murderer's identity must challenge not only moral norms but what ordinarily pass for rational and material possibilities. The murderer was the one person who could not conceivably have committed the crime. He became, in fact, the detective himself, sometimes without knowing it, thanks to a dual personality (the prosecutor Hallers is a judicial Dr. Jekyll, entrusted with the task of inquiring into the misdeeds of Mr. Hyde), sometimes knowing it full well, thanks to a borrowed identity (the bandit Ballmeyer in *Le Mystère de la chambre jaune* passes himself off as Frédéric Larsan, a policeman; the fanatical Franz Heller, in Q. Patrick's *La Mort fait appel,*[a] pretends to be the detective Mac Fee). It also happens that the same character is leading two parallel lives: in Maurice Leblanc's *813* the adventurer Arsène Lupin is alternately a Russian prince suspected by the police and the chief of police himself. Finally, a real policeman may have been led to commit a murder under the pressure of accidental circumstances.

But it is not enough that the criminal and his pursuer be one and the same: it soon happens that the criminal and the *victim* are one. A person who craves vengeance passes himself off as dead, or perhaps, knowing that he has an incurable disease, actually kills himself, in both cases leaving enough clues to bring about his enemy's conviction. Or perhaps he intended to have a go-between collect on his life insurance, and so tried to make people believe he was dead. Or finally, to turn suspicion from himself, he may have arranged for an attack on himself shortly before murdering his victim.

All these surprises soon become commonplace: readers quickly learn to distrust unrecognizable corpses and the most brilliant investigators. Authors are then forced into audacities which sometimes seem excessive. We wonder, for example, if it is really fair, in Agatha Christie's *The Murder of Roger Ackroyd,* that the culprit turns out at the end to be the narrator himself, who in the course of a long and detailed account of the crime and its investigation has left out the fact that he was the murderer, and thus remained the unsuspectable character par excellence.

In fact, we are here in the presence of an extreme case, comparable

---

[a]Originally written in English under a title we have not been able to discover.—Eds.

to those limit cases in geometry or algebra, whose whole system is disrupted when a value becomes null, infinite, or equal to another. One might also mention those bridge problems in which one must slough off an ace to win, the chess problems which necessitate the sacrifice of the queen, and, in fact, all those tricky combinations which astonish us by sacrificing habitual actions to the demands of logic.

In any case, we like the murderer to have acted alone. Not only does the reader disapprove of two criminals acting independently, he is even bothered by what seems the cheap device of substituting a group of accomplices for a single murderer, since they can provide alibis for each other or perhaps devise among themselves a murder apparently carried out by one man at a time for which each accomplice has a solid alibi. Even worse is the case in which the author bases his plot on the existence of twins or doubles. What the reader demands is that a lone man with believable human motives pull off a crime that seems to defy reason but that reason can eventually uncover.

So the intellectual character of the detective novel is easily revealed. Any number of signs give it away: in magazines among the crossword puzzles and other games whose principal attraction is the pleasure of overcoming difficulty, a cartoon strip poses a detective problem whose solution will be found in the next issue; each volume of a certain collection of detective novels also contains chess problems and sometimes even purely mathematical puzzles. It seems therefore that the same kind of enthusiasts get their fun from figuring, whether it is a matter of trains passing one another, of vessels being filled and emptied, of pieces on a chessboard, or of any other exercise in which the mind amuses itself by arriving at a definite result by following fixed rules.

Of course, these coincidental facts would not tell us much about the detective story if the whole history of the genre did not proclaim its relation to the mathematical puzzle and the chess problem. In order to determine the time and the place of the crime, or the method used, or the motive and the identity of the murderer, the same rules seem more and more to be followed, consciously or unconsciously: separate a certain human setting from the rest of the world, make sure no one can come in or leave, forbid oneself the easy explanation by means of some unknown, powerful *deus ex machina,* and provide all the facts that helped create the mystery and that the reader must know in order to solve it. Once these conditions have been met, there is no essential difference between a detective novel and a mathematical problem. The last difference disappears when the author explicitly separates the givens and the unknowns in his story, notifying the reader at a certain point that he is now in possession of all the necessary information, that he knows everything that the detective knows, and that he is in a position to discover who the criminal is if only he thinks hard and well. This sort of "challenge to the reader" is becoming more common: Hugh Austin, Ellery Queen, Kathleen Sproul, Stanislas-André Steeman, among others, have adopted it. Nothing could better demonstrate the extent to which the detective novel has become a mental exercise. But there is something even more significant: as one notices how easy it is in a narrative to gloss over a significant detail or to cover it up and to emphasize instead some inconsequential quirk or foolishness, to use various devices to turn the reader's attention from the guilty and to focus it on the innocent person who can easily be made to seem mysterious and deceitful, one is tempted to abandon the form of the novel and even the material limits of the printed volume. It is easy to see that an author, even if he follows all the rules about the content of his work, is free to influence the reader's thought processes by his manner of presenting the facts. Having noticed this, one is tempted to supply nothing but the raw materials: the reader opens a thick folder similar to the dossier of a case in progress. It is filled with police reports, the depositions of witnesses, photographs of fingerprints, railway tickets, bits of hair, matches, bloodstained pieces of cloth picked up at the scene of the crime, which together constitute the necessary evidence. Everyone must study this evidence and deduce from it the identity of the criminal: his name is sealed in an envelope which the enthusiast can always rip open in a moment of despair and which contains in addition the whole solution of the problem he was supposed to solve himself. This is, in fact, the form taken by *Murder Off Miami,* by Dennis Wheatley and J. G. Links.[2]

At this extreme point, of course, the detective novel no longer deserves its name. It demonstrates its true nature at the end of its evolution. It is not a tale but a game, not a story but a problem. This is why just at the moment when the *novel* is freeing itself from all

---

[2] London, Hutchinson and Co. (no date). [Published in 1936.—Eds.]

rules, the *detective novel* keeps inventing stricter ones. Its interest, its value, and even its originality increase with the limitations it accepts and the rules it imposes on itself. Not only does it occupy a special place in the domain of the novel, it seems to be leaving that domain altogether, since it was born by a strange reversal of perspective. In the extreme case, it has nothing more in common with the novel. It neither describes nor analyzes. It takes from reality nothing but a setting, sees in psychology nothing but a research method or an aid to investigation, and is only interested in passions and emotions to the extent that they provide the impulse that sets in motion the mechanism it has constructed. It is nothing but abstraction and demonstration. It does not attempt to touch, to move, to exalt, or even to flatter the soul with a representation of its troubles, its suffering, and its aspirations. It is cold and sterile, perfectly cerebral. It gives rise to no feeling and evokes no dream. It is careful only to leave nothing in suspense, nothing unclear. Everything mysterious that it introduces, it makes coherent. It dumps the pieces of a puzzle in a heap (this time-honored comparison is repeated again and again by the detectives themselves) and puts them together. It makes a complete and simple picture from these incomprehensible fragments. It tends to eliminate all life and humanity; its one inescapable flaw is that it cannot dispense with humanity altogether, but is obliged to give us flesh-and-blood people with feelings and passions, and not robots, numbers, or chess pieces whose conduct and character would be absolutely determinable, without the disadvantage of remaining, no matter what, just a little unpredictable and capricious. This living creature's characteristic freedom of action, of which no author can totally deprive his characters, introduces an intolerable margin of insecurity into the calculations of even the most mathematical detective. The human element is necessary and remains irreducible. One tries in vain to tame it and to put it into equations by referring to those experiments, those tests which claim to establish "psychological certitudes."

The novel and the detective novel are therefore totally different: the first takes human nature as its basis and its subject, while the second only reluctantly admits human nature because it must. The detective novel would abolish human nature altogether if it could. In fact, however, it keeps quite a lot of what it wishes it could banish, and profits from the retention. It is only because the detective novel, however much it wishes it were an intellectual puzzle, remains a novel that it attracts so many readers who are indifferent to the charms of geometry. In spite of everything, it is necessary to speak of death, of murder, of violence. The detective novel must have a hero and it must recount a drama. It is a strange ambiguity that a genre with such strictly abstract ambitions ends up interesting its readers by such obvious emotional attractions.

And so we are led to open a new line of inquiry: just when we have demonstrated that the detective novel neither ought nor desires to take part in the traditions of the novel, we notice that it cannot get away from them altogether. After showing in what ways the detective novel is the reverse of the novel, we must look for the sense in which it represents on the contrary the most naive and the most primitively novelistic of all forms of the novel.

—Translated by William W. Stowe

GERALDINE PEDERSON-KRAG

Detective Stories and the Primal Scene

In this brief, classic essay, Pederson-Krag argues that the "intense curiosity" aroused by the detective story derives from its association with the primal scene, a psychoanalytic term referring to a child's first observation, either real or imagined, of sexual intercourse between his or her parents. The three essential elements of the detective story are for her "some secret wrongdoing between two people, revealed when one of the participants is discovered to have been murdered," a perceptive, persevering detective, and "a series of observations and occurrences" to be used as clues. The secret crime corresponds to the sexual act, while "the victim is the parent for whom the reader (the child) has negative oedipal feelings." The detective is, of course, the child, and the clues are the little details picked up by the child and eventually put together to form an understanding of the scene. The great attraction of the detective story is that it offers to replay the primal scene without threatening the viewer.

Pederson-Krag's essay is the simplest of the psychoanalytic pieces reprinted here, and should be read in conjunction with those by Hutter, Hartman, and Lacan. The juxtaposition of her treatment of the primal scene and Hartman's discussion of the scene of suffering is especially enlightening.

Dr. Pederson-Krag is a noted psychoanalyst and a founder of the Pederson-Krag Clinic on Long Island (New York). This essay was first published in Psychoanalytic Quarterly *in 1949.*

The popularity of detective stories in the English-speaking countries is a phenomenon psychoanalytically interesting because of its prevalence and because the reading of such fiction so frequently becomes habitual. About one-quarter of all fiction published annually in the United States—some three hundred volumes—is of this type (1). On two of the major radio networks, one-third to one-half of dramatic programs broadcast deal with death and detection, and a large percentage of moving pictures have plots about the detection of crime. There is little novelty in this vicarious pursuit of criminals. Each mystery drama or detective story is less interesting for specific details than because the gratification lies in certain basic elements which are always present.

The first element is some secret wrongdoing between two people, revealed when one of the participants is discovered to have been murdered. The other, the criminal, is kept hidden from the reader among a cast of characters who are respectable members of society. The next element is a detective whose perception is so acute, whose knowledge so unlimited, whose perseverance so undaunted that he can expose the criminal and reveal the method by which evil was done. Usually, there is also introduced a character, typified by Sherlock Holmes's Dr. Watson, a dullard, dazzled by the detective's brilliance, to whom everything is explained as it must be explained to the reader. The third element is a series of observations and occurrences, trivial, commonplace, and apparently unconnected. The detective discovers the significance of these and forges them into a chain of clues that leads to the criminal and finally binds him. The discovery of the criminal and his crime is a logical outcome of the combination of these elements, yet on the surface these elements seem to offer nothing which explains the insatiable demand of so many readers for this formula.

Bellak (2) notes that in detective stories anxieties are built up to be released at the height of tension, providing a pleasant experience for the reader. Bergler (3) observes that there is often a sense of uncanniness which recreates the reader's infantile belief in the omnipotence of his thought. Zulliger (4) reports that his pupils worked through the œdipal anxieties aroused in adolescence by reading sensational literature. Bellak (2) demonstrates that the reader indulges his aggressive impulses by identification with the criminal; while in his identification with the detective, he becomes the mighty, blameless superego (confirmed clinically by Buxbaum [5]), and also enjoys the detective's superior intellectual accomplishments without the trouble of acquiring them. Bergler (3) described identification with the victim, by which the reader could indulge his masochism, against which he would otherwise have to defend himself, and have also the rare pleasure of watching his own funeral and of seeing his enemies get their just deserts.

One does not deny the soundness of these observations; but surely they apply to the gratification in reading every kind of fiction in which the reader identifies himself with one or several of the characters to have any interest in the book at all. In fact, the conventions of detective fiction would seem to make it more difficult than otherwise to become identified with any of the characters delineated. Aggression, for example, has its fullest expression in the adventure rather than in the mystery story. In the latter the crime is committed off stage, and the final punishment is implied. Occasionally, there may be a little shooting as an occupational hazard for the detective, but usually his work is described as a safe, tedious routine. Though the detective is a genius and a leader of men, he is often portrayed as addicted to morphine or to drink, excessively fat or thin, foppish or pedantic, or a quaint homespun philosopher. Though authors, oddly enough, seem to think these peculiarities are endearing, they should deter the average reader from imagining himself to be such characters. The victim, too, is almost never a sympathetic personality. In life he was cruel, boorish, or miserly. He makes a brief, dramatic appearance as a corpse, but he holds the center of the stage all too briefly before he is removed.

Neither the allaying of anxiety nor identifications with various characters takes into account the unique feature of the mystery story: the intense curiosity it arouses. The circumstance in which the human capacity for curiosity reaches its first and most intense expression is the primal scene. Fenichel (6) states: "The observation of sexual scenes between adults creates a high degree of sexual excitement . . . and the impression that sexuality is dangerous. This impression is caused by the fact that the quantity of excitement is beyond the child's capacity to discharge and is therefore experienced as traumatically painful; the child may also sadistically misinterpret what he perceives, or the sight of adult genitals may give rise to castration fear."

Here is the first element of the detective story—the secret crime. Carrying the parallel further, the victim is the parent for whom the reader (the child) had negative œdipal feelings. The clues in the story, disconnected, inexplicable, and trifling, represent the child's growing awareness of details it had never understood, such as the family sleeping arrangements, nocturnal sounds, stains, incomprehensible adult jokes and remarks. The criminal of the detective drama appears innocuous until the final page. In real life he was the parent toward whom the child's positive œdipal feelings were directed, the one whom the child wished least of all to imagine participating in a secret crime.

Throughout the centuries there has been a popular demand for a sadistic return to the primal scene. For our largely illiterate forebears of the sixteenth, seventeenth, and eighteenth centuries, witch hunting took the place of mystery stories. There was a need to discover witches lurking in everyday surroundings, detected by trifling blemishes on their persons, by the movements of insects, by the behavior of animals, by the testimony of unfriendly or irresponsible people, or by their own utterances under torture. This resembles the clues of the mystery tale. There were in those days many avowed witches who were psychopaths or devotees of ancient pre-Christian cults; yet, as in the detective story it is the innocent bystander who bears the brand of Cain, so in those days it was often the improbable person whom the witch finder made his quarry. The witches were hounded to death for the unforgivable sin of fornication with the Devil. Freud (7) has shown that "the Devil is an image of the father and can act as an understudy for him."

Here, too, was a reenactment of the primal scene, evidence that there was, and is, a human compulsion to repeat this experience. The primal scene, the dramatic quintessence of all œdipal and castration fears, is a shockingly traumatic event. How traumatic it is depends on the manner in which it is experienced, on the infant's psychic development at the time, and on the relationship of parents to each other and to the infant. It is noteworthy that whatever the child's reaction it always entails anxiety, a large expenditure of psychic energy, and thrusts the necessity for several choices upon the unready ego.

First the ego must decide the extent to which it will acknowledge the reality of the happening. Some children try to deny their knowledge and consequently have to obliterate much of the outer world as well. One example of this is the hebephrenic patient of Fenichel (6) who "as a child had frequently witnessed primal scenes. He had developed a sadistic conception of the sexual act, an identification with his mother, and a consequent intensive sexual fear. The original reaction to the primal scene—hostility to both parents, especially toward the father—was warded off by means of an increasing indifference toward the world."

A woman patient, until the age of five, showed precocious interest in other people's private lives and mental processes. Then a small boy told her a kindergarten classic about sexual organs and their functioning. This story served to reactivate for her repressed memories of the primal scene, and she became frightened of the curiosity she had previously tolerated well. She shrank from recognizing anything that would suggest that one person differs from another in any way. In analysis she declared ignorance of the terms by which the gender of domestic animals is designated.

Similar to this is Mahler's case (8) of a boy who chronically forgot what he was told. One reason for this was the wish to deny his knowledge of sexual intercourse between his father and a woman not his wife.

The danger of a child's knowing is exemplified by the story of Little Red Ridinghood who made impertinent comments about the size of her grandmother's organs as seen in bed. Judging from the replies, what really interested her were the functions of these parts. This story warns, "Don't be inquisitive or you will learn more than you want to know"; but the alternative, an acceptance of the primal scene, would entail anxiety and aggression. The child would have to look, overhear, correlate, speculate, and theorize, all in an atmosphere of danger derived from its own anxiety and the disapproval of adults. Since such discoveries are incompatible with accepted ideas of the parents, they are repressed, although they can occasionally be recovered with little anxiety. In this category is Bonaparte's patient (9) who as early as the fourth week of analysis produced memories of primal scenes referable to the first two years of life.

Having accepted such knowledge, the ego's task of choosing is not yet over. It must now decide whether to accept the reality of the parents' sexual activities from which the child is excluded, or to have the perilous fantasy of taking part in these activities. Little Hans took the latter course (10). He said, "In the night there was a big giraffe in the room and a crumpled one; and the big one called out because I took the crumpled one away from it. Then it stopped calling out, and then I sat down on top of the crumpled one." This was interpreted as Hans saying to his father, "Call out as much as you like, but Mummy takes me into bed all the same and Mummy belongs to me!"

A man in analysis had the wish to be the love object of a sadistic father. He imitated his mother's mannerisms, was irresponsible and financially dependent on his father, later on his wife. He appraised all his acquaintances by the extent to which they could serve as substitute fathers. He repeatedly conjured up possibilities of threat and punishment and on these occasions reacted as he had when overhearing a primal scene: he wanted to escape, was unable to do so, and developed tachycardia and dyspnea. During his first nineteen years, this patient shared a room with his parents. His symptoms were the result of his unconscious fantasy of replacing the mother in the father's bed. Fears of castration kept him a passive spectator. This recalls the classic dream of the Wolf Man (11), in which a window opened and the dreamer saw white wolves, immobile, gazing at him from the boughs of a Christmas tree. Freud, describing the fragment of reality at the core of this dream, said, "He [the dreamer] suddenly woke up and saw in front of him a scene of violent movement at which he looked with strained attention."

Whether the reaction to the primal scene has been denial or acceptance, with or without participation, the repressed memory is in every instance charged to some degree with painful affect. The mystery story attempts to present a more satisfying, less painful primal scene from the standpoint of the unconscious. This fictional primal scene satisfies the voyeurs who, like the Wolf Man, gazed with strained attention at the scene of parental coitus.

The voyeur is never entirely satisfied with his peeping which he has the compulsion endlessly to repeat like the detective story addict who rereads the same basic mystery tale without tedium. In the gradual revelation of clues that make up the bulk of the narrative, the reader is presented with one significant detail after another, a protracted visual forepleasure. Finally the crime is reconstructed, the mystery solved, that is, the primal scene is exposed. The reader has no need to take part in this by directly identifying with the characters because the gratification is obtained from being a passive onlooker.

Edgar Allan Poe, the progenitor of all modern mystery and detective fiction, with the publication of *Tales of Mystery and Imagination* in 1841, was the child of actors. Marie Bonaparte's intensive psychological study of Poe and his works traces in the greatest detail the enormous influence of the primal scene in the genesis of his tales (14). Sir Arthur Conan Doyle, creator of Sherlock Holmes in 1887, who was an ophthalmologist (frustrated by a lack of patients), was directly inspired by Poe.[1]

In participating in the detective story version of the primal scene, the reader's ego need fear no punishment for libidinal or aggressive urges. In an orgy of investigation, the ego, personified by the great detective, can look, remember, and correlate without fear and without reproach in utter contrast to the ego of the terrified infant witnessing the primal scene.

Bergler (3) observed that the sleuth is seldom a member of the official police; rather, he is a gifted amateur, often a dilettante. An inquiring child, free from anxiety, could hardly conduct official investigations. The peculiarities with which many writers endow their detectives allow the reader, who is a little frightened by what he is doing, to say, "This is not I; don't blame me." It is the child in disguise wearing father's cap or mother's coat to surprise and perhaps frighten the adults before its identity is revealed.

Dr. Watson, Sherlock Holmes's plodding companion, is more important than a literary device. He supplies the reader with a safe defense, for should the punishing superego threaten, the reader can point to this character and say, "This is I. I was simply standing by." In the complete knowledge of the crime, achieved by the detective, the ego may participate as either or both parents in the primal scene. Knowledge, as Chadwick has shown, may be the equivalent of male or female sexuality (12). However, this secondhand sexuality is often insufficient. In many books the detective or one of his surrogates, by

---

[1] *Cf.* Hanns Sachs, *Edgar Allan Poe.* Psychoanalytic Quarterly, IV, 1935, p. 294, and Marie Bonaparte, *The Murders in the Rue Morgue.* Psychoanalytic Quarterly, IV, 1935, p. 259.—Ed.

a conspicuous display of stupidity, is made the helpless prisoner of the villain. The reader cannot resist entering the parental bed, dangerous though it is. This prisoner, of course, is always rescued unscathed.

In conclusion, the reader addicted to mystery stories tries actively to relive and master traumatic infantile experiences he once had to endure passively. Becoming the detective, he gratifies his infantile curiosity with impunity, redressing completely the helpless inadequacy and anxious guilt unconsciously remembered from childhood.

REFERENCES

1. Haycraft, H.: *Murder for Pleasure.* New York: D. Appleton-Century Co., Inc., 1941.
2. Bellak, Leopold: *Psychology of Detective Stories and Related Problems.* Psa. Rev., XXXII, 1945.
3. Bergler, Edmund: *Mystery Fans and the Problem of Potential Murderers.* Amer. J. of Orthopsychiatry, XV, 1945.
4. Zulliger, Hans: *Der Abenteurer-Schundroman.* Ztschr. f. psa. Pädagogik, VII, 1933.
5. Buxbaum, Edith: *The Role of Detective Stories in a Child Analysis.* Psychoanalytic Quarterly, X, 1941.
6. Fenichel, Otto: *The Psychoanalytic Theory of the Neurosis.* New York: W. W. Norton & Co., Inc., 1945.
7. Freud, Sigmund: *A Neurosis of Demoniacal Possession in the Seventeenth Century.* Coll. Papers, IV.
8. Mahler, Margaret S.: *Pseudo Imbecility, the Magic Cap of Invisibility.* Psychoanalytic Quarterly, XI, 1942.
9. Bonaparte, Marie: Notes on the Analytical Discovery of the Primal Scene. In *Psychoanalytic Study of the Child, Vol. I.* New York: International Universities Press, 1945.
10. Freud, Sigmund: *A Phobia in a Five-Year-Old Boy.* Coll. Papers, III.
11. ———: *From the History of an Infantile Neurosis.* Coll. Papers, III.
12. Chadwick, Mary: *Notes upon the Acquisition of Knowledge.* Psa. Rev., XIII, 1926.
13. Reik, Theodor: *The Unknown Murderer.* New York: Prentice-Hall, Inc., 1945. (Ed.)
14. Bonaparte, Marie: *Edgar Allan Poe.* Paris: Editions Denoël et Steele, 1933. (Ed.)

JACQUES LACAN

Seminar on "The Purloined Letter"

Lacan analyzes Poe's tale to demonstrate the ways in which, according to his own linguistic and Freudian theories, the identity of a subject is determined by the movement of language, by a chain of signifiers (letters) that assign to him his place. In the course of the tale, the movement of the letter organizes the characters into two triangles (King–Queen–Minister; Police–Minister–Dupin) based upon their degree of blindness to its meaning; at the end, the letter reaches its destination, but not without duping Dupin.

Jacques Lacan, the best known of the French reinterpreters of Freud, was born in 1901 and died in 1982. This essay was written in 1956, published in France in Lacan's Ecrits *in 1966, and in the United States in Jeffrey Mehlman's English translation in 1972 (*Yale French Studies *48). We reprint here not only this translation of Lacan's text but also Mehlman's helpful introductory and explanatory notes.*

Despite and because of the extraordinary complexity of the "Seminar," it has been enormously influential. (For a recent response, see Barbara Johnson's The Critical Difference *[Baltimore, 1980].) The reader who wants a general introduction to Lacan's thought is urged to consult Anthony Wilden's* The Language of the Self *(Baltimore, 1968). The whole volume of* Yale French Studies *from which this article is reproduced is also of interest, as is a later volume entitled* Literature and Psychoanalysis: The Question of Reading: Otherwise *(originally YFS 55/56 [1977], now available as a separate paperback).*

Introductory Note

If "psychoanalytic criticism" is an effort to bring analytic categories to bear in the solution of critical problems, Lacan's text is certainly not an example of that discipline. One has the feeling that, on the contrary, in the confrontation between analysis and literature, the former's role for Lacan is not to solve but to open up a new kind of textual problem. The Poe text, then, is in many ways a pretext, an exemplary occasion for Lacan to complicate the question of *Beyond the Pleasure Principle*. It is indeed a "purloined letter."

The crux of the problem is in the ambiguity of the term *letter* in Lacan's analysis. It may mean either typographical character or epistle. Why?

1. As typographical character, the letter is a unit of signification without any meaning in itself. In this it resembles the "memory trace," which for Freud is never the image of an event, but a term which takes on meaning only through its differential opposition to other traces. It is a particular arrangement of "frayings" . . . The striking image of this situation in the tale is that we never know the *contents* of the crucial letter. Here then is a psychoanalysis indifferent to deep meanings, concerned more with a latent organization of the manifest than a latent meaning beneath it. In its refusal to accord any "positive" status to linguistic phenomena, this might be viewed as Lacan's Saussurean side (see text note 24).

2. As epistle, the letter allows Lacan to play on the intersubjective relations which expropriate the individual. ("To whom does a letter belong?") It is Lévi-Strauss (and Mauss) who are no doubt at the source of this effort to think of the Oedipus complex in terms of a structure of *exchange* crucial to the "fixation" of unconscious "memory traces."

These losses—of the plenitude of meaning and the security of (self-) possession—are thus the principal modes of the Lacanian *askesis* in this parable of analysis. To which we may add a third: that of metalanguage. By which we mean (a) that the Prefect is already repeating the "events" he recounts at the moment he pretends to view them objectively; (b) even Dupin (as analyst) is trapped in the fantasmatic circuit (repetitive structure, mobile scenario . . .) at the moment of his rage against the Minister. The difference between the Prefect (trapped in the transference) and Dupin (counteracting the countertransference) is that the latter is intermittently aware of his loss.

In translating the text, we found that a large measure of its difficulty was a function of Lacan's idiosyncratic use of prepositions. As a result, the reader has to play with various possibilities of subordination in a number of sentences in order to determine the "proper" one(s). For better or worse, in English we have (necessarily) chosen to normalize the use of prepositions. We have thus occasionally been obliged to chart a course through Lacan's labyrinth rather than reproduce that labyrinth whole. There has no doubt been a concomitant loss (in syntactical richness) and gain (in clarity).

The notes we have added to the text (signed —J.M.) are, on the whole, explanations of allusions or clarifications of particularly oblique points.

This text was originally written in 1956 and—along with an introductory postface—is the opening text of the *Ecrits*.

—J. M.

> *Und wenn es uns glückt,*
> *Und wenn es sich schickt,*
> *So sind es Gedanken.*[a]

● ur inquiry has led us to the point of recognizing that the repetition automatism *(Wiederholungszwang)* finds its basis in what we have called the *insistence* of the signifying chain.[1] We have elaborated that notion itself as a correlate of the *ex-sistence* (or eccentric place) in which we must necessarily locate the subject of the unconscious if we are to take Freud's discovery seriously.[2] As is known, it is in the realm of experience inaugurated by psychoanalysis that we may grasp along what imaginary lines the human organism, in the most intimate

---

[a]"And if we're successful, / And if it's fitting, / Then they are thoughts."—Eds.
[1]The translation of repetition *automatism*—rather than *compulsion*—is indicative of Lacan's speculative effort to reinterpret Freudian "overdetermination" in terms of the laws of probability. (Chance is *automaton*, a "cause not revealed to human thought," in Aristotle's *Physics*.) Whence the importance assumed by the Minister's passion for gambling later in Lacan's analysis. Cf. *Ecrits*, pp. 41–61.—J.M.
[2]Cf. Heidegger, *Vom Wesen der Wahrheit*. Freedom, in this essay, is perceived as an "ex-posure." *Dasein* ex-sists, stands out "into the disclosure of what is." It is *Dasein's* "ex-sistent in-sistence" which preserves the disclosure of beings.—J.M.

recesses of its being, manifests its capture in a *symbolic* dimension.³ The lesson of this seminar is intended to maintain that these imaginary incidences, far from representing the essence of our experience, reveal only what in it remains inconsistent unless they are related to the symbolic chain which binds and orients them.

We realize, of course, the importance of these imaginary impregnations *(Prägung)* in those partializations of the symbolic alternative which give the symbolic chain its appearance. But we maintain that it is the specific law of that chain which governs those psychoanalytic effects that are decisive for the subject: such as foreclosure *(Verwerfung)*, repression *(Verdrängung)*, denial *(Verneinung)* itself—specifying with appropriate emphasis that these effects follow so faithfully the displacement *(Entstellung)* of the signifier that imaginary factors, despite their inertia, figure only as shadows and reflections in the process.⁴

But this emphasis would be lavished in vain if it served, in your opinion, only to abstract a general type from phenomena whose particularity in our work would remain the essential thing for you and whose original arrangement could be broken up only artificially.

Which is why we have decided to illustrate for you today the truth which may be drawn from that moment in Freud's thought under study—namely, that it is the symbolic order which is constitutive for the subject—by demonstrating in a story the decisive orientation which the subject receives from the itinerary of a signifier.⁵

It is that truth, let us note, which makes the very existence of fiction possible. And in that case, a fable is as appropriate as any other narrative for bringing it to light—at the risk of having the fable's coherence put to the test in the process. Aside from that reservation, a fictive tale even has the advantage of manifesting symbolic necessity more purely to the extent that we may believe its conception arbitrary.

Which is why, without seeking any further, we have chosen our

---

³For the meanings Lacan attributes to the terms *imaginary* and *symbolic,* see J. Laplanche and J. B. Pontalis, *The Language of Psychoanalysis,* translated by Donald Nicolson-Smith (London: Hogarth Press, 1973).—J.M.
⁴For the notion of *foreclosure,* the defense mechanism specific to psychosis, see Laplanche and Pontalis.—J.M.
⁵For the notion of the signifier (and its relation to the Freudian "memory trace,") see Jeffrey Mehlman, "The Floating Signifier from Lévi-Strauss to Lacan," *Yale French Studies* 48 (1972), pp. 10–37.—J.M.

example from the very story in which the dialectic of the game of even or odd—from whose study we have but recently profited—occurs.⁶ It is, no doubt, no accident that this tale revealed itself propitious to pursuing a course of inquiry which had already found support in it.

As you know, we are talking about the tale which Baudelaire translated under the title *La lettre volée*. At first reading, we may distinguish a drama, its narration, and the conditions of that narration.

We see quickly enough, moreover, that these components are necessary and that they could not have escaped the intentions of whoever composed them.

The narration, in fact, doubles the drama with a commentary without which no *mise en scène* would be possible. Let us say that the action would remain, properly speaking, invisible from the pit—aside from the fact that the dialogue would be expressly and by dramatic necessity devoid of whatever meaning it might have for an audience: in other words, nothing of the drama could be grasped, neither seen nor heard, without, dare we say, the twilighting which the narration, in each scene, casts on the point of view that one of the actors had while performing it.

There are two scenes, the first of which we shall straightway designate the primal scene,ᵇ and by no means inadvertently, since the second may be considered its repetition in the very sense we are considering today.

The primal scene is thus performed, we are told, in the royal boudoir, so that we suspect that the person of the highest rank, called the "exalted personage," who is alone there when she receives a letter, is the Queen. This feeling is confirmed by the embarrassment into which she is plunged by the entry of the other exalted personage, of whom we have already been told prior to this account that the knowledge he might have of the letter in question would jeopardize for the lady nothing less than her honor and safety. Any doubt that he is, in fact, the King is promptly dissipated in the course of the scene which begins with the entry of the Minister D——. At that moment, in fact,

---

⁶Lacan's analysis of the guessing game in Poe's tale entails demonstrating the insufficiency of an *imaginary* identification with the opponent as opposed to the *symbolic* process of an identification with his "reasoning." See *Ecrits*, p. 59.—J.M.
ᵇSee headnote to Pederson-Krag's essay beginning on page 13.—Eds.

the Queen can do no better than to play on the King's inattentiveness by leaving the letter on the table "face down, address uppermost." It does not, however, escape the Minister's lynx eye, nor does he fail to notice the Queen's distress and thus to fathom her secret. From then on everything transpires like clockwork. After dealing in his customary manner with the business of the day, the Minister draws from his pocket a letter similar in appearance to the one in his view, and, having pretended to read it, he places it next to the other. A bit more conversation to amuse the royal company, whereupon, without flinching once, he seizes the embarrassing letter, making off with it, as the Queen, on whom none of his maneuver has been lost, remains unable to intervene for fear of attracting the attention of her royal spouse, close at her side at that very moment.

Everything might then have transpired unseen by a hypothetical spectator of an operation in which nobody falters, and whose *quotient* is that the Minister has filched from the Queen her letter and that—an even more important result than the first—the Queen knows that he now has it, and by no means innocently.

A *remainder* that no analyst will neglect, trained as he is to retain whatever is significant, without always knowing what to do with it: the letter, abandoned by the Minister, and which the Queen's hand is now free to roll into a ball.

Second scene: in the Minister's office. It is in his hotel, and we know —from the account the Prefect of police has given Dupin, whose specific genius for solving enigmas Poe introduces here for the second time—that the police, returning there as soon as the Minister's habitual, nightly absences allow them to, have searched the hotel and its surroundings from top to bottom for the last eighteen months. In vain, although everyone can deduce from the situation that the Minister keeps the letter within reach.

Dupin calls on the Minister. The latter receives him with studied nonchalance, affecting in his conversation romantic ennui. Meanwhile, Dupin, whom this pretense does not deceive, his eyes protected by green glasses, proceeds to inspect the premises. When his glance catches a rather crumpled piece of paper—apparently thrust carelessly in a division of an ugly pasteboard card rack, hanging gaudily from the middle of the mantelpiece—he already knows that he's found what he's looking for. His conviction is reenforced by the very details which seem to contradict the description he has of the stolen letter, with the exception of the format, which remains the same.

Whereupon he has but to withdraw, after "forgetting" his snuff box on the table, in order to return the following day to reclaim it—armed with a facsimile of the letter in its present state. As an incident in the street, prepared for the proper moment, draws the Minister to the window, Dupin in turn seizes the opportunity to snatch the letter while substituting the imitation, and has only to maintain the appearances of a normal exit.

Here, as well, all has transpired, if not without noise, at least without commotion. The quotient of the operation is that the Minister no longer has the letter, but, far from suspecting that Dupin is the culprit who has ravished it from him, knows nothing of it. Moreover, what he is left with is far from insignificant for what follows. We shall return to what brought Dupin to inscribe a message on his counterfeit letter. Whatever the case, the Minister, when he tries to make use of it, will be able to read these words, written so that he may recognize Dupin's hand: "Un dessein si funeste / S'il n'est digne d'Atreé est digne de Thyeste," whose source, Dupin tells us, is Crébillon's *Atreé*.[7]

Need we emphasize the similarity of these two sequences? Yes, for the resemblance we have in mind is not a simple collection of traits chosen only in order to delete their difference. And it would not be enough to retain those common traits at the expense of the others for the slightest truth to result. It is rather the intersubjectivity in which the two actions are motivated that we wish to bring into relief, as well as the three terms through which it structures them.[8]

The special status of these terms results from their corresponding simultaneously to the three logical moments through which the decision is precipitated and the three places it assigns to the subjects among whom it constitutes a choice.

That decision is reached in a glance's time.[9] For the maneuvers

---

[7] "So infamous a scheme, / If not worthy of Atreus; is worthy of Thyestes." The lines from Atreus's monologue in act 5, scene 5 of Crébillon's play refer to his plan to avenge himself by serving his brother the blood of the latter's own son to drink.—J.M.

[8] This intersubjective setting which coordinates three terms is plainly the oedipal situation. The illusory security of the initial *dyad* (King and Queen in the first sequence) will be shattered by the introduction of a *third* term.—J.M.

[9] The necessary reference here may be found in "Le Temps logique et l'Assertion de la certitude anticipée," *Ecrits*, p. 197.

which follow, however stealthily they prolong it, add nothing to that glance, nor does the deferring of the deed in the second scene break the unity of that moment.

This glance presupposes two others, which it embraces in its vision of the breach left in their fallacious complementarity, anticipating in it the occasion for larceny afforded by that exposure. Thus, three moments, structuring three glances, borne by three subjects, incarnated each time by different characters.

The first is a glance that sees nothing: the King and the police.

The second, a glance which sees that the first sees nothing and deludes itself as to the secrecy of what it hides: the Queen, then the Minister.

The third sees that the first two glances leave what should be hidden exposed to whomever would seize it: the Minister and finally Dupin.

In order to grasp in its unity the intersubjective complex thus described, we would willingly seek a model in the technique legendarily attributed to the ostrich attempting to shield itself from danger; for that technique might ultimately be qualified as political, divided as it here is among three partners: the second believing itself invisible because the first has its head stuck in the ground and all the while letting the third calmly pluck its rear; we need only enrich its proverbial denomination by a letter, producing *la politique de l'autruiche*, for the ostrich itself to take on forever a new meaning.[10]

Given the intersubjective modulus of the repetitive action, it remains to recognize in it a *repetition automatism* in the sense that interests us in Freud's text.

The plurality of subjects, of course, can be no objection for those who are long accustomed to the perspectives summarized by our formula: *the unconscious is the discourse of the Other*.[11] And we will not recall now what the notion of the *immixture of subjects,* recently introduced in our reanalysis of the dream of Irma's injection, adds to the discussion.

What interests us today is the manner in which the subjects relay

---

[10]*La politique de l'autruiche* condenses ostrich *(autruche),* other people *(autrui),* and (the politics of) Austria *(Autriche).*—J.M.

[11]Such would be the crux of the Oedipus complex: the assumption of a desire which is originally another's, and which, in its displacements, is perpetually other than "itself."—J.M.

each other in their displacement during the intersubjective repetition.

We shall see that their displacement is determined by the place which a pure signifier—the purloined letter—comes to occupy in their trio. And that is what will confirm for us its status as repetition automatism.

It does not, however, seem excessive, before pursuing this line of inquiry, to ask whether the thrust of the tale and the interest we bring to it—to the extent that they coincide—do not lie elsewhere.

May we view as simply a rationalization (in our gruff jargon) the fact that the story is told to us as a police mystery?

In truth, we should be right in judging that fact highly dubious as soon as we note that everything which warrants such mystery concerning a crime or offense—its nature and motives, instruments, and execution; the procedure used to discover the author, and the means employed to convict him—is carefully eliminated here at the start of each episode.

The act of deceit is, in fact, from the beginning as clearly known as the intrigues of the culprit and their effects on his victim. The problem, as exposed to us, is limited to the search for and restitution of the object of that deceit, and it seems rather intentional that the solution is already obtained when it is explained to us. Is *that* how we are kept in suspense? Whatever credit we may accord the conventions of a genre for provoking a specific interest in the reader, we should not forget that "the Dupin tale," this the second to appear, is a prototype, and that even if the genre were established in the first, it is still a little early for the author to play on a convention.[12]

It would, however, be equally excessive to reduce the whole thing to a fable whose moral would be that in order to shield from inquisitive eyes one of those correspondences whose secrecy is sometimes necessary to conjugal peace, it suffices to leave the crucial letters lying about on one's table, even though the meaningful side be turned face down. For that would be a hoax which, for our part, we would never recommend anyone try, lest he be gravely disappointed in his hopes.

Might there then be no mystery other than, concerning the Prefect,

---

[12] The first "Dupin tale" was "The Murders in the Rue Morgue."—J.M.

an incompetence issuing in failure—were it not perhaps, concerning Dupin, a certain dissonance we hesitate to acknowledge between, on the one hand, the admittedly penetrating, though, in their generality, not always quite relevant remarks with which he introduces us to his method and, on the other, the manner in which he, in fact, intervenes?

Were we to pursue this sense of mystification a bit further we might soon begin to wonder whether, from that initial scene which only the rank of the protagonists saves from vaudeville, to the fall into ridicule which seems to await the Minister at the end, it is not this impression that everyone is being duped which makes for our pleasure.

And we would be all the more inclined to think so in that we would recognize in that surmise, along with those of you who read us, the definition we once gave in passing of the modern hero, "whom ludicrous exploits exalt in circumstances of utter confusion."[13]

But are we ourselves not taken in by the imposing presence of the amateur detective, prototype of a latter-day swashbuckler, as yet safe from the insipidity of our contemporary *superman?*

A trick . . . sufficient for us to discern in this tale, on the contrary, so perfect a verisimilitude that it may be said that truth here reveals its fictive arrangement.

For such indeed is the direction in which the principles of that verisimilitude lead us. Entering into its strategy, we indeed perceive a new drama we may call complementary to the first, insofar as the latter was what is termed a play without words whereas the interest of the second plays on the properties of speech.[14]

If it is indeed clear that each of the two scenes of the real drama is narrated in the course of a different dialogue, it is only through access to those notions set forth in our teaching that one may recognize that it is not thus simply to augment the charm of the exposition, but that the dialogues themselves, in the opposite use they make of the powers of speech, take on a tension which makes of them a different drama, one which our vocabulary will distinguish from the first as persisting in the symbolic order.

The first dialogue—between the Prefect of police and Dupin—is

---

[13]Cf. "Fonction et champ de la parole et du langage" in *Ecrits.* Translated by A. Wilden, *The Language of the Self* (Baltimore, 1968).
[14]The complete understanding of what follows presupposes a rereading of the short and easily available text of "The Purloined Letter."

played as between a deaf man and one who hears. That is, it presents the real complexity of what is ordinarily simplified, with the most confused results, in the notion of communication.

This example demonstrates indeed how an act of communication may give the impression at which theorists too often stop: of allowing in its transmission but a single meaning, as though the highly significant commentary into which he who understands integrates it, could, because unperceived by him who does not understand, be considered null.

It remains that if only the dialogue's meaning as a report is retained, its verisimilitude may appear to depend on a guarantee of exactitude. But here dialogue may be more fertile than seems, if we demonstrate its tactics, as shall be seen by focusing on the recounting of our first scene.

For the double and even triple subjective filter through which that scene comes to us: a narration by Dupin's friend and associate (henceforth to be called the general narrator of the story)—of the account by which the Prefect reveals to Dupin—the report the Queen gave him of it, is not merely the consequence of a fortuitous arrangement.

If indeed the extremity to which the original narrator is reduced precludes her altering any of the events, it would be wrong to believe that the Prefect is empowered to lend her his voice in this case only by that lack of imagination on which he has, dare we say, the patent.

The fact that the message is thus retransmitted assures us of what may by no means be taken for granted: that it belongs to the dimension of language.

Those who are here know our remarks on the subject, specifically those illustrated by the counter case of the so-called language of bees, in which a linguist[15] can see only a simple signaling of the location of objects, in other words, only an imaginary function more differentiated than others.

We emphasize that such a form of communication is not absent in man, however evanescent a naturally given object may be for him, split as it is in its submission to symbols.

Something equivalent may no doubt be grasped in the communion established between two persons in their hatred of a common object,

---

[15]Cf. Emile Benveniste, "Communication animale et langage humain," *Diogène*, No. 1, and our address in Rome, *Ecrits*, p. 178.

except that the meeting is possible only over a single object, defined by those traits in the individual each of the two resist.

But such communication is not transmissible in symbolic form. It may be maintained only in the relation with the object. In such a manner it may bring together an indefinite number of subjects in a common "ideal": the communication of one subject with another within the crowd thus constituted will nonetheless remain irreducibly mediated by an ineffable relation.[16]

This digression is not only a recollection of principles distantly addressed to those who impute to us a neglect of nonverbal communication: in determining the scope of what speech repeats, it prepares the question of what symptoms repeat.

Thus, the indirect telling sifts out the linguistic dimension, and the general narrator, by duplicating it, "hypothetically" adds nothing to it. But its role in the second dialogue is entirely different.

For the latter will be opposed to the first like those poles we have distinguished elsewhere in language and which are opposed like word to speech.

Which is to say that a transition is made here from the domain of exactitude to the register of truth. Now that register, we dare think we needn't come back to this, is situated entirely elsewhere, strictly speaking at the very foundation of intersubjectivity. It is located there where the subject can grasp nothing but the very subjectivity which constitutes an Other as absolute. We shall be satisfied here to indicate its place by evoking the dialogue which seems to us to merit its attribution as a Jewish joke by that state of privation through which the relation of signifier to speech appears in the entreaty which brings the dialogue to a close: "Why are you lying to me?" one character shouts breathlessly. "Yes, why do you lie to me saying you're going to Cracow so I should believe you're going to Lemberg, when in reality you *are* going to Cracow?"[17]

---

[16]For the notion of *ego ideal,* see Freud, *Group Psychology and the Analysis of the Ego.* —J.M.

[17]Freud comments on this joke in *Jokes and Their Relation to the Unconscious,* New York, 1960, p. 115: "But the more serious substance of the joke is what determines the truth . . . Is it the truth if we describe things as they are without troubling to consider how our hearer will understand what we say? . . . I think that jokes of that kind are sufficiently different from the rest to be given a special position: What they are attacking is not a person or an institution but the certainty of our knowledge itself, one of our

We might be prompted to ask a similar question by the torrent of logical impasses, eristic enigmas, paradoxes, and even jests presented to us as an introduction to Dupin's method if the fact that they were confided to us by a would-be disciple did not endow them with a new dimension through that act of delegation. Such is the unmistakable magic of legacies: the witness's fidelity is the cowl which blinds and lays to rest all criticism of his testimony.

What could be more convincing, moreover, than the gesture of laying one's cards face up on the table? So much so that we are momentarily persuaded that the magician has, in fact, demonstrated, as he promised, how his trick was performed, whereas he has only renewed it in still purer form, at which point we fathom the measure of the supremacy of the signifier in the subject.

Such is Dupin's maneuver when he starts with the story of the child prodigy who takes in all his friends at the game of even and odd with his trick of identifying with the opponent, concerning which we have nevertheless shown that it cannot reach the first level of theoretical elaboration, namely, intersubjective alternation, without immediately stumbling on the buttress of its recurrence.[18]

We are all the same treated—so much smoke in our eyes—to the names of La Rochefoucauld, La Bruyère, Machiavelli and Campanella, whose renown, by this time, would seem but futile when confronted with the child's prowess.

Followed by Chamfort, whose maxim that "it is a safe wager that every public idea, every accepted convention is foolish, since it suits the greatest number," will no doubt satisfy all who think they escape its law, that is, precisely, the greatest number. That Dupin accuses the French of deception for applying the word *analysis* to algebra will hardly threaten our pride since, moreover, the freeing of that term for other uses ought by no means to provoke a psychoanalyst to intervene and claim his rights. And there he goes making philological remarks

---

speculative possessions." Lacan's text may be regarded as a commentary on Freud's statement, an examination of the corrosive effect of the demands of an intersubjective communicative situation on any naive notion of "truth."—J.M.

[18]Cf. *Ecrits,* p. 58. "But what will happen at the following step [of the game] when the opponent, realizing that I am sufficiently clever to follow him in his move, will show his own cleverness by realizing that it is by playing the fool that he has the best chance to deceive me? From then on my reasoning is invalidated, since it can only be repeated in an indefinite oscillation . . ."

which should positively delight any lovers of Latin: when he recalls without deigning to say any more that *"ambitus* doesn't mean ambition, *religio,* religion, *homines honesti,* honest men," who among you would not take pleasure in remembering . . . what those words mean to anyone familiar with Cicero and Lucretius. No doubt Poe is having a good time. . . .

But a suspicion occurs to us: might not this parade of erudition be destined to reveal to us the key words of our drama? Is not the magician repeating his trick before our eyes, without deceiving us this time about divulging his secret, but pressing his wager to the point of really explaining it to us without us seeing a thing. *That* would be the summit of the illusionist's art: through one of his fictive creations to *truly delude us.*

And is it not such effects which justify our referring, without malice, to a number of imaginary heroes as real characters?

As well, when we are open to hearing the way in which Martin Heidegger discloses to us in the word *aletheia* the play of truth,^c we rediscover a secret to which truth has always initiated her lovers and through which they learn that it is in hiding that she offers herself to them *most truly.*

Thus, even if Dupin's comments did not defy us so blatantly to believe in them, we should still have to make that attempt against the opposite temptation.

Let us track down [*dépistons*] his footprints there where they elude [*dépiste*] us.[19] And first of all in the criticism by which he explains the Prefect's lack of success. We already saw it surface in those furtive gibes the Prefect, in the first conversation, failed to heed, seeing in them only a pretext for hilarity. That it is, as Dupin insinuates, because a problem is too simple, indeed too evident, that it may appear obscure, will never have any more bearing for him than a vigorous rub of the rib cage.

Everything is arranged to induce in us a sense of the character's

---

^cSee *Being and Time* (New York, 1962), Introduction II, B.—Eds.

[19] We should like to present again to M. Benveniste the question of the antithetical sense of (primal or other) words after the magisterial rectification he brought to the erroneous philological path on which Freud engaged it (cf. *La Psychanalyse,* vol. 1, pp. 5–16). For we think that the problem remains intact once the instance of the signifier has been evolved. Bloch and Von Wartburg date at 1875 the first appearance of the meaning of the verb *dépister* in the second use we make of it in our sentence.

imbecility. Which is powerfully articulated by the fact that he and his confederates never conceive of anything beyond what an ordinary rogue might imagine for hiding an object—that is, precisely the all-too-well-known series of extraordinary hiding places, which are promptly catalogued for us, from hidden desk drawers to removable table tops, from the detachable cushions of chairs to their hollowed-out legs, from the reverse side of mirrors to the "thickness" of book bindings.

After which, a moment of derision at the Prefect's error in deducing that because the Minister is a poet, he is not far from being mad, an error, it is argued, which would consist, but this is hardly negligible, simply in a false distribution of the middle term, since it is far from following from the fact that all madmen are poets.

Yes, indeed. But we ourselves are left in the dark as to the poet's superiority in the art of concealment—even if he be a mathematician to boot—since our pursuit is suddenly thwarted, dragged as we are into a thicket of bad arguments directed against the reasoning of mathematicians, who never, so far as I know, showed such devotion to their formulae as to identify them with reason itself. At least, let us testify that unlike what seems to be Poe's experience, it occasionally befalls us—with our friend Riguet, whose presence here is a guarantee that our incursions into combinatory analysis are not leading us astray—to hazard such serious deviations (virtual blasphemies, according to Poe) as to cast into doubt that "x^2 plus px is perhaps not absolutely equal to q," without ever—here we give the lie to Poe—having had to fend off any unexpected attack.

Is not so much intelligence being exercised, then, simply to divert our own from what had been indicated earlier as given, namely, that the police have looked *everywhere:* which we were to understand—vis-à-vis the area in which the police, not without reason, assumed the letter might be found—in terms of a (no doubt theoretical) exhaustion of space, but concerning which the tale's piquancy depends on our accepting it literally: the division of the entire volume into numbered "compartments," which was the principle governing the operation, being presented to us as so precise that "the fiftieth part of a line," it is said, could not escape the probing of the investigators. Have we not, then, the right to ask how it happened that the letter was not found *anywhere,* or rather to observe that all we have been told of a more far-ranging conception of concealment does not explain, in all rigor, that the letter escaped detection, since the area combed did, in fact, contain it, as Dupin's discovery eventually proves?

Must a letter, then, of all objects, be endowed with the property of *nullibiety:* to use a term which the thesaurus known as *Roget* picks up from the semiotic utopia of Bishop Wilkins?[20]

It is evident ("a little *too* self-evident")[21] that between *letter* and *place* exist relations for which no French word has quite the extension of the English adjective: *odd*. Bizarre, by which Baudelaire regularly translates it, is only approximate. Let us say that these relations are ... *singuliers,* for they are the very ones maintained with place by the *signifier.*

You realize, of course, that our intention is not to turn them into "subtle" relations, nor is our aim to confuse letter with spirit, even if we receive the former by pneumatic dispatch, and that we readily admit that one kills whereas the other quickens, insofar as the signifier —you perhaps begin to understand—materializes the agency of death.[22] But if it is first of all on the materiality of the signifier that we have insisted, that materiality is *odd* [*singulière*] in many ways, the first of which is not to admit partition. Cut a letter in small pieces, and it remains the letter it is—and this in a completely different sense than *Gestalttheorie*[d] would account for with the dormant vitalism informing its notion of the whole.[23]

Language delivers its judgment to whoever knows how to hear it, through the usage of the article as partitive particle. It is there that spirit—if spirit be living meaning—appears, no less oddly, as more

---

[20] The very one to which Jorge Luis Borges, in works which harmonize so well with the phylum of our subject, has accorded an importance which others have reduced to its proper proportions. Cf. *Les Temps modernes,* June–July 1955, pp. 2135–36 and October 1955, pp. 574–575.

[21] Underlined by the author.

[22] The reference is to the "death instinct," whose "death," we should note, lies entirely in its diacritical opposition to the "life" of a naive vitalism or naturalism. As such, it may be compared with the logical moment in Lévi-Strauss's thought whereby "nature" exceeds, supplements, and symbolizes itself: the prohibition of incest.—J.M.

[d] An approach to psychology based on the principle that analysis of parts cannot provide an understanding of the whole.—Eds.

[23] This is so true that philosophers, in those hackneyed examples with which they argue on the basis of the single and the multiple, will not use to the same purpose a simple sheet of white paper ripped in the middle and a broken circle, indeed a shattered vase, not to mention a cut worm.

available for quantification than its letter. To begin with meaning itself, which bears our saying: a speech rich with meaning ["plein *de* signification"], just as we recognize a measure of intention ["*de* l'intention"] in an act, or deplore that there is no more love ["plus *d*'amour"]; or store up hatred ["*de la* haine"] and expend devotion ["*du* dévouement"], and so much infatuation ["tant *d*'infatuation"] is easily reconciled to the fact that there will always be ass ["*de la* cuisse"] for sale and brawling ["*du* rififi"] among men.

But as for the letter—be it taken as typographical character, epistle, or what makes a man of letters—we will say that what is said is to be understood *to the letter* [*à la lettre*], that *a letter* [*une lettre*] awaits you at the post office, or even that you are acquainted with *letters* [*que vous avez des lettres*]—never that there is *letter* [*de la lettre*] anywhere, whatever the context, even to designate overdue mail.

For the signifier is a unit in its very uniqueness, being by nature symbol only of an absence. Which is why we cannot say of the purloined letter that, like other objects, it must be *or* not be in a particular place but that unlike them it will be *and* not be where it is, wherever it goes.[24]

Let us, in fact, look more closely at what happens to the police. We are spared nothing concerning the procedures used in searching the area submitted to their investigation: from the division of that space into compartments from which the slightest bulk could not escape detection, to needles probing upholstery, and, in the impossibility of sounding wood with a tap, to a microscope exposing the waste of any drilling at the surface of its hollow, indeed the infinitesimal gaping of the slightest abyss. As the network tightens to the point that, not satisfied with shaking the pages of books, the police take to counting them, do we not see space itself shed its leaves like a letter?

But the detectives have so immutable a notion of the real that they fail to notice that their search tends to transform it into its object. A trait by which they would be able to distinguish that object from all others.

This would, no doubt, be too much to ask them, not because of their

---

[24]Cf. Saussure, *Cours de linguistique générale,* Paris, 1969, p. 166: "The preceding amounts to saying that *in language there are only differences.* Even more: a difference presupposes in general positive terms between which it is established, but in language there are only differences *without positive terms.*"—J.M.

lack of insight but rather because of ours. For their imbecility is neither of the individual nor the corporative variety; its source is subjective. It is the realist's imbecility, which does not pause to observe that nothing, however deep in the bowels of the earth a hand may seek to ensconce it, will ever be hidden there, since another hand can always retrieve it, and that what is hidden is never but what is *missing from its place,* as the call slip puts it when speaking of a volume lost in a library. And even if the book be on an adjacent shelf or in the next slot, it would be hidden there, however visibly it may appear. For it can *literally* be said that something is missing from its place only of what can change it: the symbolic. For the real, whatever upheaval we subject it to, is always in its place; it carries it glued to its heel, ignorant of what might exile it from it.

And, to return to our cops, who took the letter from the place where it was hidden, how could they have seized the letter? In what they turned between their fingers what did they hold but what *did not answer* to their description? "A letter, a litter": in Joyce's circle, they played on the homophony of the two words in English.[25] Nor does the seeming bit of refuse the police are now handling reveal its other nature for being but half torn. A different seal on a stamp of another color, the mark of a different handwriting in the superscription are here the most inviolable modes of concealment. And if they stop at the reverse side of the letter, on which, as is known, the recipient's address was written in that period, it is because the letter has for them no other side but its reverse.

What indeed might they find on its obverse? Its message, as is often said to our cybernetic joy? . . . But does it not occur to us that this message has already reached its recipient and has even been left with her, since the insignificant scrap of paper now represents it no less well than the original note?

If we could admit that a letter has completed its destiny after fulfilling its function, the ceremony of returning letters would be a less common close to the extinction of the fires of love's feasts. The signifier is not functional. And the mobilization of the elegant society whose frolics we are following would as well have no meaning if the letter itself were content with having one. For it would hardly be an

---

[25]Cf. *Our Exagmination Round his Factification for Incamination of Work in Progress,* Shakespeare & Co., 12 rue de l'Odéon, Paris, 1929.

adequate means of keeping it secret to inform a squad of cops of its existence.

We might even admit that the letter has an entirely different (if no more urgent) meaning for the Queen than the one understood by the Minister. The sequence of events would not be noticably affected, not even if it were strictly incomprehensible to an uninformed reader.

For it is certainly not so for everybody, since, as the Prefect pompously assures us, to everyone's derision, "the disclosure of the document to a third person, who shall be nameless" (that name which leaps to the eye like the pig's tail twixt the teeth of old Ubu[e]) "would bring in question the honor of a personage of most exalted station; and this fact gives the holder of the document an ascendancy over the illustrious personage whose honor and peace are so jeopardized."

In that case, it is not only the meaning but the text of the message which it would be dangerous to place in circulation, and all the more so to the extent that it might appear harmless, since the risks of an indiscretion unintentionally committed by one of the letter's holders would thus be increased.

Nothing, then, can redeem the police's position, and nothing would be changed by improving their "culture." *Scripta manent:*[f] in vain would they learn from a deluxe-edition humanism the proverbial lesson which *verba volant*[g] concludes. May it but please heaven that writings remain, as is rather the case with spoken words: for the indelible debt of the latter impregnates our acts with its transferences.

Writings scatter to the winds blank checks in an insane charge.[26] And were they not such flying leaves, there would be no purloined letters.[27]

---

[e]Title character of several wildly coarse and comic plays by Alfred Jarry.—Eds.
[f]"What is written remains."—Eds.
[g]"What is spoken flies."—Eds.
[26]The original sentence presents an exemplary difficulty in translation: "Les écrits emportent au vent les traites en blanc d'une cavalerie folle." The blank (bank) drafts (or transfers) are not delivered to their rightful recipients (the sense of *de cavalerie, de complaisance*). That is, in analysis, one finds absurd symbolic debts being paid to the "wrong" persons. At the same time, the mad, driven quality of the payment is latent in *traite*, which might also refer to the day's trip of an insane cavalry. In our translation, we have displaced the "switch-word"—joining the financial and equestrian series—from *traite* to *charge*.—J.M.
[27]*Flying leaves* (also fly-sheets) and *purloined letters—feuilles volantes* and *lettres volées* —employ different meanings of the same word in French.—J.M.

But what of it? For a purloined letter to exist, we may ask, to whom does a letter belong? We stressed a moment ago the oddity implicit in returning a letter to him who had but recently given wing to its burning pledge. And we generally deem unbecoming such premature publications as the one by which the Chevalier d'Eon[h] put several of his correspondents in a rather pitiful position.

Might a letter on which the sender retains certain rights, then, not quite belong to the person to whom it is addressed? Or might it be that the latter was never the real receiver?

Let's take a look: we shall find illumination in what at first seems to obscure matters: the fact that the tale leaves us in virtually total ignorance of the sender, no less than of the contents, of the letter. We are told only that the Minister immediately recognized the handwriting of the address and only incidentally, in a discussion of the Minister's camouflage, is it said that the original seal bore the ducal arms of the S—— family. As for the letter's bearing, we know only the dangers it entails should it come into the hands of a specific third party and that its possession has allowed the Minister to "wield, to a very dangerous extent, for political purposes," the power it assures him over the interested party. But all this tells us nothing of the message it conveys.

Love letter or conspiratorial letter, letter of betrayal or letter of mission, letter of summons or letter of distress, we are assured of but one thing: the Queen must not bring it to the knowledge of her lord and master.

Now these terms, far from bearing the nuance of discredit they have in bourgeois comedy, take on a certain prominence through allusion to her sovereign, to whom she is bound by pledge of faith, and doubly so, since her role as spouse does not relieve her of her duties as subject, but rather elevates her to the guardianship of what royalty according to law incarnates of power—and which is called legitimacy.

From then on, to whatever vicissitudes the Queen may choose to subject the letter, it remains that the letter is the symbol of a pact, and that, even should the recipient not assume the pact, the existence of

---

[h]A famous eighteenth-century nobleman, diplomat, spy, and transvestite. Until a postmortem examination, no one was sure whether he was a man or a woman. Lacan may be referring to a letter or letters that "he" signed "Chevalière d'Eon," thus by a single letter casting doubt on his own sex and confounding his correspondents.—Eds.

the letter situates her in a symbolic chain foreign to the one which constitutes her faith. This incompatibility is proven by the fact that the possession of the letter is impossible to bring forward publicly as legitimate, and that in order to have that possession respected, the Queen can invoke but her right to privacy, whose privilege is based on the honor that possession violates.

For she who incarnates the figure of grace and sovereignty cannot welcome even a private communication without power being concerned, and she cannot avail herself of secrecy in relation to the sovereign without becoming clandestine.

From then on, the responsibility of the author of the letter takes second place to that of its holder: for the offense to majesty is compounded by *high treason.*

We say the *holder* and not the *possessor.* For it becomes clear that the addressee's proprietorship of the letter may be no less debatable than that of anyone else into whose hands it comes, for nothing concerning the existence of the letter can return to good order without the person whose prerogatives it infringes upon having to pronounce judgment on it.

All of this, however, does not imply that because the letter's secrecy is indefensible, the betrayal of that secret would in any sense be honorable. The *honesti homines,* decent people, will not get off so easily. There is more than one *religio,* and it is not slated for tomorrow that sacred ties shall cease to rend us in two. As for *ambitus:* a detour, we see, is not always inspired by ambition. For if we are taking one here, by no means is it stolen (the word is apt), since, to lay our cards on the table, we have borrowed Baudelaire's title in order to stress not, as is incorrectly claimed, the conventional nature of the signifier, but rather its priority in relation to the signified.[28] It remains, nevertheless, that Baudelaire, despite his devotion, betrayed Poe by translating as "la lettre volée" (the stolen letter) his title, the purloined letter, a title containing a word rare enough for us to find it easier to define its etymology than its usage.

To purloin, says the Oxford dictionary, is an Anglo-French word, that is, composed of the prefix *pur-,* found in *purpose, purchase, purport,* and of the Old French word *loing, loigner, longé.* We recog-

---

[28] See the discussion of Lévi-Strauss's statement—"the signifier precedes and determines the signified"—in my essay cited in note 5.—J.M.

nize in the first element the Latin *pro-*, as opposed to *ante-*, insofar as it presupposes a rear in front of which it is borne, possibly as its warrant, indeed even as its pledge (whereas *ante-* goes forth to confront what it encounters). As for the second, an old French word *loigner*, a verb attributing place *au loing* (or, still in use, *longé*), it does not mean *au loin* (far off) but *au long de* (alongside); it is a question then of *putting aside*, or, to invoke a familiar expression which plays on the two meanings, *mettre à gauche* (to put to the left; to put amiss).

Thus, we are confirmed in our detour by the very object which draws us on into it: for we are quite simply dealing with a letter which has been diverted from its path; one whose course has been *prolonged* (etymologically, the word of the title), or, to revert to the language of the post office, a *letter in sufferance*.[29]

Here, then, *simple and odd*, as we are told on the very first page, reduced to its simplest expression, is the singularity of the letter, which as the title indicates, is the *true subject* of the tale: since it can be diverted, it must have a course *which is proper to it*, the trait by which its incidence as signifier is affirmed. For we have learned to conceive of the signifier as sustaining itself only in a displacement comparable to that found in electric news strips or in the rotating memories of our machines-that-think-like men, this because of the alternating operation which is its principle, requiring it to leave its place, even though it returns to it by a circular path.[30]

This is indeed what happens in the repetition automatism. What Freud teaches us in the text we are commenting on is that the subject must pass through the channels of the symbolic, but what is illustrated here is more gripping still: it is not only the subject, but the subjects, grasped in their intersubjectivity, who line up, in other words, our ostriches, to whom we here return, and who, more docile than sheep, model their very being on the moment of the signifying chain which traverses them.

If what Freud discovered and rediscovers with a perpetually in-

---

[29] We revive this archaism (for the French: *lettre en souffrance*). The sense is a letter held up in the course of delivery. In French, of course, *en souffrance* means in a state of suffering as well.—J.M.

[30] See *Ecrits*, p. 59: ". . . it is not unthinkable that a modern computer, by discovering the sentence which modulates without his knowing it and over a long period of time the choices of a subject, would win beyond any normal proportion at the game of even and odd . . ."

creasing sense of shock has a meaning, it is that the displacement of the signifier determines the subjects in their acts, in their destiny, in their refusals, in their blindnesses, in their end and in their fate, their innate gifts and social acquisitions notwithstanding, without regard for character or sex, and that, willingly or not, everything that might be considered the stuff of psychology, kit and caboodle, will follow the path of the signifier.

Here we are, in fact, yet again at the crossroads at which we had left our drama and its round with the question of the way in which the subjects replace each other in it. Our fable is so constructed as to show that it is the letter and its diversion which governs their entries and roles. If *it* be "in sufferance," *they* shall endure the pain. Should they pass beneath its shadow, they become its reflection. Falling in possession of the letter—admirable ambiguity of language—its meaning possesses them.

So we are shown by the hero of the drama in the repetition of the very situation which his daring brought to a head, a first time, to his triumph. If he now succumbs to it, it is because he has shifted to the second position in the triad in which he was initially third, as well as the thief—and this by virtue of the object of his theft.

For if it is, now as before, a question of protecting the letter from inquisitive eyes, he can do nothing but employ the same technique he himself has already foiled: leave it in the open. And we may properly doubt that he knows what he is thus doing, when we see him immediately captivated by a dual relationship in which we find all the traits of a mimetic lure or of an animal feigning death, and, trapped in the typically imaginary situation of seeing that he is not seen, misconstrue the real situation in which he is seen not seeing.[31]

And what does he fail to see? Precisely the symbolic situation which he himself was so well able to see and in which he is now seen seeing himself not being seen.

The Minister acts as a man who realizes that the police's search is his own defense, since we are told he allows them total access by his absences: he nonetheless fails to recognize that outside of that search he is no longer defended.

This is the very *autruicherie* whose artisan he was, if we may allow

---

[31] See the Laplanche and Pontalis entry on the *imaginary*.—J.M.

our monster to proliferate, but it cannot be by sheer stupidity that he now comes to be its dupe.³²

For in playing the part of the one who hides, he is obliged to don the role of the Queen, and even the attributes of femininity and shadow, so propitious to the act of concealing.

Not that we are reducing the hoary couple of *Yin* and *Yang* to the elementary opposition of dark and light. For its precise use involves what is blinding in a flash of light, no less than the shimmering shadows exploit in order not to lose their prey.

Here sign and being, marvelously asunder, reveal which is victorious when they come into conflict. A man man enough to defy to the point of scorn a lady's fearsome ire undergoes to the point of metamorphosis the curse of the sign he has dispossessed her of.

For this sign is indeed that of woman, insofar as she invests her very being therein, founding it outside the law, which subsumes her nevertheless, originarily, in a position of signifier, nay, of fetish.³³ In order to be worthy of the power of that sign, she has but to remain immobile in its shadow, thus finding, moreover, like the Queen, that simulation of mastery in inactivity that the Minister's "lynx eye" alone was able to penetrate.

This stolen sign—here, then, is man in its possession: sinister in that such possession may be sustained only through the honor it defies, cursed in calling him who sustains it to punishment or crime, each of which shatters his vassalage to the Law.

There must be in this sign a singular *noli me tangere*ⁱ for its possession, like the Socratic stingray, to benumb its man to the point of making him fall into what appears clearly in his case to be a state of idleness.³⁴

---

³²*Autruicherie* condenses, in addition to the previous terms, deception *(tricherie)*. Do we not find in Lacan's proliferating "monster" something of the *proton pseudos*, the "first lie" of Freud's 1895 *Project:* the persistent illusion which seems to structure the mental life of the patient?—J.M.

³³The fetish, as replacement for the missing maternal phallus, at once masks and reveals the scandal of sexual difference. As such it is the analytic object par excellence. The female temptation to exhibitionism, understood as a desire to *be* the (maternal) phallus, is thus tantamount to being a fetish.—J.M.

ⁱ"Touch me not" (in the Vulgate, the words of the resurrected Jesus to Mary Magdalene. John 20:17).—Eds.

³⁴See Plato's *Meno:* "Socrates, . . . at this moment I feel you are exercising magic and witchcraft upon me and positively laying me under your spell until I am just a mass

For in noting, as the narrator does as early as the first dialogue, that with the letter's use its power disappears, we perceive that this remark, strictly speaking, concerns precisely its use for ends of power—and at the same time that such a use is obligatory for the Minister.

To be unable to rid himself of it, the Minister indeed must not know what else to do with the letter. For that use places him in so total a dependence on the letter as such that in the long run it no longer involves the letter at all.

We mean that for that use truly to involve the letter, the Minister, who, after all, would be so authorized by his service to his master the King, might present to the Queen respectful admonitions, even were he to assure their sequel by appropriate precautions—or initiate an action against the author of the letter, concerning whom, the fact that he remains outside the story's focus reveals the extent to which it is not guilt and blame which are in question here but rather that sign of contradiction and scandal constituted by the letter, in the sense in which the Gospel says that it must come regardless of the anguish of whomever serves as its bearer—or even submit the letter as evidence to a qualified third person, to find out if he will have it issue in a Star Chamber for the Queen or the Minister's disgrace.

We will not know why the Minister does not resort to any of these uses, and it is fitting that we don't, since the effect of this non-use alone concerns us; it suffices for us to know that the way in which the letter was acquired would pose no obstacle to any of them.

For it is clear that if the use of the letter, independent of its meaning, is obligatory for the Minister, its use for ends of power can only be potential, since it cannot become actual without vanishing in the process—but in that case the letter exists as a means of power only through the final assignations of the pure signifier, namely, by prolonging its diversion, making it reach whomever it may concern through a supplementary transfer, that is, by an additional act of treason whose effects the letter's gravity makes it difficult to predict —or indeed by destroying the letter, the only sure means, as Dupin

---

of helplessness. If I may be flippant, I think that not only in outward appearance but in other respects as well you are like the flat stingray that one meets in the sea. Whenever anyone comes into contact with it, it numbs him, and that is the sort of thing you are doing to me now . . ."—J.M.

divulges at the start, of being rid of what is destined by nature to signify the annulment of what it signifies.

The ascendancy which the Minister derives from the situation is thus not a function of the letter, but, whether he knows it or not, of the role it constitutes for him. And the Prefect's remarks indeed present him as someone "who dares all things," which is commented upon significantly: "those unbecoming as well as those becoming a man," words whose pungency escapes Baudelaire when he translates "ce qui est indigne d'un homme aussi bien que ce qui est digne de lui" (those unbecoming a man as well as those becoming him). For in its original form, the appraisal is far more appropriate to what might concern a woman.

This allows us to see the imaginary import of the character, that is, the narcissistic relation in which the Minister is engaged, this time, no doubt, without knowing it. It is indicated as well, as early as the second page of the English text, by one of the narrator's remarks, whose form is worth savoring: the Minister's ascendancy, we are told, "would depend upon the robber's knowledge of the loser's knowledge of the robber," words whose importance the author underscores by having Dupin repeat them literally after the narration of the scene of the theft of the letter. Here again we may say that Baudelaire is imprecise in his language in having one ask, the other confirm, in these words: "Le voleur sait-il? . . ." (Does the robber know?), then: "Le voleur sait . . ." (the robber knows). What? "que la personne volée connaît son voleur" (that the loser knows his robber).

For what matters to the robber is not only that the said person knows who robbed her, but rather with what kind of a robber she is dealing; for she believes him capable of anything, which should be understood as her having conferred upon him the position that no one is, in fact, capable of assuming, since it is imaginary, that of absolute master.

In truth, it is a position of absolute weakness, but not for the person of whom we are expected to believe so. The proof is not only that the Queen dares to call the police. For she is only conforming to her displacement to the next slot in the arrangement of the initial triad in trusting to the very blindness required to occupy that place: "No more sagacious agent could, I suppose," Dupin notes ironically, "be desired or even imagined." No, if she has taken that step, it is less out of being "driven to despair," as we are told, than in assuming the charge of an impatience best imputed to a specular mirage.

For the Minister is kept quite busy confining himself to the idleness which is presently his lot. The Minister, in point of fact, is not *altogether* mad.[35] That's a remark made by the Prefect, whose every word is gold: it is true that the gold of his words flows only for Dupin and will continue to flow to the amount of the fifty thousand francs worth it will cost him by the metal standard of the day, though not without leaving him a margin of profit. The Minister, then, is not *altogether* mad in his insane stagnation, and that is why he will behave according to the mode of neurosis. Like the man who withdrew to an island to forget, what? he forgot—so the Minister, through not making use of the letter, comes to forget it, as is expressed by the persistence of his conduct. But the letter, no more than the neurotic's unconscious, does not forget him. It forgets him so little that it transforms him more and more in the image of her who offered it to his capture, so that he now will surrender it, following her example, to a similar capture.

The features of that transformation are noted, and in a form so characteristic in their apparent gratuitousness that they might validly be compared to the return of the repressed.

Thus, we first learn that the Minister in turn has *turned the letter over,* not, of course, as in the Queen's hasty gesture, but, more assiduously, as one turns a garment inside out. So he must proceed, according to the methods of the day for folding and sealing a letter, in order to free the virgin space on which to inscribe a new address.[36]

That address becomes his own. Whether it be in his hand or another, it will appear in an extremely delicate feminine script, and, the seal changing from the red of passion to the black of its mirrors, he will imprint his stamp upon it. This oddity of a letter marked with

---

[35]Baudelaire translates Poe's *"altogether* a fool" as *"absolument* fou." In opting for Baudelaire, Lacan is enabled to allude to the realm of psychosis.—J.M.

[36]We felt obliged to demonstrate the procedure to an audience with a letter from the period concerning M. de Chateaubriand and his search for a secretary. We were amused to find that M. de Chateaubriand completed the first version of his recently restored memoirs in the very month of November 1841 in which the purloined letter appeared in *Chamber's Journal.* Might M. de Chateaubriand's devotion to the power he decries and the honor which that devotion bespeaks in him (*the gift* had not yet been invented), place him in the category to which we will later see the Minister assigned: among men of genius with or without principles?

the recipient's stamp is all the more striking in its conception, since, though forcefully articulated in the text, it is not even mentioned by Dupin in the discussion he devotes to the identification of the letter.

Whether that omission be intentional or involuntary, it will surprise in the economy of a work whose meticulous rigor is evident. But in either case it is significant that the letter which the Minister, in point of fact, addresses to himself is a letter from a woman, as though this were a phase he had to pass through out of a natural affinity of the signifier.

Thus, the aura of apathy, verging at times on an affectation of effeminacy; the display of an ennui bordering on disgust in his conversation; the mood the author of the philosophy of furniture[37] can elicit from virtually impalpable details (like that of the musical instrument on the table), everything seems intended for a character, all of whose utterances have revealed the most virile traits, to exude the oddest *odor di femmina*[j] when he appears.

Dupin does not fail to stress that this is an artifice, describing behind the bogus finery the vigilance of a beast of prey ready to spring. But that this is the very effect of the unconscious in the precise sense that we teach that the unconscious means that man is inhabited by the signifier: could we find a more beautiful image of it than the one Poe himself forges to help us appreciate Dupin's exploit? For with this aim in mind, he refers to those toponymical inscriptions which a geographical map, lest it remain mute, superimposes on its design, and which may become the object of a guessing game: who can find the name chosen by a partner?—noting immediately that the name most likely to foil a beginner will be one which, in large letters spaced out widely across the map, discloses, often without an eye pausing to notice it, the name of an entire country . . .

Just so does the purloined letter, like an immense female body, stretch out across the Minister's office when Dupin enters. But just so does he already expect to find it, and has only, with his eyes veiled by green lenses, to undress that huge body.

And that is why, without needing any more than being able to listen in at the door of Professor Freud, he will go straight to the spot in

---

[37]Poe is the author of an essay with this title.
[j]"the scent of a woman." Don Giovanni catches a whiff of this scent when Donna Elvira approaches in act 1 of Mozart's opera.—Eds.

which lies and lives what that body is designed to hide, in a gorgeous center caught in a glimpse, nay, to the very place seducers name Sant' Angelo's Castle in their innocent illusion of controlling the City from within it. Look! between the cheeks of the fireplace, there's the object already in reach of a hand the ravisher has but to extend . . . The question of deciding whether he seizes it above the mantelpiece, as Baudelaire translates, or beneath it, as in the original text, may be abandoned without harm to the inferences of those whose profession is grilling.[38]

Were the effectiveness of symbols[39] to cease there, would it mean that the symbolic debt would as well be extinguished? Even if we could believe so, we would be advised of the contrary by two episodes which we may all the less dismiss as secondary in that they seem, at first sight, to clash with the rest of the work.

First of all, there's the business of Dupin's remuneration, which, far from being a closing pirouette, has been present from the beginning in the rather unself-conscious question he asks the Prefect about the amount of the reward promised him and whose enormousness the Prefect, however reticent he may be about the precise figure, does not dream of hiding from him, even returning later on to refer to its increase.

The fact that Dupin had been previously presented to us as a virtual pauper in his ethereal shelter ought rather to lead us to reflect on the deal he makes out of delivering the letter, promptly assured as it is by the checkbook he produces. We do not regard it as negligible that the unequivocal hint through which he introduces the matter is a "story attributed to the character, as famous as it was excentric," Baudelaire tells us, of an English doctor named Abernethy, in which a rich miser, hoping to sponge upon him for a medical opinion, is sharply told not to take medicine, but to take advice.

---

[38]And even to the cook herself.—J.L.

The paragraph might be read as follows: analysis, in its violation of the imaginary integrity of the ego, finds its fantasmatic equivalent in rape. . . . But whether that "rape" takes place from in front or from behind (above or below the mantelpiece) is, in fact, a question of interest for policemen and not analysts. Implicit in the statement is an attack on those who have become wed to the ideology of "maturational development" (libidinal stages et al.) in Freud (i.e., the ego psychologists).—J.M.

[39]The allusion is to Lévi-Strauss's article of the same title ("L'efficacité symbolique") in L'Anthropologie structurale.—J.M.

Do we not, in fact, feel concerned with good reason when for Dupin what is perhaps at stake is his withdrawal from the symbolic circuit of the letter—we who become the emissaries of all the purloined letters which at least for a time remain in sufferance with us in the transference? And is it not the responsibility their transference entails which we neutralize by equating it with the signifier most destructive of all signification, namely, money?

But that's not all. The profit Dupin so nimbly extracts from his exploit, if its purpose is to allow him to withdraw his stakes from the game, makes all the more paradoxical, even shocking, the partisan attack, the underhanded blow, he suddenly permits himself to launch against the Minister, whose insolent prestige, after all, would seem to have been sufficiently deflated by the trick Dupin has just played on him.

We have already quoted the atrocious lines Dupin claims he could not help dedicating, in his counterfeit letter, to the moment in which the Minister, enraged by the inevitable defiance of the Queen, will think he is demolishing her and will plunge into the abyss: *facilis descensus Averni,*[40] [k] he waxes sententious, adding that the Minister cannot fail to recognize his handwriting, all of which, since depriving of any danger a merciless act of infamy, would seem, concerning a figure who is not without merit, a triumph without glory, and the rancor he invokes, stemming from an evil turn done him at Vienna (at the Congress?) only adds an additional bit of blackness to the whole.[41]

Let us consider, however, more closely this explosion of feeling, and more specifically the moment it occurs in a sequence of acts whose success depends on so cool a head.

It comes just after the moment in which the decisive act of identifying the letter having been accomplished, it may be said that Dupin already *has* the letter as much as if he had seized it, without, however, as yet being in a position to rid himself of it.

He is thus, in fact, fully participant in the intersubjective triad, and, as such, in the median position previously occupied by the Queen and

---

[40]Virgil's line reads: *facilis descensus Averno.*
[k]"The descent to Hades is easy" (Virgil, *Aeneid* 6:126).—Eds.
[41]Cf. Corneille, *Le Cid* (II, 2): "A vaincre sans péril, on triomphe sans gloire." (To vanquish without danger is to triumph without glory).—J.M.

the Minister. Will he, in showing himself to be above it, reveal to us at the same time the author's intentions?

If he has succeeded in returning the letter to its proper course, it remains for him to make it arrive at its address. And that address is in the place previously occupied by the King, since it is there that it would reenter the order of the Law.

As we have seen, neither the King nor the Police who replaced him in that position were able to read the letter because that *place entailed blindness.*

Rex et augur,[1] the legendary, archaic quality of the words seems to resound only to impress us with the absurdity of applying them to a man. And the figures of history, for some time now, hardly encourage us to do so. It is not natural for man to bear alone the weight of the highest of signifiers. And the place he occupies as soon as he dons it may be equally apt to become the symbol of the most outrageous imbecility.[42]

Let us say that the King here is invested with the equivocation natural to the sacred, with the imbecility which prizes none other than the Subject.[43]

That is what will give their meaning to the characters who will follow him in his place. Not that the police should be regarded as constitutionally illiterate, and we know the role of pikes planted on the *campus* in the birth of the state. But the police who exercise their functions here are plainly marked by the forms of liberalism, that is, by those imposed on them by masters on the whole indifferent to eliminating their indiscreet tendencies, which is why on occasion words are not minced as to what is expected of them: *"Sutor ne ultra crepidam,* just take care of your crooks.[44] We'll even give you scientific

---

[1]"King and priest."—Eds.
[42]We recall the witty couplet attributed before his fall to the most recent in date to have rallied Candide's meeting in Venice:

> Il n'est plus aujourd'hui que cinq rois sur la terre,
> Les quatre rois des cartes et le roi d'Angleterre.

(There are only five kings left on earth: four kings of cards and the king of England.)
[43]For the antithesis of the "sacred," see Freud's "The Antithetical Sense of Primal Words." The idiom *tenir à* in this sentence means both to prize and to be a function of. The two senses—King and/as Subject—are implicit in Freud's frequent allusions to "His Majesty the Ego."—J.M.
[44]From Pliny, 35, 10, 35: "A cobbler not beyond his sole . . ."—J.M.

means to do it with. That will help you not to think of truths you'd be better off leaving in the dark."⁴⁵

We know that the relief which results from such prudent principles shall have lasted in history but a morning's time, that already the march of destiny is everywhere bringing back—a sequel to a just aspiration to freedom's reign—an interest in those who trouble it with their crimes, which occasionally goes so far as to forge its proofs. It may even be observed that this practice, which was always well received to the extent that it was exercised only in favor of the greatest number, comes to be authenticated in public confessions of forgery by the very ones who might very well object to it: the most recent manifestation of the preeminence of the signifier over the subject.

It remains nevertheless that a police record has always been the object of a certain reserve, of which we have difficulty understanding that it amply transcends the guild of historians.

It is by dint of this vanishing credit that Dupin's intended delivery of the letter to the Prefect of police will diminish its import. What now remains of the signifier when, already relieved of its message for the Queen, it is now invalidated in its text as soon as it leaves the Minister's hands?

It remains for it now only to answer that very question, of what remains of a signifier when it has no more signification. But this is the same question asked of it by the person Dupin now finds in the spot marked by blindness.

For that is indeed the question which has led the Minister there, if he be the gambler we are told and which his act sufficiently indicates. For the gambler's passion is nothing but that question asked of the signifier, figured by the *automaton* of chance.

"What are you, figure of the die I turn over in your encounter *(tychē)* with my fortune?"⁴⁶ Nothing, if not that presence of death which makes of human life a reprieve obtained from morning to morning in the name of meanings whose sign is your crook. Thus did Scheherazade for a thousand and one nights, and thus have I done for

---

⁴⁵This proposal was openly presented by a noble lord speaking to the Upper Chamber in which his dignity earned him a place.
⁴⁶We note the fundamental opposition Aristotle makes between the two terms recalled here in the conceptual analysis of chance he gives in his *Physics*. Many discussions would be illuminated by a knowledge of it.

eighteen months, suffering the ascendancy of this sign at the cost of a dizzying series of fraudulent turns at the game of even or odd." So it is that Dupin, *from the place he now occupies*, cannot help feeling a rage of manifestly feminine nature against him who poses such a question. The prestigious image in which the poet's inventiveness and the mathematician's rigor joined up with the serenity of the dandy and the elegance of the cheat suddenly becomes, for the very person who invited us to savor it, the true *monstrum horrendum*,^m for such are his words, "an unprincipled man of genius."

It is here that the origin of that horror betrays itself, and he who experiences it has no need to declare himself (in a most unexpected manner) "a partisan of the lady" in order to reveal it to us: it is known that ladies detest calling principles into question, for their charms owe much to the mystery of the signifier.

Which is why Dupin will at last turn toward us the medusoid face of the signifier nothing but whose obverse anyone except the Queen has been able to read. The commonplace of the quotation is fitting for the oracle that face bears in its grimace, as is also its source in tragedy: "Un destin si funeste, / S'il n'est digne d'Atrée, est digne de Thyeste."[47]

So runs the signifier's answer, above and beyond all significations: "You think you act when I stir you at the mercy of the bonds through which I knot your desires. Thus do they grow in force and multiply in objects, bringing you back to the fragmentation of your shattered childhood. So be it: such will be your feast until the return of the stone guest I shall be for you since you call me forth."

Or, to return to a more moderate tone, let us say, as in the quip with which—along with some of you who had followed us to the Zurich Congress last year—we rendered homage to the local password, the signifier's answer to whomever interrogates it is "Eat your Dasein."

Is that, then, what awaits the Minister at a rendezvous with destiny? Dupin assures us of it, but we have already learned not to be too credulous of his diversions.

No doubt the brazen creature is here reduced to the state of blind-

---

^m"terrifying prodigy."—Eds.
[47]Lacan misquotes Crébillon (as well as Poe and Baudelaire) here by writing *destin* (destiny) instead of *dessein* (scheme). As a result, he is free to pursue his remarkable development on the tragic Don Juan ("multiply in objects . . . stone guest").—J.M.

ness which is man's in relation to the letters on the wall that dictate his destiny. But what effect, in calling him to confront them, may we expect from the sole provocations of the Queen, on a man like him? Love or hatred. The former is blind and will make him lay down his arms. The latter is lucid but will awaken his suspicions, But if he is truly the gambler we are told he is, he will consult his cards a final time before laying them down and, upon reading his hand, will leave the table in time to avoid disgrace.[48]

Is that all, and shall we believe we have deciphered Dupin's real strategy above and beyond the imaginary tricks with which he was obliged to deceive us? No doubt, yes, for if "any point requiring reflection," as Dupin states at the start, is "examined to best purpose in the dark," we may now easily read its solution in broad daylight. It was already implicit and easy to derive from the title of our tale, according to the very formula we have long submitted to your discretion, in which the sender, we tell you, receives from the receiver his own message in reverse form. Thus, it is that what the "purloined letter," nay, the "letter in sufferance" means is that a letter always arrives at its destination.

—*Translated by Jeffrey Mehlman*

---

[48]Thus, nothing shall (have) happen(ed)—the final turn in Lacan's theater of lack. Yet within the simplicity of that empty present the most violent of (pre-)oedipal dramas —Atreus, Thyestes—shall silently have played itself out.—J.M.

ERNST KAEMMEL

Literature under the Table: The Detective Novel and its Social Mission

In this essay the East German scholar Ernst Kaemmel attempts to explain, with reference to social and economic conditions, the facts that the detective novel, despite its limited literary value, is enormously popular in the capitalistic countries and that it does not exist in the socialist ones. Examination of the history and conventional features of the genre reveal it to be a child of capitalism. The crimes invariably represent attacks upon private property and the whole social order designed to protect it; the authorized institutions of bourgeois society are incapable of bringing the perpetrator to justice, yet this can be achieved by an individual who is outside the institutions and is endowed with remarkable capabilities. The bourgeois reader's realization of the failure of capitalism is thereby invoked; yet the possibility of revolutionary political action by the oppressed classes is precluded by the romantic glorification of the isolated individual. "It is obvious that a detective literature of this sort is hardly conceivable in a socialist state, above all for lack of the corresponding social phenomena. It is a product of capitalism and, with the latter's collapse, will likewise disappear one day." Yet a socialist version of the detective novel can be imagined, one in which state agencies, with the cooperation of the people, would track down an occasional individualistic criminal. Such a version would no longer be a trivial pastime, but would educate readers and thereby acquire a serious literary value. The West German Richard Alewyn and the Australian Stephen Knight advance different explanations for the popularity of the detective novel in capitalist countries.

Ernst Kaemmel, born in 1890, spent the last years of his life in East Berlin, where he was a professor of literature. This essay originally appeared in 1962 in the East German publication Neue deutsche Literatur.

What is a detective novel? Why is there virtually a glut of this kind of literature in the capitalist world and why is there—with few exceptions—nothing comparable in the socialist camp? What attracts its readers and what repels them? The detective novel is, to be sure, a kind of literature on the surface, but one under the table—to put it differently, the literary critical and literary historical outlawing of this branch of literature impedes scholarly interest in it and careful judgment about it. The detective novel plays an important role in the capitalist world; at the same time, its influence reaches into our own world—its very existence is a problem. It would be worthwhile to take a closer look at this problem; perhaps some argument can be suggested to help explain the peculiar false-bottom quality of this literary genre, its limited literary value contrasted with its enormous popularity and its large influence.

In the capitalist world, the detective novel is probably the most popular branch of belles-lettres, and its effect upon readers corresponds pretty well to this popularity. There are estimates, especially in the Anglo-Saxon secondary literature, which, though they may be quite imprecise in detail, nevertheless give some idea of the sheer quantity of this branch of literature. According to the article on "Mystery Stories" in the *Encyclopaedia Britannica* (1946), in England and the United States about 1,300 different detective novels appeared from 1841 to 1920 and about 8,000 from 1920 to 1940; for the period from 1940 to 1960, *Publishers' Weekly* estimates the number of published detective novels at 15,000 to 16,000. Moreover, editions of individual novels are almost unbelievably large. The total distribution of the detective novels of the author Ellery Queen (the pseudonym of F. Danney and Manfred B. Lee), who himself appears in his books under the name Ellery Queen as a master detective, was estimated to have reached twenty million copies by 1950, while Agatha Christie has allegedly published one hundred million copies of fifty different detective novels. The American author Erle Stanley Gardner, a former lawyer, had editions of ten million copies in the cheap pocket editions of his novels at the end of the 1940s; at that time, six to seven million copies of the regular editions of his novels were sold each year. The great popularity of this genre shows that we are dealing here not only with a literary problem but above all with a social one. For this reason we are justified in asking what the social situation was out of which the detective novel arose, what its social and literary missions are, what development it has undergone, and what influence it has exerted. These questions will guide the following remarks.

The detective novel is a child of capitalism. It arose in the most highly developed countries of premonopolistic capitalism, in England and the United States in the second half of the nineteenth century, and it achieved its classic expression at the end of the nineteenth century and the beginning of the twentieth. In the last forty years, under the conditions of decaying imperialism in the United States, it has sunk to the so-called "hard-boiled" variety and to the potboilers of a Mickey Spillane, and has reached its temporary nadir in horror stories and horror movies.

Without a doubt, belles-lettres assisted at the birth of the detective novel, which developed out of the adventure novels of the late eighteenth century and the romantic, sensationalist novels and thrillers of the nineteenth century. Proponents of the theory that the detective novel is derived from riddle literature overlook the fact that riddle literature addresses quite different areas of human life, ones beyond belles-lettres. In the course of its development, the detective novel became concentrated very quickly upon portraying a (fictional) detective's solution of a murder or another capital crime in a fictional plot. In this way it freed itself from criminal reportage (like Löwenthal's *Golden Gallows*), from memoirs (for example, Manolescu's *Memoirs of a Confidence Man*), the criminal story without a detective (for example, Fontane's "Under the Pear-Tree"), the adventure novel (for example, Stevenson's *Treasure Island*), the thriller (for example, Eugène Sue's *The Mysteries of Paris*), the ghost story (for example, Daphne du Maurier's *Jamaica Inn*), and the picaresque novel (Thomas Mann's *Confessions of Felix Krull, Confidence Man*). The detective novel has become an independent branch of literature with sharply defined characteristics, one that proceeds according to certain constant rules.

The forefathers of the detective novel are considered to be a series of famous writers of the nineteenth century, above all Edgar Allan Poe with his "The Murders in the Rue Morgue" and Charles Dickens with a whole series of novels, such as *Bleak House* and *The Mystery of Edwin Drood*. But a decisive step in its development is not to be found until the end of the 1880s with Sir Arthur Conan Doyle. He invented the figures of the master detective Sherlock Holmes and of his friend Watson, and the gigantic (and even today not quite exhausted) success which his fairy tales have had, comparatively meager as they are literarily and in part quite implausible, shows clearly that they corresponded to a quite specific stage in the development of capitalist society. Let us bear in mind the subject matter, too, the portrayal of the solution of a murder by a private detective in a fictional story. What is involved is the interpretation of the circumstances of a case, in most instances also that of an attack upon the social relations of a society based upon exploitation. A murder is never committed out of passion or revenge, it is not the result of overwhelming emotion, but is instead always an act based upon economic motives; it touches upon the basic law of capitalist society, upon private property. Neither society itself nor the institutions it has created, especially the police, prove themselves capable of solving it. What is required is the activity of the private detective, who allows justice to rule and the criminal to be punished. Alone, without the support of society, indeed even against its will, the individual is capable of repairing the rupture in the moral order. That also means that the individual, isolated and self-reliant, can correct the mistakes and weaknesses of the social order. This is, to be sure, a crass misunderstanding of social forces; but the success of detective literature in the capitalist world at least shows how strongly the defects of its social order are felt.

The private detective is a typical phenomenon of Anglo-Saxon life. He is a kind of auxiliary organ of the police, authorized to perform investigations, interrogations, and so forth, but only on the basis of a license—and always on his own account and at his own risk. In literature, he is equipped with supernatural attributes so that he can perform his task; his mental acuity permits the solution of the crime

Literature under the Table

and the discovery of the criminal. This exaggeration of the mental powers generally makes reason absolute, but does not permit the narrowly defined and rigid scheme of the detective novel to vary. As a further consequence, the reader does not become conscious of its real social mission; instead, the whole thing takes on the appearance of a quiz, in whose solution the reader's combinatory impulse (solution of the murder) and simultaneously his ethical requirements (sense of justice—reconstitution of the violated order of law) are taken account of.

The criminal case to be solved by the detective is introduced into the plot as being enigmatic or inexplicable. In this way, the question of the type, meaning, and detailed circumstances of the murder or capital crime is posed. The necessary tension is achieved by misleading the reader and the detective by narrative retardations which culminate in the establishment of an erroneous theory, which is finally demolished bit by bit, so that the reader goes step by step from error to truth. A rigid technique of novelistic construction develops from this scheme. First, the external facts of the case are given; this is followed by the posing of the problem, the introduction of the detective and his indispensable assistant, the appearance of the antagonist (mostly a police officer, sheriff, district attorney, police prefect, or the like), the description of the circle of suspects, the construction of a theory, the gradual purification of the theory from errors, until finally the detective finds the solution; the reader is then informed of this in the form of a revelation. Neither the murder nor the trial nor the punishment is portrayed in classic detective literature.

This formula for the composition of a detective novel (in the Anglo-Saxon secondary literature there are textbooks on the manufacture of criminal novels—for example, Rodell, *Mystery Fiction, Theory and Technique,* New York, 1952, based on lectures at a New York university)[a] shows that a job is being done here in an absolutely workmanlike manner, with a craftsman's rules. In fact, this is a genuine handicraft in the art of entertainment, a lucrative trade. If the craftsman's rules have been followed, the work itself will not miss its effect, even if it is literarily sloppy and meager and full of theatricality. There are certain fundamental principles which must not be violated. The

---

[a]Marie F. Rodell, *Mystery Fiction: Theory and Technique* (New York: Duell, Sloan, and Pearce, 1943). The notion that these were university lectures appears unfounded.—Eds.

detective (his role can also be taken over by a clever police officer) must have an assistant, a "Watson." The reader himself must be cleverer than the assistant; the assistant is "the great big simpleton." Furthermore, the whole course of the action must be seen by the reader with the eyes of the detective. Finally, the whole work of the detective must rest upon logically strict conclusions drawn from the accurate judgment of details unnoticed by others. Naturally, this is only possible within the framework of a fictional story, for what is strict is obviously, in fact, only the author's report but not the conclusions drawn from the circumstances, for these are arbitrarily drawn by the author.

All of this applies to so-called classic detective literature as it is embodied above all in Sherlock Holmes and his friend Watson. There are not many literary figures which have led and still lead so strong a life. Doyle gave the address of Sherlock Holmes as Baker Street 221b in London. Baker Street is one of the formerly boring, quiet, genteel streets that cross Oxford Street. But there has never been a number 221B there. The London Post Office has a box in which even today thousands of letters are preserved which were sent to this address between 1900 and 1930. Sherlock Holmes was a representative of law, justice, and capitalist order; his readers, generally middle-class and lower middle-class people, whose interest in this literature was based above all on its depictions of society (almost all these novels take place in polite society) and on the acuity and superiority of the detective, with whom they were inclined to identify themselves, expect the violated order to be reconstituted in a suspenseful story.

The decline of detective literature began when, instead of Sherlock Holmes, Nick Carter and the tribe of the Carters appeared on a lower level in cheap magazines. While the readers of the classic criminal novels were able to appreciate the private detective's acuity and successes, the stories on the Nick Carter level are unreeled more coarsely and without making a claim upon mental powers. Naturally, there are a number of authors of detective novels (like, for example, Dorothy Sayers, Agatha Christie, and so on) who are still producing criminal novels in the old style, but America has taken over the leadership in developing this field, and there the hard-boiled school has entirely supplanted the old type. Obviously, thirty years of production of classic criminal novels have exhausted the motifs and made the types rigid and the titles stereotyped, so that the uncreative, ever-recurring method of portrayal has given the classic criminal novel the characteristics of a barren system. It was from this dead end that the hard-boiled authors, who oriented themselves towards Hemingway, thought they were escaping. Suddenly—what is impossible in classic detective novels—detailed descriptions of murder and of brutal mistreatment appear, the police and the detective are portrayed as amoral gangster types, social life appears to be a swamp of corruption. The hero has changed into an unromantic cynic. Negative phenomena of social life are accepted as simple facts without any relevance. In most of the detective novels of the hard-boiled school, there does not appear a single nice, decent, or good character; the reader comes upon a turbulent collection of criminal types who smoke each other out. The transition to the gangster milieu has been completed.

It is obvious that a detective literature of this sort is hardly conceivable in a socialist state, above all for lack of the corresponding social phenomena. It is a product of capitalism and, with the latter's collapse, will likewise disappear one day. It is possible that a literature will remain and develop that, using some of the technical devices of the classic detective novel, takes as its object criminal offenses of the most various sorts; that is, it discovers and reveals acts against law and against society in a literary plot (cf. Radtke's "Frogman in the Oder," the novels of Wolfgang Schreyer, and the books of Friedrich Karl Kaul, which hold a middle position between criminal novel, detective novel, and adventure novel). But the method, like the successful search for the criminal, will be as different from classic detective literature as the social orders themselves differ from one another, for it is scarcely conceivable that the investigation of a criminal in a socialist society could be the solo performance of a private man, an outsider, if necessary against the collective work of the police and of the organs of state, indeed against the cooperation of the populace. And in this sense one can conceive of a development from classic schematic detective literature to a really modern criminal literature, whose main purpose would then no longer be to pass the time and to titillate the nerves. It would have attained the function of transmitting knowledge, and thereby for the first time a serious literary function.

—*Translated by Glenn W. Most*

RICHARD ALEWYN

The Origin of the Detective Novel

Alewyn attempts to answer the twin questions of why the detective novel is so popular nowadays and why it is only a century old. He lists and criticizes the traditional arguments—psychological, political, historical —for and against the genre, and postulates three essential features of all such novels: first, a murder at the beginning and its explanation at the end; second, an innocent person is suspected and the guilty one is not; and third, the detection is the work, not of the police, but of an outsider. All these features are found, long before Poe, in E. T. A. Hoffmann's story, "Das Fräulein von Scuderi" (1818). In fact, the detective novel is not the child of the rationalistic and conservative nineteenth century but of the mystical and irrationalistic German romantic movement, and its ultimate precursors are Gothic novels. Instead of rendering everyday reality, rational order, and bourgeois security safe and sound, the detective novel serves instead to shake them up.

Alewyn's view of the detective novel's relation to bourgeois society stands in interesting contrast to those expressed by Kaemmel, Grossvogel, Knight, and Miller. Richard Alewyn, who died in 1980, was a professor of Germanic philology, most recently in Bonn. This essay is translated from his 1974 volume of essays, Probleme und Gestalten.

A body is discovered. The circumstances permit no other diagnosis than murder. But who did it? That is the question that occupies and frightens everyone but that is not answered until the end of the story has been reached. The question becomes more urgent after a second murder has been committed, and a third. The search becomes feverish. Clues are found, pursued, and lost again. Hypotheses are constructed and refuted. But slowly some proven facts are sifted out. Their correct interpretation and correlation provide the answer to the mute question posed by the corpse, the reconstruction of the course of events, and the detection of the criminal.

What I have presented to you is a model in which you will recognize a literary phenomenon familiar to everyone: the detective novel. Reading a detective novel is one of the things people are willing to do but are not willing to talk about, at least not in good society and especially not among academics. Its material is indelicate, its style not always the most refined, its popularity knows no limits—reasons enough to disqualify it morally, esthetically, and socially, even if not to lessen its fascination. A couple of figures may provide evidence: in the United States alone, about 500 detective novels appear each year in book form, not counting the thousands of detective stories that are disseminated in magazines, radio, and television. One author sold in a single year four million volumes, while the total sales of another author's detective novels exceed 100 million copies. The pestilence began in America and England, but has spread over the whole world. And not only as opium for the people. We could name respectable representatives of politics and business, of literature and theology, who have confessed to this addiction. One can consider this disturbing, amusing, or perplexing; but one cannot ignore it.

What makes this phenomenon remarkable is not only its distribution, but also the fact that it is a modern invention. According to general opinion, the detective novel is not much more than a century old. The American Edgar Allan Poe is considered to be the discoverer of its formula, and his "Murders in the Rue Morgue" (1841) is taken as the classic example of the genre. But it did not begin its triumphal procession until fifty years later, under the leadership of Sherlock Holmes, the master detective created by Conan Doyle in London. Since then, however, the fruitfulness of this genre has never dried up, in spite of the frequent prophecies of its death.

How is it possible that so successful a fashion was not discovered earlier? Only if no need corresponded to it earlier. And, conversely, the current attractiveness of the detective novel can only be explained by its satisfying widespread needs. Whoever could succeed in figuring out what a detective novel really is would therefore not only have answered a question of literary history, he would perhaps also have acquired information about the masses of its readers and thus about the psychological condition of man in our time. Tell me what you read and I will tell you who you are.

What is a detective novel? This question has seldom been posed impartially. Though so many have thought, written, and spoken about it, most of them can be easily divided into two camps: its opponents and its defenders. It is not our intention to become embroiled in this debate, not because the question of a thing's value is unimportant, but because it cannot be answered as long as that thing is not recognized and understood. And the debate up to now has been so rich in misrecognitions and misunderstandings that inspecting its arguments provides the most unavoidable and most profitable starting point.

Everyone is familiar with the psychological argument. The objection is made against the detective novel that it deals with crimes of violence and numbs its readers to them or stimulates them to imitate them by showing them in a romantic light and removing the natural inhibitions against them. Hence, the detective novel is a school of crime. Against this, the response is that real criminals read no detective novels; they have no need to. Conversely, the readers of detective novels have no need to become criminals, since their reading permits them to rid themselves of their dormant criminal instincts innocently and harmlessly. Thus, the reader of the detective novel is subjected to the same catharsis as the viewer of Greek tragedy.

Both arguments have some plausibility and could certainly be corroborated. But we mention them only because they speak of an object which has often been mistaken for our own, which in practice probably intersects often enough with ours but is not identical with it, namely, the crime novel. In appearance, the difference is merely technical: the crime novel tells the story of a crime, the detective novel that of the solution of a crime. But this difference has far-reaching consequences. In the crime novel, the criminal is presented to the reader before the crime is, and the circumstances of the crime before its result. In the detective novel, on the other hand, the sequence is reversed. When the reader learns the identity of the criminal, the novel is necessarily at an end; he is informed of the result of the crime earlier than its circumstances; and he does not witness these circumstances, but instead learns of them by subsequent reconstruction. If the crime novel recommends itself by permitting the reader to empathize with the murderer and to experience the crime with him in his own mind, the detective novel denies its reader such sensational effects. Hence, the latter reader has neither a contagion to fear nor a cure to hope for, and if he is not spared excitement, it is of a different nature.

But, we hear the opponents say, even if the criminal remains anonymous until the end, that still does not alter the regrettable fact that the detective novel always has to do with a murder. In response, its defenders can do little more than confess their embarrassment. They can neither deny the fact nor explain it convincingly. But they can point out that it is just as inevitable that the murderer be tracked down and bagged at the end. Hence, the detective novel teaches that crime does not pay, and thereby becomes a school of morality and justice. But this argument would be more convincing if the murderers were not represented so often as being more sympathetic than their victims and if their pursuers, the police and detectives, were always justified in considering themselves the champions of goodness.

But most of the apologists have gone even further: according to them, the detective novel is not only a school of justice but also an expression of democratic civic consciousness. They have started out from the correct observation that the detective novel has developed most fruitfully in England, the United States, and France, countries with liberal traditions, while it has never really succeeded in taking root in Germany or in Southern and Eastern Europe, and they have found it significant that the detective novel has been suppressed under totalitarian regimes. What is more plausible, they suppose, than to understand the detective novel as a democratic institution? They have also provided an explanation: in autocratically ruled countries, they suggest, the public is in the opposition and hence automatically stands on the side of the person who breaks the law. Here, therefore, only the crime novel, in which the criminal is glorified, could flourish. The detective novel, on the other hand, in which the reader's sympathies are involved in the hunt for the criminal, his feelings satisfied and his convictions confirmed at the end by the restoration of the order of law, could only be conceived on the soil of democracy.

Every sentence in this argument has an error of fact or a mistake in logic. But let us try to keep listening. The apologists have pointed to an innovation in criminal procedure, allegedly not much older than the detective novel, namely, the introduction of circumstantial proof. Before the nineteenth century, we hear, nobody had bothered about circumstantial evidence. When no eyewitnesses could be found, the courts had been satisfied with torturing the defendant until he confessed. It is only since he, too, has enjoyed the protection of the laws himself that the public prosecutor has been obliged to prove the defendant's guilt to the court by a consistent chain of circumstantial evidence. But what else is the detective novel than such a circumstantial proof? Are not here, too, the circumstances of the crime consistently reconstructed, and thereby the criminal convicted, on the basis of clues? Hence, isn't the detective novel practically a textbook of liberal legal procedures, and could it have arisen before these arose?

Before we express our doubts about this argument, too, let us listen a bit longer. The apologists have pointed finally to certain public institutions created by the nineteenth century. They have claimed that there can only be detective novels once there are detectives, who have only existed since the creation in England in 1829 of a nonuniformed police force, from which Scotland Yard arose in 1842, and since the simultaneous organization in France of the Sûreté Nationale for investigating crimes. The spirit which produced these public institutions is, according to these writers, the same as the one that animates the detective novel.

But is all that, in fact, correct? We do not wish to ask now whether the claims concerning legal and cultural history (which have been taken over even by such clever and informed authors as Dorothy Sayers and Ernst Bloch) hold water. We need only pose a single question, one which can be answered by anyone who has read even only a couple of detective novels: is it then correct that in the detective novel it is an agency of the government which tracks down the murderer? Certainly, the police are usually at the scene of the crime en masse and get to work with commendable zeal. But do they accomplish anything other than finding a few tracks that quickly come to nothing or than throwing their nets around the wrong man? Would the criminal ever be found if a generally quite unauthorized person did not get involved, one who takes up the investigation to amuse himself or as a favor, without being appointed to do so by his office and often against the resistance of the police?

Doubtless, connoisseurs of detective literature will know that there are also successful detectives in the official police and will think, for example, of Georges Simenon's amiable Inspector Maigret or F. W. Croft's valiant Inspector French. But they will also concede that these are exceptions. (Estimates vary between ten and twenty percent.) Opposed to them stands the long series of amateur detectives that begins with E. A. Poe's Dupin and Conan Doyle's Sherlock Holmes and is gloriously continued by Chesterton's Father Brown, Agatha Christie's Hercule Poirot, Dorothy Sayers's Lord Peter Wimsey, Margery Allingham's Albert Campion, by Ellery Queen, by Raymond Chandler's Philip Marlowe, Rex Stout's Nero Wolfe, Erle Stanley Gardner's Perry Mason, and many others.

If a strange custom is observed so conscientiously, it is certainly more than a mere whim, and identifying it more than mere pedantry. There can be no doubt about its meaning. To be sure, the police and the detectives usually—if not always—cooperate cordially; but neither is the one side free from fits of jealousy nor the other from feelings of superiority, and both sentiments are not unjustified. Furthermore, the police are usually—by no means always—honestly and zealously on the job, but they are, even at their best, nothing more than capable routinists and ordinarily blind, narrow-minded, and unimaginative. And although the police have at their disposal an unlimited apparatus of persons and resources, they seldom avoid a dead end or a false clue. It is really impossible to derive from this a high opinion of the effectiveness of the agencies of the constitutional state.

But where the professionals make fools of themselves, the amateur shines. If anything at all is supposed to be glorified here, then it is certainly not the criminal, and not the state and police either, but instead the individual; and if we are looking for a political and sociological position for the detective or the detective novel, then it would make more sense to think of the liberalistic spirit of self-help which has been so impressively developed in the Anglo-Saxon countries and which has often enough not been especially pious towards the state.

But detectives are not only individuals; they are also outsiders. What lives they lead! They have no wife, they have no children, they have no profession, they live in messy rooms, they lead an irregular life, they turn the night into day, they smoke opium or raise orchids; indeed, they have unconcealed artistic inclinations, they quote Dante or play the violin. These detectives have the souls neither of civil servants nor even of citizens; these detectives are eccentrics and bohemians. This fact, too, has been often acknowledged, and not without astonishment; but it has never been explained. What does it mean when detective novels attribute with such striking unanimity precisely to these outsiders the success they withhold from the police? Certainly, not a vote of confidence for public institutions nor an acknowledgment of a social conformism. Instead, the suspicion obtrudes itself that precisely these aberrations from the social and psychological norm explain the success of the detective.

This leads us to examine a further attempt to explain the origin of the detective novel in terms of the spirit of the nineteenth century. It has been said that this century brought the exact sciences to victory. As a child of the Enlightenment, it banished the darkness that until then had lain upon all areas of life and thought. It determined to explain reality by methodically collecting and logically ordering facts. But, it has been asked, what is the detective novel if not a model of this procedure? What else happens here than that a secret is elucidated by exact observation and controlled combination? And could that have been conceivable in the autocratic or totalitarian social orders in which thinking was prohibited?

Again, we do not wish to take up the terrible simplification at the basis of this theory, but only to examine the detective novel itself. In this case, to be sure, we will not have it so easy. There is no doubt that what is involved here is a process of the discovery of truth. At the beginning is a riddle, at the end comes the solution; the theme is nothing other than the search for this solution, and a large part of the tension is derived from this. Empiricism and logic, the methods of scientific thought, are also the methods with which the detective operates. He must combine many scattered and hidden traces with one another in such a way that a consistent correlation results. But does the object of these investigations have anything to do with our reality, and are their methods used in the same way as they are in the exact sciences?

I wish only briefly to point out that the world of the detective novel is constructed differently from that of our everyday experience. One of the recognized rules, for example, is that the criminal is one of the characters known to the reader from the beginning. It is considered impermissible to make an unknown character passing by chance the murderer. There are various reasons for this, but one is that it would otherwise be impossible for the reader to participate in the investigation. Hence, a circle of characters which is limited from the beginning is required. Frequently, this limitation is further marked by physical barriers. A weekend party at an isolated country house, a snowbound express train, a luxury yacht on a Mediterranean cruise, or a hermetically sealed house are therefore favored locations. These are artifical situations: they are possible in reality, but not especially frequent.

But the circumstances of the murder are just as carefully prepared. So that it can later be consistently reconstructed through mere combination, it must not only have been consistently planned but also brought off according to plan. Details of the sort that constantly require us in everyday life to change our plans and to postpone appointments—an unexpected call or visit, a downpour, or an occupied telephone booth—are not foreseen in the murderer's plan. The detective novel takes place in a world without chance, a world which is certainly possible, but is not the ordinary one.

But in other respects as well, what happens in the detective novel has little in common with everyday life. To begin with, a crime is already something that scarcely ever occurs in the experience of normal people; again, among all crimes, murder is fortunately the rarest. But not only does the detective novel insist upon murder with a curious pedantry: it makes it its object precisely to dream up cases of such a complexity as rarely or never appear even in the experience of the police. And the reason for this is not only, as has been supposed, that the classic methods of murder, poison and the dagger, have become so clichéd that every new author is compelled to surpass his predecessors by more exotic inventions. The unusual murder stood already at the cradle of the detective novel. E. A. Poe's first murderer was very far from being everyday; it was an orangutan, and not by chance. Poe had his detective confess (and many have agreed) that the more exotic the method of a murder, the easier its solution. Hence, if it is true that the detective finds out the truth about a reality, this reality is not the usual one and is certainly not the one that obeys the laws of the natural sciences.

But what about the methods with which the detective operates? Certainly, he draws his conclusions from observations; it is not the obvious and most palpable facts that interest him, however, but rather extremely inconspicuous and insignificant things: a nail that has been broken off, a little bit of cigar ash, a clock that stopped or that did not stop—things that say nothing to an ordinary person, that have absolutely no significance in ordinary life, but that for the detective become the signs of a secret writing whose deciphering solves the riddle. But this art of reading clues and interpreting signs is denied to the ordinary person; indeed, in ordinary life it has no utility.

"Nothing deceives more than a naked fact," Sherlock Holmes is fond of saying and his successors are fond of repeating. But normal people (and to these belong especially the representatives of the police) inevitably let themselves get led astray by such "naked facts," palpable and evidently obvious facts of a case. And here we must mention an institution we have previously omitted, one which, though it has seldom been recognized, belongs, like the amateur detective, to the basic requirements of the detective novel: the motif of the false clue. Inevitably, all the circumstances point unanimously at the beginning to one person, who, in reality, is entirely innocent. And this error can be repeated until all the main characters of the novel have come into the gravest suspicion one after the other, with a single exception: the one who, in reality, is the criminal. It is a generally practiced rule that the most suspected person is innocent and the least suspected the criminal; naturally, the validity of this rule is not annulled, but only confirmed, when the author for once reverses the procedure in consideration of the clever reader and permits the really guilty party to seem so suspicious that he seems unsuspicious.

Misleading the reader in this way is designed to startle him and thereby to increase his pleasure. But it also betrays a doubt about the nature of the world and the aptitude of the organs of our experience, and it contains above all a scathing judgment of the reliability of circumstantial proof. So far from spreading trust in reason and science, it serves rather to undermine it. Just as little as the usual in the detective novel is the real, so little is the probable in it the true. Its world is not constructed according to the realistic and rationalistic model of positivism. Therefore, we shall have to seek its home elsewhere.

The Origin of the Detective Novel

Before we inquire into this, we wish to recall once more the institutions which we bumped into while examining the popular theories about the spirit and origin of the detective novel and which we had to add to our first model. This model was: an enigmatic murder and its solution. The first addition was: this solution is the work, not of the police, but of an amateur who is an outsider socially and an eccentric psychologically. The second addition was: the apparently guilty person is, in reality, innocent, the apparently most innocent person is, in reality, the guilty one. These are seemingly technical formalities, but the conscientiousness and unanimity with which they are observed betrays an unconscious need, which requires explanation.

And now, after so much dry theory, I am happy to tell, or rather to retell, a story. It takes place in Paris at the time of Louis XIV. The city has been alarmed for some time by a series of murders, all performed according to the same pattern. The victims are always isolated pedestrians who are supplied with expensive gifts and are on their way late at night to an amorous tryst. They are found in the morning, stabbed to death with the same weapon and robbed of their jewels. Police protection is increased and a special court is established, which succeeds in spreading a fear that causes even the most innocent to begin to tremble but not in getting hold of the murderer or even in preventing the continuation of his crimes. It is only when the respected goldsmith Cardillac is discovered murdered that the criminal is thought to have been found: Olivier Bresson, Cardillac's apprentice and lodger and the fiancé of his daughter Madelon, is arrested.

All the evidence speaks against him. He was found in Cardillac's room with the corpse, as was, with him, the weapon with which not only Cardillac but also all the earlier victims had been killed. He can supply no plausible explanation of the circumstances. He claims that his master left the house at midnight and ordered him to follow him at a distance of fifteen steps. From this distance he had seen Cardillac attacked by an unknown man. The murderer had vanished in the darkness, while he himself had dragged the dying man into his house and had also brought the murder weapon with him.

These statements are entirely implausible, as is demonstrated at length. For one thing, Olivier cannot explain what might have caused Cardillac to go out so late. Second, it appears to be impossible both that he could have left the house unnoticed at that hour and that Olivier could have brought him back unnoticed. Other people who live in the house attest (and this is checked and confirmed) that neither the lock nor the hinges of the house door can be moved without creating a loud noise which can be heard as far as the fourth floor. But on the third floor, two witnesses had spent the whole night without sleep. They clearly heard Cardillac bolt the door from inside at nine o'clock in the evening, as was his custom, and then nothing more until after midnight, when they heard, above the ceiling of their room, first heavy steps, then a muffled fall, and then a loud groan. The situation—well known to the theory and practice of the detective novel as the "locked room murder"—permits no other conclusion than that the murder was performed in the house. No other suspect comes into question but Olivier.

But then the earlier murders as well, which were performed with the same weapon under similar circumstances, must be laid to his account, and this suspicion becomes a certainty when, with the arrest of Olivier, the murders immediately cease. Neither the police nor the public doubt Olivier's guilt, especially as he was the fiancé of the daughter and sole heir of Cardillac and consequently would not have lacked an obvious motive.

Here we have the apparently consistent circumstantial proof which nevertheless goes completely astray. Olivier is not the murderer, but the unwilling and unhappy accessory who—as so often in detective novels—is compelled to silence by his regard for someone close to him. The real murderer is none other than Cardillac, who, as someone known as an honest craftsman and, moreover, as the apparently last victim in a long series of murders, is the apparently least suspicious character. A neurotic compulsion (whose origin, by the way, is explained according to psychoanalytic method) drove him to use murderous methods to take possession again of the jewels he had manufactured. A secret passage permitted him to leave the house without being noticed. During the last of these sorties he had been stabbed with his own dagger in self-defense by an officer he had attacked, and had been brought back into the house by Olivier, who had secretly followed him.

It is not through the work of the police that all this is brought to light. On the contrary, their methods practically prevented the solution. The terror they spread sealed the lips of Cardillac's murderer. The solution is rather the work of an outsider, Mlle de Scuderi, a little old lady who is as clever as she is plucky and who is a poet. She solves the crime, not, to be sure, like her later colleagues in the detective novel, by actively taking the investigation in hand, yet still not by accident, but by means of capabilities which the representatives of the court and the police entirely lack and which make her a poet, too: warmheartedness, wisdom, and an infallible emotional certainty. These capabilities encourage the unwilling murderer of Cardillac to entrust himself to her. It is to these capabilities (and to an earlier personal connection) that she already owed a confession that Olivier, to spare his beloved, had denied the police.

Next to some subordinate motifs, we find all together in this story the three elements that constitute the detective novel: first, the murder, or the series of murders, at the beginning and its solution at the end; second, the innocent suspect and the unsuspected criminal; and third, the detection, not by the police, but by an outsider, an old maid and a poet; and then fourth, the extraordinarily frequent, though not obligatory, element of the locked room. The story is entitled "Das Fräulein von Scuderi" ("Mlle de Scuderi"). Its author is the German romantic E. T. A. Hoffmann. It appeared in 1818, almost a quarter-century before E. A. Poe's "Murders in the Rue Morgue," with which, according to previous opinion, the history of the detective novel begins.

I do not intend to claim by this that Poe knew Hoffmann's story and was influenced by it. Determining this priority would have only an academic interest, and the history of the detective novel would not have to be rewritten if it were simply a matter of a lucky bull's eye. But the case is quite different. To be sure, this is the only time that all the essential characteristics of the detective novel are found together in a single story by E. T. A. Hoffmann (in Poe, by the way, this happens nowhere), but individually they can be found easily everywhere in his works. In "Marquise de la Pivardière," retold from Pitaval, only the detective is missing. More importantly, the vast majority of his stories are constructed on the same pattern: a mystery and its solution. At the beginning one learns of an enigmatic event, or one encounters an unknown man with strange habits or an obscure past, or one is introduced into a whole circle of persons, a household or a clan or a court society, above whom a mystery hovers, or one enters a castle in a gloomy landscape or stands in front of an uninhabited house in a lively city, where there is something uncanny. The riddle awakens the reader's drive to investigate, when not that of one of the characters in the story, and this drive to investigate gives rise to discoveries that often yield new riddles but that confirm both the reader and the characters in the story in their sense of a subterranean connection. For a long time, all speculations or investigations lead to nothing or lead astray; but at the end, as is usually the case in the detective novel, everything obscure is clarified in a coherent report.

In this regard, E. T. A. Hoffmann is not alone. Mysteries and their solution provide the theme and the scheme of the romantic novel in Germany. All the novels of Tieck, Novalis, Brentano, and Eichendorff begin with riddles and questions and end with solutions and answers. If the characters in romantic novels are so willing to wander, this is also because a restlessness drives them on or a yearning draws them, but they are always also in search of something they once possessed but lost, their home, their father and mother, or a beloved. And during this search, it befalls them to encounter everywhere clues that say nothing to others but in which they recognize signs and messages, and these clues entwine themselves more and more closely into contexts in which everything that seemed isolated is connected and everything that seemed accidental attains a deeper significance, until at the end everything that had been lost is found again and all the riddles are solved. For romanticism, mystery is the condition of the world and all external appearance is merely the hieroglyph of a concealed meaning.

It is this romantic mystery that takes on the shadow of the uncanny in E. T. A. Hoffmann. But in his "Nachtstücke" ("Night Pieces"), the uncanny is always the sense of a crime concealed in the past or in the future. Hoffmann, like Poe after him, is one of the virtuosi of terror, and he is not the first who discovered and exploited this stimulus. Tieck had preceded him in Germany, and both Hoffmann and Tieck drew from a murky current which at the end of the eighteenth century had arisen in England and flooded all of Europe and had fertilized romanticism: the "Gothic" horror story.

The horror story is the abstinence neurosis of the aging Enlightenment. To a race starved by rationalism and bored with bourgeois security, it offered the forbidden fruits of mystery and of fear. If one strips away its nerve-shattering packaging—old castles in desolate mountains, around which at night the storm howls and the moon sheds an uncertain light—there remains a core similar to the simplest model of the detective novel; many inexplicable and uncanny phenomena turn out to be clues to secret connections, and these again reveal themselves slowly to be the consequences or omens of terrible crimes, whose roots are buried deep in the past and which are completely solved at the end when the criminal is unmasked and brought to justice.

These novels are often entitled *Mysteries:* between 1794 and 1850 over seventy novels appeared in England carrying this word in their title. Detective novels are still called mystery stories in English. The detective stories of E. T. A. Hoffmann and E. A. Poe are nothing but lateral shoots from this common root.

Now the detective novel is distinguished from the horror story by its locale. It does not carry its reader off into the dark Middle Ages. To be sure, it still occasionally makes itself at home in remote country houses and sleepy provincial towns, but it is happy to take residence in the modern metropolises and takes pleasure in turning precisely their well-known streets and buildings into the scene of extremely unusual occurrences and thereby making them strange in an uncanny manner. But this procedure, too, has its prehistory. In the middle of the nineteenth century, the Gothic mysteries had already receded when Eugène Sue's *The Mysteries of Paris* (1842–1843) unleashed a new wave of mystery novels in all of Europe, from whose fascination Balzac and Dickens, too, could not free themselves. In these novels, the apparently so prosaic and secure everyday life of the modern metropolis turned out to be nothing but a thin and brittle cover, undermined by a labyrinth of criminal conspiracies. Without being able to compete with the gloomy, colossal paintings of these metropolitan mysteries, E. T. A. Hoffmann had nevertheless here, too, already provided the model.

Romanticism had been just as dissatisfied with the trivial surface of the world and of life as the detective novel would be. Everywhere, in nature and in the soul, it tracked down hidden powers and secret meanings. It looked not only outside reality, but also *within* it, not on its surface, but into its depths. "Everything external is something internal transformed into the condition of mystery," says Novalis, and he means that for the favored gaze every phenomenon is a riddle whose key lies hidden in its depths. The whole world is a secret writing, and this applies to society no less than to nature.

It was E. T. A. Hoffmann who, thirty years before Eugène Sue and eighty years before Conan Doyle, developed this notion by turning not only lonely castles and cloisters but also the streets and squares, houses and places of entertainment of Paris and Berlin, Dresden, and Frankfurt, familiar to every native, into the scene of strange, mysterious, and criminal events, and lodging the unusual and the improbable in the middle of the everyday. In his story "Das öde Haus" ("The Deserted House"), in which behind the inconspicuous facade of a well-known and exactly specifiable house in Berlin, on the street Unter den Linden, gloomy secrets are revealed, he expresses the conviction "that the real phenomena in life often take on a much more marvelous form than everything the most active fantasy tries to invent." It sounds like an echo of this when Conan Doyle and his disciples repeat or vary countless times the saying, "Life is more fantastic than fantasy." And conversely, E. T. A. Hoffmann would not have hesitated to sign Conan Doyle's creed: "Nothing deceives more than a naked fact." Romanticism saw reality as the detective novel does: an everyday and peaceful and deceptive surface, with abysses of mystery and danger underneath.

But in both cases, not everybody is capable of recognizing and disclosing these dark depths. Rather, two kinds of men correspond to these two levels of reality. The first are the prosaic and profane ones who have made themselves at home in everyday reality and resist every insight that could shake their confidence in the rational order of the world and in the reliability of common sense, and who consequently are blind to the unusual and not up to dealing with the improbable. Romanticism calls them Philistines. But then there are the others, a small minority, who are pretty useless for practical life because they are strangers to it, eccentrics and outsiders, but to whom, according to E. T. A. Hoffmann, "the power to recognize the wonders of our life is given like a special sense." Romanticism calls them artists.

These are the men who—again according to E. T. A. Hoffmann—"in every ordinary phenomenon, be it person, act, or event, immediately perceive the eccentric element to which we find nothing comparable in our ordinary life and which we therefore call marvelous, who notice, for example, what thousands of passers-by overlook, that there is something odd about a certain house in Unter den Linden." To such a person it can also happen that he "often follows for days on end unknown persons who have something wondrous in their gait, clothing, tone, or look, that he brings together things from the antipodes and imagines from them connections no one thinks of." Could one give a better description of the talent and activity of the detective?

The romantics populated their novels with people of this sort. They are called "artists," less because they practice some art than because their eccentric character and their extravagant life style exclude them from the society of ordinary men and make them useless for everyday life. Without family and without profession, without residence and without possessions, they are at war with society and state. Citizens and civil servants they consider a nuisance or ridiculous. But these émigrés or exiles are the ones who know how to read the clues and to interpret the signs which remain invisible or incomprehensible to normal men. For they are prepared for the reality of the unusual and immune against the deception of the probable. To this type of person belongs Mlle de Scuderi. To it belong also Poe's Dupin and Conan Doyle's Sherlock Holmes and all the other outsiders among the detectives.

In this way, the literary source and the spiritual home of the detective novel are secured. It is a child of rationalism only insofar as all romanticism has rationalism as its father. In this way, too, the question of its essence can be posed anew, and the question of the source of the fascination it exerts. So far from confirming everyday reality, the rational order, and bourgeois security, it serves instead to jeopardize them. Perhaps, in the course of such an investigation, the answer to the question which has often been put but never satisfactorily answered suggests itself—the question which is the scandal of all the opponents and the embarrassment of all the friends of the detective novel: Why in the world is the detective novel not satisfied with a more gratifying theme than a murder?

Postscript 1974: My thesis that the first detective story was written by E. T. A. Hoffmann has found more disagreement than agreement, especially since Mlle de Scuderi does not proceed actively and methodically enough. That is true and is suggested above. But even E. A. Poe did not create a single complete detective story. In the "Murders in the Rue Morgue," which is always cited as the model, the murderer is missing. For a wild orangutan cannot commit murder, only manslaughter. To say this is not to split hairs. For a murder presupposes a motive and a plan, the most important factors in the detective story, the ones that make it possible to track down the criminal. Moreover, the motif of the innocent suspect appears here, but is entirely peripheral. Poe's "The Purloined Letter" is not concerned with a murder but with a stolen document. In "The Murder of Marie Roget," a hypothesis is proposed that is never verified, for the murderer remains undiscovered. Finally, in "Thou Art the Man," the impartial detective is lacking. The innocent suspect himself discovers the criminal.

—*Translated by Glenn W. Most*

HELMUT HEISSENBÜTTEL

Rules of the Game of the Crime Novel

Heissenbüttel distinguishes between two types of detective: the one who proceeds by ratiocination (Poe, Doyle) and the hard-boiled one who uses violence (Hammett, Chandler). The detective novel does not aim at the object of serious literature: the portrayal of human beings and the investigation of their motivations. Instead, it uses stylized versions of these themes in order to constitute a group of exemplary figures in specific locations with respect to the corpse. The group turns out to be a paradigm of late bourgeois sociological connectedness. This constitution of the group is brought about by the death of the victim. But the connection can only become apparent when the criminal unmasks himself as the one who must be sacrificed. Unexpectedly, the enormous number of variants of the detective novel and its evolution over the last half-century (which Heissenbüttel examines in some detail) reveal it to be one of the openest forms of modern literature; it is also one of the few kinds of modern literature which all readers can enjoy.

Original as it is, Heissenbüttel's argument has clear connections with the formalism of Caillois and Eco and the sophisticated social analysis of Alewyn, Jameson, Marcus, Knight, and Miller. Helmut Heissenbüttel is a radio editor, poet, critic, and essayist. His article appeared in the West German publication Der Monat *in 1963.*

1.

I have read 600 or 700 crime novels and continue to be a fairly regular reader of newly published books of this kind and of ones that I have missed in the past. It is difficult to make a survey of this reading: there are so many nuances and variations. Certain works are easily rejected, however. I have trouble reading Edgar Wallace or Ellery Queen, though I have tried several times. Similarly, I have gradually lost my taste for stories that put across nothing but the fame and the cleverness of their heroes, those, for example, about Peter Cheyney's detective, Lemmy Caution, or Carter Brown's police lieutenant, Al Wheeler. Mickey Spillane's Mike Hammer is another one of these. This branch of the genre is widespread, but it really represents a borderline case.

There is a classic pair of opposites among detectives: the one who, roughly or even brutally, thrashes his opponents (and naturally is himself also thrashed on occasion) until he has found out who done it; and the other who, by a mixture of investigation of facts and combinatory puzzle solving, brings what was at first confused and opaque into plausible connections and makes it transparent.

These two types play a role in the historic development of the genre. With Edgar Allan Poe's Auguste Dupin, the detective who is capable of solving the case through logical deduction alone makes his appearance. Dupin has a positivistic bent. He trusts in the omnipotent ability of human reason to provide enlightenment. On the other hand, what his enlightenment is directed towards is the quintessence of horror and inhumanity. The murderer is an ape. In this extreme polarization of reason and inhumanity, "The Murders in the Rue Morgue" seems like a programmatic statement which was never again to be expressed so purely. Sherlock Holmes, too, the most celebrated follower of Dupin, possesses this confidence in the solubility of problems. The emphasis is different in Chesterton's Father Brown. Liberal Christianity brakes the clerical detective's compulsion to disclose. The later followers of Dupin and Sherlock Holmes become more and more strongly stereotyped sociologically. Inspector French, Hercule Poirot, Lord Peter Wimsey, Dr. Gideon Fell, Albert Campion, Chief Inspector Alleyn, John Appleby, Nigel Strangeways, Professor Gervase Fen, Roger Crammond, Nero Wolfe, Dr. Martin Buell, Hildegard Withers, Inspector Napoleon Bonaparte (and a host of others) wear a conventional bourgeois mask in comparison to their forefathers. Their new prototype is the most famous one, Georges Simenon's Parisian Police Commissioner Maigret. It seems that with him a new lineage is founded; I shall return to this later.

The other species of the detective profession, the "hard-boiled" sort, does not enter literary life in as clearly defined a way as did Dupin and Sherlock Holmes. Its origin is in part to be derived from stories like those of Bret Harte, Mark Twain, or Ambrose Bierce. Early forms can be found in Europe, for example, in Sven Elvestad's detective Asbjörn Krag, who was famous in Germany in the twenties. But the real prototypes are considered to be Dashiell Hammett's detectives, such as Samuel Spade and Nick Charles (like their inventor, mostly small and inconspicuous employees of an agency), and Raymond Chandler's Philip Marlowe. It is especially Marlowe, the lost soul of Puritan treatises who nevertheless incarnates in all its perfection that justice which he sees corrupted in the representatives of a metropolitan and sophisticated upper class, who has found a large following. And James Hadley Chase has perhaps described the most original variants, for in his case the intermediate position between justice and injustice is taken seriously: the fronts seem to switch from case to case, and the activities of the "Enlightener" are ambiguous. An impressive, grotesque variant is found in the black detectives Gravedigger Jones and Coffin Ed Johnson of Chester Himes.[a]

2.

If one looks more closely at both these family trees of literary detectives, one can scarcely avoid the suspicion that, in spite of all the breadth of variation of the types, nevertheless this distinction is something technical, perhaps only regional. Roughly speaking, the difference is one of methods: on the one hand, logical thought; on the other, raw violence. But at the same time one notices that the logician, too, cannot do without an act of violence and that the hard-boiled detective in his turn depends upon the logical solution of his puzzle of facts.

One can quite well consider them as one and the same person. Their differences are internal, deriving as they do from their different degrees of capability. But capability to do what? To answer this, one must recognize how far the crime novel must really be considered as a realistic narrative in real specifiable milieus, real specifiable chronologies, with fictional but human figures. Appearances speak for this. But it also has been long noticed and objected that the representa-

[a] See his *Blind Man with a Pistol* (New York, 1969).—Eds.

tion of crime in the crime novel contradicts every criminological inventory, statistical and otherwise.

Mary Hottinger, the capable publisher of crime stories and valiant defender of the genre, has this to say on the subject:

> This odd position of the detective story is also evident when we compare it with the excellent series of *Notable British Trials* or the *Famous Trials*. Both series command a very wide and cultivated readership, consisting not only of criminal lawyers. They contain verbatim transcripts of important trials, with an introduction and an afterword by a respected legal scholar. The interest here, though, is always in the accused, while in the detective novel the criminal is seldom interesting and almost never appealing. There the interest is concentrated on the detective. This gap between trial reports and the detective story throws some light on the genre.[b]

The light that this gap throws on the genre illuminates one thing in particular, namely, that the cases dealt with in the crime novel are invented, indeed constructed. The examples that Erle Stanley Gardner reports from the real practice of his "Court of Last Resort" prove themselves entirely unsuitable for one of his Perry Mason novels. They must be adapted. The difference between a case of the sort solved by the literary detective and one of the legal practice of any country is, above all, that the real case results from complexities that only permit violent solutions, while the case in a novel must be constructed with a view towards its plausible solubility. This means that all the realistic elements, be they psychological, economic, or social in nature, must from the very beginning be so arranged that they can be combined into games with patterns that can be both encoded and decoded. Two possibilities for stylization result: abnormality and reduction. The descendants of Poe's orangutan are found in abnormality. Here the crime novel is transformed into the thriller, the horror story. Reduction leads to a further insight. It turns out that the crime novel has no interest in precisely that object in which the novel of so-called serious literature is interested: the representation of characters and the exploration of their motives in reflection and action. What looks like the exploration of motives turns out to be merely

[b]Mary Hottinger, *Mord: Angelsächsische Kriminalgeschichten von Edgar Allan Poe bis Agatha Christie* (Zurich, 1959).—Eds.

turning over previously provided play counters. The crime novel is an exemplary story that practices something according to a certain scheme.

3.

Here something must be added that likewise is not clearly enough differentiated in general. The crime novel is not a story that reports criminal acts *tout court*. The few examples that tell of robberies, smugglings, swindles, and the like are incidental. Just as little can the distinction (which is drawn over and over) between criminal stories and detective novels be maintained: this occurs especially in England and America, where a terminological distinction is made between crime stories and detective stories. The crime novel, as it has developed historically and as it plays a specific and undeniable role nowadays, is always a detective novel. Its foundation is provided by a fixed scheme containing three factors to begin with: the corpse, the detective, and the suspects. The victim, who is murdered either before the beginning of the story or on its first pages, sets everything in motion. The corpse is, as it were, the lever that provides the impulse to the story. On the other side stands the discoverer, who strives to solve the murder's complexity. All the other figures presented are either the detective's assistants (or else malicious delayers of his activity) or suspects. No character is portrayed for his or her own sake. All the extras are firmly bound to the schema.

Ernst Bloch has shown how the crime novel derives its narrative movement from the "reconstruction of the unnarrated," at which no one claims to have been present: "If, on the other hand, new murders occur in the course of the detective story itself, they, too, are still a black spot, connected with the initial darkness, increasing it, sometimes indeed impeding the solution. But the main thing always remains: the alpha, where none of the figures appearing in sequence admits to having been present, and the reader least of all: it happens —like the fall of man or even of the angels (pardon the mythical coloring)—outside of history."[c]

It is not necessary to prolong the perspective to Oedipus as Bloch does to recognize the exemplary and fundamental character of this

[c]Ernst Bloch, *Literarische Aufsätze*, Gesamtausgabe, vol. 9 (Frankfurt/Main, 1965), p. 254.—Eds.

kind of narrative. It is always one and the same story that is told. There is only one story of the corpse that is discovered and of the reconstruction of the murder, a reconstruction that gradually places the figures of the suspects, thrown together at first in an arbitrary manner, into a more and more orderly pattern. What pattern? At first one can only say that this pattern takes as its genuine and unique goal what appears in the "serious" novel only incidentally on the last pages, when the later fortunes of the characters, with whom we suffered and feared while we read, are quickly indicated.

In the one story that is told over and over again with almost infinite variability, there is no concern for the rehabilitation of the victim. As a reconstructed character, the corpse has the very least valuable personal position at the end of the exemplum. Its death is avenged, not in order to atone for personal guilt, but rather so as to be able to organize a group of exemplary figures in such a way that at the end one can pick out that figure who can take upon himself or be burdened with the atonement, not for the murder, but for the possible guilt of the other suspects, because he at the end represents the necessary loss pattern.

The particular path by which a conviction is reached plays a decisive role in each crime novel. The classical scheme of the Agatha Christie story begins with a situation that apparently excludes any solution (*Murder on the Orient Express, Murder in Mesopotamia,* and others). The murder is represented in such a way as to make it implausible that any of those present could have done the deed. Then facts come up that make a solution seem possible. These facts stand in irresolvable contradiction to one another. At this point, Hercule Poirot appears. In order to supplement the so far insufficient information, he looks into a few things that have not been checked up on yet, enlarges on them by using a little provocation, asking hypothetical questions whose answers bring the available facts into a new relation, and so on. The motive plays a special role in this gradually growing complex of clues. This is not conceived, however, as something too terribly psychological or subjectively penetrating; it appears rather in factual form. The activity of the detective has in such cases a wholly material goal. . . .[d] The detective tries to reconstruct a trace out of

---

[d] Here follows a long list of examples.—Eds.

individual accidental marks. He is like someone who out of individual strokes deciphers at first a script and then a text. The crucial thing, to stay with this image, is the script. The important thing is to practice a combinatorial skill in completing the trace. It is characteristic of many crime novels of the classic type that at the end the recounting of the murder itself is performed only superficially and with catchwords, sometimes indeed incompletely. Here Bloch's distinction can be made even sharper: what is important is not the reconstruction of the unnarrated, but rather the reconstruction of the trace of the unnarrated.

In this way it becomes clear that the narrative of the crime novel is fundamentally trapped in an abstractly functioning schematism with its own rigorous regularity. The story that is told works or does not work depending upon how these regularities are followed or neglected. The schematism is, so to speak, of a formal type. It does not produce, but it does guarantee the infinite variability of the one story. Within the framework of its rigorously calculable schema, the reconstruction of the trace of the unnarrated permits ever new combinations of possible contents.

4.

Now even such an abstract narrative can naturally not dispense with what is called its content. This content, one can say at first, consists in an ever new approximation to real scenes and milieus. The story gets dressed, as it were, in clothes of scene and milieu, always newly tailored. This does not happen in a merely psychological, sociological, or even ethnological humanization; it happens, remarkably enough, topographically. One variable is kept constant by anchoring the story topographically. Walter Benjamin has made this clear for earlier crime novels. In *One-Way Street* he says:

> The furniture style of the second half of the nineteenth century has received its only adequate description, and analysis, in a certain type of detective novel at the dynamic center of which stands the horror of apartments. The arrangement of the furniture is at the same time the site plan of deadly traps, and the suite of rooms prescribes the fleeing victim's path. . . . This character of the bourgeois apartment, tremulously awaiting the nameless murderer like a lascivious old lady her gallant, has been penetrated by a number of authors who,

as writers of "detective stories"—and perhaps also because in their works part of the bourgeois pandemonium is exhibited—have been denied the reputation they deserve.[e]

What Benjamin here calls "bourgeois pandemonium" appears in the pattern of the earlier crime novel as a clear representation of a polarization of good and evil, reason and monstrosity. This changes after Doyle and Chesterton. What stays the same is the topographical anchoring. While Benjamin's diagnosis still seems immediately applicable to Anthony Berkeley's London Club, Dorothy Sayers's (and Lord Peter's) Bellona Club is a more ordinary place, appearing naturally in the cityscape of certain London districts. It is like this, too, in John Dickson Carr.

The between-ness of places in many novels of Agatha Christie remains remarkable: interiors that are not, strictly speaking, interiors at all (the inside of an airplane or a sleeping car or the middle deck of a Nile steamer); interiors that stretch out feelers, as it were, without turning our surroundings into pure landscape; bits of landscape that acquire the character of interiors as they are treated like rooms.

Features that Benjamin in his analysis found out of the ordinary have changed; the ordinary, the everyday entanglement of people with places, still appears today to be one of the most prominent characteristics of the genre. But it must not be overlooked that it is not a matter of describing places and areas in the sense of serious literature. Interior and landscape are not transformed into language for their own sake; they do not appear in language as they really are. If I unmistakably learn in Hammett something about the topography of San Francisco, in Chandler about that of slums and luxury streets in Los Angeles, in Gardner something about estates and motels in California, in F. and R. Lockridge and Margaret Scherf about certain remote parts of New York City, in Margot Neville about Sydney, in Arthur W. Upfield about Australian small towns and farms, this familiarity with locations is always a familiarity with scenes of crime. I learn something about the place, not in its transformation into language, but rather in the summarizing of facts into a physiognomy of the scene of the crime. The reconstruction of the trace of the unnarrated is

[e]Walter Benjamin, *One-Way Street*, translated by Edmund Jephcott (London, 1979), pp. 48–49.—Eds.

performed with the help of topographic penetration. The location that is identified as the scene of the crime does not appear as a landscape in the artistic or romantic sense. It appears as a typologically imprinted living space. The model constructed by the crime novel appears at first as a place that has preserved the trace of typically human activity; the place appears as something that is made up of the traces of this activity. Conversely, the place has preserved in itself something immediately human (traces of psychology, emotions, happiness and unhappiness, sociability, and so on) as the play figures of the exemplary case itself. What is human is reified into the location. What Robbe-Grillet, for example, advocates theoretically[f] has been fulfilled by the crime novel long before him in its own way.

Benjamin speaks of this as a matter of "the only adequate description and analysis." What should be noticed in his remarks is the fact that the reconstruction of the scene of the crime is performed in the name of one of the participants (namely, of that one who performs the analysis), and that is the detective. He reconstructs. He can do this because of his special position, in which he is alone with the corpse. He reconstructs because, when examined more closely, he turns out to be equipped with capabilities that mark him out as a superhuman being. He is immortal and has a higher knowledge, omnipotence. Neither characteristic should be interpreted as something accidental, as exaggerated subjectivism, or as the secret self-glorification of the author: they must be taken literally. The detective knows from the beginning where his path will take him. The difficulties he has concern the path on which he must go. Kafka's sentence holds for him: "There is a goal, but no path; what we call path is delay." If he boasts at the end of his initial lack of knowledge, this is merely a mask he ties ironically around his face while he winks. In Hammett's *Thin Man* it says near the end: " 'You mean you thought that from the beginning?' Nora demanded, fixing me with a stern eye. 'No, darling, though I ought to be ashamed of myself for not seeing it . . .' "

5.

I used to think that, as happened with Gilbert Keith Chesterton and Dorothy Sayers as well, the detective must be interpreted as a theo-

---

[f] See *For a New Novel* (New York, 1966).—Eds.

logical figure, as a kind of archangel disguised as a citizen. I now think that such an interpretation oversimplifies the problem. Certainly, the detective has some characteristics of such an "emissary"; certainly, the crime novel is more at home in the narrative space of a secularized literature of legends and allegories than in the neighborhood of the realistic, psychological, or postrealistic novel. However, the reconstruction of the trace in the scene of the crime cannot be interpreted as an act of theological insight. But as what then?

If the reconstruction of the trace turns out at the end to be something that can also be understood as the gradual revelation of a pattern, this revelation has to do not with the scene of the crime but with the characters in the story, more precisely with the group of suspects (not the detective's assistants or opponents). The first characteristic shared by this group of suspects is that they each had some relation to the corpse. These relations are limited to emotional, familial, and economic ties. The gangster appears only as a marginal figure or, with a special function, in the latest phase of the genre. The ties of the characters to the corpse reveal themselves furthermore to be the same ones that make the characters recognizable among themselves as a group. They can also be described as the molecular affinities which structure late bourgeois society: the ones that reveal themselves to be the last sociological cement between the individual persons in a situation in which class divisions no longer exist and despotic methods are not yet binding enough. The pattern formed at the end by the group of suspects is determined by this last binding agent of late bourgeois society. The group proves to be a pattern of late bourgeois sociological bonding. This constitution of the group is purchased at the cost of the victim's death. What divides them has, as it were, been precipitated in pure form. But the tie can only come to light when the other one, the murderer, has been unmasked as the one who must be sacrificed. Corpse and murderer are indissolubly bound to one another. In certain cases, namely those in which the group itself is the murderer (as in *Murder on the Orient Express* by Agatha Christie), the corpse and the murderer become identical. For, in contrast to real jurisprudence, the group is never capable of becoming guilty. In this case, the guilt returns entirely to the corpse.

6.

Clearly, this model is not quite valid for the development of the genre in the last fifteen or twenty years. The decisive point of transition seems to be found in the stories of the deeds of Police Commissioner Maigret, as Georges Simenon has described them. Maigret is one of those detectives who at the same time occupy an important official position. In addition to his own extraordinary gifts, he can call on a large apparatus to help him. Significantly, however, this does not make him into a representative of the power of the state; instead, he finds himself in a permanent state of guerrilla warfare against its deputies. To his immortality, then, and his supernatural insight, must be added his ability to make a place for himself in the official hierarchy and to maintain himself in it (the threat of being fired always appears more effective than that of death; he is seriously wounded only when he encounters particularly backward forms of state power, as in *Maigret and the Killer*). The tendency to disguise the detective has always been great. "A laughable little man, whom no one took seriously" is the description of Hercule Poirot. "The most capable detectives look like ministers, and the most cunning gamblers like bank clerks," asserts Gardner's lawyer, Mason. In the figure of Maigret, this disguising reaches what might be called its perfection. Maigret is the very model of the urban petty bourgeois with roots in the country. Simenon has enlarged and furnished the whole repertoire of this petty bourgeois existence with finesse and authorial economy. The "emissary" is completely incarnated in a sociologically unequivocal type.

This incarnation only results in Maigret's being able to get in contact with suspects practically without making any detours. His human and psychological sympathy seems more immediate. More than his predecessors and his colleagues, he lives as an equal in the midst of his suspects. At the same time, the character of the social model is more often sketched out. Every Maigret novel appears to be an extract from a larger whole. One has the impression that all the individually described groups could come together to form an overlapping social body. In this more realistic coloring-in (and disguising), analysis seems more like a sketch. We mustn't take this impression literally, however; it does not hold up, but turns out to be rather a new, refined kind of disguise. Something else seems more important.

Maigret's greater closeness to the group of suspects also brings him nearer to the perpetrator, his victim. The anguished association of the detective and his prey comes more strongly to the fore here than in earlier kinds of crime novels. This association can be found elsewhere, in Margery Allingham, Phyllis Hambledon, Helen Nielsen, or Thomas Muir, but never in such a pronounced and fundamental way. Maigret is always heading toward identifying himself with the criminal. This is less true, however, where the group of suspects seems very rudimentary or exotic. In such cases he draws back (as in *Maigret and the Gangsters* or *Maigret in Arizona*). He identifies himself most strongly in those cases where the criminal has acted as a practically avowed representative of the group. In these cases it can happen that he conceals the criminal, or lets him judge himself. He takes a part of the burden upon himself, not, as it might seem, out of sympathy with the guilty party, not out of fellow feeling, but because he (and in this connection, of course, the author) recognizes that something demands this stronger identification between the perpetrator and the discoverer, that something objective effectively changes the function of the detective. This change can by all means have overtones of criticism and bitterness, as in *Maigret and the Lazy Burglar;* it has become more apparent in Simenon's thirty years of activity as a writer than in any other province of the crime novel.

Actually, this change corresponds to a development which can be identified in other places. Seen from outside, the setting and the characters of the crime novel seem to be getting more everyday, more familiar, so to speak. The stories by F. and R. Lockridge, Helen Nielsen (whose books provide the single most impressive parallel with Simenon), Margaret Scherf, Thomas Muir, Guy Collingford, Margot Neville are characteristic in this regard, and so are those of Ben Benson, the Gordons, Ivan T. Ross, and P. J. Merrill. A certain kind of stereotypical deliberation recurs as a characteristic of the novels in this group. A figure from the group of suspects raises the commonplaceness of the group's daily life as a protest against the schematic nature of the process of uncovering the killer. This figure remarks that such horrible things simply cannot happen in this normal life, that they are not, after all, living in a detective novel. Here reflection on the fictive quality of the exemplary tale is twisted into a hallucinatory trick, as if it were actually a matter of a harmless report on facts.

This starting handicap belongs to the new arsenal of disguises with which the story is concealed. The growth in plausible realism leads to the discussion of crime itself and of criminals. So it is in the narratives of the Gordons and Ben Benson. In the works of Ivan T. Ross the criminal is seen as a potential savior led astray. He possesses this character, however, not as a member of a definable group, but as a kind of Everyman. The grouping becomes gradually less clear; the molecular bonds of the classic grouping get weaker, and more general relations take their place. The model character himself steps into the horizon of the story. The possibility of transferring the exemplary tale into our own field of experience becomes greater. The distance lessens. It is happening here and now, in our very midst.

In this situation a remarkable event takes place: the detective and the perpetrator become a single person, as they do in Stanley Ellin's two astonishing novels, *The Eighth Circle* and *Dreadful Summit*. In any case, the detective is the guilty one. Margaret Millar has developed another variant in her novels. There are more examples in Helen Nielsen and in P. J. Merrill's *Slender Thread* and Fletcher Flora's *Killing Cousins*. The perpetrator becomes more or less aware of his role as necessary victim and is therefore forced to take over both functions. The reconstruction of the trace becomes a self-unmasking. This self-unmasking does not serve the constitution of a group, however, since the group appears as something given from the very beginning. What stands out here is its inalterability, in which internal bonds appear as nothing but flourishes. The possibility of the widest generalization is balanced by a kind of immanent social criticism which is not directed at any determinable object. At the same time, the character of the topographical anchoring changes. The scene of the crime becomes a typical, no longer uniquely referential location: common quarters of a large city, anonymous small towns and villages, technical or touristic landscapes.

It seems as if above everything else the corpse loses its conclusiveness in this process. It becomes something unreal. It disappears, as in Margaret Millar and Stanley Ellin, as if there were something in the air that decomposed it, dematerialized it.

This raises once again the question of why in the crime novel it must always and in all circumstances be a murder that serves as lever, as can opener so to speak. The answer to such a question might be that in the late bourgeois society the compulsion towards constituting a group can evidently only become effective under a threat, the threat of annihilation. The corpse appears not as someone who was rightly or wrongly persecuted, as the accidental victim of an emotional act or of criminal greed. It is the object which represents the threat. The threat is immanent in the character of the molecular bonds of the group. But in order to reveal these bonds positively as something to be constructed, the short circuit of the murder must happen; to this murder the criminal, then, as the posthumous guarantor of the grouping, is chained, just as the corpse of the victim is.

This schema has dissolved, but the gamelike character of the exemplary narrative has not disappeared. It seems, on the contrary, as if it has become clearer and more aware of itself. What this means is at first glance hard to say. Perhaps the growing polarization between the realistic plausibility of the physical set and the walk-on characters, on the one hand, and the increasing irreality of the corpse, on the other, will make the character of the purely hypothetical game absolute. The unending variability of a single story would then appear to be in the same class as that of chess or of a card game.

7.

Unexpectedly, the crime novel seems in this regard to be one of the openest forms of current literature. This is because it has simultaneously developed one of the few self-contained domains of modern literature. What bothers many critics in it—its laconic and anonymous language, its schematically reductive psychology, its "inartistic" description—all this belongs to its internal characteristics. It has its own linguistic tradition, which is only connected with the rest of literature in some points; it also has (and this is often overlooked) its own linguistic and stylistic criteria, which are entirely tailored to the needs of what might be called allegorical narrative.

What is more, the crime novel is something which is missed by so many critics of modern literature, namely, legitimate reading matter for all. Everyone can feel at home in it. The critics, to be sure, seem unhappy about just this.

—Translated by Glenn W. Most and William W. Stowe

UMBERTO ECO

Narrative Structures in Fleming

Eco provides a highly formalistic analysis of the narrative and conceptual structures of Ian Fleming's novels: "I intend here to examine in detail this narrative machine in order to identify the reasons for its success. It is my plan to devise a descriptive table of the narrative structure in the works of Ian Fleming while evaluating for each structural element the probable influence upon the reader's sensitivity." Eco describes the array of characters and values that structure the novels' meanings, as well as the ludic elements that shape their narratives, to produce a convincing analysis of Fleming's literary techniques and the ideology they serve. Far from elevating Fleming to the status of major novelist, furthermore, Eco treats him throughout as a mystery writer in the tradition of Mickey Spillane. "In fact, in every detective story and in every hard-boiled novel, there is no basic variation, but rather the repetition of a habitual scheme in which the reader can recognize something he has already seen and of which he has grown fond."

Umberto Eco is an Italian semiotician and literary scholar, one of the two or three most influential exponents of the structuralist analysis of narrative. He holds a chair at the University of Bologna, and has taught and lectured in a number of universities around the world. His first detective novel, Il nome della rosa (The Name of the Rose) was published in Milan in 1980 and in the United States in 1983 (Harcourt Brace Jovanovich, Publishers). The article that follows was originally published in Italian in 1965 (in Il caso Bond, edited by O. Del Buono and U. Eco), and reprinted, in a revised version of R. A. Downie's translation, in Eco's The Role of the Reader: Explorations in the Semiotics of Texts (Bloomington and London, 1979). As the last sentence of this excerpt suggests, we have reprinted only the first three sections of Eco's long essay here.

In 1953 Ian Fleming published *Casino Royale*, the first novel in the 007 series. Being a first work, it is subject to the then current literary influence, and in the fifties, a period which had abandoned the traditional detective story in favor of the hard-boiled novel, it was impossible to ignore the presence of Mickey Spillane.

To Spillane *Casino Royale* owes, beyond doubt, at least two characteristic elements. First, the girl Vesper Lynd, who arouses the confident love of Bond, is in the end revealed as an enemy agent. In a novel by Spillane the hero would have killed her, whereas in Fleming's the woman has the grace to commit suicide; but Bond's reaction has the Spillane characteristic of transforming love into hatred and tenderness into ferocity: "The bitch is dead, now," Bond telephones to his London office, and so ends his romance.

Second, Bond is obsessed by an image: that of a Japanese expert in codes whom he killed in cold blood on the thirty-sixth floor of the RCA building at Rockefeller Center with a bullet shot from a window of the fortieth floor of the skyscraper opposite. By an analogy that is surely not accidental, Mike Hammer seems to be haunted by the memory of a small Japanese he killed in the jungle during the war, though with greater emotive participation (Bond's homicide, authorized officially by the double zero, is more ascetic and bureaucratic). The memory of the Japanese is the beginning of the undoubted nervous disorders of Mike Hammer (his sadomasochism and his suspected impotence); the memory of his first homicide could have been the origin of the neurosis of James Bond, except that, within the ambit of *Casino Royale,* either the character or his author solves the problem by nontherapeutic means: Fleming excludes neurosis from the narrative possibilities. This decision was to influence the structure of the following eleven novels by Fleming and presumably forms the basis for their success.

After helping to blow up two Bulgarians who had tried to get rid of him, after suffering torture in the form of a cruel abuse of his testicles, after enjoying the elimination of Le Chiffre by a Soviet agent, having received from him a cut on the hand, cold-bloodedly carved while he was conscious, and after risking his love life, Bond, relaxing during his well-earned convalescence in a hospital bed, confides a chilling doubt to his French colleague, Mathis. Have they been fighting for a just cause? Le Chiffre, who had financed communist spies among the French workers—was he not "serving a wonderful purpose, a really vital purpose, perhaps the best and highest purpose of all"? The difference between good and evil—is it really something neat, recognizable, as the hagiography of counterespionage would like us to believe? At this point Bond is ripe for the crisis, for the salutary recognition of universal ambiguity, and he sets off along the route traversed by the protagonist of le Carré. But at the very moment he questions himself about the appearance of the devil and, sympathizing with the Enemy, is inclined to recognize him as a "lost brother," Bond is treated to a salve from Mathis: "When you get back to London you will find there are other Le Chiffres seeking to destroy you and your friends and your country. M will tell you about them. And now that you have seen a really evil man, you will know how evil they can be and you will go after them to destroy them in order to protect yourself and the people you love. You know what they look like now and what they can do to people. . . . Surround yourself with human beings, my dear James. They are easier to fight for than principles. . . . But don't let me down and become human yourself. We would lose such a wonderful machine."

With this lapidary phrase Fleming defines the character of James Bond for the novels to come. From *Casino Royale* there remains the scar on his cheek, the slightly cruel smile, the taste for good food, and a number of subsidiary characteristics minutely documented in the course of this first volume; but, persuaded by Mathis's words, Bond is to abandon the treacherous life of moral meditation and of psychological anger, with all the neurotic dangers that they entail. Bond ceases to be a subject for psychiatry and remains at the most a physiological object (except for a return to psychic diseases in the last, untypical novel in the series, *The Man with the Golden Gun*), a magnificent machine, as the author and the public, as well as Mathis, wish. From that moment Bond does not meditate upon truth and justice, upon life and death, except in rare moments of boredom, usually in the bar of an airport but always in the form of a casual daydream, never allowing himself to be infected by doubt (at least in the novels; he does indulge in such intimate luxuries in the short stories).

From the psychological point of view, the conversion has taken place quite suddenly, on the basis of four conventional phrases pronounced by Mathis, but the conversion should not be justified on a psychological level. In the last pages of *Casino Royale,* Fleming, in fact, renounces all psychology as the motive of narrative and decides to transfer characters and situations to the level of an objective structural strategy. Without knowing it Fleming makes a choice familiar to many contemporary disciplines: he passes from the psychological method to the formalistic one.

In *Casino Royale* there are already all the elements for the building of a machine that functions basically on a set of precise units governed by rigorous combinational rules. The presence of those rules explains and determines the success of the "007 saga"—a success which, singularly, has been due both to the mass consensus and to the appreciation of more sophisticated readers. I intend here to examine in detail this narrative machine in order to identify the reasons for its success. It is my plan to devise a descriptive table of the narrative structure in the works of Ian Fleming while evaluating for each structural element the probable incidence upon the reader's sensitivity. I shall try therefore to distinguish such a narrative structure at five levels:

1. the opposition of characters and of values;
2. play situations and the story as a "game";
3. a Manichean ideology;
4. literary techniques;
5. literature as collage.

My enquiry covers the range of the following novels listed in order of publication (the date of composition is presumably a year earlier in each case):

Casino Royale (1953);
Live and Let Die (1954);
Moonraker (1955);
Diamonds are Forever (1956);

Narrative Structures in Fleming

From Russia, With Love (1957);
Dr. No (1958);
Goldfinger (1959);
Thunderball (1961);
On Her Majesty's Secret Service (1963);
You Only Live Twice (1964).

I shall refer also to the stories in *For Your Eyes Only* (1960) and to *The Man with the Golden Gun* (1965), but shall not take into consideration *The Spy Who Loved Me* (1962), which seems quite untypical.

The opposition of characters and of values

The novels of Fleming seem to be built on a series of oppositions which allow a limited number of permutations and interactions. These dichotomies constitute invariant features around which minor couples rotate as free variants. I have singled out fourteen couples, four of which are opposing characters, the others being opposing values, variously personified by the four basic characters:

1. Bond–M;
2. Bond–Villain;
3. Villain–Woman;
4. Woman–Bond;
5. Free World–Soviet Union;
6. Great Britain–Non-Anglo-Saxon Countries;
7. Duty–Sacrifice;
8. Cupidity–Ideals;
9. Love–Death;
10. Chance–Planning;
11. Luxury–Discomfort;
12. Excess–Moderation;
13. Perversion–Innocence;
14. Loyalty–Disloyalty.

These pairs do not represent "vague" elements but "simple" ones that are immediate and universal, and, if we consider the range of each pair, we see that the variants allowed, in fact, include all the narrative devices of Fleming.

Bond–M is a dominated–dominant relationship which characterizes from the beginning the limits and possibilities of the character of Bond and which sets events moving. Psychological and psychoanalytical interpretations of Bond's attitude toward M have been discussed in particular by Kingsley Amis.[a] The fact is that, even in terms of pure fictional functions, M represents to Bond the one who has a global view of the events, hence his superiority over the "hero" who depends upon him and who sets out on his various missions in conditions of inferiority to the omniscient chief. Frequently, his chief sends Bond into adventures the upshot of which he had discounted from the start. Bond is thus often the victim of a trick—and it does not matter whether things happen to him beyond the cool calculations of M. The tutelage under which M holds Bond—obliged against his will to visit a doctor, to undergo a nature cure *(Thunderball),* to change his gun *(Dr. No)*—makes so much the more insidious and imperious his chief's authority. We can therefore see that M represents certain other values such as Duty, Country, and Method (as an element of programming contrasting with Bond's own inclination to rely on improvisation). If Bond is the hero, hence in possession of exceptional qualities, M represents Measure, accepted perhaps as a national virtue. But Bond is not so exceptional as a hasty reading of the books (or the spectacular interpretation which films give of the books) might make one think. Fleming always affirmed that he had thought of Bond as an absolutely ordinary person, and it is in contrast with M that the real stature of 007 emerges, endowed with physical attributes, with courage and fast reflexes, but possessing neither these nor other qualities in excess. It is rather a certain moral force, an obstinate fidelity to the job—at the command of M, always present as a warning—that allows him to overcome superhuman ordeals without exercising any superhuman faculty.

The Bond–M relationship presupposes a psychological ambivalence, a reciprocal love–hate. At the beginning of *The Man with the Golden Gun,* Bond, emerging from a lengthy amnesia and having been conditioned by the Soviets, tries a kind of ritual parricide by shooting at M with a cyanide pistol; the gesture loosens a longstanding series of narrative tensions which are aggravated every time M and Bond find themselves face to face.

[a] *The James Bond Dossier* (New York: NAL, 1965).—Eds.

Started by M on the road to Duty (at all costs), Bond enters into conflict with the Villain. The opposition brings into play diverse values, some of which are only variants of the basic couples listed above. Bond represents Beauty and Virility as opposed to the Villain, who often appears monstrous and sexually impotent. The monstrosity of the Villain is a constant point, but to emphasize it we must here introduce a methodological notion which will also apply in examining the other couples. Among the variants we must consider also the existence of vicarious characters whose functions are understood only if they are seen as "variations" of one of the principal personages, some of whose characteristics they carry on. The vicarious roles function usually for the Woman and for the Villain; one can see as variations of M certain collaborators of Bond—for example, Mathis in *Casino Royale,* who preaches Duty in the appropriate M manner (albeit with a cynical and Gallic air).

As to the characteristics of the Villain, let us consider them in order. In *Casino Royale* Le Chiffre is pallid and smooth, with a crop of red hair, an almost feminine mouth, false teeth of expensive quality, small ears with large lobes, and hairy hands. He never smiles. In *Live and Let Die* Mr. Big, a Haitian, has a head that resembles a football, twice the normal size and almost spherical. "The skin was gray-black, taut and shining like the face of a week-old corpse in the river. It was hairless, except for some gray-brown fluff above the ears. There were no eyebrows and no eyelashes and the eyes were extraordinarily far apart so that one could not focus on them both, but only on one at a time.... They were animal eyes, not human, and they seemed to blaze." His gums are pale pink.

In *Diamonds Are Forever* the Villain appears in three different, vicarious roles. Two are Jack and Seraffimo Spang, the first of whom has a humped back and red hair ("Bond did not remember having seen a red-haired hunchback before"), eyes which might have been borrowed from a taxidermist, big ears with rather exaggerated lobes, dry red lips, and an almost total absence of neck. Seraffimo has a face the color of ivory, black puckered eyebrows, a bush of shaggy hair, and jutting, ruthless jaws; if it is added that Seraffimo used to pass his days in a Spectreville of the Old West dressed in black leather chaps embellished with silver spurs, pistols with ivory butts, a black belt and ammunition—also that he used to drive a train of 1870 vintage furnished with a Victorian carriage—the picture is complete. The third vicarious figure is Señor Winter, who travels with a label on his suitcase which reads "My blood group is F" and who is really a killer in the pay of the Spangs. Señor Winter is a gross and sweating individual, with a wart on his hand, a placid visage, and protruding eyes.

In *Moonraker* Hugo Drax is six feet tall, with "exceptionally broad" shoulders, a large and square head, and red hair. The right half of his face is shiny and wrinkled from unsuccessful plastic surgery, the right eye different from and larger than the left and "painfully bloodshot." He has heavy moustaches, whiskers to the lobes of his ears, and patches of hair on his cheekbones: the moustaches conceal with scant success a prognathous upper jaw and a marked protrusion of his upper teeth. The backs of his hands are covered with reddish hair. Altogether he evokes the idea of a ringmaster at the circus.

In *From Russia, With Love* the Villain generates three vicarious figures. Red Grant, the professional murderer in the pay of SMERSH, has short, sandy-colored eyelashes; colorless, opaque blue eyes; a small, cruel mouth; innumerable freckles on his milk-white skin; and deep, wide pores. Colonel Grubozaboyschikov, head of SMERSH, has a narrow and sharp face; round eyes like two polished marbles, weighed down by two flabby pouches; a broad, grim mouth; and a shaven skull. Finally, Rosa Klebb, with the humid, pallid lip stained with nicotine, the raucous voice, flat and devoid of emotion, is five-feet-four, with no curves, dumpy arms, short neck, too sturdy ankles, and gray hair gathered in a tight "obscene" bun. She has shiny, yellow-brown eyes, wears thick glasses, and has a sharp nose with large nostrils that is powdered white. "The wet trap of a mouth, that went on opening and shutting as if it was operated by wire under the chin" completes the appearance of a sexually neuter person.

In *From Russia, With Love,* there occurs a variant that is discernible only in a few other novels. There enters also upon the scene a strongly drawn being who has many of the moral qualities of the Villain, but uses them in the end for good, or at least fights on the side of Bond. An example is Darko Kerim, the Turkish agent in *From Russia, With Love.* Analogous to him are Tiger Tanaka, the head of the Japanese secret service in *You Only Live Twice,* Draco in *On Her Majesty's Secret Service,* Enrico Colombo in "Risico" (a story in *For Your Eyes Only*), and—partially—Quarrel in *Dr. No.* They are at the same time representative of the Villain and of M, and we shall call them "ambiguous representatives." With these Bond always stands in a kind of competitive alliance: he likes them and hates them at the same time, he uses them and admires them, he dominates them and is their slave.

In *Dr. No* the Villain, besides his great height, is characterized by the lack of hands, which are replaced by two metal pincers. His shaved head has the appearance of a reversed raindrop; his skin is clear, without wrinkles; the cheekbones are as smooth as fine ivory; his eyebrows are dark as though painted on; his eyes are without eyelashes and look "like the mouths of two small revolvers"; his nose is thin and ends very close to his mouth, which shows only cruelty and authority.

In *Goldfinger* the eponymous character is a textbook monster— that is, he is characterized by a lack of proportion: "He was short, not more than five feet tall, and on top of the thick body and blunt, peasant legs was set, almost directly into the shoulders, a huge and it seemed exactly round head. It was as if Goldfinger had been put together with bits of other people's bodies. Nothing seemed to belong." His vicarious figure is that of the Korean, Oddjob, who, with fingers like spatulas and fingertips like solid bone, could smash the wooden balustrade of a staircase with a karate blow.

In *Thunderball* there appears for the first time Ernst Starvo Blofeld, who crops up again in *On Her Majesty's Secret Service* and in *You Only Live Twice*, where in the end he dies. As his vicarious incarnations we have in *Thunderball* Count Lippe and Emilio Largo: both are handsome and personable, however vulgar and cruel, and their monstrosity is purely mental. In *On Her Majesty's Secret Service* there appear Irma Blunt, the *longamanus* of Blofeld, a distant reincarnation of Rosa Klebb, and a series of Villains in outline who perish tragically, killed by an avalanche or by a train. In *You Only Live Twice*, the primary role is resumed by Blofeld, already described in *Thunderball:* a childlike gaze from eyes that resemble two deep pools, surrounded "like the eyes of Mussolini" by clear whites, eyes having the symmetry and silken black lashes that recall the eyes of a doll; a mouth like a badly healed wound under a heavy squat nose; altogether an expression of hypocrisy, tyranny, and cruelty, on a Shakespearean level. Blofeld weighs twenty stone. As we learn in *On Her Majesty's*

Secret Service, he lacks earlobes. His hair is a wiry, black crewcut.

To make more constant the Bond–Villain relationship, there is also a racial quality common to all Villains, along with other characteristics. The Villain is born in an ethnic area that stretches from Central Europe to the Slav countries and to the Mediterranean basin: usually he is of mixed blood and his origins are complex and obscure. He is asexual or homosexual, or at any rate is not sexually normal. He has exceptional inventive and organizational qualities which help him acquire immense wealth and by means of which he usually works to help Russia: to this end he conceives a plan of fantastic character and dimensions, worked out to the smallest detail, intended to create serious difficulties either for England or for the Free World in general. Gathered in the figure of the Villain, in fact, are the negative values which we have distinguished in some pairs of opposites, the Soviet Union and other non–Anglo-Saxon countries (the racial convention blames particularly the Jews, the Germans, the Slavs, and the Italians, always depicted as half-breeds), Cupidity elevated to the dignity of paranoia, Planning as technological methodology, satrapic Luxury, physical and psychical Excess, physical and moral Perversion, radical Disloyalty.

Le Chiffre, who organizes the subversive movement in France, comes from a mixture of Mediterranean and Prussian or Polish strains and has Jewish blood revealed by small ears with large lobes. A gambler not basically disloyal, he still betrays his own bosses and tries to recover by criminal means money lost in gambling. He is a masochist (at least so the Secret Service dossier proclaims). He has bought a great chain of brothels, but has lost his patrimony by his exalted manner of living.

Mr. Big is a black who enjoys with Solitaire an ambiguous relationship of exploitation (he has not yet acquired her favors). He helps the Soviet by means of his powerful criminal organization founded on the voodoo cult, finds and sells in the United States treasure hidden in the seventeenth century, controls various rackets, and is prepared to ruin the American economy by introducing, through the black market, large quantities of rare coins.

Hugo Drax displays indefinite nationality—he is English by adoption—but, in fact, he is German. He holds control of columbite, a material indispensable to the construction of reactors, and gives to the

British crown the means of building a most powerful rocket. He plans, however, first to make the rocket fall, when tested atomically, on London, and then to flee to Russia (equation: Communist–Nazi). He frequents clubs of high class and is passionately fond of bridge, but only enjoys cheating. His hysteria does not permit one to suspect any sexual activity worthy of note.

Of the secondary characters in *From Russia, With Love*, the chief are from the Soviet Union and, in working for the communist cause, enjoy comforts and power: Rosa Klebb, sexually neuter, "might enjoy the act physically, but the instrument was of no importance"; Red Grant, a werewolf who kills for pleasure, lives splendidly at the expense of the Soviet government in a villa with a swimming pool. The science-fiction plot consists of the plan to lure Bond into a complicated trap, using for bait a woman and an instrument for coding and decoding ciphers, and then to kill and to checkmate the English counterspy.

Dr. No is a Chinese–German half-breed who works for Russia. He shows no definite sexual tendencies (having in his power Honeychile, he plans to have her torn to pieces by the crabs of Crab Key). He has a flourishing guano industry and plans to cause guided missiles launched by the Americans to deviate from their course. In the past he has built up his fortune by robbing the criminal organization of which he had been elected cashier. He lives, on his island, in a palace of fabulous pomp.

Goldfinger has a probable Baltic origin, but also has Jewish blood. He lives splendidly from commerce and from smuggling gold, by means of which he finances communist movements in Europe. He plans the theft of gold from Fort Knox (not its radioactivation, as the film indicates) and, to overcome the final barrier, sets up an atomic attack on a NATO installation and tries to poison the water of Fort Knox. He does not have a sexual relationship with the woman he dominates, but limits himself to the acquisition of gold. He cheats at cards by using expensive devices such as binoculars and radios; he cheats to make money, even though he is fabulously rich and always travels with a stock of gold in his luggage.

Blofeld is of a Polish father and a Greek mother. He exploits his position as a telegraph clerk to start in Poland a flourishing trade in secret information and becomes chief of the most extensive independent organization for espionage, blackmail, rapine, and extortion. Indeed, with Blofeld Russia ceases to be the constant enemy—because of the general international relaxation of tension—and the part of the malevolent organization assumed by SPECTRE has all the characteristics of SMERSH, including the employment of Slav–Latin–German elements, the use of torture, the elimination of traitors, and the sworn enmity to all the powers of the free world. Of the science-fiction plans of Blofeld, that of *Thunderball* is to steal from NATO two atomic bombs and with these to blackmail England and America; that of *On Her Majesty's Secret Service* envisages the training in a mountain clinic of girls with suitable allergies to condition them to spread a mortal virus intended to ruin the agriculture and livestock of the United Kingdom; and in *You Only Live Twice,* Blofeld, affected by a murderous mania, organizes a fantastic suicide garden near the coast of Japan, which attracts legions of heirs of the kamikaze who are bent on poisoning themselves with exotic, refined, and lethal plants, thus doing grave and complex harm to the human patrimony of Japanese democracy. Blofeld's tendency toward satrapic pomp shows itself in the kind of life he leads in the mountain of Piz Gloria and, more particularly, on the island of Kyashu, where he lives in medieval tyranny and passes through his *hortus deliciarum*[b] clad in metal armor. Previously, Blofeld showed himself to be ambitious of honors (he aspired to be known as the Count of Blenville), a master of planning, an organizing genius, as treacherous as needs be, and sexually impotent—he lived in marriage with Irma Blofeld, also asexual and hence repulsive. To quote Tiger Tanaka, Blofeld "is a devil who has taken human form."

Only the evil characters of *Diamonds Are Forever* have no connections with Russia. In a certain sense the international gangsterism of the Spangs appears to be an earlier version of SPECTRE. For the rest, Jack and Seraffimo possess all the characteristics of the canon.

To the typical qualities of the Villain are opposed the Bond characteristics, particularly Loyalty to the Service, Anglo-Saxon Moderation opposed to the excess of the half-breeds, the selection of Discomfort and the acceptance of Sacrifice opposed to the ostentatious Luxury of the enemy, the genial improvisation (Chance) op-

[b]"garden of delights."—Eds.

posed to the cold Planning which it defeats, the sense of an Ideal opposed to Cupidity (Bond in various cases wins from the Villain in gambling, but as a rule returns the enormous winnings to the Service or to the girl of the moment, as occurred with Jill Masterson). Some oppositions function not only in the Bond–Villain relationship but also in the behavior of Bond. Thus, Bond is normally loyal but does not disdain overcoming a cheating enemy by a deceitful trick and blackmailing him (see *Moonraker* or *Goldfinger*). Even Excess and Moderation, Chance and Planning are opposed in the acts and decisions of Bond. Duty and Sacrifice appear as elements of internal debate each time Bond knows he must prevent the plan of the Villain at the risk of his life, and in those cases the patriotic ideal (Great Britain and the Free World) takes the upper hand. He calls also on the racist need to show the superiority of the Briton. Also opposed in Bond are Luxury (the choice of good food, care in dressing, preference for sumptuous hotels, love of the gambling table, invention of cocktails, and so on) and Discomfort (Bond is always ready to abandon the easy life—even when it appears in the guise of a Woman who offers herself—to face a new aspect of Discomfort, the acutest point of which is torture).

We have discussed the Bond–Villain dichotomy at length because, in fact, it embodies all the characteristics of the opposition between Eros and Thanatos, the principle of pleasure and the principle of reality, culminating in the moment of torture (in *Casino Royale* explicitly theorized as a sort of erotic relationship between the torturer and the tortured). This opposition is perfected in the relationship between the Villain and the Woman; Vesper is tyrannized and blackmailed by the Soviets, and therefore by Le Chiffre; Solitaire is the slave of Mr. Big; Tiffany Case is dominated by the Spangs; Tatiana is the slave of Rosa Klebb and of the Soviet government in general; Jill and Tilly Masterson are dominated, to different degrees, by Goldfinger, and Pussy Galore works under his orders; Domino Vitali is subservient to the wishes of Blofeld through the physical relationship with the vicarious figure of Emilio Largo; the English girls of Piz Gloria are under the hypnotic control of Blofeld and the virginal surveillance of Irma Blunt; Honeychile, wandering pure and untroubled on the shores of his cursed island, has a purely symbolic relationship with the power of Dr. No, except that at the end Dr. No offers her naked body to the crabs (she has been dominated by the Villain through the vicarious effort of the brutal Mander and has justly punished Mander by causing a scorpion to kill him, anticipating the revenge of No—who had recourse to crabs); and, finally, Kissy Suzuki lives on her island in the shade of the cursed castle of Blofeld, suffering a purely allegorical domination shared by the whole population of the place. In an intermediate position is Gala Brand, who is an agent of the Service but who becomes the secretary of Hugo Drax and establishes a relationship of submission to him. In most cases the Villain-Woman relationship culminates in the torture the woman undergoes along with Bond; here the Love-Death pair functions also, in the sense of a more intimate erotic union of the two through their common ordeal.

Dominated by the Villain, however, Fleming's woman has already been previously conditioned to domination, life for her having assumed the role of the villain. The general scheme is (1) the girl is beautiful and good; (2) she has been made frigid and unhappy by severe trials suffered in adolescence; (3) this has conditioned her to the service of the Villain; (4) through meeting Bond she appreciates her positive human chances; (5) Bond possesses her but in the end loses her. This curriculum is common to Vesper, Solitaire, Tiffany, Tatiana, Honeychile, and Domino; rather vague as for Gala; equally shared by the three vicarious women of Goldfinger (Jill, Tilly, and Pussy—the first two have had a sad past, but only the third has been violated by her uncle; Bond possesses the first and the third; the second is killed by the Villain; the first is tortured with gold paint; the second and third are Lesbians, and Bond redeems only the third; and so on); more diffuse and uncertain for the group of girls on Piz Gloria (each has had an unhappy past, but Bond, in fact, possesses only one of them; similarly, he marries Tracy, whose past was unhappy because of a series of unions, dominated by her father, Draco, and who is killed in the end by Blofeld, who realizes at this point his domination and who ends by Death the relationship of Love which she entertained with Bond); Kissy Suzuki's unhappiness is the result of a Hollywoodian experience which has made her chary of life and of men.

In every case Bond loses the woman, either by her own will or by that of another (in the case of Gala, it is the woman who marries somebody else, although unwillingly) and either at the end of the novel or at the beginning of the following one (as happened with

Tiffany Case). Thus, in the moment in which the Woman solves the opposition to the Villain by entering with Bond into a purifying–purified, saving–saved relationship, she returns to the domination of the negative. Every woman displays an internal combat between the couple Perversion–Purity (sometimes external, as in the relationship of Rosa Klebb and Tatiana) which makes her similar to the Richardsonian persecuted virgin. The bearer of purity, notwithstanding and despite her perversion, eager to alternate lust with torture, she would appear likely to resolve the contrast between the privileged race and the non–Anglo-Saxon half-breed, since she often belongs to an ethnically inferior breed; but insofar as the erotic relationship always ends with a form of death, real or symbolic, Bond resumes willy-nilly his purity as an Anglo-Saxon bachelor. The race remains uncontaminated.

Play situations and the story as a "game"
The various pairs of oppositions (of which we have considered only a few possible variants) seem like the elements of an *ars combinatoria*[c] with fairly elementary rules. It is clear that in the engagement of the two poles of each couple there are, in the course of the novel, alternative solutions: the reader does not know at which point of the story the Villain defeats Bond or Bond defeats the Villain, and so on. But toward the end of the book, the algebra has to follow a prearranged pattern: as in the Chinese game that 007 and Tanaka play at the beginning of *You Only Live Twice,* hand beats fist, fist beats two fingers, two fingers beat hand. M beats Bond, Bond beats the Villain, the Villain beats Woman, even if at first Bond beats Woman; the Free World beats the Soviet Union, England beats the Impure Countries, Death beats Love, Moderation beats Excess, and so on.

This interpretation of the story in terms of a game is not accidental. The books of Fleming are dominated by situations that we call "play situations." First are several archetypal situations such as the Journey and the Meal; the Journey may be by Machine (and here occurs a rich symbolism of the automobile, typical of our century), by Train (another archetype, this of obsolescent type), by Airplane, or by Ship. But a meal, a pursuit by machine, or a mad race by train always takes the

[c]In logic, a method for combining a limited number of principles in a variety of permutations; introduced by Ramón Lull (c. 1232–1316).—Eds.

form of a game. Bond decides the choice of foods as though they formed the pieces of a puzzle, prepares for the meal with the same scrupulous attention as that with which he prepares for a game of bridge (see the convergence, in a means–end connection, of the two elements in *Moonraker*), and he intends the meal as a play. Similarly, train and machine are the elements of a wager made against an adversary: before the journey is finished, one of the two has finished his moves and given checkmate.

At this point it is useless to record the occurrence of the play situations, in the true and proper sense of conventional games of chance, in each book. Bond always gambles and wins, against the Villain or some vicarious figure. The detail with which these games are described is the subject of further consideration in section 4 [omitted here], which deals with literary technique; here it must be said that, if these games occupy a prominent space, it is because they form a reduced and formalized model of the more general play situation that is the novel. The novel, given the rules of combination of oppositional couples, is fixed as a sequence of "moves" inspired by the code and constituted according to a perfectly prearranged scheme. The invariable scheme is the following:

    A. M moves and gives a task to Bond;
    B. Villain moves and appears to Bond (perhaps in vicarious forms);
    C. Bond moves and gives a first check to Villain or Villain gives first check to Bond;
    D. Woman moves and shows herself to Bond;
    E. Bond takes Woman (possesses her or begins her seduction);
    F. Villain captures Bond (with or without Woman, or at different moments);
    G. Villain tortures Bond (with or without Woman);
    H. Bond beats Villain (kills him, or kills his representative or helps at their killing);
    I. Bond, convalescing, enjoys Woman, whom he then loses.

The scheme is invariable in the sense that all the elements are always present in every novel (so that it might be affirmed that the fundamental rule of the game is "Bond moves and mates in eight moves"). That the moves always be in the same sequence is not imperative. A minute detailing of the ten novels under consideration would yield several examples of a set scheme we might call ABC-DEFGHI (for example, *Dr. No*), but often there are inversions and variations. Sometimes Bond meets the Villain at the beginning of the volume and gives him a first check, and only later receives his instructions from M. For example, *Goldfinger* presents a different scheme, BCDEACDFGDHEHI, where it is possible to notice repeated moves: two encounters and three games played with the Villain, two seductions and three encounters with women, a first flight of the Villain after his defeat and his ensuing death, and so on. In *From Russia, With Love*, the company of Villains increases—through the presence of the ambiguous representative Kerim, in conflict with a secondary Villain, Krilenku, and the two mortal duels of Bond with Red Grant and with Rosa Klebb, who was arrested only after having grievously wounded Bond—so that the scheme, highly complicated, is BBBBDA(BB-C)EFGH(I). There is a long prologue in Russia with the parade of the Villain figures and the first connection between Tatiana and Rosa Klebb, the sending of Bond to Turkey, a long interlude in which Kerim and Krilenku appear and the latter is defeated, the seduction of Tatiana, the flight by train with the torture suffered by the murdered Kerim, the victory over Red Grant, the second round with Rosa Klebb, who, while being defeated, inflicts serious injury upon Bond. In the train and during his convalescence, Bond enjoys love interludes with Tatiana before the final separation.

Even the basic concept of torture undergoes variations, being sometimes a direct injustice, sometimes a kind of succession or course of horrors that Bond must undergo, either by the explicit will of the Villain *(Dr. No)* or by accident during an escape from the Villain, but always as a consequence of the moves of the Villain (for example, a tragic escape in the snow, pursuit, avalanche, and hurried flight through the Swiss countryside in *On Her Majesty's Secret Service*).

Occurring alongside the sequence of fundamental moves are numerous side issues which enrich the narrative by unforeseen events, without, however, altering the basic scheme. For a graphic representation of this process, we may summarize the plot of one novel—*Diamonds Are Forever*—by placing on the left the sequence of the fundamental moves, on the right the multiplicity of side issues:

	Long, curious prologue which introduces one to diamond smuggling in South Africa
Move A. M sends Bond to America as a sham smuggler	
Move B. Villains (the Spangs) appear indirectly in the description of them given to Bond	
Move D. Woman (Tiffany Case) meets Bond in the role of go-between	
	Detailed journey by air, in the background two vicarious Villains; play situations; imperceptible duel between hunters and prey
Move B. First appearance in the plane of vicarious Villain Winter (Blood Group F)	
Move B. Meeting with Jack Spang	
	Meeting with Felix Leiter, who brings Bond up to date about the Spangs
Move E. Bond begins the seduction of Tiffany	
	Long interval at Saratoga at the races; to help Leiter, Bond, in fact, "damages" the Spangs
Move C. Bond gives a first check to the Villain	
	Appearance of vicarious Villains in the mud bath and punishment of the treacherous jockey, anticipating symbolically the torturing of Bond; the whole Saratoga episode represents a play situation in miniature; Bond

Move B. Appearance of Seraffimo Spang

decides to go to Las Vegas; detailed description of the district

Another long and detailed play situation; play with Tiffany as croupier gambling at table, indirect amorous skirmish with the woman, indirect gamble with Seraffimo; Bond wins money

Move C. Bond gives a second check to Villain

Next evening, long shooting match between cars; association of Bond and Ernie Cureo

Move F. Spang captures Bond

Long description of SPECTRE and the train-playing of Spang

Move G. Spang has Bond tortured

With the aid of Tiffany, Bond begins a fantastic flight by railway trolley through the desert followed by the locomotive-plaything driven by Seraffimo; play situation

Move H. Bond defeats Seraffimo, who crashes into the mountain on the locomotive

Rest with his friend Leiter; departure by ship; long, amorous convalescence with Tiffany; exchanges of coded telegrams

Move E. Bond finally possesses Tiffany
Move B. Villain reappears in the form of Winter

	Play situation on board ship; mortal gamble played by infinitesimal moves between the two killers and Bond; play situation becomes symbolized on reduced scale in the lottery on the course of the ship; the two killers capture Tiffany; acrobatic action by Bond to reach the cabin and kill the killers
Move H. Bond overcomes vicarious Villains finally	
	Meditations on death in the presence of the two corpses; return home
Move I. Bond knows he can enjoy well-earned repose with Tiffany, and yet . . .	
	. . . deviations of the plot in South Africa, where Bond destroys the last link of the chain
Move H. Bond defeats for the third time the Villain in the person of Jack Spang	

For each of the ten novels it would be possible to trace a general plan. The collateral inventions are rich enough to form the muscles of the separate skeletons of narrative; they constitute one of the great attractions of Fleming's work, but they do not testify, at least not obviously, to his powers of invention. . . . It is easy to trace the collateral inventions to definite literary sources, and hence these act as familiar reference marks to romanesque situations acceptable to readers. The true and original story remains immutable, and suspense is stabilized curiously on the basis of a sequence of events that are entirely predetermined. The story of each book by Fleming, by and large, may be summarized as follows: Bond is sent to a given place to avert a "science-fiction" plan by a monstrous individual of uncertain origin and definitely not English who, making use of his organizational or productive activity, not only earns money, but helps the cause of the enemies of the West. In facing this monstrous being, Bond meets a woman who is dominated by him and frees her from her past, establishing with her an erotic relationship interrupted by capture by the Villain and by torture. But Bond defeats the Villain, who dies horribly, and rests from his great efforts in the arms of the woman, though he is destined to lose her. One might wonder how, within such limits, it is possible for the inventive writer of fiction to function, since he must respond to a demand for the sensational and the unforeseeable. In fact, in every detective story and in every hard-boiled novel, there is no basic variation, but rather the repetition of a habitual scheme in which the reader can recognize something he has already seen and of which he has grown fond. Under the guise of a machine that produces information, the criminal novel produces redundancy; pretending to rouse the reader, it, in fact, reconfirms him in a sort of imaginative laziness and creates escape by narrating, not the Unknown, but the Already Known. In the pre-Fleming detective story, however, the immutable scheme is formed by the personality of the detective and of his colleagues, while within this scheme are unraveled unexpected events (and most unexpected of all is the figure of the culprit). On the contrary, in the novels of Fleming, the scheme even dominates the very chain of events. Moreover, the identity of the culprit, his characteristics, and his plans are always apparent from the beginning. The reader finds himself immersed in a game of which he knows the pieces and the rules—and perhaps the outcome—and draws pleasure simply from following the minimal variations by which the victor realizes his objective.

We might compare a novel by Fleming to a game of football in which we know beforehand the place, the numbers and personalities of the players, the rules of the game, and the fact that everything will take place within the area of the great pitch—except that in a game of football we do not know until the very end who will win. It would be more accurate to compare a novel by Fleming to a game of basketball played by the Harlem Globetrotters against a local team. We know with absolute confidence that the Globetrotters will win: the pleasure lies in watching the trained virtuosity with which they defer the final moment, with what ingenious deviations they reconfirm the foregone conclusion, with what trickeries they make rings round their opponents. The novels of Fleming exploit in exemplary measure that element of foregone play which is typical of the escape machine geared for the entertainment of the masses. Perfect in their mechanism, such machines represent the narrative structure which works upon a material which does not aspire to express any ideology. It is true that such structures inevitably entail ideological positions, but these do not derive so much from the structured contents as from the way of structuring them.

A Manichean ideology

The novels of Fleming have been variously accused of McCarthyism, fascism, the cult of excess and violence, racism, and so on. It is difficult, after the analysis we have carried out, to maintain that Fleming is not inclined to consider the British superior to all Oriental or Mediterranean races or that Fleming does not profess to heartfelt anticommunism. Yet it is significant that he ceased to identify the wicked with Russia as soon as the international situation rendered Russia less menacing according to the general opinion. It is significant also that, while he is introducing the gang of Mr. Big, Fleming is profuse in his acknowledgment of the new African nations and of their contribution to contemporary civilization (Negro gangsterism would represent a proof of the industrial efficiency attained by the developing countries); when the Villain is supposed to have Jewish blood, Fleming is always fairly unexplicit; he never shows more than a cautious, middle-class chauvinism. Thus arises the suspicion that our author does not characterize his creations in such and such a manner as a result of an ideological opinion but purely for rhetorical purposes. By "rhetoric" I mean an art of persuasion which relies on *endoxa*, that is, on the common opinions shared by the majority of readers.

Fleming is, in other words, cynically building an effective narrative apparatus. To do so he decides to rely upon the most secure and universal principles and puts into play precisely those archetypal elements that have proved successful in fairy tales. Let us recall for a moment the pairs of oppositional characters: M is the King and Bond is the Knight entrusted with a mission; Bond is the Knight and the Villain is the Dragon; the Lady and Villain stand for Beauty and the Beast; Bond restores the Lady to the fullness of spirit and to her senses—he is the Prince who rescues Sleeping Beauty; between the

Free World and the Soviet Union, England and the non–Anglo-Saxon countries is realized the primitive epic relationship between the Privileged Race and the Lower Race, between White and Black, Good and Bad. Fleming is a racist in the sense that any artist is one if, to represent the devil, he depicts him with oblique eyes; in the sense that a nurse is one who, wishing to frighten children with the bogeyman, suggests that he is black. It is singular that Fleming should be anticommunist with the same lack of discrimination as he is anti-Nazi and anti-German. It isn't that in one case he is reactionary and in the other democratic. He is simply Manichean for operative reasons: the sees the world as made up of good and evil forces in conflict.

Fleming seeks elementary oppositions; to personify primitive and universal forces, he has recourse to popular standards. In a time of international tensions, popular notions of "wicked communism" exist beside those of the unpunished Nazi criminal. Fleming uses them both in a sweeping, uncritical manner.

At the most, he tempers his choice with irony, but the irony is completely masked and is revealed only through incredible exaggeration. In *From Russia, With Love,* the Soviet men are so monstrous, so improbably evil that it seems impossible to take them seriously. And yet, in his brief preface, Fleming insists that all the narrated atrocities are absolutely true. He has chosen the path of fable, and fable must be taken as truthful if it is not to become a satirical fairy tale. The author seems almost to write his books for a twofold reading public, those who take them as gospel truth and those who see their humor. In order to work as ambiguous texts, however, they must appear authentic, credible, ingenious, and plainly aggressive. A man who chooses to write in this way is neither a fascist nor a racist; he is only a cynic, an expert in tale engineering.

If Fleming is a reactionary at all, it is not because he identifies the figure of "evil" with a Russian or a Jew. He is reactionary because he makes use of stock figures. The very use of such figures (the Manichean dichotomy, seeing things in black and white) is always dogmatic and intolerant—in short, reactionary—whereas he who avoids set figures, who recognizes nuances and distinctions and who admits contradictions is democratic. Fleming is conservative as, basically, the fable—any fable—is conservative; his is the static, inherent, dogmatic conservatism of fairy tales and myths, which transmit an elementary wisdom, constructed and communicated by a simple play of light and shade, by indisputable archetypes which do not permit critical distinction. If Fleming is a "fascist," he is so because of his inability to pass from mythology to reason.

The very names of Fleming's protagonists suggest the mythological nature of the stories by fixing in an image or in a pun the character from the start, without any possibility of conversion or change. (One cannot be called Snow White and not be white as snow, in face and in spirit.) The wicked man lives by gambling? He will be called Le Chiffre. He is working for the Reds? He will be called Red—and Grant if he works for money, duly granted. A Korean professional killer by unusual means will be Oddjob. One obsessed with gold is Auric Goldfinger. A wicked man is called No. Perhaps the half-lacerated face of Hugo Drax will be conjured up by the incisive onomatopoeia of his name. Beautiful, transparent, telepathic Solitaire evokes the coldness of the diamond. Chic and interested in diamonds, Tiffany Case recalls the leading jewelers in New York and the beauty case of the mannequin. Ingenuity is suggested by the very name of Honeychile; sensual shamelessness, by that of Pussy Galore. A pawn in a dark game? Such is Domino. A tender Japanese lover, quintessence of the Orient? Such is Kissy Suzuki. (Would it be accidental that she recalls the name of the most popular exponent of Zen spirituality?) We pass over women of less interest such as Mary Goodnight or Miss Trueblood. And if the name Bond has been chosen, as Fleming affirms, almost by chance, to give the character an absolutely common appearance, then it would be by chance, but also by guidance, that this model of style and success evokes the luxuries of Bond Street or treasury bonds.

By now it is clear how the novels of Fleming have attained such a wide success: they build up a network of elementary associations to achieve something original and profound. Fleming also pleases the sophisticated readers who here distinguish, with a feeling of esthetic pleasure, the purity of the primitive epic impudently and maliciously translated into current terms and who applaud in Fleming the cultured man, whom they recognize as one of themselves, naturally the most clever and broadminded.

Such praise Fleming might merit if he did not develop a second facet much more cunning: the game of stylistic oppositions, by virtue of which the sophisticated reader, detecting the fairy-tale mechanism, feels himself a malicious accomplice of the author, only to become a victim, for he is led on to detect stylistic inventions where there is, on the contrary—as will be shown[d]—a clever montage of *déjà vu*.

—Translated by R. A. Downie

ROLAND BARTHES

Delay and The Hermeneutic Sentence

The detective story is the perfect model of the "hermeneutic tale," the fiction whose form and action are based on one or more artfully protracted questions. Barthes provides the groundwork for this way of understanding the genre in two brief sections of S/Z (1970), where he introduces and elaborates on the notion of the "hermeneutic code." By interpreting certain narrative elements (events, words, descriptions) as implied questions, answers, or obstacles to the questioning–answering process, Barthes shows how narratives create suspense and challenge thought. Although the excerpts we have chosen are schematic rather than analytic and do not refer directly to the detective novel, they are, as Frank Kermode and Dennis Porter make clear, important documents for the contemporary understanding of the genre.

Roland Barthes' writing on narrative represents only one aspect of an extensive corpus of literary and cultural criticism and theory. His influence as a creator and defender of the French Nouvelle Critique *is still spreading. We have here reprinted two short sections (XXXII and XXXVII) from S/Z, his book-length analysis of a tale, "Sarrasine," by Balzac. S/Z was published in Paris in 1970, and in New York, in an English translation by Richard Miller, in 1974.*

XXXII. Delay

Truth is brushed past, avoided, lost. This accident is a structural one. In fact, the hermeneutic code has a function, the one we (with Jakobson[a]) attribute to the poetic code: just as rhyme (notably) structures the poem according to the expectation and desire for recurrence, so the hermeneutic terms structure the enigma according to the expectation and desire for its solution. The dynamics of the text (since it implies a truth to be deciphered) is thus paradoxical: it is a static dynamics: the problem is to *maintain* the enigma in the initial void of its answer; whereas the sentences quicken the story's "unfolding" and cannot help but move the story along, the hermeneutic code performs an opposite action: it must set up *delays* (obstacles, stoppages, deviations) in the flow of the discourse; its structure is essentially reactive, since it opposes the ineluctable advance of language with an organized set of stoppages: between question and answer there is a whole dilatory area whose emblem might be named "reticence," the rhetorical figure which interrupts the sentence, suspends it, turns it aside (Virgil's *Quos ego . . .* [b]). Whence, in the hermeneutic code, in comparison to these extreme terms (question and answer), the abundance of dilatory morphemes: the *snare* (a kind of deliberate evasion of the truth), the *equivocation* (a mixture of truth and snare which frequently, while focusing on the enigma, helps to thicken it), the *partial answer* (which only exacerbates the expectation of the truth), the *suspended answer* (an aphasic stoppage of the disclosure), and *jamming* (acknowledgment of insolubility). The variety of these terms (their inventive range) attests to the considerable labor the discourse must accomplish if it hopes to *arrest* the enigma, to keep it open. Expectation thus becomes the basic condition for truth: truth, these narratives tell us, is what is *at the end* of expectation. This design brings narrative very close to the rite of initiation (a long path marked with pitfalls, obscurities, stops, suddenly comes out into the light); it implies a return to order, for expectation is a disorder: disorder is supplementary, it is what is forever added on without solving anything, without finishing anything; order is complementary, it completes, fills up, saturates, and dismisses everything that risks adding on: truth is what completes, what closes. In short, based on the articulation of question and answer, the hermeneutic narrative is constructed according to our image of the sentence: an organism probably infinite in its expansions, but reducible to a diadic unity of

---

[a] I.e., Roman Jakobson (1896–1982), the linguist.—Eds.
[b] See *Aeneid* 1:135. The technical term is aposiopesis.—Eds.

subject and predicate. To narrate (in the classic fashion) is to raise the question as if it were a subject which one delays predicating; and when the predicate (truth) arrives, the sentence, the narrative, are over, the world is adjectivized (after we had feared it would not be). Yet, just as any grammar, however new, once it is based on the diad of subject and predicate, noun and verb, can only be a historical grammar, linked to classical metaphysics, so the hermeneutic narrative, in which truth predicates an incomplete subject, based on expectation and desire for its imminent closure, is dated, linked to the kerygmatic civilization of meaning and truth, appeal and fulfillment.

XXXVII. The Hermeneutic Sentence

The proposition of truth is a "well-made" sentence; it contains a subject (theme of the enigma), a statement of the question (formulation of the enigma), its question mark (proposal of the enigma), various subordinate and interpolated clauses and catalyses (delays in the answer), all of which precede the ultimate predicate (disclosure). Canonically, Enigma 6 *(Who is La Zambinella?*[c]) would be set forth as follows:

Question:	"*This is La Zambinella.* (subject, theme)	*Who is she* (formulation)	? (proposal)
Delays:	"*I will tell you:* (promise of answer)	*a woman,* (snare)	*a creature outside nature* (ambiguity)
	a . . . (suspended answer)	*relative of the Lantys,* (partial answer)	
	no one knows. (jammed answer)		
Answer:	*A castrato dressed as a woman.* (disclosure)		

This canon can be modified (just as there are several kinds of sentence), provided that the principal hermeneutemes (the "knots" or "kernels") are present at some point in the discourse: the discourse

[c] La Zambinella is the character who embodies the central enigma in Balzac's novella. —Eds.

can condense several hermeneutemes into a single statement (into a single signifier) by making some of them implicit (thematization, proposal, and formulation); it can also invert the terms of the hermeneutic order: an answer can be given before the question has been asked (it is suggested that La Zambinella is a woman even before she appears in the story); or a snare can remain set after the truth has been revealed (Sarrasine continues to ignore La Zambinella's true sex even though it has been revealed to him). This freedom of the hermeneutic sentence (which is something like the freedom of the flexional sentence) exists because the classic narrative combines two points of view (two pertinences): a rule of communication, which keeps the networks of destination separate, so that each one can continue to operate even if its neighbor is already "burned out" (Sarrasine can continue to receive a false message although the reader's circuit is already saturated: the sculptor's blindness becomes a new message, object of a new system henceforth destined solely for the reader); and a pseudological rule, which tolerates a certain freedom in the order in which predicates are presented, once the subject has been proposed: this freedom actually reinforces the preeminence of the subject (of the star), whose perturbation (literally, whose jeopardy) seems accidental and provisional; or rather, from the question's provisional nature, we infer its accidents: once the subject is provided with its *"true"* predicate, everything falls into place, the sentence can end.

—*Translated by Richard Miller*

F. R. JAMESON

On Raymond Chandler

Jameson begins by examining the interaction between Chandler's stylistic genius and his sensitivity to the peculiar qualities of American society: his use of slang, his collage of a variety of levels of diction, his ear for the language of deceit and inauthenticity are perfect instruments for analyzing a fragmented modern society. Disguised as murder mysteries, Chandler's works are, in fact, searches for knowledge of the underlying reality of American society.

Jameson's approach to the detective novel has most in common with those of Steven Marcus, Stephen Knight, and D. A. Miller. Jameson himself is probably best known for two influential works, Marxism and Form *(1971) and* The Prison House of Language *(1972). In addition to teaching in the French Department at Yale, he has continued in the vanguard of both Marxist critics and commentators on and in the mode of the new French criticism here represented by Roland Barthes and Jacques Lacan. His essay on Chandler first appeared in* The Southern Review *in 1970.*

I

A long time ago when I was writing for the pulps I put into a story a line like "He got out of the car and walked across the sun-drenched sidewalk until the shadow of the awning over the entrance fell across his face like the touch of cool water." They took it out when they published the story. Their readers didn't appreciate this sort of thing—just held up the action. I set out to prove them wrong. My theory was that the readers just *thought* they cared about nothing but the action; that really, although they didn't know it, the thing they cared about, and that I cared about, was the creation of emotion through dialogue and description.[a]

That the detective story represented something more to Raymond Chandler than a mere commercial product, furnished for popular entertainment purposes, can be judged from the fact that he came to it late in life, with a long and successful business career behind him. He published his first and best novel, *The Big Sleep*, in 1939, when he was fifty years old, and had studied the form for almost a decade. The short stories he had written over that period are for the most part sketches for the novels, episodes that he will later take over verbatim as chapters in the longer form: and he developed his technique by imitating and reworking models produced by other detective story writers: a deliberate, self-conscious apprenticeship at a time of life when most writers have already found themselves.

Two aspects of his earlier experience seem to account for the personal tone of his books. As an executive of the oil industry, he lived in Los Angeles for some fifteen years before the Depression put him out of business, enough time to sense what was unique about the city's atmosphere, in a position to see what power was and what forms it took. And as a born American, he spent his school years, from the age of eight, in England, and had an English public school education.

For Chandler thought of himself primarily as a stylist, and it was his distance from the American language that gave him the chance to use it as he did. In that respect his situation was not unlike that of Nabokov: the writer of an adopted language is already a kind of stylist by force of circumstance. Language can never again be unselfconscious for him; words can never again be unproblematical. The naive and unreflecting attitude towards literary expression is henceforth proscribed, and he feels in his language a kind of material density and resistance: even those clichés and commonplaces which for the native speaker are not really words at all, but instant communication, take on outlandish resonance in his mouth, are used between quotation marks, as you would delicately expose some interesting specimen: his sentences are collages of heterogeneous materials, of

---

[a]From a letter of May 7, 1948, to Frederick Lewis Allen, reprinted in *Raymond Chandler Speaking*, edited by Dorothy Gardiner and Kathrine Sorley Walker (Boston: Houghton Mifflin, 1977), p. 219.—Eds.

odd linguistic scraps, figures of speech, colloquialisms, place names, and local sayings, all laboriously pasted together in an illusion of continuous discourse. In this, the lived situation of the writer of a borrowed language is already emblematic of the situation of the modern writer in general, in that words have become objects for him. The detective story, as a form without ideological content, without any overt political or social or philosophical point, permits such pure stylistic experimentation.

But it offers other advantages as well, and it is no accident that the chief practitioners of art for art's sake in the recent novel, Nabokov and Robbe-Grillet, almost always organize their works around a murder: think of *Le Voyeur* and *La Maison de Rendezvous;* think of *Lolita* and *Pale Fire*. These writers and their artistic contemporaries represent a kind of second wave of the modernist and formalistic impulse which produced the great modernism of the first two decades of the twentieth century. But in the earlier works, modernism was a reaction against narration, against plot: here the empty, decorative event of the murder serves as a way of organizing essentially plotless material into an illusion of movement, into the formally satisfying arabesques of a puzzle unfolding. Yet the real content of these books is an almost scenic one: the motels and college towns of the American landscape, the island of *Le Voyeur,* the drab provincial cities of *Les Gommes* or of *Dans le labyrinthe*.

In much the same way, a case can be made for Chandler as a painter of American life: not as a builder of those large-scale models of the American experience which great literature offers, but rather in fragmentary pictures of setting and place, fragmentary perceptions which are by some formal paradox somehow inaccessible to serious literature.

Take, for example, some perfectly insignificant daily experience, such as the chance encounter of two people in the lobby of an apartment building. I find my neighbor unlocking his mailbox; I have never seen him before, we glance at each other briefly, his back is turned as he struggles with the larger magazines inside. Such an instant expresses in its fragmentary quality a profound truth about American life, in its perception of the stained carpets, the sand-filled spittoons, the poorly shutting glass doors: all testifying to the shabby anonymity which is the meeting place between the luxurious private lives that stand side by side like closed monads, behind the doors of the private apartments: a dreariness of waiting rooms and public bus stations, of the neglected places of collective living that fill up the interstices between the privileged compartments of middle-class living. Such a perception, it seems to me, is in its very structure dependent on chance and anonymity, on the vague glance in passing, as from the windows of a bus, when the mind is intent on some more immediate preoccupation: its very essence is to be inessential. For this reason it eludes the registering apparatus of great literature: make of it some Joycean epiphany and the reader is obliged to take this moment as the center of his world, as something directly infused with symbolic meaning; and at once the most fragile and precious quality of the perception is irrevocably damaged, its slightness is lost, it can no longer be half glimpsed, half disregarded.

Yet put such an experience in the framework of the detective story and everything changes: I learn that the man I saw does not even live in my building, that he was, in reality, opening the murdered woman's mailbox, not his own; and suddenly my attention flows back onto the neglected perception and sees it in renewed, heightened form without damaging its structure. Indeed, it is as if there are certain moments in life which are accessible only at the price of a certain lack of intellectual focus: like objects at the edge of my field of vision which disappear when I turn to stare at them head on. Proust felt this keenly. His whole esthetic is based on some absolute antagonism between spontaneity and self-consciousness. For Proust we can only be sure we have lived, we have perceived, after the fact of the experience itself; for him the deliberate project to meet experience face to face in the present is always doomed to failure. In a minor way the unique temporal structure of the best detective story is a pretext, a more organizational framework, for such isolated perception.

It is in this light that the well-known distinction between the atmosphere of English and American detective stories is to be understood. Gertrude Stein, in her *Lectures in America*, sees the essential feature of English literature to be the tireless description of "daily life," of lived routine and continuity, in which possessions are daily counted up and evaluated, in which the basic structure is one of cycle and repetition. American life, American content, on the other hand, is a formless one, always to be reinvented, an uncharted wilderness in which the very notion of experience itself is perpetually called into question and revised, in which time is an indeterminate succession out of which a few decisive, explosive, irrevocable instants stand out in relief. Hence, the murder in the placid English village or in the fogbound London club is read as the sign of a scandalous interruption in a peaceful continuity; whereas the gangland violence of the American big city is felt as a secret destiny, a kind of nemesis lurking beneath the surface of hastily acquired fortunes, anarchic city growth, and impermanent private lives. Yet in both, the moment of violence, apparently central, is nothing but a diversion: the real function of the murder in the quiet village is to allow its daily life to be felt more strongly; while the principal effect of the violence of the American detective story is to allow it to be experienced backwards, in pure thought, without risks, as a contemplative spectacle which gives not so much the illusion of life as the illusion that life has already been lived, that we have already had contact with the archaic sources of that Experience of which Americans have always made a fetish.

II

We looked at each other with the clear innocent eyes of a couple of used car salesmen.[b]

European literature is metaphysical or formalistic, because it takes the nature of the society, of the nation, for granted and works out beyond it. American literature never seems to get beyond the definition of its starting point: any picture of America is bound to be wrapped up in a question and a presupposition about the nature of American reality. European literature can choose its subject matter and the width of its lens; American literature feels obliged to put everything in, knowing that exclusion is also part of the process of definition, and that it can be called to account as much for what it doesn't say as for what it does.

The last great period of American literature, which ran more or less from one world war to the other, explored and defined America in a geographical mode, as a sum of separate localisms, as an additive unity, at its outside limit an ideal sum. But since the War, the organic differences from region to region have been increasingly obliterated by standardization; and the organic social unity of each region has been

---
[b]We have not found the source of this quotation.—Eds.

increasingly fragmented and abstracted by the new closed lives of the individual family units, by the breakdown of cities and the dehumanization of transportation and of the media which lead from one monad to another. Communication in this new society is upwards, through the abstract connecting link, and back down again. The isolated units are all haunted by the feeling that the center of things, of life, of control, is elsewhere, beyond immediate lived experiences. The principal images of interrelationship in this new society are mechanical juxtapositions: the identical prefabricated houses in the housing project, swarming over the hills; the four-lane highway full of cars bumper to bumper and observed from above, abstractly, by a traffic helicopter. If there is a crisis in American literature at present, it should be understood against the background of this ungrateful social material, in which only trick shots can produce the illusion of life.

Chandler lies somewhere between these two literary situations. His whole background, his way of thinking and of seeing things, derives from the period between the wars. But by an accident of place, his social content anticipates the realities of the fifties and sixties. For Los Angeles is already a kind of microcosm and forecast of the country as a whole: a new centerless city, in which the various classes have lost touch with each other because each is isolated in his own geographical compartment. If the symbol of social coherence and comprehensibility was furnished by the nineteenth-century Parisian apartment house (dramatized in Zola's *Pot-Bouille*) with its shop on the ground floor, its wealthy inhabitants on the second and third, petty bourgeoisie further up, and workers' rooms on top along with the maids and servants, then Los Angeles is the opposite, a spreading out horizontally, a flowing apart of the elements of the social structure.

Since there is no longer any privileged experience in which the whole of the social structure can be grasped, a figure must be invented who can be superimposed on the society as a whole, whose routine and life pattern serve somehow to tie its separate and isolated parts together. Its equivalent is the picaresque novel, where a single character moves from one background to another, links picturesque but not intrinsically related episodes together. In doing this the detective in a sense once again fulfills the demands of the function of knowledge rather than that of lived experience: through him we are able to see, to know, the society as a whole, but he does not really stand for any genuine close-up experience of it. Of course, the origin of the literary detective lies in the creation of the professional police, whose organization can be attributed not so much to a desire to prevent crime in general as to the will on the part of modern governments to know and thus to control the varying elements of their administrative areas. The great continental detectives (Lecoq, Maigret) are generally policemen; but in the Anglo-Saxon countries, where governmental control sits far more lightly on the citizens, the private detective, from Holmes to Chandler's Philip Marlowe, takes the place of the government functionary.

As an involuntary explorer of the society, Marlowe visits either those places you don't look at or those you can't look at: the anonymous or the wealthy and secretive. Both have something of the strangeness with which Chandler characterizes the police station: "A New York police reporter wrote once that when you pass in beyond the green lights of the precinct station you pass clear out of this world into a place beyond the law."[c] On the one hand those parts of the American scene which are as impersonal and seedy as public waiting rooms: run-down office buildings, the elevator with the spittoon and the elevator man sitting on a stool beside it; dingy office interiors, Marlowe's own in particular, seen at all hours of the clock, at those times when we have forgotten that offices exist, in the late evening, when the other offices are dark, in the early morning before the traffic begins; police stations; hotel rooms and lobbies, with the characteristic potted palms and overstuffed armchairs; rooming houses with managers who work illegal lines of business on the side. All these places are characterized by belonging to the mass, collective side of our society: places occupied by faceless people who leave no stamp of their personality behind them; in short, the dimension of the interchangeable, the inauthentic:

> Out of the apartment houses come women who should be young but have faces like stale beer; men with pulled-down hats and quick eyes that look the street over behind the cupped hand that shields the match flame; worn intellectuals with cigarette coughs and no money in the bank; fly cops with granite faces and unwavering eyes; cokies

[c] We have not found the source of this quotation.—Eds.

and coke peddlers; people who look like nothing in particular and know it, and once in a while even men that actually go to work. But they come out early, when the wide cracked sidewalks are empty and still have dew on them.[d]

The presentation of this kind of social material is far more frequent in European art than in our own: as if somehow we were willing to know anything about ourselves, the worst kind of secret, just as long as it was not this nameless, faceless one. But it suffices to compare the faces of actors and participants in almost any European movie with those in American ones to note the absence in ours of the whole-grain lens and the dissimilarity between the product offered and the features of people around us in the street. What makes this somewhat more difficult to observe is that, of course, our view of life is conditioned by the art we know, which has trained us not to see what the texture of ordinary people's faces is, but rather to invest them with photographic glamour.

The other side of American life with which Marlowe comes into contact is the reverse of the above: the great estate, with its retinue of servants, chauffeurs, and secretaries; and around it, the various institutions which cater to wealth and preserve its secrecy: the private clubs, set back on private roads in the mountains, patrolled by a private police which admits members only; the clinics in which drugs are available; the religious cults; the luxury hotels with their hotel detectives; the private gambling ships, anchored out beyond the three-mile limit; and a little further away, the corrupt local police which rule a municipality in the name of a single family or man, and the various kinds of illegal activity which spring up to satisfy money and its wants.

But Chandler's picture of America has an intellectual content as well: it is the converse, the darker concrete reality, of an abstract intellectual illusion about the United States. The federal system and the archaic federal Constitution developed in Americans a double image of their country's political reality, a double system of political thoughts which never intersect with each other. On the one hand, a glamorous national politics whose distant leading figures are invested with charisma, an unreal, distinguished quality adhering to their for-

[d]From *The High Window,* in *The Raymond Chandler Omnibus* (New York: Modern Library, 1975), p. 358.—Eds.

eign policy activities, their economic programs given the appearance of intellectual content by the appropriate ideologies of liberalism or conservatism. On the other hand, local politics, with its odium, its ever-present corruption, its deals and perpetual preoccupation with undramatic, materialistic questions such as sewage disposal, zoning regulations, property taxes, and so forth. Governors are halfway between the two worlds, but for a mayor, for example, to become a senator involves a thoroughgoing metamorphosis, a transformation from one species into another. Indeed, the qualities perceived in the political macrocosm are only illusory qualities, the projection of the dialectical opposite of the real qualities of the microcosm: everyone is convinced of the dirtiness of politics and politicians on the local level, and when everything is seen in terms of interest, the absence of greed becomes the feature which dazzles. Like the father whose defects are invisible to his own children, the national politicians (with occasional stunning exceptions) seem to be beyond personal self-interest, and this lends an automatic prestige to their professional affairs, lifts them onto a different rhetorical level entirely.

On the level of abstract thought, the effect of the preordained permanency of the Constitution is to hinder the development of any speculative political theorizing in this country, and to replace it with pragmatism within the system, the calculation of counterinfluences and possibilities of compromise. A kind of reverence attaches to the abstract, a disabused cynicism to the concrete. As in certain types of mental obsession and dissociation, the American is able to observe local injustice, racism, corruption, educational incompetence, with a practiced eye, while he continues to entertain boundless optimism as to the greatness of the country, taken as a whole.

The action of Chandler's books takes place inside the microcosm, in the darkness of a local world without the benefit of the federal Constitution, as in a world without God. The literary shock is dependent on the habit of the political double standard in the mind of the reader: it is only because we are used to thinking of the nation as a whole in terms of justice that we are struck by these images of people caught in the power of a local county authority as absolutely as though they were in a foreign country. The local power apparatus is beyond appeal, in this other face of federalism; the rule of naked force and money is complete and undisguised by any embellishments of theory. In an eerie optical illusion, the jungle reappears in the suburbs. In this sense the honesty of the detective can be understood as an organ of perception, a membrane which, irritated, serves to indicate in its sensitivity the nature of the world around it. For if the detective is dishonest, his job boils down to the technical problem of how to succeed on a given assignment. If he is honest, he is able to feel the resistance of things, to permit an intellectual vision of what he goes through on the level of action. And Chandler's sentimentalism, which attaches to occasional honest characters in the earlier books, but which is perhaps strongest in *The Long Goodbye,* is the reverse and complement of this vision, a momentary relief from it, a compensation for it: where everything is seen in a single light, there is not much possibility for subtlety or variety of feelings to develop, there is available only the ground tonality and its opposite.

The detective's journey is episodic because of the fragmentary, atomistic nature of the society he moves through. In European countries, people no matter how solitary are still somehow engaged in the social substance; their very solitude is social; their identity is inextricably entangled with that of all the others by a clear system of classes, by a national language, in what Heidegger describes as the *Mitsein,* the being-together-with-others.

But the form of Chandler's books reflects an initial American separation of people from each other, their need to be linked by some external force (in this case the detective) if they are ever to be fitted together as parts of the same picture puzzle. And this separation is projected out onto space itself: no matter how crowded the street in question, the various solitudes never really merge into a collective experience, there is always distance between them. Each dingy office is separated from the next; each room in the rooming house from the one next to it; each dwelling from the pavement beyond it. This is why the most characteristic leitmotif of Chandler's books is the figure standing, looking out of one world, peering vaguely or attentively across into another:

> Across the street was an Italian funeral home, neat and quiet and reticent, white painted brick, flush with the sidewalk. Pietro Palermo Funeral Parlors. The thin green script of neon sign lay across its façade, with a chaste air. A tall man in dark clothes came

> out of the front door and leaned against the white wall. He looked very handsome. He had dark skin and a handsome head of iron-gray hair brushed back from his forehead. He got out what looked at that distance to be a silver or platinum and black enamel cigarette case, opened it languidly with two long brown fingers, and selected a gold-tipped cigarette. He put the case away and lit the cigarette with a pocket lighter that seemed to match the case. He put that away and folded his arms and stared at nothing with half-closed eyes. From the tip of his motionless cigarette a thin wisp of smoke rose straight up past his face, as thin and straight as the smoke of a dying campfire at dawn.[e]

In psychological or allegorical terms, this figure on the doorstep represents Suspicion, and suspicion is everywhere in this world, peering from behind a curtain, barring entry, refusing to answer, preserving the privacy of the monad against snoopers and trespassers. Its characteristic manifestations are the servant coming back out into the hallway, the man in the car lot hearing a noise, the custodian of a deserted farm looking outside, the manager of the rooming house taking another look upstairs, the bodyguard appearing in the doorway.

Hence, the detective's principal contact with the people he meets is a rather external one; they are seen briefly in their own doorways, for a purpose, and their personalities come out against the grain, hesitant, hostile, stubborn, as they react to the various questions and drag their feet on the answers. But seen another way, the very superficiality of these meetings with the characters is artistically motivated: for the characters themselves are pretexts for their speech, and the specialized nature of this speech is that it is somehow external, indicative of types, objective, remarks bounced across to strangers:

> Her eyes receded and her chin followed them. She sniffed hard.
> "You been drinkin' liquor," she said coldly.
> "I just had a tooth out. The dentist gave it to me."
> "I don't hold to it."
> "It's bad stuff except for medicine," I said.
> "I don't hold with it for medicine neither."
> "I think you're right," I said. "Did he leave her any money? Her husband?"

[e]From *The High Window*, in *The Raymond Chandler Omnibus*, p. 358.—Eds.

"I wouldn't know." Her mouth was the size of a prune and as smooth. I had lost out.[f]

This kind of dialogue is also characteristic of the early Faulkner; it is quite different from that of Hemingway, which is much more personal and fluid, created from the inside, somehow reenacted and personally reexperienced by the author. Here clichés and stereotyped speech patterns are heated into life by the presence behind them of a certain form of emotion, that which you would feel in your dealings with strangers: a kind of outgoing belligerence, or hostility, or the amusement of the native, or bantering, helpful indifference: a communicativeness always nuanced or colored by an attitude. And whenever Chandler's dialogue, which in the early books is very good, strays from this particular level to something more intimate and more expressive, it begins to falter; for his forte is the speech pattern of inauthenticity, of externality, and derives immediately from the inner organic logic of his material itself.

In the art of the twenties and thirties, however, such dialogue had the value of social schematism. A set of fixed social types and categories underlay it, and the dialogue was itself a way of demonstrating the coherence and peculiar organization the society possessed, of apprehending it in miniature. Anyone who has watched New York movies of the thirties is aware how linguistic characterization feeds into a picture of the city as a whole: the stock ethnic and professional types, the cabbie, the reporter, the flatfoot, the high society playboy and flapper, and so forth. Needless to say, the decay of this kind of movie results from the decay of such a picture of the city, which no longer presents any convenience as a way of organizing reality. But already the Los Angeles of Chandler was an unstructured city, and the social types are here nowhere near as pronounced. By the chance of a historical accident, Chandler was able to benefit from the survival of a purely linguistic, typological way of creating his characters after the system of types that had supported it was already in decay. A last hold, before the dissolving contours of the society made these linguistic types disappear also, leaving the novelist faced with the problem of the absence of any standard by which dialogue can be judged realistic or lifelike (except in certain very specialized situations).

[f]From *Farewell, My Lovely*, in *The Raymond Chandler Omnibus*, pp. 206–207.—Eds.

In Chandler the presentation of social reality is involved immediately and directly with the problem of language. He thought of himself primarily as a stylist, and there can be no doubt that he invented a distinctive kind of language, with its own humor and imagery, its own special movement. But the most striking feature of this style is its use of slang, and here Chandler's own remarks are instructive:

> I had to learn American just like a foreign language. To use it I had to study it and analyze it. As a result, when I use slang, colloquiálisms, snide talk, or any kind of offbeat language, I do it deliberately. The literary use of slang is a study in itself. I've found that there are only two kinds that are any good: slang that has established itself in the language and slang that you make up yourself. Everything else is apt to be passé before it gets into print. . . .[g]

And Chandler comments on O'Neill's use in *The Iceman Cometh* of the expression "the big sleep," "in the belief that it was an accepted underworld expression. If so, I'd like to see whence it comes, because I invented the expression."[h]

But slang is eminently serial in its nature: it exists as objectively as a joke, passed from hand to hand, always elsewhere, never fully the property of its user. In this, the literary problem of slang forms a parallel in the microcosm of style to the problem of the presentation of the serial society itself, never present fully in any of its manifestations, without a privileged center, offering the impossible alternative between an objective and abstract lexical knowledge of it as a whole and a lived concrete experience of its worthless components.

III

Part of the appeal of Chandler's books for us is a nostalgic one. They are among a whole class of objects we have come to call "camp," including Humphrey Bogart movies, certain comic books, hard-boiled detective stories, and monster movies, among other things. Pop art is the principle contemporary manifestation of this nostalgic interest: it is not unlike art about other art, for in spite of its simplicity it has two levels within it, a simplified outer expression, and an inner period

---

[g]From a letter of March 18, 1949, to Alex Barrish, reprinted in *Raymond Chandler Speaking*, p. 80.—Eds.
[h]From a letter of May 18, 1950, to Hamish Hamilton, reprinted in *Raymond Chandler Speaking*, pp. 88–89.—Eds.

atmosphere which is its object and which is evoked by balloon speeches, the enlarged dots of newspaper print, the faded faces of celebrities and well-known imaginary characters. Rather than art about art, it would be more accurate to say that it is art whose content is not direct experience, but already formed ideological artifacts.

Yet the experience of nostalgia remains itself to be explained. It is not a constant of all periods, and yet when it does appear, it is generally characterized by an attachment to a moment of the past wholly different from our own, which offers a more complete kind of relief from the present. The romantics, for example, reacted against the growth of an industrial society by recalling examples of pastoral, hierarchically organized ones from history or from travel. And limited sections of our own society continue to feel this kind of nostalgia, for Jeffersonian America, for example, or for the conditions of the frontier. Or else they satisfy their nostalgia in a concrete way by tourism in countries whose life and ways are the equivalent of some precapitalistic stage of historical development.

But the nostalgia which gave birth to pop art fastens for its object on the period immediately preceding our own, one apparently from a larger historical perspective not very different from it: its objects all come from a span of years too often referred to simply as the thirties and which, in reality, extends from the New Deal well across the parenthesis of the Second World War, and up to the beginning of the cold war. This period is marked by strong political and ideological movements, and with the revival of political life in the sixties these too have been the object of admiration and nostalgia; but they are themselves results and not causes, and are far from being its most significant features.

The atmosphere of a given period is crystallized first of all in its objects: the double-breasted suits, the long dresses of the new look, the fluffy hairdos, and the styling of the automobiles. But our nostalgia for this particular time is distinct from the evocation of museum-piece objects from the past in that it seeks out not so much the life style behind them as the objects themselves. It aims at a world like our own in its general conditions, industrialism, market capitalism, mass production, and is unlike it only in being somewhat simpler. It is partly a fascination with dating, aging, the passage of time for its own sake: like looking at photographs of ourselves in old-fashioned clothing in order to have a direct intuition of change, of historicity. (And, undoubtedly, the existence of the movies as a form does much to account for the peculiar intensity of this nostalgia: we can not only see the past alive before us tangibly, without having to rely on our own imagination of it, more than that, we can feel this past personally by seeing actors young whom we ourselves have grown familiar with as older figures, even by seeing movies we dimly remember from our own pasts.) But this historicity is itself a historical thing. It is as far from the ritual cycle of the seasons as is the turnover in clothing fashions. It is a rapid change intimately linked with the production and marketing of objects for sale.

For the beginning of the cold war also marked the beginning of the great postwar boom, and with it, the prodigious expansion in advertising, the use of television as a more vivid and suggestive way of selling competing and similar products—one that mingles them more intimately with our lives than did the newspaper or the radio.

The older products had a certain stability about them, a certain permanence of identity that can still be captured here and there in farm country, for example, where a few sparse signs point to the attachment to a few indispensable products. Here, the brand name is still synonymous with the object itself: a car is a "Ford," a lighter is a "Ronson," a hat is a "Stetson." In this early stage of the marketing of industrial products, the brands require a stable, relatively unchanging identity in order to become identified and adopted by the public, and the relatively primary and simplified advertising is merely a way of recalling something already familiar to the public mind. To be sure, the advertisements tend to blend with the image of the brand itself, but for that very reason in this period the advertisements also change very little and have a kind of stability of their own. Thus, the older kinds of products remain relatively integrated into the landscape of natural objects; they still fulfill easily identifiable needs, desires which are still felt to be relatively "natural"; lying midway between nature (land, climate, foodstuffs) and human reality, they correspond to a world in which the principal activity is still the overcoming of the resistance of nature and of things and in which human need and desire arise as a function of that struggle.

But with the postwar boom the premium comes to be placed on rapid change and evolution of products rather than on their stability and identity. In automobiles, in cigarettes, in soaps, among other things, this wild proliferation and transformation of marketable objects can be observed. Nor can scientific or technical advance (the invention of cigarette filters, of the automatic transmission, of the long-playing record) be held responsible for it. On the contrary, most of these technical innovations were feasible earlier; it is only when frequent styling changes are desirable that they are appealed to. The cause of this wholesale alteration in our purchasable environment would appear to be twofold: first, the increasing wealth and diversification of the various manufacturing companies which no longer have to depend on a single brand and which can now invent and eliminate brands at their convenience; second, the increasing autonomy of advertising, which is able to float any number of unfamiliar new objects in a hurry—in a kind of time exposure in which the older, slower familiarity is artificially reproduced by around-the-clock stimuli.

What is being created in these advertising exposures is not so much an object, a new type of physical thing, but rather an artificial need or desire, a kind of mental or ideological symbol by which the consumer's craving to buy is associated with a particular type of packaging and label. Evidently, in a situation in which most basic needs have already been satisfied it is necessary to evolve ever newer and more specialized ones in order to continue to be able to sell products. But the change has its psychological dimension as well, and corresponds to the turnover from a production economy to a service one. Fewer and fewer people are involved with objects as tools, with natural objects as raw materials; more and more are involved with objects as semi-ideas, busy marketing and consuming objects which they never really apprehend as pure materiality, as the product of work on resisting things. In such a world, material needs are subliminated into more symbolic satisfactions; the initial desire is not the solution of a material problem, but the style and symbolic connotations of the product to be possessed.

The life problems of such a world are radically different in kind from those of the relatively simple world of needs and physical resistance which preceded it. They involve a struggle, not against things and relatively solid systems of power, but against ideological fantasms, bits and pieces of spiritualized matter, the solicitations of various kinds of dreamlike mirages and cravings, a life to the second power, not heightened and intensified but merely refined and confused, unable to find a footing in the reality of things. Such a world clearly poses the most difficult problems for the artist trying to register it. It is full of merely spiritualized, or in our conventional terminology, merely "psychological" problems which do not seem to stand in any direct, observable relationship to the objective realities of the society. At their upper limit, presented for themselves alone, these problems lose themselves in supersubtleties and uninteresting introspection; while the presentation of the objective reality itself strikes the modern reader as old-fashioned and without any relevance to his lived experience.

But the most immediate and visible effects of this situation are stylistic. In the time of Balzac manufactured objects, products, have an immediate and intrinsic novelistic interest, and not only because they record as furnishings the taste and personality of their owners. In this earliest period of industrial capitalism, they are in the very process of being invented and marketed by contemporaries, and where some books tell the very story of their evolution and exploitation, others allow them to stand mute around or behind the characters themselves, as testimony to the nature of the world being created at that moment and to the stage which human energies have been able to reach. In the era of stable products, however, to which Chandler's books belong, there is no longer any feeling of the creative energy embodied in a product: the latter are simply there, in a permanent industrial background which has come to resemble that of nature itself. Now the author's task is to make an inventory of these objects, to demonstrate, by the fullness of his catalogue, how completely he knows his way around the world of machines and machine products, and it is in this sense that Chandler's descriptions of furniture, his description of women's clothing styles, will function: as a naming, a sign of expertise and know-how. And at the limits of this type of language, the brand-names themselves: "I went in past him, into a dim pleasant room with an apricot Chinese rug that looked expensive, deep-sided chairs, a number of white drum lamps, a big Capehart in the corner." "I got a half-bottle of Old Taylor out of the deep drawer of the desk." "The sweetish smell of his Fatima poisoned the air for me." (Hemingway is, of course, the chief representative of this style of brand-name dropping, but it has currency throughout the literature of the thirties.)

By the time we come to that cross-country inventory of Americana which is Nabokov's *Lolita*, the attitude to objects has changed significantly. Precisely in order for his descriptions to be representative, Nabokov hesitates to use the actual brand names of the products: the esthetic reason, that such language is of a different nature from the language of the narration generally and cannot be crudely introduced into it, is part of a more general realization that the physical product itself has long since been dissolved as a permanence. Like the "substances" of philosophy, of mathematics, of the physical sciences, it has long since lost its essentiality and become a locus of processes, a meeting place for social manipulation and human raw material. Where Nabokov occasionally does use names, they are brand names invented in imitation of the real, and as such his use is a way of rendering not the product but the process of nomination. But in general he describes the jumble of commercial products in the American landscape from the outside, as pure appearance without any reference to functionality, since in the new American culture of the fifties functionality, practical use in the satisfaction of need and desire, is no longer of any great importance.

Warhol's Coca-Cola bottles or Campbell's soup cans represent a different kind of attitude towards objects: the attempt to seize them, not in their material, but in their dated historical reality, as a certain moment and style of the past. It is a fetish representing the will to return to a period when there was still a certain distance between objects, when the manufactured landscape still had a certain solidity. The Warhol image is a way of making us stare at a single commercial product, in hopes that our vision of all those around us will be transformed, that our new stare will infuse those also with depth and solidity, with the meaning of remembered objects and products, with the physical foundation and dimensions of the older world of need.

The comic strip drawing does much the same thing for the world of culture, as jammed as the airwaves with bits and pieces of stories, imagined characters, cheaply manufactured fantasies of all kinds, even where newspaper and historical truth have come to be assimilated to the products of the entertainment industry. Now suddenly all the floating figures and shapes are simplified down, stamped with exaggeration, blown up and reduced to the size of children's daydreams. The transfer to the fixed object which is the painting takes place in imitation of the material consumption by the child of the comic books themselves, which he handles and uses as objects. For the nostalgia for this earlier world operates just as strongly on the forms as on the content of its materials. Humphrey Bogart, for example, obviously stands for the hero who knows how to find his way around the dangerous anarchy of the world of the thirties and forties. He is distinguished from the other stars of his period in that he is able to show fear, and his fear is the organ of perception and exploration of the dark world lying about him. As an image, he is related to Marlowe (indeed, briefly coincides with him in the movie version of *The Big Sleep*), and a descendant of the Hemingway hero of the earlier part of the same period, in whom the trait of purely technical know-how was even more pronounced.

On the other hand, his revival has its formal dimension as well, whether we are consciously aware of it or not. For in our recognition of Humphrey Bogart as a culture hero is also included a regret for the smaller black-and-white ninety-minute movie in which he traditionally appeared, and beyond that, for that period in the history of the medium when work was done in a small, fixed form, in a series of small works rather than isolated, enormous, and expensive production. (This evolution in the movie industry parallels the movement in serious literature away from the fixed form of the nineteenth century towards the personally invented, style-conscious individual forms of the twentieth.)

Thus, the perception of the products with which the world around us is furnished precedes our perception of things-in-themselves and forms it. We first use objects, only then gradually do we learn to stand away from them and to contemplate them disinterestedly, and it is in this fashion that the commercial nature of our surroundings influences and shapes the production of our literary images, stamping them with the character of a certain period. In Chandler's style the period identifies itself in his most characteristic feature, the exaggerated comparison, the function of which is at the same time to isolate the object in question and to indicate its value: "She was in oyster-white lounging pajamas trimmed with white fur, cut as flowingly as a summer sea frothing on the beach of some small and exclusive island." "Even on Central Avenue, not the quietest-dressed street in the world, he looked about as inconspicuous as a tarantula on a slice of angel food." "There was a desk and a night clerk with one of those moustaches that gets stuck under your fingernail." "This is the ultimate end of the fog belt, and the beginning of that semidesert region where the sun is as light and dry as old sherry in the morning, as hot as a blast furnace at noon, and drops like an angry brick at nightfall."

As in the hard-boiled movies, the narrator's voice-over works in counterpoint to the things seen, heightening them subjectively through his own reactions to them, through the poetry his comparisons lend them, and letting them fall back again into their sordid, drab reality through the deadpan humor which disavows what it has just maintained. But where the movies already present a divided structure of vision and sound ready to be played off against each other, the literary work must rely on some deeper division in its material itself. Such a tone is possible for it only against the background of a certain recognizable uniformity of objects, among which the outlandish comparison serves as a pause, drawing a circle momentarily around one of them, causing it to stand out as typical of one of the two zones of the novel's content, as either very expensive or very shabby. It avoids the flat and naturalistically prosaic on the one hand, and the poetic and unreal on the other, in a delicate compromise executed by the tone of the narration. And because it is a spoken account in its very essence, the voice-over stands as testimony, like the records of old songs or old comedians, to what everyday life was like in a world similar enough to our own to seem very distant.

IV

My theory was that the readers just *thought* they cared about nothing but the action; that really, although they didn't know it, the thing they cared about, and that I cared about, was the creation of emotion through dialogue and description. The things they remembered, that haunted them, were not, for example, that a man got killed, but that in the moment of his death he was trying to pick a paper clip off the polished surface of a desk and it kept slipping away from him, so that there was a look of strain on his face and his mouth was half open in a kind of tormented grin, and the last thing in the world he thought about was death. He didn't even hear death knock on the door. That damn little paper clip kept slipping away from his fingers.[i]

Raymond Chandler's novels have not one form, but two, an objective form and a subjective one, the rigid external structure of the detective story on the one hand, and a more personal distinctive rhythm of events on the other, arranged, as is the case with any novelist of originality, according to some ideal molecular chain in the brain cells, as personal in their encephalographic pattern as a fingerprint, peopled with recurrent phantoms, obsessive character types, actors in some forgotten psychic drama through whom the social world continues to be interpreted. Yet the two kinds of form do not conflict with each other; on the contrary, the second seems to have been generated out of the first by the latter's own internal contradictions. Indeed, it results from a kind of formula on Chandler's part:

> It often seems to this particular writer that the only reasonably honest and effective way of fooling the reader that remains is to make the reader exercise his mind about the wrong problem, to make him, as it were, solve a mystery (since he is almost sure to solve something) which will land him in a bypath because it is only tangential to the central problem.[j]

For the detective story is not only a purely intellectual mode of knowing events, it is also a puzzle in which the faculties of analysis and reasoning are to be exercised, and Chandler here simply generalizes a technique of outwitting the reader. Instead of the innovation that will only work once (the most famous is, of course, that of Agatha Christie in *The Murder of Roger Ackroyd*, where, as is well known, the murderer turns out to be the narrator himself), he invents a principle for the construction of the plot itself.

It is, of course, the presence of this kind of plot construction in all of his books, the persistence of this fixed intellectual purpose, that accounts for their similarity as forms. Yet the two aspects of the works hardly seem commensurable, seem to involve different dimensions that miss each other in passing: the intellectual purpose is a purely

---

[i]From the letter cited in note a.—Eds.
[j]From "Casual Notes on the Mystery Novel," in *Raymond Chandler Speaking*, p. 69. —Eds.

temporal one, it abolishes itself when it is successful and when the reader realizes that he has been misled and that the real solution to the murder is to be found elsewhere. The form is, on the other hand, more spatial in character: even after the temporal reading of the book is finished we have a feeling of its continuity spread out before us in a pattern, and the earlier, misleading twists of the plot (which the pure mind rejects as illusory filling just as soon as it guesses the secret to the puzzle) remain for the imagination of form as an integral part of the road traveled, the experiences gone through. In Chandler's books we are therefore confronted with the paradox of something slight in density and resonance being at the source of some incomparable larger solid, of a kind of nothingness—creating being, of a shadow projecting three-dimensionality out from itself. It is as though an object designed for some purely practical purpose, a machine of some kind, suddenly turned out to be of interest on a different level of perception, on the esthetic, for example; for the rather negative technical device, the quantitative formula for purely intellectual deception given above in Chandler's own words, is responsible in a kind of dialectical accident for the positive qualitative nature of his forms, their lopsided, episodic movements, the characteristic effects and emotions related to them.

The initial deception takes place on the level of the book as a whole, in that it passes itself off as a murder mystery. In fact, Chandler's stories are first and foremost descriptions of searches, in which murder is involved, and which sometimes end with the murder of the person sought for. The immediate result of this formal change is that the detective no longer inhabits the atmosphere of pure thought, of puzzle solving and the resolution of a set of given elements. On the contrary, he is propelled outwards into the space of his world and obliged to move from one kind of social reality to another incessantly, trying to find clues to his client's whereabouts.

Once set in motion, the search has unexpectedly violent results. It is as if the world of the beginning of the book, the imaginary Chandler Southern California, lay in a kind of uneasy balance, an equilibrium of large and small systems of corruption, in a tense silence as of people straining to listen. The appearance of the detective breaks the balance, sets the various mechanisms of suspicion ringing, as he triggers the electric eyes, snooping and preparing to make trouble in a way which isn't yet clear. The upshot is a whole series of murders and beatings: it is as though they existed already in a latent state, the acts that had merited them having already been committed, like chemical substances juxtaposed, waiting for a single element to be withdrawn or added in order to complete a reaction which nothing can stop. The appearance of the detective is this element, allowing the predetermining causes to run their course suddenly, to burst into flame on exposure to the open air.

But as has already been made apparent in Chandler's description of his own plot construction, this trail of bloodshed is a false scent, designed to draw the reader's attention to guilt in the wrong places. The diversion is not dishonest, inasmuch as the guilt uncovered along the way is also real enough; the latter is simply not that with which the book is directly involved. Hence, the episodic nature of the diversionary plot: the characters are drawn in heightened, sharp fashion because we will never see them again. Their entire essence must be revealed in a single brief meeting. Yet these meetings take place on a different plane of reality from that of the main plot of the book. It is not only that the intellectual function of our mind is busy weighing and selecting them (are they related in some way to the search or are they not?) in a set of operations which it does not have to perform on the materials of the main plot (the client and his or her household, the person sought and his or her connections). The very violence and crimes themselves are here apprehended on a different mode: since they are tangential and secondary for us, we learn of them in a manner not so much realistic (novelistic) as lengendary, much as we would hear about occasional violence in the newspaper or over the radio. Our interest in them is purely anecdotal, and is already a kind of distance from them. Whether we know it yet or not therefore, these characters of the secondary plot exist for us in a different dimension, like glimpses through a window, noises from the back of a store, unfinished stories, unrelated activities going on in the society around us simultaneously with our own.

The climax of the book must therefore involve a return to its beginning, to the initial plot and characters. Obviously the person searched for must be found. But in a perhaps less obvious way, the guilty party (since a murder, a crime, is always in some way involved in the search) must turn out to be in one way or another a member of the family, the client, or a member of his entourage. Chandler's novels are all variations on this pattern, almost mathematically predictable combinations and permutations of these basic possibilities: the missing person is dead and the client did it, or the missing person is guilty and the body found was that of somebody else, or both the client and a member of her entourage are guilty and the missing person is not really missing at all, and so forth.

In a sense this pattern is in itself little more than a variation on the law of the least likely party, since it seems to make little sense that a criminal would go to a detective in the first place and ask him to solve a murder of which he or she was, in reality, guilty. And then there is a secondary, sociological shock: the comparison between all the secondary, relatively institutionalized killings (gangland murders, police brutality) and the private-life, domestic crime which is the book's central event and which turns out to be just as sordid and violent in its own way.

But the principal explanation of this pattern of a return to the beginning is to be found in the ritual unveiling of the murderer itself. A kind of intellectual satisfaction might be derived from a demonstration of the necessity for such-and-such a minor character, met only briefly in passing, to be the murderer, but we have already seen that the emotional effect of the revelation of the murderer depends on a certain familiarity with its innocent mask; and the only characters in Chandler whom we stay with long enough to develop this familiarity, whom we ever get to know in any kind of depth of character analysis, are those of the opening, of what has been called the main plot.

(In ingenious and metaphysical detective stories such as Robbe-Grillet's *Les Gommes* or Doderer's *Ein Mord den Jeder begeht,* the logic inherent in this situation is pushed to its conclusion and the murderer turns out to be the detective himself, in that abstract equation of $I = I$ which Hegel saw as the source of all self-conscious identity. In a more Freudian way, Chandler's imitators—most notably Ross Macdonald—have experimented with situations in which, after a search through time as well as through space, the criminal and the victim or the client and the criminal turn out to be related to each other, in one oedipal variation or another. Yet in all this the detective story plot merely follows the basic tendency of all literary plots or intrigue in general, which is marked by the resolution of multiplicity back into some primal unity, by a return to some primal starting point, in the marriage of hero and heroine and the creation of the original family cellular unit, or the unveiling of the hero's mysterious origins, and so forth.)

On the other hand, it would be wrong to think of Chandler's stories as conforming in their final effect with the description we have given of the unveiling of the murderer in the classical detective story. For the discovery of the criminal here is only half of a more complicated revelation, and takes place, not only as the climax of a murder mystery, but also as that of a search. The search and the murder serve as alternating centers for our attention in a kind of intricate Gestalt pattern; each serves to mask off the weaker, less convincing aspects of the other, each serves to arrest the blurring of the other out into the magical and the symbolic and to refocus it in a raw and sordid clarity. When our mind is following the motif of the murder, the search ceases to be a mere literary technique, a pretext on which to hang a series of episodes, and is invested with a kind of depressing fatality, like a circular movement narrowing down. When on the contrary we focus on the search as the organizing center of the events described, the murder becomes a purposeless accident, the senseless breaking off of a thread, of a trail.

Indeed, it would not be too much to say that there takes place in Chandler a demystification of violent death. The fact of the search tends to arrest the transformation involved in the revelation of the murderer. There is no longer behind the unveiling that infinity of possibilities of evil, that formlessness behind a determinate mask. One character has simply been transformed into another; a name, a label, has wavered and then gone to fix itself to someone else. For the attribute of being a murderer can no longer function as a symbol of pure evil when murder itself has lost its symbolic qualities.

Chandler's demystification involves the removal of purpose from the murder event. The classical detective story always invests murder with purpose by its very formal perspective. The murder is, as we have seen, a kind of abstract point which is made to bear meaning and significance by the convergence of all lines upon it. In the world of the classical detective story nothing happens which is not related to the central murder: therefore it is purposeful, if for no other reason than to organize all that raw material around itself. (The actual purpose, the motive and cause, is worked up after the fact by the author, and never matters very much.) But in Chandler the other random violence of the secondary plot has intervened to contaminate the central murder. And by the time we reach its explanation, we have come to feel all violence in the same light, and it strikes us as being just as shoddy and cheap, just as physically abrupt and as morally insignificant.

Murder comes to seem moreover in its very essence accidental and without meaning. It was the optic of the classical detective story, the distortion of its formal perspective, that made the murder look like the almost disembodied result of a process of purely mental planning and premeditation, like the jotting down on paper of the results of mathematical operations performed in the head. Now, however, the gap between intention and execution is glaringly evident: no matter what planning is involved, the leap to physical action, the committing of the murder itself, is always abrupt and without prior logical justification in the world of reality. Thus, the reader's mind has been used as an element in a very complicated esthetic deception: he has been made to expect the solution of an intellectual puzzle, his purely intellectual functions are operating emptily, in anticipation of it, and suddenly, in its place, he is given an evocation of death in all its physicality, when there is no longer any time to prepare himself for it properly, when he is obliged to take the strong sensation on its own terms.

The final element in Chandler's characteristic form is that the underlying crime is always old, lying half forgotten in the pasts of the characters before the book begins. This is the principal reason why the reader's attention is diverted from it: he assumes it to be part of the dimension of the present, of the events going on before him in the immediacy of his narrated universe. Instead, it is buried in that world's past, in time, among the dead evoked in the memorable closing page of *The Big Sleep*.

And suddenly the purely intellectual effect of Chandler's construction formula is metamorphosed into a result of unmistakable esthetic intensity. From the point of view of abstract curiosity we might expect the reader to have a reaction not altogether unmixed: satisfaction at the solution of the puzzle, irritation at having been misled through so much extraneous material which had no real bearing on it. And on the esthetic level the irritation remains, but transfigured.

For now, at the end, all the events of the book are seen in a new and depressing light: all that energy and activity wasted to find somebody who had, in reality, been dead for so long, for whom the time of the present was little more than a process of slow physical dissolution. And suddenly, at the thought of that dissolution, and of the mindless lack of identity of the missing person so long called by name, the very appearance of life itself, of time in the present, of the bustling activity of the outside world, is stripped away and we feel in its place the presence of graves beneath the bright sunlight; the present fades to little more than a dusty, once-lived moment which will quickly take its place in the back years of an old newspaper file. And our formal distraction at last serves its fundamental purpose: by diverting us with the ritual detective story aim of the detection of the criminal, and of his transformation into the Other, it is able to bring us up short, without warning, against the reality of death itself, stale death, reaching out to remind the living of its own moldering resting place.

MICHAEL HOLQUIST

Whodunit and Other Questions: Metaphysical Detective Stories in Postwar Fiction

Kitsch is familiar, comforting, reassuring; art unsettles, questions, provokes. Kitsch provides an escape, art a confrontation. The classic detective story, Holquist argues, was the kitsch for modernist intellectuals, providing an escape from the unsettling irrationality of myth and the newly discovered unconscious and some reassurance that reason does indeed possess the power to conquer evil. Postmodernist writers, while hardly confident, optimistic rationalists, have rejected mythic modes and psychological realism to experiment with the possibilities, the limitations, and the power of conscious perception and the search for knowledge. In the process, they have made the same use of the detective novel that their predecessors made of myth. The result is the "metaphysical" detective story, which adopts the "method" of the detective novel but not its "telos," forcing the reader to put together clues, not to reach a solution, but to understand the process of understanding. "If, in the detective story, death must be solved, in the new metaphysical detective story, it is life *which must be solved."*

Holquist's essay in literary history can be profitably juxtaposed with Richard Alewyn's. Holquist himself is a specialist in Russian literature and literary theory, currently on the faculty of Indiana University. His article was first published in New Literary History *(vol. 3, 1971–1972).*

I

This paper seeks to make two points: first, what the structural and philosophical presuppositions of myth and depth psychology were to modernism (Mann, Joyce, Woolf, and so forth), the detective story is to postmodernism (Robbe-Grillet, Borges, Nabokov, and so on); secondly, if such is the case, we will have established a relationship between two levels of culture, kitsch and the avant-garde, often thought to be mutually exclusive.

II

Popular culture is a skeleton in our academic closets. And like other disturbing topics it generates discourse which seems inevitably to end in a polarity. Clement Greenberg states the dilemma very clearly:

> One and the same civilization produces simultaneously two such different things as a poem by T. S. Eliot and a Tin Pan Alley song, or a painting by Braque and a *Saturday Evening Post* cover . . . ; a poem by Eliot and a poem by Eddie Guest—what perspective of culture is large enough to enable us to relate them in an enlightening relation to each other?"[1]

Greenberg's uneasiness is shared by the majority of critics who have addressed the problem at all.[2] He and many others find disturbing what appears to be an absolute cut-off between their own traditions and responses and those of the millions who sit, beer can in hand, glued to the television set. In this view the distance between Sophocles and the sitcom, the museum and the dimestore seems immeasurable. And it no doubt *is* if seen as so many sociologists do, as a static synchronic relationship. But the cultural historian perceives a different, more dynamic and ultimately a more hopeful connection between popular and high culture. Viewed historically, it is clear that there has

---

[1] "Avant-Garde and Kitsch," in *Mass Culture: The Popular Arts in America*, ed. Bernard Rosenberg and David Manning White (Glencoe, Ill., 1958), p. 98.

[2] A brilliant (and occasionally hysterical) case in point would be Gunther Anders's essay, "The Phantom World of TV," also in *Mass Culture*, pp. 358–367. Further evidence may be found in Gillo Dorfles' *Kitsch, an Anthology of Bad Taste* (London, 1969); Karlheinz Deschner, *Kitsch, Konvention und Kunst* (München, 1962); Walter Nutz, *Der Trivialroman: seine Formen und seine Hersteller* (Köln und Opladen, 2.e Auflage, 1966); and two rich collections of essays: Gerhard Schmidt-Henkel, Horst Enders, et al., eds. *Trivialliteratur* (Berlin, 1964), and Norman Jacobs, ed., *Culture for the Millions: Mass Media in Modern Society* (Boston, 1964).

been and continues to be a dialectical apposition between the two poles. In order for our argument to proceed it is not necessary to advance new definitions for terms we are using, each of which has a history. Rather we shall appeal to the clichés which have grown up around each. Kitsch and the avant-garde are both in a problematic relationship to the mainstream tradition of high culture, which is perhaps most economically defined by the curricula of our universities. A college catalogue is a kind of telephone book for the city of culture. In the area of literature thumbnail descriptions of culture may be found in all those courses which begin the first semester with Homer and the Bible. These models are to college graduates what the oral tradition is to the savage. Not included in such lists will be works defined by those who compile them as being below the canon (kitsch) or beyond it (avant-garde). Both phenomena are of relatively recent origin, a point which has been made for kitsch by Gillo Dorfles[3] and for the avant-garde by Renato Poggioli.[4] Why both tendencies should have not developed earlier is an exceedingly complex question. But certainly mass industrialization might be adduced as a cause in both cases. Kitsch springs not from artists or craftsmen but from the machine. Our increasingly sophisticated technology represents new possibilities for mass culture. At the same time it represents a new threat to the avant-garde. As has so often been pointed out, newly developed means for the rapid and widespread transmission of ideas have relentlessly closed the distance between what is known to the *cognoscenti* and to the man in the street. Today's experiment becomes tomorrow's habit: reproductions of Jackson Pollock paintings are to be found in motel rooms all across the country.

The more uniform mass culture becomes, the more violently the

---

[3] "... in every age before our own, there was no such thing as ... kitsch. ... In ages other than our own, particularly in antiquity, art had a completely different function compared to modern times: it was connected with religious, ethical, or political subject matter, which made it in a way 'absolute,' unchanging, eternal (always of course within a given cultural milieu)." Dorfles, op. cit., pp. 9–10. P. O. Kristeller argues that the interdependence of art and other human activities and concerns, such as those cited by Dorfles, broke down somewhere at the end of the seventeenth, beginning of the eighteenth century, in his magisterial survey of the problem: "The Modern System of the Arts," *Renaissance Studies II: Papers on Humanism and the Arts* (New York, 1965), pp. 163–227.

[4] "... it is by now an undoubted fact that the term and concept of avant-garde art reach no further back in time than the last quarter of the past century." *The Theory of the Avant-Garde,* tr. Gerald Fitzgerald (New York, 1971), p. 13.

avant-garde strains after idiosyncrasy, creating a situation in which the truth of an old dichotomy becomes daily more apparent: art is difficult, kitsch is easy. The difficulty of experimental art in the last one hundred years hardly needs demonstrating. But the assumption of mass culture that everything is, or should be, understandable, easily and quickly accessible, bears some further reflection. Kitsch seems to appropriate art by robbing it of the demonic, not just its "aura" as Walter Benjamin has argued,[5] but its dangers. Even if you assume that art is therapeutic, you must first experience the pity and terror of a tragedy before winning the catharsis it may then provide. Such unsettling emotions are precisely what kitsch operates against in its urge to avoid all difficulties, whether of perception, execution, or reception. It gives not pain but bromides, not deep questions but easy answers. It opposes to Hamlet's dilemma the advice of the gum huckster: "Chew your little troubles away."

Gunther Anders has suggested that the best metaphor for kitsch may be modern travel:

> For modern man does not attach value to his traveling because of any interest in the regions he visits, actually or vicariously; he does not travel to become experienced but to still his hunger for omnipresence and for rapid change as such. . . . A publicity poster of a well-known airline, utterly confusing provincialism and globalism, appeals to its customers with these words: "When you use our services, you are everywhere at home."[6]

Tourists travel from the Istanbul Hilton to the Athens Hilton, the only differences being in the quality of the plumbing and the "motif" of the hotel restaurants. There is no strangeness. Our international airports are all the same; they collectively constitute a country all their own, have more in common with each other than they have with the countries in which they are actually located. And that is what kitsch is—a country all its own, unlike any other, but giving the sense of reassuring sameness. It is not real, but it is familiar.

If so much is assumed, we may differentiate between various genres of literary kitsch by focusing on the particular pattern of reassurance

---

[5] In "The Work of Art in the Age of Mechanical Reproduction," *Illuminations*, ed. Hannah Arendt, tr. Harry Zohn (New York, 1969), pp. 217–252.
[6] *Mass Culture*, p. 364.

each provides. For instance, it is clear that much recent spy fiction is aimed at allaying fears aroused by two human activities which seem to have got out of human control, science on the one hand and diplomacy on the other. The pattern of spy thrillers changes quite markedly after Hiroshima. Instead of the elegant, patriotic heroes of E. Phillips Oppenheim, who merely prevent one or two countries from going to war (by stealing naval secrets, or something equally innocuous), we now have amoral supermen who save the entire planet from atomic destruction—the suggestion being that while the world may be full of mad scientists and bumbling statesmen, a lone hero can still keep us all from being blown up. At a time when enormous destruction is in the hands of faceless committees, it is reassuring indeed to follow the adventures of a single man who, by exploiting the gifts of courage and resourcefulness which have always characterized the hero, can offset the ineffectiveness of government as well as the irresponsibility of the scientists.

The same pattern of easy reassurance is to be found in the increasingly less comic comic strips, where, as in *Dick Tracy*, the brutality of crime is always overcome by the brutality of Chester Gould. Other strips have become the elephant's graveyard for those novels which really are dead: *On Stage* is a *Frauenroman*[a] in pictures, constantly engaging issues of current concern (the generation gap, women's lib, and so forth) merely to provide easy answers only slightly more sophisticated than the equally formulaic "they all lived happily ever after."

So much for generalities. What, then, is the particular pattern of reassurance provided by detective fiction? In order to answer this question we must first of all determine what is meant by detective story, and in order to do that a brief look at its history will be necessary.

III

Very little crime fiction is of the classical detective story variety. Crime is very old, detective fiction very new. There have always been critics ready to see crime fiction everywhere, such as Peter Haworth,[7] who puts forward as examples of the genre such ancient tales as the

---

[a] A novel either about women or intended primarily for female readers.—Eds.
[7] In *Classic Crimes in History and Fiction* (New York, 1927).

"History of Susanna" from the *Apocrypha*, the story of King Rhampsinitus' treasure house from Herodotus, tales from the *Gesta Romanorum*,[b] and so on. Régis Messac[8] begins his study of the genre with Archimedes' discovery of his famous principle of hydrostatics. A. E. Murch's standard history[9] opens with seventeenth-century British rogue tales, such as Dekker's *The Belman of London* (1608). And it has long been a favorite trick of classicists to teach *Oedipus Rex* as a detective story. Such eclectic definitions of the genre create obvious difficulties.

What is meant in this paper by detective story is rather the tale of pure puzzle, pure ratiocination, associated with Poe, Conan Doyle, Agatha Christie. As Jacques Barzun and W. H. Taylor have recently written: "A detective story should be mainly occupied with detecting,"[10] which would exclude Gothic romances, psychological studies of criminals, and hard-boiled thrillers.

The paradox that there is nevertheless no detective fiction before the nineteenth century can be explained in many ways, all too complicated to go into here, except for adducing the obvious reason that you cannot have detective fiction before you have detectives.[c] It is a curious fact that the institution of the modern metropolitan police force as we now know it did not exist before the nineteenth century. It was the early decades of that century which saw the almost simultaneous foundation of the Sûreté in Paris and the precursors of Scotland Yard, the Bow Street Runners, in London.

But the foundation of these forces was not enough in itself to inspire the creation of the fictional detective. For one thing they did not immediately inspire confidence in their methods or their morals. One of the founders of the Sûreté was Eugène François Vidocq (1775–1857), a notorious thief and adventurer whose early successes in the bureau were made possible by his intimate—indeed personal—knowledge of the French underworld. In 1828 he published his *Mémoires*, which contain improbable and hyperbolic accounts of his double life. It is a fact that this fictive account has had a greater effect on the

[b]An anonymous medieval collection of stories and anecdotes, compiled about 1400 in Latin.—Eds.
[8]*Le "Detective Novel" et l'influence de la pensée scientifique* (Paris, 1929), p. 54.
[9]*The Development of the Detective Novel* (New York, 1958).
[10]*A Catalogue of Crime* (New York, 1971), p. 5.
[c]Cf. the essay by Knight, reprinted in this volume.—Eds.

history of detective stories than his actual career with the historical Sûreté. As for the Bow Street Runners, we have the words of Dickens himself that they "kept company with thieves and such like . . ." and were to be found in the lowest and most degraded gin mills, where they were quite at home.[11]

It took some time before people believed in the police as forces for good. And this bit of historical sociology explains, in a small way, why the rise of the practicing detective did not coincide with the rise of tales and novels about him. Because the emphasis was still on crime; the forces of law had not yet become glamorous. It had always been true, of course, that while evil was reprehensible, it was also fascinating in a way virtue simply was not. Thus, the few genres which may lay claim to the title of criminal—but not detective—fiction before the nineteenth century have as their heroes the villains who were hanged at Tyburn, in such romances as Francis Kirkman's *The Counterfeit Lady Unveiled* (1673) or Elkanah Settle's *The Complete Memoires of the Life of that Notorious Imposter Will Morrell* (1694). The degree to which these and other such seventeenth-century criminal biographies depart from the tradition of the true detective story may be gleaned from the fact that such tales are today remembered mainly for the role they played in establishing the tradition of the realistic novel.[12]

No, we must restate the reason for the seemingly tardy development of detective fiction. We said it had to wait for the historical advent of the institution of the detective. We must now add that the detective who made detective fiction possible was himself a fiction: detective stories have their true genesis not in Vidocq or any other real life detective. The father of them all, is, rather, Edgar Allan Poe's Chevalier Dupin.

We may argue about the birth of tragedy, whence arose comedy, the antiquity of the lyric, or the rise of the novel. But about the first detective story there can be no such uncertainty. We know the precise time and place of its origin. It was in *Graham's Magazine* of April

---

[11]In an 1862 letter to W. Thornbury, quoted by Dorothy Sayers in her essay "The Omnibus of Crime," *The Art of the Mystery Story,* ed. Howard Haycraft (New York, 1946), p. 75.
[12]See, for instance, Spiro Peterson, "Foreword," *The Counterfeit Lady Unveiled and Other Criminal Fiction of Seventeenth-Century England* (New York, 1961), p. xii.

1841, in Philadelphia, Pennsylvania, U.S.A., that "The Murders in the Rue Morgue" appeared, and the character which there made his entrance, sprung full blown from the bulging brow of Poe, has, under different aliases, been with us ever since.

Why is Poe the creator of the classical detective story? A clue may be found in Joseph Wood Krutch's statement to the effect that "Poe invented the detective story that he might not go mad."[13]

Poe's biography, of course, is a paradigm for that of the romantic artist:[14] a precociously brilliant child, raised by foster parents, a seventeen-year-old dropout from the University of Virginia, then a dropout from his father's business, dismissal from West Point in a scandal—his beloved child bride wasting away of an incurable disease, a life devoted to art, but threatened by heavy drinking and drugs. He died on an uncompleted journey, after being found wandering the streets of Baltimore in a raving delirium. The world was a place of chaos for Poe, a vale not only of tears but also of unspeakable horrors; sometimes he caught this world in the metaphor of a crumbling mansion, haunted amidst its weird landscape; at other times it was the black labyrinthine canals of Renaissance Venice, or the great whirlpool of the maelstrom. But it is in the very depths to which he experienced, and was able to capture in words, the chaos of the world, that we must search for the key to the ordered, ultrarational world of the detective story.

It was to this powerful impulse toward the irrational that he opposed the therefore necessarily potent sense of reason which finds its highest expression in "The Murders in the Rue Morgue" and "The Purloined Letter." Against the metaphors for chaos, found in his other tales, he sets, in the Dupin stories, the essential metaphor for order: the detective.

The detective, the instrument of pure logic, able to triumph because

[13]Quoted in Howard Haycraft, *Murder for Pleasure: The Life and Times of the Detective Story* (New York, 1941), p. 9.
[14]Richard Alewyn ("Das Rätsel des Detektivromans" in *Definitionen: Essays zur Literatur*, ed. Adolf Frisé [Frankfurt a. M., 1963]) has argued that the detective novel is a product not of rationalism or realism, but of romanticism. . . . As support for this he outlines the biography of an archetypal romantic artist, charged with a sense of the everyday world as only a thin layer of deception over an abyss of dark symbols which the artist seeks to penetrate. Alewyn then asks "Could one better describe the talent and the profession of the detective?" [A translation of Alewyn's essay is included in this volume.—Eds.]

he alone in a world of credulous men holds to the Scholastic principle of *adequatio rei et intellectus,* the adequation of mind to things, the belief that the mind, given enough time, can understand everything. There are no mysteries, there is only incorrect reasoning. This is the enabling discovery Poe makes for later authors; he is the Columbus who lays open the world of radical rationality which is where detectives have lived ever since.

Consider some of the other specific conventions which Poe first uses:

> the first if exceedingly awkward use of the least likely person theme; the first instance of the scattering of false clues by the real criminal; and the first extortion of a confession by means of the psychological third degree....[15]

Poe created

> the transcendent and eccentric detective; the admiring and slightly stupid foil; the well-intentioned floundering and unimaginativeness of the official guardians of the law; the locked room convention; ... deduction by putting oneself in another's position...; concealment by means of the ultra-obvious; the staged ruse to force the culprit's hand; even the expansive and condescending explanation when the chase is done...[16]

These are the basic conventions of the classical detective story, and so fixed are they that some of the more hallowed among them are actually included in an oath which must be taken by new members of the British association of detective story writers, the Detection Club. Consider, for example, the following two articles which must be sworn to:

> Do you solemnly swear never to conceal a vital clue from the Reader?—Do you promise to observe a seemly moderation in the use of Gangs, Conspiracies, Death Rays, Ghosts, Hypnotism, trapdoors, Chinamen, ... and utterly and forever to forswear Mysterious Poisons Unknown to Science?[17]

The vow not to use ghosts and death rays may seem amusing—certainly, in their elephantine way, the founders of the club intended

---
[15] Haycraft, *Murder for Pleasure,* p. 10.
[16] Ibid., p. 12.
[17] Haycraft, *The Art of the Mystery Story,* p. 198.

it to be so; but it contains great wisdom, too. For these elements are foreign to the world of the detective story—they belong to other worlds of sheer convention, pure fiction, the ghost story and science fiction. There is an important point to be learned about conventions here. They do not exist in isolation; to do their work they must determine whole landscapes, conjure up specific plots which are peculiar to them alone. Conventions must be *familiar*.

Each fictive world has its own magic, its own form of reassuring omnipotence. In the fairy tale, a good heart and patience in the face of misfortune will always avail; so, in cowboy stories, will a good heart and a quick gun. In spy stories a peculiar kind of committed amorality coupled with an ability to survive unusual amounts (and kinds) of physical punishment overcome atomic destruction again and again. In the Tarzan novels great physical strength and intimacy with nature conquers all. (Tarzan is, in a sense, the last of the noble savages. He is, it will be remembered, a member of the House of Lords.)

We have spoken of several subgenres of popular literature, each of which is defined by its own system of conventions and its own reassuring magic. The basic clichés of the detective story especially should now be clear. But what is its peculiar magic, how does it reassure in a way other popular modes do not? Its magic is, as we saw in the case of Poe, the power of reason, *mind* if you will. It is not, as is so often said, the character of great detectives which accounts for their popularity.[18] If character *means* anything, we must admit that most of them have very little of it. Take Sherlock Holmes, for example. He does not really *exist* when he is not on a case. The violin, the drugs merely keep him in a state of suspended animation until the inevitable knock on the door comes, announcing a new problem. He does not solve crimes, he solves puzzles. There is no death in his world—only the statement of riddles. You will remember that famous bit of "Sherlockismus" which begins, "I would call your attention to the curious incident of the dog in the nighttime." Watson says, "The dog did nothing in the nighttime." And Holmes replies, "*That* was the curious incident."

[18] As, for instance, William S. Baring-Gould: "What, we may ask, inspires the great devotion to [Sherlock] Holmes displayed by three generations of readers? . . . it is *the character* of Holmes that grips us." In his Introduction to *The Adventures of the Speckled Band and other Stories of Sherlock Holmes* (New York, 1965), p. xi.

This is a metaphor for what happens in all the stories. *Nothing really happens,* but it is all therefore *curious.* Holmes is less a detective than a mathematician: he *is* his function. Therefore, other people simply are not people for him. Watson is regarded, as he himself admits in an unguarded moment, as merely "the whetstone for [Sherlock's] mind." The degree to which Holmes is pure mind may also be seen in the official iconography of him; in the later illustrations he is all nose and bulging brow.[19]

It is this supremely rational quality which accounts for the popularity of such stories—the magic of mind in a world that all too often seems impervious to reason. Popular—but with whom? Detective stories, at least of the sort we are here concerned with, are not popular in the sense everyone reads them. Who does? Not surprisingly—in light of what we've said about their emphasis on mind—it is largely intellectuals who keep Agatha Christie and Rex Stout writing into an indecent old age.[20]

Not only do intellectuals read detective stories, they write them. It is significant that in such tales the body is usually discovered in the *library,* for their authors tend to be oppressively bookish. Many of them are scholars of real note, such as Michael Innes, in real life J. I. M. Stewart, a well-known expert on the modern novel and one of the editors of the *Oxford History of English Literature,* or Nicholas Blake, in real life C. Day Lewis, Oxford professor of Poetry from 1951–1956 and translator of Virgil's *Aeneid;* or Dorothy Sayers, one of the first women to receive an Oxford degree and a ranking Dante translator and critic. The list could be extended to include American academics,[21] who, for some reason, cling much more tenaciously to their pseudonyms.

But for every intellectual who writes detective fiction, there are

---

[19]He begins to look something like Edgar Allan Poe, as a matter of fact.
[20]This is difficult to prove, of course, but it is taken for granted by most students of the subject. See, for instance, Marjorie Nicolson's delightful essay, "The Professor and the Detective," in Haycraft's *Art of the Mystery Story,* pp. 110–127. It is clear, at any rate, that detective fiction is the one aspect of popular culture which most exercises the imagination of intellectuals.
[21]For example, chosen at random: C. Daly King, Yale Ph.D., and author of several books on psychology, as well as at least six detective novels, all written in the 1930s, or Alfred Harbage, the Elizabethan scholar and professor at Harvard; Walter Blair, expert on American humor, professor at Chicago.

several more who write *about* it.²² And when they do, some very strange things happen. Consider what W. H. Auden has to say on the subject. Such tales are an occasion to write about sin and purgation:

> I suspect that the typical reader of detective stories is, like myself, a person who suffers from a sense of sin. From the point of view of ethics, desires and acts are good and bad, and I must choose the good and reject the bad, but the *I* which makes this choice is ethically neutral; it only becomes good or bad in its choice. To have a sense of sin means to feel guilty at there being an ethical choice to make, a guilt which, however 'good' I may become, remains unchanged.²³

This quote is from an essay on the detective story, and one can't help suspecting its aim of rationalization; the product not of the guilt about which Auden is here so eloquent but rather of the guilt of reading detective stories.

Auden's friend C. Day Lewis, perhaps because he writes them, has even more extravagant claims to make for detective stories.

> We may imagine some James Frazier of the year 2042 discoursing on "The Detective Novel—the Folk-Myth of the Twentieth Century." He will, I fancy, connect the rise of crime fiction with the decline of religion at the end of the Victorian era . . . When a religion has lost its hold upon men's hearts they must have some other outlet for the sense of guilt . . . [the future anthropologist] will call attention to the pattern of the detective novel, as highly formalized as that of a religious ritual, with its initial necessary sin (the murder), its victim, its high priest (the detective). He will conjecture—and rightly—that the devotee identified himself both with the detective and the murderer, representing the dark side of his own nature. He will note a significant parallel between the formalized denouement of the detective novel and the Christian

---

[22] We have already mentioned Jacques Barzun; one might also cite Jacques Lacan's essay on "The Purloined Letter" ("Le séminaire sur 'La lettre volée,' " *Ecrits*, I [Paris, 1966], pp. 19–78) [reprinted in this volume—Eds.]; or W. K. Wimsatt's critique of Poe's work on the mystery of Mary Rogers (*PMLA*, LVI [1941], 230–248). Gide's fascination with American hard-boiled fiction is well known. As George Grella has written, "the detective story, unlike most kinds of popular literature, prizes intellectual gifts above all." ("Murder and Manners: The Formal Detective Novel," *Novel*, IV [1970], 36).

[23] "The Guilty Vicarage," in *The Dyer's Hand and Other Essays* (New York, 1968), p. 158.

conception of the Day of Judgment, when with a flourish of trumpets, the mystery is made plain and the goats are separated from the sheep.[24]

C. Day Lewis, like Matthew Arnold, fears that religion has declined.[25] Arnold hopes literature—high culture—will take its place. Lewis suggests detective stories *have* taken its place. It can be shown that in a sense, Arnold was right; literature in the modern period did try, consciously or unconsciously, to substitute for religion. But Lewis has completely missed the point about detective stories, particularly the ones he has in mind.

The molders of the modernist tradition, however, sensed, as did Arnold, that Christianity was losing its power to console and explain, to flood a hostile world with meaning. Such masters as Joyce and Mann sought to fill this religious void with different symbols, more often than not taken from mythical systems older than Christianity. Mann is exceedingly self-conscious about his own attempts to light the Christmas tree of the world again, as can be seen in his account of how *Dr. Faustus* grew into a novel, and in the published correspondence he had with Karoly Kerényi.[26] The case of *Ulysses* is obvious. Eliot appends learned footnotes to *The Wasteland,* explaining his symbols on the basis of work done by Sir James Frazer and Jessie L. Weston. Yeats's whole life is a search for a mythical system on which he could ground his poetry. And they all used—in one way or another—Freud, who when confronted by the death of God in the universe, discovered a new cosmos inside man himself. The Freudian system gave a new —and profound—dimension to *all* symbols, independent of, or underlying, whatever religious meaning they might (or more importantly, might *not*) still have.

Modernism had dual roots in psychology and myth; Freud and Frazer were the Siamese twins who presided museulike at the creation of *The Waves* or *Ulysses.* The emphasis was on the innermost inner life, resulting in a psychological impulse that was lyrical, nonsocietal,

---

[24]"The Detective Story—Why," in Haycraft, *The Art of the Mystery Story,* p. 399.
[25]It is significant that so many authors of detective stories were in one way or another deeply involved with religious issues. Lewis is also a well-known apologist for Anglican Christianity, as was Dorothy Sayers in her later years. Ronald Knox, a student and author of detective fiction, was also a theologian, indeed a monsignor. G. K. Chesterton's Catholicism is as present in his Father Brown stories as in his essays.
[26]*Gespräch in Briefen* (Zürich, 1960).

relational—constantly exposing itself to the danger of esthetic solipsism. Nineteenth-century novels had unfolded in an extreme specificity of time and place—there is a sense in which they are all historical novels. They took place in Paris or London, whereas modernist novels essentially take place in a country of the mind, inside. To this degree they are ahistorical, their time is Bergsonian,[d] not chronological. Thus, these works are marked by an emphasis on recurring patterns of experience, those paradigmatic human occasions that seem to happen outside of time: the trauma of being cast into the world in birth, the sorrows of travel, the joys of love, and the mystery of death. These are the matter of all art, but in the modernist period there was a conscious attempt to get at the archetypal, ahistorical meaning of such events, and the most frequent method for doing so was to dramatize subtly—and sometimes not so subtly—parallels between archetypal occurrences of ancient myth and modern experience, much as Freud was to seek a pattern in the Oedipus story which would unlock certain secrets of twentieth-century behaviour.

Now it is precisely during the twenties and thirties of this century, when modernism was in its deep-diving prime, achieving its most completely realized persons and its densest world, that the detective story had its golden age. It is a period when the two strands, experimental literature—high culture, on the one hand, and popular literature—the detective story, on the other, are more than ordinarily split in their techniques, basic assumptions, and effect. It is the age when Agatha Christie, John Dickson Carr, Dorothy Sayers, and Michael Innes, to name only a few, are at their peak. And far from seeking to populate the corporeal world with symbols, they are concerned further to purify their own narrow world of impossibly eccentric Oxbridge colleges, improbably quaint little English villages, that hermetic world of cruise ships, the Blue trains, and weekends at country houses. Plots become more *outré* (such as *The Murder of Roger Ackroyd*), weapons more exotic (such as poisoned toothpaste) —but the basic conventions remained essentially unchanged.

A small digression is in order here: during the 1930s there did arise a new (if we exclude Wilkie Collins in the nineteenth century) kind

[d]Henri Bergson (1859–1941) was a French philosopher who propounded a theory of time as subjectively felt and intensive duration rather than as objectively measurable and uniformly linear.—Eds.

of detective story represented in England by Dorothy Sayers's new style which became apparent after her 1935 novel *Gaudy Night,* and represented in America by Raymond Chandler and later Dashiell Hammett. The British and American types are quite distinct from each other, but both have in common an attempt to break away from the rigid conventions of detective fiction. Each strand resulted in stories of crime which depended for their appeal on the devices of mainstream fiction; literature, if you will. They sought to write novels, not detective novels as such. The characters were more fully rounded, the settings more ordinary—or at least less formulaic—the plots less implausible. The detective is more human and so are the criminals and victims. You get, at least in the hard-boiled American school, something more like real blood, actual corpses instead of mere excuses for yet another demonstration of the detective's superhuman skills. Chandler did for detective fiction what John le Carré was later to do for spy fiction. Books in this third—call it novelistic—stream (Ross Macdonald, John D. MacDonald and Donald Hamilton continue the tradition in America, as Graham Greene and James Hadley Chase did in England)—books in this third stream are obviously *not*—whatever their other merits may be—what I have been talking about as the classical detective story. The third stream is impure—and I mention it only as an exception.

But to return to our argument: it was during the same period when the upper reaches of literature were dramatizing the limits of reason by experimenting with such irrational modes as myth and the subconscious, that the lower reaches of literature were dramatizing the power of reason in such figures as Inspector Poirot and Ellery Queen. What must be remembered here is that it is essentially the same group of intellectuals who were reading both. We began by assuming that literature is difficult, popular literature easy, and we are now in a position to be more specific about this formulation. What is difficult about a Mann novel, for example, is not only its style and architechtonic complexities, but—and perhaps above all—its unsettling message: all the certainties of the nineteenth century—positivism, scientism, historicism—seem to have broken down. Dangerous questions are raised, the world is a threatening, unfamiliar place, inimical more often than not to reason. Is it not natural to assume, then, that during this period when rationalism is experiencing some of its most damaging attacks, that intellectuals, who experienced these attacks first and most deeply, would turn for relief and easy reassurance to the detective story, the primary genre of popular literature which they, during the same period, were, in fact, consuming? The same people who spent their days with Joyce were reading Agatha Christie at night—and if the pattern of reassurance we've adduced as peculiar to the detective story is accepted, we should not long have to wonder why.

At any rate, in order for our argument to proceed, it is necessary only to keep in mind the polar opposition between the high art of the novel with its bias toward myth and depth psychology and the popular art of the detective story with its flatness of character and setting during the flowering of modernism. Because it is just this opposition which is bridged in the period following World War II.

Postmodernism—or at least that strand of it which here concerns us and which is arguably the most defining strand—can best be understood as springing from a different view of man, and therefore a different view of art from that which obtained in modernism. It has at its heart the exact opposites of the two tendencies which define modernism. The esthetics of postmodernism is militantly *anti*psychological (if that word is taken in its usual meaning) and radically *anti*mythical. It is about things, not people, as Robbe-Grillet points out when he says:

> All around us, defying our pack of animistic or domesticating adjectives, things are there. Their surface is smooth, clear, and intact, without false glamor, without transparency. [Let me interject—they are not symbolical, the forest is a forest, not a forest of symbols. But it is not, therefore, less mysterious.] The whole of our literature has not yet managed even to begin to penetrate them, to alter their slightest curve.[27]

And far from wishing to deal with recurring patterns whose universality will be emphasized, novelists in the postmodern period ingeniously —and sometimes, it must be admitted, rather strenuously—seek to avoid the familiar. Nathalie Saurraute writes: demands for universality

[27]"A Path for the Future of the Novel," in Maurice Nadeau, ed., *The French Novel since the War*, tr. A. M. Sheridan Smith (New York, 1969), p. 185.

with regard to the novel, are all the more familiar to the author who, being himself a reader, and often a very perceptive one, has also experienced them. The result is that when he starts to tell a story and says to his self he must . . . write down for the mocking eye of the reader "The Marquise went out at five o'clock," he hesitates, he hasn't the heart, he simply can't bring himself to do it.[28]

Now, if, as such figures as Robbe-Grillet and Borges have been, you are interested in disestablishing the mythic and psychological tendencies of the tradition you are defining yourself against, what better way for doing so could recommend itself than that of exploiting what had already become the polar opposite of that tradition in its own time? Detective stories had always been recognized as escape literature. But escape from what? Among other things, escape from *literature itself*, as we emphasized above in the dichotomy between the detective story with its exterior simplicities and modernism with its interior complexities. Thus, when after World War II Robbe-Grillet was searching for ways to overcome the literary tradition of the novel he so naturally turned to the detective story as a mode. What myth was to experimental fiction before World War II, detective fiction is to avant-garde prose after World War II. The possibilities for symbolic action and depth psychology which Homer provides for James Joyce are replaced in the later period by the ambiguous events, the psychologically flat and therefore mysterious world which Holmes and Poirot make available to Robbe-Grillet and Borges.

That is to say that postmodernism exploits detective stories by expanding and changing certain possibilities in them, just as modernism had *modified* the potentialities of myth. There is a difference in the way that Homer and Joyce come at Ulysses, and there is also a difference in the way that Agatha Christie and Borges come at the detective story. Robbe-Grillet is quite explicit about this. In a 1956 essay on the *nouveau roman* he speaks of it in terms of an inverted detective story. He says:

> The exhibits described in a thriller . . . provide a fairly accurate illustration of the situation. The various elements collected by the detectives—an object abandoned at the scene of the crime, a movement immobilized in a photograph, a phrase overheard by a witness

[28]"The New Novel," in Nadeau, op. cit., p. 181.

—these would all seem at first sight to call for an explanation, to exist only as a function of their role in an affair which is beyond them. But now various hypotheses begin to be built: the examining magistrate tries to establish a logical and necessary connection between the things; you think everything is going to resolve itself into a trite collection of causes and effects . . . But the plot starts to thicken alarmingly, witnesses contradict one another, the suspect multiplies his alibis, new factors crop up which had previously been overlooked . . . And you have to keep coming back to the recorded evidence: the exact position of a piece of furniture, the shape and frequency of a fingerprint, a word written in a message. The impression grows on you that nothing else is true. Whether they conceal or reveal a mystery, these elements that defy all systems have only one serious, obvious quality—that of being there. And that is how it is with the world around us. We thought we had come to terms with it by giving it a meaning, and the whole art of the novel, in particular, seemed dedicated to this task. But that was only an illusory simplification and, far from becoming clearer and nearer, all that was happening was that the world was gradually losing its life in the process. Since its reality consists above all in its presence, what we have to do now, then, is to build a literature which takes this into account.[29]

If Robbe-Grillet knew more about the history of detective fiction he would not have chosen the type of tale he does, in fact, adduce as a metaphor for his own method. He would rather have chosen as his example the four murder classics published by Dennis Wheatley and J. G. Links in the late 1930s.

Although each story was remarkably intricate, the dossiers' particular originality lay in their presentation or construction; construction in the literal sense, for the dossiers contain the actual evidence of the murders, photographs of the victims and central characters, bits and pieces of material, cigarettes, pills, and so on.[30]

In fact, very much the same sort of thing Robbe-Grillet has listed as evidence in his essay—and in his novel. The Wheatley–Links dossiers received a mixed reception. The *Times* reviewer wrote that if this were the start of a new fashion,

[29]Robbe-Grillet, op. cit., p. 188.
[30]Reg Gadney, "The Murder Dossiers of Dennis Wheatley and J. G. Links," *The London Magazine*, VIII (1969), 41.

the critics, it may be imagined, will be replaced by analysts—experts who, instead of hovering lengthily over literary merits will be able to pronounce with finality such verdicts as "The hay in Mr. Blank's pastoral scenes is definitely the best he has given us yet," or, "Miss Dash's picture of nursery life is marred by an unimaginative use of tapioca."[31]

Another critic made the same point with less hyperbole: ". . . the principal actors in the dossier are not [the characters in it], but the real cretonne, the detachable match end, and the engaging twist of hair."[32] The dossiers became increasingly complicated, until, in the fourth and last one, the reader

> had to remember the complete details of sixteen people and backgrounds, and then pick out the five or six key details. For example, a man has asthma and might therefore smoke an herbal cigarette: but to discover this the reader would have to take the butt ends and actually smoke them.[33]

The solution to the mystery was always found under a seal on the last page of the book.

Now, with some important differences which must be kept in mind, it can be seen that these long-forgotten toys provide an easily grasped metaphor for certain essential characteristics of recent experimental fiction. What the reviewer jokes about in the Wheatley dossiers has become a serious business in Robbe-Grillet: "experts . . . instead of hovering lengthily over literary merits" will in fact be constrained to examine the objects themselves; the principal actors have in Robbe-Grillet ceased to be the characters, and have rather become the things of the world. Just as Wheatley and Links wished through *their* objects to create a greater reality, so does Robbe-Grillet, in his vastly subtler way, wish to do so with his. But the basic difference between the British murder mystery and the French New Novel is the different sense each has of the operation plot performs. The solution to a novel like *The Voyeur*, for instance, is not to be found under a seal on its last page. Indeed, *The Voyeur* has no last page in the sense in which that term is normally used. No, the solu-

---

[31] Quoted by Gadney, op. cit., p. 46.
[32] Ibid., p. 46.
[33] Ibid., p. 49.

tion cannot be had by breaking a seal in a book—the solution must be found in the experience of the reader himself, as a brief examination of *The Voyeur* will show.

We will not have time to discuss the manifold clues which the reader is tempted to gather, to put together in an orderly sequence, such as the at-first-seemingly-significant, recurring motifs of the figure eight, the newspaper clipping, the precise distance (twenty feet) which a gull keeps between himself and Mathias, or the difference between gumdrops and caramels. But in order to see the trick which is contained in each of these booby traps, we should examine at least one set of those parallels which teem in *The Voyeur*. There are three different movie posters which are described at the beginning, middle, and end of the book.

The first one looks like this:

> In front of the door a bulletin board, supported from behind by two wooden uprights, offered the weekly program of the local movie house . . . In the garishly colored advertisement, a colossal man dressed in Renaissance clothes was clutching a young girl wearing a kind of long pale nightgown; the man was holding her wrists behind her back with one hand, and was strangling her with the other. The upper part of her body and her head were bent backward in her effort to escape her executioner, and her long blond hair hung down to the ground. The setting in the background represented a tremendous pillared bed with red covers.[34]

What are the significant points here? First, what kind of a plot does this poster call to mind? It is an absurd, theatrical situation, very much like that found in cheap historical novels or thrillers; colossal men, young girls in long pale nightgowns, a tremendous bed with the conventional red covers on it of conventional fictive passion. The hyperbole of the specific adjectives—colossal, tremendous—is subsumed by the "garish colors" of the whole thing. But notice also what is happening: a young girl is being strangled, just as Mathias strangles Violet/Jacqueline. What we have here is the first part of a very complicated, serial joke, which is a key to the nonplot of *The Voyeur*. That is, in this scene, Robbe-Grillet sets up what he *might* have done, had he written a conventional murder novel. This first poster is a meta-

---

[34] Alain Robbe-Grillet, *The Voyeur*, tr. Richard Howard (New York, 1966), p. 34.

phor for what would have been the traditional literary treatment of his subject—garish, hyperbolic, narrative.

The second poster is a metaphor for the novel he actually writes, a metaphor for the structure of *The Voyeur* itself:

> The new advertisement represented a landscape. At least Mathias thought he could make out a moor dotted with clumps of bushes in its interlacing lines but something else must have been superimposed: here and there certain outlines or patches of color appeared which did not seem to be part of the original design. On the other hand, they could not be said to constitute another drawing entirely; they appeared to have no relation to one another, and it was impossible to guess their intention. They succeeded, in any case, in so blurring the configurations of the moor that it was doubtful whether the poster represented a landscape at all ... Underneath was spread in huge letters what must have been the name of the film: "Monsieur X on the Double Circuit." Not conforming to the trends of recent productions, this title—which was scarcely enticing, having little or no relation to anything human—provided remarkably little information about what type of film it described. Perhaps it was a detective story, or a thriller.[35]

First of all, this is a physical landscape roughly similar to the one in which the novel's crime is committed—the lonely, moorlike grazing ground where the girl tends her flock, the clumps of bushes under which Mathias forgets his three cigarette butts. But more importantly, there is a suggestion of two different posters, one on top of the other, in other words, a palimpsest, and remaining, therefore, still slightly visible under the new text.

Robbe-Grillet says that this palimpsest effect of the two superimposed posters so blurs "the configurations of the moor that it was doubtful whether [they] represented a landscape at all." And indeed, it is not a landscape. Perhaps it was a detective story or a thriller. And of course it is, and we can tell from its title just which detective story it is: *Monsieur X on the Double Circuit.* Monsieur X is, of course, Mathias, who is on several double circuits, each of which is marked by the double circuit of a figure eight. He is on a double circuit from mainland to island, from present to his past, from the village to the outlying cottages by the sea and back again, and so forth. But

[35] Ibid., p. 143.

Mathias's tale is not just a detective story. This title, as Robbe-Grillet says, does not conform "to the trends of recent productions, [it] was scarcely enticing, having little or no relation to anything human." What better description of *The Voyeur?* It is about things, not humans, and it certainly does not conform to recent productions by other, more traditional writers. And it is nonconventional in a specific way, specifically suggested by the double track of the palimpsest metaphor: it is a new text, a new kind of plot, written over the face of the old detective story, whose traditional elements still are legible underneath the new message.

The third poster comes up very near the end of the book:

> On the other side of the monument he notices that the bulletin board is covered with a completely white sheet of paper pasted on the surface of the wood. At this moment the garageman comes out of his tobacco shop carrying a little bottle and a fine brush. Mathias asks him what happened to the sign that was up the day before: it wasn't the right one, the garageman answers, for the film they had sent along with it; the distributor had made an error in the shipment. He would have to announce next Sunday's program by a handmade ink inscription. Mathias leaves the man already busy with his task firmly tracing a large letter O.[36]

The former poster was the wrong one—its suggestion of clashing messages was adequate to the *method* of the novel, but not to its *telos*. That is, the palimpsest of old and new detective fiction does not, in itself, indicate the specific difference between the two levels. That is given to us here: the new metaphysical detective story finally obliterates the traces of the old which underlie it. It is nonteleological, is not concerned to have a neat ending in which all the questions are answered, and which can therefore be forgotten. No, the new story is purged of such linear teleology; it is not, like the old posters, mass produced, printed in the sense other books are. It is rather a fresh sheet of paper, on which the reader, as in our example, must hand letter his own answers. That is the meaning of the new title here: it is not yet written out, not yet completed. The double cycle has been broken, the bottom half of the figure eight has been stripped away to reveal the letter O, the only letter which also may be a cipher—zero.

[36] Ibid., p. 214.

This zero works in several ways: it is a clue to the author's polemical intention in that it realizes the metaphor contained in the antiliterary manifesto of Robbe-Grillet's friend Roland Barthes, *Le Dégré zéro de l'écriture* (1953).[e] But more to the point, it represents the real end of the novel: its telos is the lack of telos, its plot consists in the calculated absence of plot. It is not a story—it is a process; the reader, if he is to experience the book, must do what detectives do, must turn it into a series of objects, must then collate all the clues which Robbe-Grillet has provided. But all these clues end—when put together—in zero, or a circle, the line which has no end. It is not a story—it is not about Mathias or a little girl—it is not about fictive people. It is about —or rather—it is a real process. It is a kind of callisthenics of perception. In absorbing the book, the reader exercises the muscles which control his inner, "private," eye.

Robbe-Grillet was not the first to subvert the clichés of detective fiction in the service of a programmatic attempt to achieve less "literary" plots. He had been preceded in this direction by Nabokov and Borges. Patricia Merivale has pointed out that both men

> exploit for their own thematic purposes, all the narrative tricks and devices of the Gothic fantasy writers of the last two centuries, and they blend mannerism and Gothicism together in their single most important parodic pattern, the metaphysical detective story . . .[37]

Five of Nabokov's major fictions end in fatal gunshots, and several of his most important protagonists, such as Humbert Humbert in *Lolita* (1955) or Kinbote in *Pale Fire* (1962), are cosmic detectives, who wish to solve the crime of their own existence.

Borges, in particular, is a great reader of detective stories: in 1951 he published (in Spanish) an anthology which included classical representatives of the genre by Agatha Christie, Ellery Queen, and G. K.

---

[e] Appeared in English as *Writing Degree Zero* (New York, 1968).—Eds.
[37] "The Flaunting of Artifice in Vladimir Nabokov and Jorge Luis Borges," *Wisconsin Studies in Contemporary Literature,* VIII (1967), 295. While recognizing as much, and even pointing to parallels in Robbe-Grillet, Miss Merivale does not directly engage the problem of why these men should choose *precisely* the detective story as a point of departure. Her concern is the subject of her title, of course; but even so, in her otherwise admirable study, she establishes a grammar, but not a semantics, for the parody in both Nabokov and Borges.

Chesterton and others.[38] And he himself writes at least two kinds of detective stories: the first of which is fairly conventional, at least when compared to the rest of his work; examples of this type would be the tales collected under the title *Six Problems for Indio Parodi* (1942). His other experiments with the form are probably the purest example of the metaphysical detective story. It is this tendency he has also in common with Robbe-Grillet, a point made several times by students of both, who usually compare *The Erasers* (1953) with Borges's short story *Death and the Compass*.[39] The first is the story of a detective who knows he must be at a certain place at a certain time in order to catch the criminal, but when he shows up he himself commits the murder. The Borges tale uses the same twist to achieve the opposite effect: when the detective works out where the next in a series of murders must occur, he shows up only to become the victim.

We have seen how two leading postmodernists play with the conventions of the detective story, mining the genre for plots and surprises. Just as earlier Mann had depended on his readers' knowledge of the Faust legend, and therefore could achieve certain effects by changing the familiar story in crucial ways, so Robbe-Grillet and Borges depend on the audience's familiarity with the conventions of the detective story to provide the subtext they may then play with by defeating expectations.

The most common expectation, based on reading classical detective stories, which postmodernism defeats is that of syllogistic *order*. Like Poe, Robbe-Grillet and Borges have a deep sense of the chaos of the world, but unlike Poe, they cannot assuage that sense by turning to the mechanical certainty, the hyperlogic of the classical detective

---

[38]Chesterton is of particular interest here. English and American audiences have long been baffled by the extravagant praise Borges bestows on such otherwise uncanonical authors as Robert Louis Stevenson or the author of *The Man Who Was Thursday*. But it should be remembered that Howard Haycraft coined the phrase (as far as can be determined) "metaphysical detective story" in 1941 (*Murder for Pleasure*, p. 78) to describe Chesterton's unique contribution to the genre.

[39]As in Merivale, op. cit., pp. 296–297. Another twist on the relationship between detective and criminal is found in a 1936 story of the Polish master, Witold Gombrowicz ("Premeditated Crime"). An old man has died, apparently of natural causes, yet the detective convinces the dead man's son that he (the son) has murdered his father. There are no clues, so the son obligingly chokes the corpse, leaving fingerprints, which "together with the murderer's clear confession at the trial, were finally considered as adequate legal basis."

story. Postmodernists use as a foil the assumption of detective fiction that the mind can solve all: by twisting the details just the opposite becomes the case. Take as an example Borges's story *The Garden of Forking Paths*. Its whole effect depends on the clash between two levels, one a disturbing philosophical proposition about a temporal, instead of a spatial, labyrinth, the other a frame story, a kind of narrative sandwich which has all the clichés of detective (and certain of spy) fiction. The ending is very well made, with a kind of O. Henry-like twist—but this tying up of loose ends at the conclusion has the opposite effect from that which obtains, say, in a Sherlock Holmes story. The neatness of the ending, its pat explanation, far from having the reassuring effect of demonstrating the mind's capacity to order the world in the Borges tale, looks shaky, hollow; its logic is unconvincing in the face of the complexity which has preceded it.

Thus, the metaphysical detective story does not have the narcotizing effect of its progenitor; instead of familiarity, it gives strangeness, a strangeness which more often than not is the result of jumbling the well-known patterns of classical detective stories. Instead of reassuring, they disturb. They are not an escape, but an attack. By exploiting the conventions of the detective story such men as Borges and Robbe-Grillet have fought against the modernist attempt to fill the void of the world with rediscovered mythical symbols. Rather, they dramatize the void. If, in the detective story, death must be solved, in the new metaphysical detective story it is *life* which must be solved.

And in this attack on the reader lies all the difference between art and kitsch. I hope our tentative historical model has suggested at least one way in which the kaleidoscope of popular and high culture constantly rearrange their patterns of relationship to each other. In art there is always the potential for reduction to kitsch, especially in an age in which we possess the technology to print the Mona Lisa on bath towels. That is unfortunate, but not the cause for alarm it is so often felt to be. If we really believe in culture, we should have faith in its capacity to survive even such indignities. And one of the ways that art does survive is by going on the counterattack, exploiting kitsch for new effects of which kitsch in its complacency, its urge to reassure, was itself unaware. That is the lesson of the metaphysical detective story in our own time. It sees the potential for *real* violence—violence to our flabby habits of perception—in the *phony* violence of the detective story. And out of it postmodernism contrives to perform the traditional function of all art, which Wallace Stevens has defined as "the violence from within which protects us from the violence without."

FRANK KERMODE

Novel and Narrative

The current crisis in narrative, Kermode argues, is neither totally regrettable nor quite without precedent. On the contrary, the attack on "the novel" by "the New Novel" reveals the strengths of the old form and some long-neglected capabilities of narrative itself by reviving certain practices with regard to closure, characterization, and mimesis that were current in medieval romance. As his primary exhibits, Kermode chooses two texts, Bentley's detective classic, Trent's Last Case, *and Michel Butor's by now near-classic variation on the detective theme,* L'Emploi du temps (Passing Time). *The first of these, for all its gamelike simplicity, "inevitably provides information which, if we are not docile, we may process independently of the intention or instruction of the author, who is therefore neither the source of a message nor an authority on reading." The second uses the form of the detective novel, but emphasizes just those qualities Kermode found only latent in* Trent's Last Case, *and refuses to provide the classic closure that the form leads us to expect, refuses to solve the crime and reestablish a comforting order in the world. Kermode compares the effect of the two novels, and then most usefully extends the comparison by relating it to Roland Barthes'* S/Z, *thereby elucidating both the detective stories and that difficult but crucial text in contemporary literary theory.*

Frank Kermode is a distinguished literary critic, currently on the faculty at Columbia University. Among his publications, those of most interest to readers of detective fiction would include The Sense of an Ending *(1967) and* The Genesis of Secrecy *(1979). The essay reprinted here first appeared in 1974 in* Theory of the Novel: New Essays, *edited by John Halperin.*

I

We could save ourselves much trouble by agreeing that a novel is a fictional prose narrative of a certain length, which allows for a great deal of variation between novels. But it is obvious that people want to expand it; they plump it out in various ways, and this enables them to make such observations as "This is not really a novel," or "Where have all the novelists gone?" They can specify a novel with much more accuracy than my simple formula allows; the trouble is that in doing so they represent accident as essence. This is one reason why the death of the novel is so often announced. Provisional and local characteristics are mistaken for universal requirements. The difficulty is made worse by the desire of those who understand this to dissociate themselves vigorously from the old novels that exhibit such restrictions; not only do they wish, understandably, to write novels which are free of those local and provincial restrictions so long mistaken for essential elements of the kind; not only do they sensibly want to enquire into what sort of a thing a novel really is, what goes on in the mind that reads it; they also, and less happily, assert that the newness of what they are doing distinguishes it decisively from anything that has been done before. So both sides may agree that the old novel is dead, one rejoicing and the other lamenting. The New Novel is parricide and usurper, and the oedipal parallel is strengthened, some might say, by the self-inflicted blindness of the son.

If we have the patience to look at the difficulty more closely, we may find that a family resemblance persists, as between Laius and Oedipus, who were both lame, both deceived by oracles, and both married to the same woman. Novels new and old may have congenital defects, may take oracles too literally, and have an intimate relationship with the reader. Differences, of course, exist, though commentary and advertisement exaggerate them. Certain old habits have been discontinued; for example, the old assumption that a novel must be concerned with the authentic representation of character and milieu, and with social and ethical systems that transcend it—what may be called the kerygmatic assumption—is strongly questioned. The consequence is a recognizable estrangement from what used to be known as reality; and a further consequence, which can equally be defended as having beneficent possibilities, is that the use of fiction as an instrument of research into the nature of fiction, though certainly not new, is much more widely recognized. But if we admit novelty to this extent, we must at once add that none of these new things was outside the scope of the long narrative of the past; what we are *learning* about narrative may be, in a sense, new, but narrative was always potentially what we have now learned to think it, insofar as our thinking is right; though perhaps for good reasons the aspects that interest us seemed less important and were the subject of fewer or even no enquiries.

It seems doubtful, then, whether we need to speak of some great divide—a strict historical *coupure*—between the old and new. There are differences of emphasis, certainly, as to what it is to read; and there are, within the narratives themselves, rearrangements of emphasis and interest. Perhaps, as metacritics often allege, these are to be attributed to a major shift in our structures of thought; but although this may be an efficient cause of the mutation of interests it does not appear that the object of those interests—narrative—imitates the shift.

II

Compare an older historical problem. W. P. Ker tells us in his *Epic and Romance* that the yielding of the first of these kinds to the second was an epochal event: "The change of temper and fashion represented by the appearance and vogue of the medieval French romances is a change involving the whole world and going far beyond the compass of literature and literary history."[1] He is talking about what later came to be called the Renaissance of the twelfth century, of which the change from a "stronger kind of poetry"[2] to another, more eclectic, less heroic, more ambiguous, was but a part. Within the larger changes in society he detects not only changes in poetry and rhetoric, but also new kinds of storytelling, which "imply the failure of the older manner of thought, the older fashion of imagination."[3] "Failure" here is too strong, surely: "change" would serve. It must be said that the reexamination of the nature and design of an instrument, in this case fiction, might well be related to other kinds of cultural change, as Ker suggests. But within the history of narrative this is interesting mainly as an example of how, from time to time, it becomes possible and desirable to think about the nature of narrative, not as if it were given and self-evident, but as if it were susceptible of widely different developments. "No later change in the forms of fiction," says Ker, "is more important than the twelfth-century revolution. . . . It . . . finally put an end to the old local and provincial restrictions upon narrative."[4]

This is perhaps extravagant; "finally" is also too strong. But we can add to Ker's authority that of Eugène Vinaver, who speaks of related matters in his remarkable book *The Rise of Romance*. Look first at the kinds of difficulty encountered in the *Chanson de Roland:* its discrete, discontinuous scenes, its lack of "temporal and rational links and transitions."[5] It seems impossible to speak of its possessing an overall structure, or a narrative syntax, for that would imply sequence, connection, subordination—not this parataxis. The same event may dominate successive strophes: Roland dies three times, always with a difference, almost as if in a novel by M. Robbe-Grillet. Vinaver insists that if we try to lay out these strophes as temporally successive we shall distort the work, which appears not to be as interested as we have come to be in the registration of an even flow of time and causality. Romance, on the other hand, does have continuous narrative of a sort, but the problems it sets us are equally difficult. So much is not explained. The writers seem consciously to require their readers to work on their texts *(gloser la lettre)* and supply meanings to them *(de lor sen le sorplus mettre)*.[6] The reader's job is like the writer's own, the progressive discovery of nonlinear significances, the reading, in narrative, of clues to what is not narrative. Creative inferences of this kind are necessary in all competent reading; here the fact is recognized and exploited in what seems a peculiar way. The coherence of a narrative may be of such a kind as to frustrate certain cultural expectations.

The complexities of Chrétien de Troyes are such that he may still, in up-to-date books, be accused of "lapses of coherence."[7] His Grail story is particularly vexatious, and scholars have solved it by inventing a Quest sequence: Miraculous Weapon, Dolorous Stroke, Waste Land, Healing. But this sequence, and a fortiori its mythic archetype as we discover it in the work of Jessie L. Weston, occurs neither in Chrétien nor in any early text. (Such is our rage for order that when Eliot dissolved this myth in *The Waste Land* his critics crystallized it out again.) Chrétien was not aiming at this kind of coherence, and to provide it is to violate his text—to import irrelevant constraints into the interpretation of the narrative. What he sought to produce was what Vinaver—adapting a famous formula of Cleanth Brooks's—calls "a pattern of *un*resolved stresses."[8] He did not assume that all good fiction must be of the kind of which it can be predicated that everything "fits in."[9] This position may be hard to hold; in the thirteenth century what Vinaver calls "the restraints of design"[10]—the requirements of sequence and closure—grew strong again.

Certain qualities which we may, on a narrow view, associate with well-formed narratives, are absent from that of Chrétien: closure, character, authenticated reference to settled notions of reality. The modern rejection of these qualities is, in part, a rediscovery of properties of narrative known in the twelfth century: the qualities Vinaver calls *entrelacement,* and polyphony, of resistance to closure, and to certain other expectations bred by narratives of a different emphasis.

What we discover, then, from listening to Ker and Vinaver on the *Chanson* and Chrétien is that discoveries about the nature and possibilities of narrative may, perhaps must, take place at times when there are in progress revaluations of much larger cultural scope, but that the discoveries themselves are about narrative, and are not necessarily of a character that connects them in an obvious way with the changes that accompany them. Nor do they constitute an irreversible evolution; that is why in both works there are what we think of as anticipations of the fire-new research of our contemporaries. We note also the recurrent desire to reimpose local and provincial restrictions. Narrative is prior to all such, and we need to understand how it works without identifying it with its local and transient manifestations.

III

I want now, for a moment, to talk about a single novel; for reasons which I shall try to make clear, it is a detective story. This kind of narrative began to develop in the nineteenth century and reached a very remarkable degree of specialization in the twentieth. It is therefore a good example of the overdevelopment of one element of narrative at the expense of others: it is possible to tell a story in such a way that the principal object of the reader is to discover, by an interpretation of clues, the answer to a problem posed at the outset. All other considerations may be subordinated to this interpretative, or, as I shall call it, hermeneutic activity. Clearly, this emphasis requires, to a degree much greater than in most stories (though all have hermeneutic aspects) the disposition, in a consecutive narrative, of information which requires us to ask both how it "fits in," and also how it will all "come out"; and this information bears upon an event, usually a murder, that precedes the narrative which bears the clues. Clearly, there is a peculiar distortion of more usual narrative conventions (though readers rapidly acquire the competence to meet the new demands). I have chosen a recognized classic of the genre, *Trent's Last Case*. There is not much detailed study of such books, partly because they are by some thought unworthy of it, but also because there is a taboo on telling what happens in the end. This taboo, which, observed, frustrates comment, is relevant to my enquiry, because one of the most powerful of the local and provincial restrictions is that a novel must *end*, or pretend to; or score a point, by disappointing the expectation that it will do so. There must be *closure* or at least an allusion to it. The taboo sacralizes closure; it suggests that to give away the solution that comes at the end is to give away all, so intense is the hermeneutic specialization. But in the present context profanity is necessary and also good.

The detective story is much more concerned than narratives normally are with the elucidation of a series of events which closed either before or only shortly after its own starting point. The narrative is ideally required to provide, by variously enigmatic clues, all the evidence concerning the true character of those earlier events that the investigator and the reader require to reconstruct them. Clues are of many kinds. Some information is simply conveyed; other information looks simple but isn't. Still more appears to have a bearing on the problem but does not, or does have a bearing while seeming not to. Of course, another kind of information must also be provided and processed, the kind that moves the narrative along, establishes a milieu, or characterizes the detective—as a priest, a don, an aborigine, or a peculiar old lady—or explains why so many people disliked the deceased, and so on. This information may or may not be irrelevant to the hermeneutic enterprise on which the reader is embarked; also it can conceal clues or introduce false ones. It will certainly, insofar as it takes his attention, distract the reader from his hermeneutic task. And the interplay between narrative and hermeneutic processes is so complex that information which has no bearing on the prenarrative events may be processed by an attentive reader in senses which alter the whole bearing of the book. Ideally, however, we are always sorting out the hermeneutically relevant from all the other information, and doing so much more persistently than we have to in other kinds of novel. For although all have hermeneutic content, only the detective story makes it preeminent.

In *Trent's Last Case*[a] the title itself is enigmatic: we don't find out why it's his *last* case until the final paragraph. The first sentence of the book is: "Between what matters and what seems to matter, how should the world we know judge wisely?" This has the characteristic ambiguity. The narrator explains it thus: very rich financiers, such as Manderson, the victim in this book, are extremely important in the international money markets, though they have no effect at all on the world in which wealth is really produced. (Notice also the false complicity of "the world we know," which suggests that our reading is always going to be the one prescribed by the narrator.) Of course, the words refer equally to the difficulty of distinguishing what, hermeneutically, matters and does not matter in the pages that follow. It is worth adding that it does not matter whether this ambiguity was intended or not. An important and neglected rule about reading narratives is that once a certain kind of attention has been aroused we read according to the values appropriate to that kind of attention whether or not there is a series of definite gestures to prompt us; of course, we may also decide not to be docile, and evade these local and provincial restrictions.

The millionaire Manderson is found dead in the grounds of his house.[11] He has been shot through the eye. No weapon is found, and there are scratches on his wrists. He is oddly dressed in a mixture of day and evening clothes; his false teeth are missing; his watch is not in the pocket designed for it; his shoelaces are badly tied. Yet he was known to be a neat dresser; he had clearly put on some of his clothes with his usual leisurely care; and he had parted his hair. Trent finds among Manderson's otherwise perfect shoes a pair slightly damaged, as if by the insertion of too large a foot. This enables him, though reluctantly, to suspect Manderson's English secretary, Marlowe. He duly finds Marlowe's pistol to have been used in the killing, and he finds the right fingerprints on Manderson's tooth glass and elsewhere.

[a]By E. C. Bentley (1913).—Eds.

However, Marlowe has a perfect alibi: he had driven through the night to Southampton on business of Manderson's. Trent correctly concludes that death must have occurred much earlier than had been supposed—the ambiguity of evidence on this point has been scrupulously indicated—and that Marlowe, on the previous evening, had dumped the body where it was found, entered the house wearing Manderson's shoes, conducted a daring imitation of his employer—even conversing with the butler and Mrs. Manderson—and then, having planted the clues which suggested that his employer died the following morning, departed for Southampton. Trent writes all this out and takes the document to the young widow, whom he likes but suspects of an attachment to Marlowe, and perhaps even of complicity. He leaves her to decide whether the facts ought to be revealed.

This is the famous "false bottom" of the book. Almost every clue, including some I haven't alluded to, has been caught up into a satisfactory pattern. Nothing happens for some time, until Trent meets Mrs. Manderson again, is assured of the mistake he has made concerning her relations with Marlowe, and proposes marriage. He confronts Marlowe, who is able to give a satisfactory explanation of his conduct on the night of the murder; he was the victim of Manderson's fiendish plot (well motivated by much talk of the millionaire's ingenuity and jealousy) to achieve revenge on his wife's supposed lover by sending him on a journey with a large quantity of money and diamonds belonging to his employer. Manderson would shoot himself; Marlowe would be found to have shot his master and absconded with the loot. Luckily Marlowe was a skilled chess player as well as a clever actor; he saw through Manderson's plot in the nick of time, correctly interpreting certain anomalies in his behavior, and, turning the car round, found Manderson dead near the spot where they had parted. Believing in the impossibility of establishing his innocence otherwise, he behaved then exactly as Trent had deduced, driving the body back, replacing his pistol in his room, and executing the charade in the house before leaving for Southampton.

The position now is that while the police still accept the explanation —good enough for them, it's implied—that Manderson was murdered by the emissaries of an American union he had antagonized, Trent believes that he committed suicide as part of his crazy scheme for revenge. But this is still another false bottom, and gentle old Mr.

Cupples, scholarly confident of Trent and uncle of Mrs. Manderson, now reveals that he happened to be nearby when Manderson pointed the pistol at himself. Darting forward and seizing the weapon, he accidentally shot the financier. This incident is not, by the way, unclued; it is prepared for by concealed clues in the opening pages. Trent did not notice them, nor did we. He will not inform the police, but he does despair of human reason, which is why he calls this his last case.

If Trent had attended as closely to Cupples as to Marlowe he might not have missed these clues. The reason why he overlooked them is simple: Cupples is honest, English, and upper-middle class. Trent prides himself on knowing the intrinsic value of people, but they rarely win his esteem unless they conform closely to that description. They must not be policemen, servants, or Americans. The characters who, as he senses it, are incapable of evil are Mrs. Manderson, Marlowe, and Cupples. Manderson, on the other hand, is too rich, too puritanical, too ruthless, and not English. In a way the police are right; the killer is an American, as it happens Manderson himself rather than American labor desperadoes.

Tricking us about the clues is, of course, the writer's business here; but it is important that in order to do so he may be obliged to provide information which he cannot stop us from processing in a quite different fashion. Thus, it is important that Manderson is jealous, a plotter, an exploiter of the poor, and that this reflects on his nation. Mr. Cupples himself remarks that in these unprecedentedly bad times the "disproportion between the material and the moral constituents of society" is especially marked in the U.S.A. In trying to throw suspicion on American labor the book willy-nilly invites the reader to make inferences on an entirely new system. We gather that money-lust, godless and narrow morality, social unease, insane plotting, napoleonism, eventually madness, are typical of Americans. Not content with merely nationalist snobbery, Marlowe ventures a racial explanation. He has looked into Manderson's genealogy and found early Mandersons mating with Indian women. "There is a very great deal of aboriginal blood," he says, "in the genealogical makeup of the people of America." He is, wrongly, under the impression that this discovery of the Indian taint was what set his employer against him. But the charge remains true, even if he wasn't ashamed of his aboriginal blood, since Cupples can speak of his "apparently hereditary temper of suspicious jealousy." Mrs. Manderson is much better off married to Trent.

Bentley dedicated his book to Chesterton, who was capable of believing that Jewish financiers started the Boer War to induce youths to slaughter one another. As a reading of history this might be thought to fall short of competence, but taken together with what is known of the Edwardian Englishman's attitude to colonials it helps to explain a certain chauvinism in the tale, though Bentley presumably meant it to remain inexplicit. Yet the processing of clues leads us inevitably to the conclusion that this novel has a cultural significance which, if we had to attempt a formal description of the text, we might subsume under some such heading as "early twentieth-century myth of America." The processing of hermeneutic material has entailed the provision of other matter from which we may infer an ideological system: American is to English as the first to the second term in each member of this series: rich–not rich, uneducated–educated, cruel–gentle, exploiter–paternalist, insensitive–sensitive, and so on, down to colored–white. So the hermeneutic spawns the cultural.

It also spawns the symbolic. For example: Trent solves the riddle only in part (the whole solution requires the aid of the old Cupples —a goodish name for Tiresias); he supplants a man who, since he is old enough to be his wife's father, is also old enough to be Trent's. There's a good deal of displacement, of course, but the myth is oedipal. So we see that Bentley's novel, though primarily a hermeneutic game, inevitably provides information which, if we are not docile, we may process independently of the intention or instruction of the author, who is therefore neither the source of a message nor an authority on reading. All narratives are like this, whether they belong to the nursery, the analyst's casebook, or the library shelf. Bentley's genre is evidently one in which hermeneutic information predominates; but to provide it in a narrative is to activate other systems of reading or interpretation. Trusting the tale can have unforeseen consequences, as all readers of *Studies in Classic American Literature*[b] ought to know. The multiple, perhaps unfathomable possibilities which inhere in a narrative "of a certain magnitude" declare themselves under this kind

[b]By D. H. Lawrence (1923).—Eds.

of examination, even though the text is generically so limited, so resistant to plurisignificance.

IV

It happens—to continue with this example of highly developed hermeneutic interest—that in rejecting the old novel some self-conscious makers of the new have taken a special interest in detective stories. Their reasons for doing so are that they mistrust "depth"; they regard orthodox narrative, with its carefully developed illusions of sequentiality and its formal characterization, as a kind of lie. Thus, they admire the detective story, in which the hermeneutic preoccupation is dominant at the expense of "depth," in which "character" is unimportant, and in which there are necessarily present in the narrative sequence enigmas which, because they relate to a quite different and earlier series of events, check and make turbulent its temporal flow. The presence of ambiguous clues is also of great interest, especially if you give up the notion—and here is a major change—that they ought to lock together with great exactness, and abandon the attempt at full hermeneutic closure (all loose ends tied up).

As early as 1942, in a comment on his own *Pierrot mon amour*, Raymond Queneau was talking about " 'an ideal detective story' in which not only does the criminal remain unknown but one has no clear idea whether there has even been a crime or who the detective is." Eleven years later Alain Robbe-Grillet published the first of the new wave of new novels, *Les Gommes*,[c] which is an approach to that ideal. His detective goes much more seriously wrong than Trent, and it turns out, if that is not too strong an expression, that the murder he is investigating has not yet been committed, and that when it is, the murderer is the detective Wallas, and the victim his own father, perhaps. Since Wallas appears to be physically attracted by someone who appears to be his stepmother, is repeatedly asked riddles about what animal is thus and thus in the morning, at noon, and so on, and searches devotedly for an eraser of which the brand name may be *Oedipe*, he has inherited Trent's oedipal qualities; but he lives in a very different kind of narrative, in which events and characters are doubled; in which objects—including a famous tomato—are described in

[c]Appeared in English as *The Erasers* (New York, 1964).—Eds.

hallucinated detail but have at best very obscure hermeneutic relevance; and which is in itself as it were false, not just false-bottomed. Trent lives without trouble in a book which has a double flow of time, but Wallas gets hopelessly swamped in it. Trent masters most of the clues; the clues master Wallas. And the erasers are always at work, rubbing out the novel. The closure is, in Barthes' expression, *à la fois posé et déçu*.[d] Novels, it seems, may erase themselves instead of establishing a permanent fixed reality. There are many internal relations and echoes which have no significance outside the text, point to no external meaning. The book seems to be trying to seal itself off from everything outside it.

The fashion prevailed: Michel Butor's *L'Emploi du temps*,[e] written a few years later, is also, in its curious and complicated and unclosed way, a detective story. A young Frenchman, passing a year in the bleak English northern city of Bleston, finds himself at war with it; after seven months of passivity he rouses himself to defeat the city in the remaining five by recapturing the lost time, writing an account of those lost months. The double flow of time becomes extremely turbulent. In May Revel is recounting, straightforwardly, the events of October; in June the events of June mingle with those of November; and so on, with increasing complexity, until in September the events of September, July, March, August, and February are all boiling up together, as he not only recalls the past but frantically rereads his manuscript. The young writer concerns himself incessantly with maps of the city—they have a magical relation to its labyrinths. Among his stories the most interesting is *Le Meurtre de Bleston (The Bleston Murder,* but also *The Murder of Bleston),* a work of great topographical accuracy. Revel meets its author, and reveals his identity, an indiscretion which perhaps causes an attempt on the author's life.

The Bleston Murder is, by all accounts, an elaborately clued story. And in *L'Emploi du temps* there are hundreds of clues of many kinds; but they do not work traditionally. We can see how Revel forms them into hermeneutic sequences, and we even try to do it ourselves; but they do not work out. They lie in the past of the manuscript: the Cain window in the Old Cathedral, suggesting not only fratricide but the first city and also Bleston, is incomplete, like the novel itself and other

[d]"Simultaneously set up and disappointed."—Eds.
[e]Appeared in English as *Passing Time* (London, 1965).—Eds.

works of art in it; it is related—but how?—to all the other cities that are mentioned—Petra, Baalbek, Rome in flames, and the labyrinth at Cnossos. In the same way the mythical Ariadne underlies, but not with a perfect fit, the girl Rose; and Theseus (a mythical twin of Oedipus) underlies, with imperfect fit, the author. The book becomes arbitrarily encyclopedic: the Old Cathedral offers one systematic world view, the New Cathedral, with its careful carvings of plants and animals in proper modern botanical and zoological orders, a world view appropriate to the nineteenth century; the detective story murder took place there, and was finally avenged in the red light from the Cain window in the Old Cathedral. But all these and many other hints about the hermeneutic fit are false; all remains unclosed, incomplete, and we watch Revel fail in his attempt to hammer it all into a unity, to make the clues work like clues in a detective story.

J. C. Hamilton, author of *The Bleston Murder*, lectures intermittently on the genre. It must, he says, have two murders; the murderer is the victim of the second, which is committed by the detective, his weapon an "explosion of truth." The detective is, as so often in the tradition, at odds with the police (for Butor an allegory of the best possible relationship between himself and the reader) because he is concerned, not with the preservation of an old order, but with the institution of a new; so he cheats the police (as Trent did). The climax of his existence is the moment when his accurate vision transforms and purifies reality. Furthermore, he is a true Oedipus, "not only because he solves a riddle, but also because he kills the man to whom he owes his title and because this murder was foretold him from the day of his birth."[12] Hamilton argues further that "in the best of such works the novel acquires, as it were, a new dimension," giving among his reasons for saying this the view that such novels have narrative which "is not merely the projection on a flat surface of a series of events" but which, in addition, "rebuilds these as it were spatially."[13] Revel adds that in exploring events anterior to its opening, such a novel has a truth missing from other kinds, for we muse on our disasters after they have happened, and live our lives in these crosscurrents of past and present. It was for this reason that he felt obliged to abandon the simplicities of May, when he set down what happened in October, in favor of the detective story writer's complex movements in the labyrinth of time and memory.

But the attempt fails; the clues don't fit, or close; all the receding series of objects, works of art, mythical equivalents, are askew. No blinding explosion of truth will destroy Bleston. And these myriad dissymmetries, displacing the symmetries, force us to peer, each from his own angle, into the text, make our own adjustments, institute within the text a new order of reality, our own invention. Butor himself speaks of "spatial polyphony." Barthes, examining such phenomena, will speak of "stereographic space"; in terms of the relations established within it we produce our own reading, so changing our view and, ideally, ourselves, altering our opinion as to what matters and what does not. For ordinarily we go on living in a state of truce with the world, supposing an identity between it and the arbitrary notion we happen to hold of it. The novel can be a criticism of common consciousness. It can show that our normal "fitting" is bogus; it attacks the way in which we "legitimate" our beliefs. Without forgetting that it could always do these things—it would not sound strange to say that George Eliot's novels are criticisms of common consciousness—we can allow that we are forced to produce, rather than merely assent to, an order, and that the order must be new.

Thus are the hermeneutic specializations of the detective story transformed in the interests of *truth,* in the cause of enabling us to live in the world as it is, as it simply *is,* lacking all meaning but that signified in our texts. Every novel, on this view, should be an affront to the simple hermeneutic expectation that it will *work out,* because it can only work out if we accept the false implication that the world itself is simply coded, full of discoverable relations and offering closure. Since, as sociologists assure us, "conceptual machineries of universe-maintenance are themselves products of social activity, as are all forms of legitimation,"[14] we need not be surprised that in adapting the detective novel to their purposes these French writers change it with revolutionary intent; they are usually willing to see in what they are doing a model of larger changes in politics, or more generally in the institution of a modern *Weltanschauung.* For them the oedipal detective, no longer concerned with puzzles guaranteed soluble and limited, becomes a herald of the new order. The problem of reading, and not less of rereading, because it requires us to remake ourselves, to move about in worlds not conventionally realized, becomes the central problem. The novel is "deconstructed"; mysteries like those of Chrétien once more challenge the reader. He must forget how he used to read, deluded by local and provincial restrictions; he must cease to invent structural myths, and instead develop the creative activity which narrative always demands in some measure, but which may be deadened by overfamiliarity and by trained expectations too readily satisfied.

This is, I think, to allow the new its full quantum of novelty. It amounts to a lively awareness of, and a new way of stating, what has always been at least intuitively known: the "openness" and the "intransitivity," and the essential "literariness" of texts. This new awareness is such that it ought to change conventional attitudes to all, and not merely new, texts; but there is, of course, a difficulty here, namely, the restrictiveness of the criticism to which the new critics aggressively oppose themselves.

V

How are we to give up the kind of reading which reinforces and complies with "local and provincial restrictions"? We began to do so long ago; occasionally one regrets the bad communications with Paris, for we, who have had Professor Empson and the New Criticism with us for forty years, hardly need to be told that texts can be polysemous, and will hardly believe that all professors deny this. But such differences will not excuse our neglect of what is being said; nor will our mistrust for the politics, philosophy, and polemics of the new French criticism. They have something to teach practical critics about method—and not only in their operations on new texts. Roland Barthes, an early champion of Robbe-Grillet, was carried away by the theoretical possibilities of the early *nouveau roman;* he proclaimed, before its authors were able to, that the desired "anéantissement de l'anecdote"[15f] had finally been achieved. Later, with other structuralist critics, he grew interested in the attempt of the Russian formalists of forty years earlier to find methods of describing a story or novel as a linguist describes a sentence—without regard, that is, to the meaning it may communicate, only to its structure. This suited his view that literature must struggle against the temptations of meaning[16]

---

[f] "the annihilation of the anecdote."—Eds.

—that the "science of literature," as he called this new enterprise, should, like linguistics, operate within systems not of *pleins* but of *vides*.[g] He devised the expression *écrivance* to distinguish an older literature of reference from the true *écriture*.[h] The neoformalist or structuralist enterprise was in full swing about six years ago, and much machinery was devised for the scientific description of texts.[17] But Barthes grew discontented with it; it was unequal to the really important task of describing a text in its individuality and difference. In *S/Z* (1970) he developed new procedures, and tested them on Balzac's story *Sarrasine*.[i]

A text, he argues, is not to be referred to a structural model, but understood as a series of invitations to the reader to *structurate* it. It is a network of significations, of *signifiants* lacking transcendent *signifiés*,[j] and a reader can enter it anywhere. He must produce, not consume it; he must as it were *write* it; and insofar as it avoids external reference it may be called *scriptible*. Classic texts he calls *lisible;* they lack the plurality of the *scriptible,* possessing meaning which can only be ideological, and in some respects, such as story, possessing also a directionality that must be avoided by the *scriptible*. In other words, the *lisible* has local and provincial restrictions, the *scriptible* (of which no example is available) has not.[k]

Barthes' analysis is conducted in terms of five codes, which are to account for what we do in the process of reading a text, to one or more of which each *lexie,* or unit of discourse, is assigned. These codes, though as yet unsatisfactory, are rather promising. Two have to do with what we think of as narrative, distinguished as the proairetic and hermeneutic codes: that is, the sequence of actions (dependent on choices), and the proposing of enigmas which are eventually, after delay, concealment, deception, and so on, solved. The other codes relate to information not processed sequentially: semantic, cultural, and symbolic, they stand as it were on the vertical rather than the horizontal axis of the work, and remain rather vague, especially in

[g]"not of fullnesses but of emptinesses."—Eds.
[h]An English equivalent might be "scrivening" as opposed to "writing."—Eds.
[i]Two sections of *S/Z* are reprinted in this volume.—Eds.
[j]"of *signifiers* lacking transcendent *signifieds*" (the terms are derived from the linguist F. de Saussure [1857–1913]).—Eds.
[k]The standard translation renders *lisible* as "readerly" and *scriptible* as "writerly." "Readable" and "writable" would be closer.—Eds.

view of the prohibition against organizing some of them on a thematic basis. To study these codes is not to study meanings, but only to describe the plurality of the work as apprehended by (presumably competent) readings. In *lisible* writing (Balzac's, for instance) this plurality is limited. In a *scriptible* text it would not be so. The *lisible* adheres to an obsolete *épistème*,[1] a kerygmatic civilization of meaning and truth. But even in the *lisible* there is movement from code to code: the same signifier may operate in both symbolic and hermeneutic codes (the castration of Zambinella in Balzac's story, or the false clues about American violence in *Trent's Last Case*). Despite the constraints of limited plurality—the commitment to closure—symbolic, hermeneutic, and proairetic may, in the *lisible,* stand in an and/or relation. We now see clearly what the authors of the *lisible* were prevented from seeing. Above all we understand that there is no *message* that is passed from writer to reader: "dans le texte, seul parle le lecteur."[18] [m]

If we ignore his ideological bias—itself a local and provincial restriction—we may find the codes of Barthes a very promising way of approaching the task of describing what happens when we read a narrative. On the question of the hermeneutic operations of the reader, he seems, in *S/Z,* very limited, partly no doubt because of the character of the text examined. But there seems little doubt that he has got behind the arbitrary constraints that have been mistaken for rules; the kind of reading he describes will perhaps enable us to cleanse our perceptions in the matter of narrative. One instance might be that we should alter our notions of acceptable closure, so exploited by the specialized hermeneutic of the detective story. The questioning of this by Queneau and Robbe-Grillet was a prelude to a new understanding that hermeneutic and other forms of closure are contingent, not necessary, aspects of narrative. This, rather than a purely modern dissociation of narrative from kerygma,[n] is the lesson of the New Novel and also of the codes.

For it seems wrong to argue that all this establishes a sharp distinc-

---

[l]Conceptual framework defining a period of history (the term is derived from the French philosopher M. Foucault).—Eds.
[m]"In the text, only the reader speaks."—Eds.
[n]The preaching and proclamation of the Christian gospels, especially as in the early church.—Eds.

tion between something called the novel, with all those qualities and conditions that seemed essential but turn out to be period trappings, and some leaner narrative that has cast them off. We have seen how even the classic detective novel, with its not always perfectly fitting clues and its uncontrollable play between hermeneutic and symbolic codes, prefigures "stereoscopy." New insights into the nature of modern fiction are equally insights into the novel—for all novels verge on the stereographic insofar as they satisfy the reader (a crude criterion, admittedly, but defensible).

Because *Sarrasine* is interesting in this way, though it was published in 1830, Barthes calls it a *texte-limite;*[o] although it is an instance of what he calls, sardonically, *Pleine Littérature,*[p] it stresses, by its very subject, namely castration, and in many of the ciphers which reflect it, an interest in want, in emptiness; it exploits the collision of castration with sex, of emptiness with plenitude, of Z with S. So that although it is on the wrong side of that firm line which, for Barthes, cuts off the modern from the classic, *Sarrasine* happens to be a book that not only illustrates the limited plurality of the classic, but adumbrates the *Littérature Vide*[q] which, in the present *épistème*, succeeds it just as sign is held to have succeeded symbol.

The inference appears to be that all the novels of the past in which we find much to admire partake of the modern precisely insofar as they are not patient of interpretation that assumes limited meaning. Barthes, under the influence of a domestic French quarrel, always talks as if establishment critics deny that position. Outside France this is, of course, untrue. In a sense he is saying, in a new way, something we have long known about the plurality of good texts.

Yet some critics do continue to feel some *horreur du vide.*[r] The invention of myths to explain Chrétien's allusions to the Grail stories is a handy example of a continuing critical passion for closure, the more interesting in that there are fictions more or less contemporary with these mythical inventions that are expressly designed to frustrate closure. James provides classic instances, notably in *The Sacred*

[o]"limit-text," by analogy to a limiting case in mathematics.—Eds.
[p]"Full Literature."—Eds.
[q]"Empty Literature."—Eds.
[r]Traditionally, "abhorrence of the vacuum," a physical principle; here Kermode is also referring to the critics' horror of empty literature.—Eds.

Fount. It does seem to be taking us a long time to understand the implication of these experiments in enforced plurality and imperfect closure. Yet the success of our interpretative enterprises on the novels of, say, Dickens, is evidence that in our unmethodical way we have made good guesses about such implications, and noticed that there seems no easily ascertainable limit to the number of *structurations* they will bear: what we reject we reject intuitively. More simply still, the very length of anything we call a novel should warn us that it will contain much information of which the critic, no matter how committed to the single full interpretation, makes no use. He explains it away or ignores it; sometimes behaving as if he thought there are things necessary for novels to do—because they are novels and need to seem "true"—that are nevertheless hardly his business ("pour faire 'vrai' il faut à la fois être précis et insignifiant,"[s] as Barthes[19] remarks). At best he is dealing with a remarkably small proportion of the information provided in the text, information which may, as we all know, be processed in so many ways that a plurality of readings is ensured.

As I've noted, novelists themselves long ago exploited this knowledge that their medium was inherently pluralistic; to the name of James one need add only that of Conrad, who invented the hermeneutic gap long before Robbe-Grillet expanded it to engulf the whole text. These writers saw ways of using the fact that the senses of a narrative are always, in some measure, *en jeu;*[t] they exploited this discovery and wrote to show how crucial it was despite the obscurity in which it had remained. So Barthes has found a possibly useful way of talking about something which the researches of novelists had already brought to light.

To take a simple example: in *Under Western Eyes* Rasumov leaves Russia to serve as an *agent provocateur.* We are not told until later how he contrived to do so: his cover was provided by an oculist. The novel has a great many allusions, few of which could be regarded as important to the narrative, to eyes and seeing. Some of these relate to the difference between Russians and others, to the difference between Russia and Switzerland; and others are concentrated in the representation of Miss Haldin. All this could be schematized in terms

---

[s]"In order to give the effect of the 'true' one must be at the same time precise and insignificant."—Eds.
[t]"In play."—Eds.

of Barthes' codes as proairetic, hermeneutic (he provides for delay in the solving of an enigma), semantic, cultural, and symbolic; and the fluent interplay between the codes is evident. It is indeed very complex, much more so than in Balzac; and it is from writing of this kind that the need to invent formal means to describe the pluralities grows, rather than from a wish to develop an instrument capable of analyzing any narrative (though Barthes might deny this). A copious interplay of plural significances was the invention of novelists examining the potential of narrative; our competence to read them is dependent upon the existence of texts requiring such competence.

It is, by the way, perfectly correct to say, as Barthes would, that the question as to whether Conrad intended the visit to the oculist to signify in all these ways is beside the point. It is simply in the nature of the case. This is the sense in which it is true that "dans le texte seul parle le lecteur." And having learned from certain texts how to speak, the reader will do it in others, including the classic, the *lisible;* that is why we can always find new things to say about a classic text; we can structurate it anew. There has been a change in our reading, not in the texts; we know that a novel does not simply encode a message from an author, and this knowledge became explicit when we had to deal with novels like *Under Western Eyes,* which asserts the fallibility of all that it seems to assert right down to its last page, which offers not closure but a hermeneutic booby-trap.[20] Its views on Russia, whatever they may be said to be, are not Conrad's; his were not Western eyes. Here is a difference in points of view that produces an authentic stereography. And that expression "points of view" will serve to remind us that there have been earlier attempts, in the Anglo-American tradition, to come to terms with the problems that engage Barthes. They are inherent in narrative; he did not discover them, nor has he shown that they came into being with the great cultural changes of the modern era.

VI

The French theorists want a novel without transcendental reference as they want a world without God. They want it to be impossible for anybody to "recuperate" the local and provincial which is inherent in the *lisible.* And in the course of their research they have made discoveries. They have noticed, as D. H. Lawrence did, that the novel may be a way of demonstrating that it is possible to live, because it is possible to read, without accepting official versions of reality. The excitement of the discovery has led them to believe that there may be a kind of novel in better faith than any before it by virtue of its abandoning the old assumptions and cultivating the text of pure sign, without external reference, without symbolism, without structure, receptive of all structures the reader produces. But this exaggerates —perhaps for ideological purposes—the novelty of some aspects of narrative, which, though now given much attention, are a selection from the set of permanent possibilities. As we saw at the outset, it was as possible for Roland to die three times as it is for a Robbe-Grillet personage; and Chrétien understood something of the now-fashionable "emptiness." Nor would it be difficult to multiply historical instances; after all, when we speak of a classic what we mean is a text that has evaded local and provincial restrictions.

There has, in short, been a renewal of attention to aspects of narrative which did not cease to exist because they were not attended to. When we remake our great novels—as we must, and as we have, of recent years, remade the nineteenth-century English classics—we shall find that they all have certain qualities of *Sarrasine,* as Barthes defines them, and also certain qualities of twelfth-century romance, as Marie de France defines them. They will always invite us to plural glosses on the letter, to ingenious manipulation of the codes; it is their nature to demand that we produce rather than consume them, and that we liberate them from local and provincial restrictions, including, so far as that is possible, our own. As to Barthes, it may seem odd to suggest that he has outlined a method for the formal description of a classic; but I believe that is what he has done, and the keenness and brilliance of his insights into *Sarrasine* tells us the same story. If you continue to speak well of narrative it follows that you will speak well of the novel.

NOTES

1. 1896; ed. of 1931, p. 6.
2. P. 49.
3. P. 322.
4. P. 349.

5. 1971, p. 5.
6. Marie de France, quoted by Vinaver, p. 16.
7. R. S. Loomis, *Arthurian Tradition and Chrétien de Troyes* (1949), p. 6; quoted in Vinaver, p. 40.
8. P. 47n.
9. P. 51.
10. P. 52.
11. It is only fair to say that this banal summary does no justice to a very entertaining puzzle.
12. *Passing Time,* translated by Jean Stewart, ed. of 1965, p. 143.
13. P. 158.
14. P. L. Berger and T. Luckmann, *The Social Construction of Reality,* (1966) ed. of 1967, p. 108.
15. *Essais critiques* (1964), p. 65.
16. *Essais critiques,* p. 267.
17. See *Communications* 8 (1966), and T. Todorov, ed., *Théorie de la littérature* (1965).
18. *S/Z,* p. 157.
19. *S/Z,* p. 75.
20. For a fuller discussion of the example, see "The Structures of Fiction," *Modern Language Notes* 84 (1969), 891–915.

STEVEN MARCUS

Dashiell Hammett

Using the Flitcraft story in The Maltese Falcon *as a starting point, Marcus examines Hammett's depiction of ethical duplicity and his characters' paradoxically persistent belief in the prophylactic, even the redemptive, powers of "normalcy." Hammett's Op typically discovers that not only normality but "reality" itself is so elusive as to be practically nonexistent: "What he soon discovers is that the 'reality' that anyone involved will swear to is, in fact, itself a construction, a fabrication, a fiction, a faked and alternate reality—and that it has been gotten together before he ever arrived on the scene." Marcus blames this pervasive duplicity on three elements in Hammett's society, all of which gave rise to conventional social fiction making. First was Prohibition, which forced a large number of otherwise "law-abiding" citizens to collaborate with organized crime, under the eyes of often indulgent authorities. Then there was organized crime itself, parading as legitimate, respectable business. Finally, there was the capitalist system, whose similarities with organized crime are for Marcus not accidental. The Op plies his trade in a world pervaded by conventional, criminal, and commercial hypocrisy. Inevitably, he is himself contaminated by this world. Hammett does not idealize him as an untainted truth seeker, but sees him realistically as a small, fat, sometimes unnecessarily violent little man.*

Marcus's study of the relation between a certain kind of detective novel and the society that spawned it takes its place here with the related studies of Alewyn, Jameson, Knight, and Miller. Steven Marcus himself is a writer and critic based at Columbia University. We have here reprinted part two of his introduction to The Continental Op, *a collection of stories by Dashiell Hammett, selected and edited by Marcus and published in 1974.*

I was first introduced to Dashiell Hammett by Humphrey Bogart. I was twelve years old at the time, and mention the occasion because I take it to be exemplary, that I share this experience with countless others. (Earlier than this, at the very dawn of consciousness, I can recall William Powell and Myrna Loy and a small dog on a leash and an audience full of adults laughing; but that had nothing to do with Hammett or anything else as far as I was concerned.) What was striking about the event was that it was one of the first encounters I can consciously recall with the experience of moral ambiguity. Here was this detective you were supposed to like—and did like—behaving and speaking in peculiar and unexpected ways. He acted up to the cops, partly for real, partly as a ruse. He connived with crooks, for his own ends and perhaps even for some of theirs. He slept with his partner's wife, fell in love with a lady crook, and then refused to save her from the police, even though he could have. Which side was he on? Was he on any side apart from his own? And which or what side was that? The experience was not only morally ambiguous; it was morally complex and enigmatic as well. The impression it made was a lasting one.

Years later, after having read *The Maltese Falcon* and seen the movie again and then reread the novel, I could begin to understand why the impact of the film had been so memorable, much more so than that of most other movies. The director, John Huston, had had the wit to recognize the power, sharpness, integrity, and bite of Hammett's prose—particularly the dialogue—and the film script consists almost entirely of speech taken directly and without modification from the written novel. Moreover, this unusual situation is complicated still further. In selecting with notable intelligence the relevant scenes and passages from the novel, Huston had to make certain omissions. Paradoxically, however, one of the things that he chose to omit was the most important or central moment in the entire novel. It is also one of the central moments in all of Hammett's writing. I think we can make use of this oddly "lost" passage as a means of entry into Hammett's vision or imagination of the world.

It occurs as Spade is becoming involved with Brigid O'Shaughnessy in her struggle with the other thieves, and it is his way of communicating to her his sense of how the world and life go. His way is to tell her a story from his own experience. The form this story takes is that of a parable. It is a parable about a man named Flitcraft. Flitcraft was a successful, happily married, stable, and utterly respectable real estate dealer in Tacoma. One day he went out to lunch and never returned. No reason could be found for his disappearance, and no account of it could be made. " 'He went like that,' Spade said, 'like a fist when you open your hand.' "

Five years later Mrs. Flitcraft came to the agency at which Spade was working and told them that " 'she had seen a man in Spokane who looked a lot like her husband.' " Spade went off to investigate and found that it was indeed Flitcraft. He had been living in Spokane for a couple of years under the name of Charles Pierce. He had a successful automobile business, a wife, a baby son, a suburban home, and usually played golf after four in the afternoon, just as he had in Tacoma. Spade and he sat down to talk the matter over. Flitcraft, Spade recounts, "had no feeling of guilt. He had left his family well provided for, and what he had done seemed to him perfectly reasonable. The only thing that bothered him was a doubt that he could make that reasonableness clear" to his interlocutor. When Flitcraft went out to lunch that day five years before in Tacoma, " 'he passed an office-building that was being put up. . . . A beam or something fell eight or ten stories down and smacked the sidewalk alongside him.' " A chip of smashed sidewalk flew up and took a piece of skin off his cheek. He was otherwise unharmed. He stood there " 'scared stiff,' " he told Spade, " 'but he was more shocked than really frightened. He felt like somebody had taken the lid off life and let him look at the works.' "

Until that very moment Flitcraft had been " 'a good citizen and a good husband and father, not by any outer compulsion, but simply because he was a man who was most comfortable in step with his surroundings. . . . The life he knew was a clean orderly sane responsible affair. Now a falling beam had shown him that life was fundamentally none of these things. . . . What disturbed him was the discovery that in sensibly ordering his affairs he had got out of step, and not into step, with life.' " By the time he had finished lunch, he had reached the decision " 'that he would change his life at random by simply going away.' " He went off that afternoon, wandered around for a couple of years, then drifted back to the Northwest, " 'settled in Spokane and got married. His second wife didn't look

like the first, but they were more alike than they were different.' "
And the same held true of his second life. Spade then moves on to
his conclusion: " 'He wasn't sorry for what he had done. It seemed
reasonable enough to him. I don't think he even knew he had settled
back into the same groove that he had jumped out of in Tacoma.
But that's the part of it I always liked. He adjusted himself to beams
falling, and then no more of them fell, and he adjusted himself to
their not falling.' " End of parable. Brigid, of course, understands
nothing of this, as Spade doubtless knew beforehand. Yet what he
has been telling her has to do with the forces and beliefs and contingencies that guide his conduct and supply a structure to his apparently enigmatic behavior.

To begin with, we may note that such a sustained passage is not the
kind of thing we ordinarily expect in a detective story or novel about
crime. That it is there, and that comparable passages occur in all of
Hammett's best work, clearly suggests the kind of transformation that
Hammett was performing on this popular genre of writing. The transformation was in the direction of literature. And what the passage in
question is about among other things is the ethical irrationality of
existence, the ethical unintelligibility of the world. For Flitcraft the
falling beam "had taken the lid off life and let him look at the works."
The works are that life is inscrutable, opaque, irresponsible, and
arbitrary—that human existence does not correspond in its actuality
to the way we live it. For most of us live as if existence itself were
ordered, ethical, and rational. As a direct result of his realization in
experience that it is not, Flitcraft leaves his wife and children and goes
off. He acts irrationally and at random, in accordance with the nature
of existence. When after a couple of years of wandering aimlessly
about he decides to establish a new life, he simply reproduces the old
one he had supposedly repudiated and abandoned; that is to say, he
behaves again as if life were orderly, meaningful, and rational, and
"adjusts" to it. And this, with fine irony, is the part of it, Spade says,
that he " 'always liked,' " which means the part that he liked best. For
here we come upon the unfathomable and most mysteriously irrational part of it all—how despite everything we have learned and
everything we know, men will persist in behaving and trying to behave
sanely, rationally, sensibly, and responsibly. And we will continue to
persist even when we know that there is no logical or metaphysical,

no discoverable or demonstrable reason for doing so.[1] It is this sense of sustained contradiction that is close to the center—or to one of the centers—of Hammett's work. The contradiction is not ethical alone; it is metaphysical as well. And it is not merely sustained; it is sustained with pleasure. For Hammett and Spade and the Op, the sustainment in consciousness of such contradictions is an indispensable part of their existence and of their pleasure in that existence.

That this pleasure is itself complex, ambiguous, and problematic becomes apparent as one simply describes the conditions under which it exists. And the complexity, ambiguity, and sense of the problematical are not confined to such moments of "revelation"—or set pieces—as the parable of Flitcraft. They permeate Hammett's work and act as formative elements in its structure, including its deep structure. Hammett's work went through considerable and interesting development in the course of his career for twelve years as a writer. He also wrote in a considerable variety of forms and worked out a variety of narrative devices and strategies. At the same time, his work considered as a whole reveals a remarkable kind of coherence. In order to further the understanding of that coherence, we can propose for the purposes of the present analysis to construct a kind of "ideal type" of a Hammett or Op story. Which is not to say or to imply in the least that he wrote according to a formula, but that an authentic imaginative vision lay beneath and informed the structure of his work.

Such an ideal-typical description runs as follows. The Op is called in or sent out on a case. Something has been stolen, someone is missing, some dire circumstance is impending, someone has been murdered—it doesn't matter. The Op interviews the person or persons most immediately accessible. They may be innocent or guilty—it doesn't matter; it is an indifferent circumstance. Guilty or innocent, they provide the Op with an account of what they know, of what they assert really happened. The Op begins to investigate; he compares these accounts with others that he gathers; he snoops about; he does research; he shadows people, arranges confrontations between those who want to avoid one another, and so on. What he soon discovers

[1] It can hardly be an accident that the new name that Hammett gives to Flitcraft is that of an American philosopher [Charles Sanders Peirce (1839–1914).—Eds.]—with two vowels reversed—who was deeply involved in just such speculations.

is that the "reality" that anyone involved will swear to is, in fact, itself a construction, a fabrication, a fiction, a faked and alternate reality —and that it has been gotten together before he ever arrived on the scene. And the Op's work therefore is to deconstruct, decompose, deplot and defictionalize that "reality" and to construct or reconstruct out of it a true fiction, that is, an account of what "really" happened.

It should be quite evident that there is a reflective and coordinate relation between the activities of the Op and the activities of Hammett, the writer. Yet the depth and problematic character of this self-reflexive process begin to be revealed when we observe that the reconstruction or true fiction created and arrived at by the Op at the end of the story is no more plausible—nor is it meant to be—than the stories that have been told to him by all parties, guilty or innocent, in the course of his work. The Op may catch the real thief or collar the actual crook—that is not entirely to the point. What is to the point is that the story, account, or chain of events that the Op winds up with as "reality" is no more plausible and no less ambiguous than the stories that he meets with at the outset and later. What Hammett has done—unlike most writers of detective or crime stories before him or since—is to include as part of the contingent and dramatic consciousness of his narrative the circumstance that the work of the detective is itself a fiction-making activity, a discovery or creation by fabrication of something new in the world, or hidden, latent, potential, or as yet undeveloped within it. The typical "classical" detective story—unlike Hammett's—can be described as a formal game with certain specified rules of transformation. What ordinarily happens is that the detective is faced with a situation of inadequate, false, misleading, and ambiguous information. And the story as a whole is an exercise in disambiguation—with the final scenes being a ratiocinative demonstration that the butler did it (or not); these scenes achieve a conclusive, reassuring clarity of explanation, wherein everything is set straight, and the game we have been party to is brought to its appropriate end. But this, as we have already seen, is not what ordinarily happens in Hammett or with the Op.

What happens is that the Op almost invariably walks into a situation that has already been elaborately fabricated or framed. And his characteristic response to his sense that he is dealing with a series of deceptions or fictions is—to use the words that he uses himself repeatedly—"to stir things up." This corresponds integrally, both as metaphor and in logical structure, to what happened in the parable of Flitcraft. When the falling beam just misses Flitcraft, "he felt like somebody had taken the lid off life." The Op lives with the uninterrupted awareness that for him the lid has been taken off life. When the lid has been lifted, the logical thing to do is to "stir things up" —which is what he does.[2] He actively undertakes to deconstruct, decompose, and thus demystify the fictional—and therefore false— reality created by the characters, crooks or not, with whom he is involved. More often than not he tries to substitute his own fictional-hypothetical representation for theirs—and this representation may also be "true" or mistaken, or both at once. In any event, his major effort is to make the fictions of others visible as fictions, inventions, concealments, falsehoods, and mystifications. When a fiction becomes visible as such, it begins to dissolve and disappear, and presumably should reveal behind it the "real" reality that was there all the time and that it was masking. Yet what happens in Hammett is that what is revealed as "reality" is a still further fiction-making activity—in the first place the Op's, and behind that yet another, the consciousness present in many of the Op stories and all the novels that Dashiell Hammett, the writer, is continually doing the same thing as the Op and all the other characters in the fiction he is creating. That is to say, he is making a fiction (in writing) in the real world; and this fiction, like the real world itself, is coherent but not necessarily rational. What one both begins and ends with, then, is a story, a narrative, a coherent yet questionable account of the world. This problematic penetrates to the bottom of Hammett's narrative imagination and shapes a number of its deeper processes—in *The Dain Curse,* for example, it is the chief topic of explicit debate that runs throughout the entire novel.

Yet Hammett's writing is still more complex and integral than this. For the unresolvable paradoxes and dilemmas that we have just been describing in terms of narrative structure and consciousness are reproduced once again in Hammett's vision and representation of society,

---

[2]These homely metaphors go deep into Hammett's life. One of the few things that he could recall from his childhood past was his mother's repeated advice that a woman who wasn't good in the kitchen wasn't likely to be much good in any other room in the house.

of the social world in which the Op lives. At this point we must recall that Hammett is a writer of the 1920s and that this was the era of Prohibition. American society had in effect committed itself to a vast collective fiction. Even more, this fiction was false not merely in the sense that it was made up or did not in fact correspond to reality; it was false in the sense that it was corrupt and corrupting as well. During this period every time an American took a drink he was helping to undermine the law, and American society had covertly committed itself to what was in practice collaborative illegality.[3] There is a kind of epiphany of these circumstances in "The Golden Horseshoe." The Op is on a case that takes him to Tijuana. In a bar there, he reads a sign:

ONLY GENUINE PREWAR AMERICAN AND
BRITISH WHISKEYS SERVED HERE

He responds by remarking that "I was trying to count how many lies could be found in those nine words, and had reached four, with promise of more," when he is interrupted by some call to action. That sign and the Op's response to it describe part of the existential character of the social world represented by Hammett.

Another part of that representation is expressed in another kind of story or idea that Hammett returned to repeatedly. The twenties were also the great period of organized crime and organized criminal gangs in America, and one of Hammett's obsessive imaginations was the notion of organized crime or gangs taking over an entire society and running it as if it were an ordinary society doing business as usual. In other words, society itself would become a fiction, concealing and belying the actuality of what was controlling it and perverting it from within. One can thus make out quite early in this native American writer a proto-Marxist critical representation of how a certain kind of society works. Actually, the point of view is pre- rather than proto-Marxist, and the social world as it is dramatized in many of

[3]Matters were even murkier than this. The Eighteenth Amendment to the Constitution was in effect from January 1920 to December 1933, nearly fourteen years. During this period Americans were forbidden under penalty of law to manufacture, sell, or transport any intoxicating liquor. At the same time no one was forbidden to buy or drink such liquor. In other words, Americans were virtually being solicited by their own laws to support an illegal trade in liquor, even while Congress was passing the Volstead Act, which was intended to prevent such a trade.

these stories is Hobbesian rather than Marxist.[4] It is a world of universal warfare, the war of each against all, and of all against all. The only thing that prevents the criminal ascendancy from turning into permanent tyranny is that the crooks who take over society cannot cooperate with one another, repeatedly fall out with each other, and return to the Hobbesian anarchy out of which they have momentarily arisen. The social world as imagined by Hammett runs on a principle that is the direct opposite of that postulated by Erik Erikson[b] as the fundamental and enabling condition for human existence. In Hammett, society and social relations are dominated by the principle of basic mistrust. As one of his detectives remarks, speaking for himself and for virtually every other character in Hammett's writing, "I trust no one."

When Hammett turns to the respectable world, the world of respectable society, of affluence and influence, of open personal and political power, he finds only more of the same. The respectability of respectable American society is as much a fiction and a fraud as the phony respectable society fabricated by the criminals. Indeed, he unwaveringly represents the world of crime as a reproduction in both structure and detail of the modern capitalist society that it depends on, preys off, and is part of. But Hammett does something even more radical than this. He not only continually juxtaposes and connects the ambiguously fictional worlds of art and of writing with the fraudulently fictional worlds of society; he connects them, juxtaposes them, and sees them in dizzying and baffling interaction. He does this in many ways and on many occasions. One of them, for example, is the Maltese Falcon itself, which turns out to be and contains within itself the history of capitalism. It is originally a piece of plunder, part of what Marx called the "primitive accumulation"; when its gold encrusted with gems is painted over, it becomes a mystified object, a commodity itself; it is a piece of property that belongs to no one—

[4]Again it can hardly be regarded as an accident that the name Hammett gives to the town taken over by the criminals in *Red Harvest* is "Personville"—pronounced "Poisonville." And what else is Personville except Leviathan, the "artificial man" represented by Hobbes as the image of society itself.
[b]American psychologist (b. 1902). Marcus is alluding to his theories of the relation between a child's development and his later social behavior. In this context, Erikson speaks of basic trust and basic mistrust. See *Childhood and Society* (New York, 1963), pp. 247–251; *Identity: Youth and Crisis* (New York, 1968), pp. 82f, 96–107.—Eds.

whoever possesses it does not really own it. At the same time it is another fiction, a representation or work of art—which turns out itself to be a fake, since it is made of lead. It is a rara avis indeed. As is the fiction in which it is created and contained, the novel by Hammett. It is into this bottomlessly equivocal, endlessly fraudulent, and brutally acquisitive world that Hammett precipitates the Op. There is nothing glamorous about him. Short, thickset, balding, between thirty-five and forty, he has no name, no home, no personal existence apart from his work. He is, and he regards himself as, "the hired man" of official and respectable society, who is paid so much per day to clean it up and rescue it from the crooks and thieves who are perpetually threatening to take it over. Yet what he—and the reader—just as perpetually learn is that the respectable society that employs him is itself inveterately vicious, deceitful, culpable, crooked, and degraded. How, then, is the Op to be preserved, to preserve himself, from being contaminated by both the world he works against and the world he is hired to work for?

To begin with, the Op lives by a code. This code consists in the first instance of the rules laid down by the Continental Agency, and they are "rather strict." The most important of them by far is that no operative in the employ of the agency is ever allowed to take or collect part of a reward that may be attached to the solution of a case. Since he cannot directly enrich himself through his professional skills, he is saved from at least the characteristic corruption of modern society —the corruption that is connected with its fundamental acquisitive structure. At the same time, the Op is a special case of the Protestant ethic, for his entire existence is bound up in and expressed by his work, his vocation. He likes his work, and it is honest work, done as much for enjoyment and the exercise of his skills and abilities as it is for personal gain and self-sustainment. The work is something of an end in itself, and this circumstance also serves to protect him, as does his deliberate refusal to use high-class and fancy moral language about anything. The work is an end in itself and is therefore something more than work alone. As Spade says, in a passage that is the culmination of many such passages in Hammett:

> "I'm a detective and expecting me to run criminals down and then let them go free is like asking a dog to catch a rabbit and let it go.

It can be done, all right, and sometimes it is done, but it's not the natural thing."

Being a detective, then, entails more than fulfilling a social function or performing a social role. Being a detective is the realization of an identity, for there are components in it which are beyond or beneath society—and cannot be touched by it—and beyond and beneath reason. There is something "natural" about it. Yet if we recall that the nature thus being expressed is that of a manhunter, and Hammett's apt metaphor compels us to do so, and that the state of society as it is represented in Hammett's writing reminds us of the state of nature in Hobbes, we see that even here Hammett does not release his sense of the complex and the contradictory, and is making no simple-minded appeal to some benign idea of the "natural."

And indeed the Op is not finally or fully protected by his work, his job, his vocation. (We have all had to relearn with bitterness what multitudes of wickedness "doing one's job" can cover.) Max Weber has memorably remarked that "the decisive means for politics is violence." In Hammett's depiction of modern American society, violence is the decisive means indeed, along with fraud, deceit, treachery, betrayal, and general, endemic unscrupulousness. Such means are in no sense alien to Hammett's detective. As the Op says, " 'detecting is a hard business, and you use whatever tools come to hand.' " In other words, there is a paradoxical tension and unceasing interplay in Hammett's stories between means and ends; relations between the two are never secure or stable. And as Max Weber[c] further remarked, in his great essay "Politics as a Vocation": "the world is governed by demons, and he who lets himself in for . . . power and force as means, contracts with diabolic powers, and for his action it is *not* true that good can follow only from good and evil only from evil, but that often the opposite is true. Anyone who fails to see this is, indeed, a political infant." Neither Hammett nor the Op is an infant; yet no one can be so grown up and inured to experience that he can escape the consequences that attach to the deliberate use of violent and dubious means.

These consequences are of various orders. "Good" ends themselves

---

[c]German sociologist and political theorist (1864–1920). The article Marcus alludes to appears in English in *From Max Weber's Essays in Sociology,* edited and translated by H. H. Gerth and C. Wright Mills (New York, 1946). The section quoted is on p. 121.
—Eds.

can be transformed and perverted by the use of vicious or indiscriminate means. (I am leaving to one side those even more perplexing instances in Hammett in which the ends pursued by the Op correspond with ends desired by a corrupted yet respectable official society.) The consequences are also visible inwardly, on the inner being of the agent of such means, the Op himself. The violence begins to get to him:

> I began to throw my right fist into him.
> I liked that. His belly was flabby, and it got softer every time I hit it. I hit it often.

Another side of this set of irresolvable moral predicaments is revealed when we see that the Op's toughness is not merely a carapace within which feelings of tenderness and humanity can be nourished and preserved. The toughness is toughness through and through, and as the Op continues his career, and continues to live by the means he does, he tends to become more callous and less and less able to feel. At the very end, awaiting him, he knows, is the prospect of becoming like his boss, the head of the agency, the Old Man, "with his gentle eyes behind gold spectacles and his mild smile, hiding the fact that fifty years of sleuthing had left him without any feelings at all on any subject." This is the price exacted by the use of such means in such a world; these are the consequences of living fully in a society moved by the principle of basic mistrust. "Whoever fights monsters," writes Nietzsche, "should see to it that in the process he does not become a monster. And when you look long into an abyss, the abyss also looks into you."[d] The abyss looks into Hammett, the Old Man, and the Op.

It is through such complex devices as I have merely sketched here that Hammett was able to raise the crime story into literature. He did it over a period of ten years. Yet the strain was finally too much to bear—that shifting, entangled, and equilibrated state of contradictions out of which his creativity arose and which it expressed could no longer be sustained. His creative career ends when he is no longer able to handle the literary, social, and moral opacities, instabilities, and contradictions that characterize all his best work. His life then splits apart and goes in the two opposite directions that were implicit

[d] *Beyond Good and Evil*, in *Basic Writings of Nietzsche*, translated and edited by W. Kaufmann (New York, 1968), p. 279 (Aphorism 146).—Eds.

in his earlier, creative phase, but that the creativity held suspended and in poised yet fluid tension. His politics go in one direction; the way he made his living went in another—he became a hack writer, and then finally no writer at all. That is another story. Yet for ten years he was able to do what almost no other writer in this genre has ever done so well—he was able to really write, to construct a vision of a world in words, to know that the writing was about the real world and referred to it and was part of it; and at the same time he was able to be self-consciously aware that the whole thing was problematical and about itself and "only" writing as well. For ten years, in other words, he was a true creator of fiction.

GEOFFREY H. HARTMAN

Literature High and Low: The Case of the Mystery Story

Beginning and ending with references to Sophocles' Oedipus the King, but focusing primarily upon the novels of Raymond Chandler and Ross Macdonald, Hartman's essay is addressed to the twin questions of what detective fiction shares with traditional forms of high or serious literature and what separates it from them. The essential characteristic of mystery fiction is a strictly delimited scene of suffering, which need not be narrated but may be only alluded to and whose disclosure is the central anchoring point of the story. Psychoanalysts have equated this scene with the Freudian primal scene, but Hartman is more interested in its literary implications. Typically, the mystery story emphasizes visual proof of this scene, and thereby conservatively rationalizes and defuses the possibilities for anarchy it might imply. On the other hand, "sophisticated art is closer to being an antimystery than a mystery. It limits, even while expressing, this passion for ocular proof": great art calls into question such easy notions of problem solving, culpability, and truth. Mystery novelists trivialize serious issues by reducing them to a fashionable science: sociology (Chandler), psychology (Macdonald, whom, unusually, Hartman prefers). "Thus the trouble with the detective novel is not that it is moral but that it is moralistic; not that it is popular but that it is stylized; not that it lacks realism but that it picks up the latest realism and exploits it. A voracious formalism dooms it to seem unreal, however 'real' the world it describes." In spite and because of his evident fascination with and sensitivity to the genre, Hartman concludes by vigorously condemning it.

As psychoanalytically inspired analysis and original cultural criticism, Hartman's article shares parts of its subject and its approach with many of the pieces in this collection. See especially Pederson-Krag and Lacan for psychoanalysis and Alewyn and Grossvogel for evaluative criticism of the genre.

Geoffrey Hartman is Professor of English and Comparative Literature at Yale University. A version of this article appeared in the New York Review of Books *(May 18, 1972);* it was revised for inclusion in Hartman's own collection, The Fate of Reading and Other Essays *(Chicago, 1975).*

The terms reversal *(peripeteia)* and recognition *(anagnorisis)* are well known. They name, according to Aristotle, the essential ingredients of complex plots in tragedy. Reversal he defines as a change which makes the action veer in a different direction to that expected, and he refers us to the messenger from Corinth who comes to cheer Oedipus and eventually produces the recognition leading to an opposite result. Recognition is often linked to this kind of reversal, and is defined as a change from ignorance to knowledge. "Then once more I must bring what is dark to light," Oedipus says in the prologue of the play—and does exactly that, however unforeseen to him the result. In most detective stories, clearly, there is both a reversal and a recognition, but they are not linked as powerfully as in tragedy. The reversal in detective stories is more like an unmasking; and the recognition that takes place when the mask falls is not prepared for by dramatic irony. It is a belated, almost last-minute affair, subordinating the reader's intelligence to such hero-detectives as Ross Macdonald's Archer, who is no Apollo but who does roam the California scene with cleansing or catalyzing effect.

I wish, however, to draw attention to a third term, left obscure in the *Poetics.* Aristotle calls it *tò pathos,* "The Suffering," or as Butcher translates it, the "Scene of Suffering." *Tò pathos,* he says—and it is all he says—"is a destructive or painful action, such as death on the stage, bodily agony, wounds and the like."[1]

Aristotle is probably referring to what happens at the conclusion of *Oedipus Rex,* though chiefly offstage: the suicide of Jocasta and self-blinding of Oedipus. Or to the exhibition of the mangled head of

Pentheus by his deluded mother, in Euripides' *Bacchae*. He may also be thinking of the premise on which the tragic plot is built, the blood deed from which all consequences flow, and which, though premised rather than shown, is the real point of reference.[2] I wish to suggest that some such "heart of darkness" scene, some such *pathos,* is the relentless center or focus of detective fiction and that recognition and reversal are merely paths toward it—techniques which seek to evoke it as strongly and visually as possible.[a]

I don't mean that we must have the scene of suffering—the actual murder, mutilation, or whatever—exhibited to us. In *The Chill,* and in Ross Macdonald's novels generally, violence is as offstage as in *Oedipus Rex.* (The real violence, in any case, is perpetrated on the psyche.) But to solve a crime in detective stories means to give it an exact location: to pinpoint not merely the murderer and his motives but also the very place, the room, the ingenious or brutal circumstance. We want not only proof but, like Othello, ocular proof. Crime induces a perverse kind of epiphany: it marks the spot, or curses it, or invests it with enough meaning to separate it from the ordinary space–time continuum. Thus, though a Robbe-Grillet may remove the scene of pathos, our eyes nervously inspect all those graphic details which continue to evoke the detective story's lust for evidence.

The example of Robbe-Grillet—I want to return to it later—suggests that sophisticated art is closer to being an antimystery rather than a mystery. It limits, even while expressing, this passion for ocular proof. Take the medieval carol, "Lully, lulley," and regard how carefully it frames the heart of darkness scene, how with a zooming motion at once tactful and satisfyingly ritual, it approaches a central mystery:

> Lully, lulley,
> The faucon hath born my mak away
>
> He bare him up, he bare him down,
> He bare him into an orchard brown.
>
> In that orchard there was an halle
> Which was hanged with purpill and pall.

[a]Compare Pederson-Krag's treatment of the "primal scene" in her article reprinted in this volume.—Eds.

And in that hall there was a bed,
It was hanged with gold so red.

And in that bed there lith a knight,
His wounds bleding day and night.

By that bed side kneleth a may,
And she wepeth both night and day.

And by that bed side there stondeth a stone,
Corpus Christi wreten there on.

Here we have a scene of pathos, "death on the stage, bodily agony, wounds, and the like," but in the form of picture and inscription, a still life we can contemplate without fear. It is a gentle falcon, even if it be a visionary one, that lifts us in this ballad from the ordinary world into that of romance. This is no bird of prey attracted to battlefield carnage. And though the heart of the romance is dark enough, it is also comforting rather than frightening because interpreted by the inscription. We do not have to overcome an arresting moment of pity or fear, we do not even have to ask, as in the Parsifal legends, "What does this mean?" in order to redeem the strange sight. Its redeeming virtue is made clear to everyone borne away on this ritual trip.

The relation of the ballad to the modern mystery story is a complicated one, and my purpose here is not historical genealogy. The ballad revival had its influence not only on the gothic novel with its mystifications but also on the tension between brevity and elaboration in Melville's *Billy Budd,* the tales of Henry James, and the Gaucho stories of Borges. The modern elliptical ballad as well as the "novel turned tale"[3] qualify the element of mystery in a definably new, even generic way.

Consider Wordsworth's "The Thorn," first published in a collection called *Lyrical Ballads* (1798). The movement of this ballad is so slow, the dramatic fact so attenuated, that we begin to sense the possibility of a plotless story. A line of descent could easily be established between pseudonarratives like "The Thorn," which converge obsessively on an ocular center of uncertain interest (has a crime been committed near the thorn, or is the crime an illusion to stimulate crude imaginations?) and lyrical movies like Antonioni's *Blow Up* or

Resnais's *Marienbad*. The center they scan is an absence; the darkness they illumine has no heart. There is pathos here but no defined scene of pathos. Instead of a whodunit we get a whodonut, a story with a hole in it.[4]

Wordsworth's poem begins and ends with a thornbush seen by the poet "on the ridge of Quantock Hill, on a stormy day, a thorn which I had often passed in calm and bright weather without noticing it. I said to myself, "Cannot I by some invention do as much to make this Thorn permanently an impressive object as the storm has made it to my eyes at this moment?' " The narrator's eye therefore remains on the thorn, or the thorn (if you wish) in his eye: as always in Wordsworth the path from thing to meaning via an act of imaginative perception (an "invention") is fully, almost painfully, respected. Though consciousness moves toward what it fears to find, a scene of ballad sorrow and bloodiness, it never actually presents that beautiful and ominous "still" which the Corpus Christi poem composes for us. The corpse has vanished and will not be found. The strange spot is not approached on the wings of a falcon, nor does it ever become a burning bush. Instead, we approach it from within a peculiar consciousness, whose repetitive, quasi-ritual stepping from one object to another, from thorn to pond to hill of moss, as well as spurts of topographical precision—"And to the left, three yards beyond,/ You see a little muddy pond"—suggests we are behind the camera eye of a mad movie maker or . . . on the way to Robbe-Grillet.

But what exactly are we on the way to? Robbe-Grillet, after hints in Henry James, Gide, Faulkner, and Camus, has killed the scene of pathos. We all know that a corpse implies a story; yet Robbe-Grillet's contention that a story kills, that a story is a corpse, may be news for the novel. In his fiction the statement "He has a past" is equivalent to "He is doomed" or "It is written." So Oedipus, or a Robbe-Grillet hero, is safe as long as he has no past. So the detective in *The Erasers* commits the crime he is sent to solve: he enacts the prefigurative or formalistic force of traditional storymaking which insists on its corpse or scene of suffering. If, moreover, we identify that scene of suffering with what Freud calls the primal scene—the "mystery" of lovemaking which the child stumbles on—then we also understand why Robbe-Grillet is opposed to character or plot based on a psychoanalytic model. For him Freudianism is simply another form of mystery religion, one which insists on its myth of depth and hidden scene of passion. Robbe-Grillet formulates therefore what might be called the modern script-tease, of which Antonioni's *Blow Up* and *L'Avventura,* Bergman's *A Passion,* and Norman Mailer's *Maidstone,*[5] are disparate examples. What they share is the perplexing absence of *tò pathos:* one definitively visualized scene to which everything else might be referred.

I have brought you, safely I hope, from ancient to modern mystery stories by following the fortunes of the scene of pathos. But one comment should be added concerning this scene and its structure. Comparing the scene of suffering with Freud's primal scene, we gain a clue as to why it is able to motivate entire novels or plays.

It resembles, first of all, a highly condensed, supersemantic event like riddle, oracle, or mime. Now whether or not the power of such scenes is linked to our stumbling as innocents on sexual secrets—on seeing or overhearing that riddling mime[6]—it is clear that life is always in some way too fast for us, that it is a spectacle we can't interpret or a dumbshow difficult to word. The detective novel allows us to catch up a little by involving us in the interpretation of a mystery that seems at first to have no direct bearing on our life. We soon realize, of course, that "mystery" means that something is happening too fast to be spotted. We are made to experience a consciousness (like Oedipa's in Thomas Pynchon's *Crying of Lot 49*) always behind and running; vulnerable therefore, perhaps imposed on. But we are also allowed to triumph (unlike Oedipa) over passivity when the detective effects a catharsis or purgation of consciousness and sweeps away all the false leads planted in the course of the novel.

No wonder the detective's reconstitution of the scene of pathos has something phantasmagoric about it. So quick that it is always "out of sight," the primal scene's existence, real or imagined, can only be mediated by a fabulous structure in which coincidence and convergence play a determining role. Time and space condense in strange ways, like language itself, and produce absurdly packed puns of fate. What is a clue, for instance, but a symbolic or condensed corpse, a living trace or materialized shadow? It shrinks space into place (furniture, and so forth) exactly as a bullet potentially shrinks or sensitizes time. The underdetermined or quasi-invisible becomes, by a reversal, so overdetermined and sharply visible that it is once again hard on the eyes. Bullet, clue, and pun have a comparable phenomenological shape: they are as magical in their power to heighten or oppress imagination as Balzac's "Oriental" device of the fatal skin[b] in *La Peau de Chagrin*.

Is it less Oriental, magical, or punning when, in a Ross Macdonald story, the same gun is used for killings fifteen years apart or the murders of father and then son take place in the same spot also fifteen years apart (*The Underground Man*)? Or when, as in *The Chill*, a man's "mother" turns out to be his wife? Or when, in Mrs. Radcliffe's *Romance of the Forest*, a marriageable girl happens to be brought to the very castle chamber where her true father was killed while she was still an infant? Recall also the speed with which things move in *Oedipus Rex*, and how a messenger who on entry is simply a UPI runner from Corinth proves to be an essential link in Oedipus' past, part of the chain that preserved him from death and for a second death—the consciousness to befall him. There is nothing more fearfully condensed than the self-image Oedipus is left with: "A man who entered his father's bed, wet with his father's blood."

I am haunted therefore by André Breton's image of "le revolver aux cheveux blancs." There has always been something like this grayhaired gun, some magic weapon in the service of superrealism. The movie camera that "shoots" a scene is the latest version of this venerable gadget. Our reality-hunger, our desire to know the worst and the best, is hard to satisfy. In Sophocles' day it was oracular speech that prowled the streets and intensified the consciousness of men. "This day will show your birth *and* will destroy you." Try to imagine how Tiresias' prophecy can come to pass. A lifetime must depend on a moment or on one traumatic recognition.

Tragedy as an art that makes us remember death is not unlike a memory vestige forcing us back to birth—to the knowledge that man is born of woman rather than self-born, that he is a dependent and mortal being. We become conscious of human time. The detective story, however, allows *place* to turn the tables on *time* by means of its decisive visual reanimations. The detective's successful pursuit of vestiges turns them into quasi-immortal spores; and while this resusci-

---

[b] A magical skin that gave its possessor certain powers, but shrank in proportion to his use of these powers.—Eds.

tation of the past partakes of the uncanny,[7] it also neatly confines the deadly deed or its consequences to a determinate, visualized, field.

This observation brings me to a central if puzzling feature of the popular mystery. Its plot idea tends to be stronger than anything the author can make of it. The *surnaturel* is *expliqué*,[c] and the djinni returned to the bottle by a trick. For the mystery story has always been a genre in which appalling facts are made to fit into a rational or realistic pattern. The formula dominating it began to emerge with the first instance of the genre, Horace Walpole's *Castle of Otranto* (1764), which begins when a child who is the heir apparent of a noble house is killed by the enormous helmet of an ancestral statue which buries him alive. After this ghostly opening Walpole's novel moves, like its descendants, from sensation to simplification, from bloody riddle to quasi-solution, embracing as much "machinery" as possible on the way.

The conservative cast of the mystery story is a puzzle. Born in the Enlightenment, it has not much changed. As mechanical and manipulative as ever, it explains the irrational, after exploiting it, by the latest rational system: Macdonald, for instance, likes to invent characters whose lives have Freudian or oedipal explanations. In *The Underground Man*, the murderer turns out to be a murderess, a possessive mother with an overprotected son. The real underground man is the underground woman. With a sense of family nightmare as vivid as it is in Walpole, the novel advances inward, from the discovery of the corpse to the frozen psyche of the murderess, Mrs. Snow. All the characters are efficiently, even beautifully sketched, but they are somehow too understandable. They seem to owe as much to formula as the plot itself, which moves deviously yet inexorably toward a solution of the mystery.

A good writer, of course, will makes us feel the gap between a mystery and its laying to rest. He will always write in a way that resists the expected ending: not simply to keep us guessing (for, as Edmund Wilson remarked, "The secret is nothing at all") but to show us more about life—that is, about the way people die while living. What is uncovered is not death but death-in-life.[8]

[c]"The supernatural is explained."—Eds.

Perhaps endings (resolutions) are always weaker than beginnings, and not only in the "explained mystery" kind of detective story. What entropy is involved? Pynchon's *The Crying of Lot 49,* more imaginative than Mailer's *Barbary Shore,* and one of the few genuinely comic treatments in America of the detective story formula, suggests an answer. It is not simply a matter of beginnings and endings but of two sorts of repetition, one of which is magical or uncanny, the other deadly to spirit. Magical repetition releases us into the symbol: a meaning that sustains us while we try to thread secondary causes, trivialities, middles-and-muddles—the rich wastings of life in pre-energy-conserving America. As Pynchon's novel unfolds, we are literally wasted by its riches; those cries and sights; that treasure of trash; and to redeem it all only the notion of anamnesis, which reintroduces the idea of a "first" cause, counterbalances the drag:

> *She was meant to remember.* . . . She touched the edge of its voluptuous field, knowing it would be lovely beyond dreams simply to submit to it; that not gravity's pull, laws of ballistics, feral ravening, promised more delight. She tested it, shivering: I am meant to remember. Each clue that comes is *supposed* to have its own clarity, its fine chances for permanence. But then she wondered if the gem-like "clues" were only some kind of compensation. To make up for her having lost the direct, epileptic Word, the cry that might abolish the night.

Oedipa's vision of being trapped in an "excluded middle," that is, having to desire always some first or last event that would resolve life in terms of something or nothing, meaning or meaninglessness, is reenforced, in the novel's last pages, by a haunting blend of metaphors:

> It was like walking among matrices of a great digital computer, the zeros and ones twinned above, hanging like balanced mobiles right and left, ahead, thick, maybe endless. Behind the hieroglyphic streets there would either be a transcendent meaning, or only the earth. . . . either an accommodation reached, in some kind of dignity, with the Angel of Death, or only death and the daily, tedious preparations for it.

If Pynchon's novel ends strongly, it is because it doesn't end. "It's time to start," says Genghis Cohen, of the auction, and by a kind of "honest forgery" (a sustained theme in the book) we find ourselves with Oedipa, absurdly, lyrically, at the threshold of yet another initiation.[9] This outwitting of "the direct, epileptic Word" is like purifying the imagination of *tò pathos;* for the ritual "crying" evoked but not rendered at the close of Pynchon's book is simply a version of that "long-distance" call which perhaps began everything.

The detective story structure—strong beginnings and endings and a deceptively rich, counterfeit, "excludable" middle—resembles almost too much that of symbol or trope.[10] Yet the recent temptation of linguistic theorists to collapse narrative structure into this or that kind of metaphoricity becomes counterproductive if it remains blind to the writer's very struggle to outwit the epileptic Word. Take a less symbolic novel than Pynchon's, one in the European tradition of self-conscious realism. In Alfred Andersch's *Efraim's Book* the narrator generates an entire novel by writing *against* a final disclosure.[11] Efraim keeps interpolating new incidents, although he knows the book will trump him in the end. A journalist shuttling between London, Berlin, and Rome, he is moved to write a book whose climax is the embarrassing secret he continually delays telling. Efraim is a post-Auschwitz Jew and uprooted intellectual who broods on the human condition, yet the secret obsessing him is simply that his wife is unfaithful. It is as if Andersch wants to reduce the dilemmas of moral existence in postwar Europe to a humiliating sexual disclosure.

We are not deceived by this deflation any more than by the inflated secret of detective stories. I prefer Andersch's novel, a work of political and artistic intelligence, to most mystery stories, but there is much in it that suggests it is in flight from the detective novel mood—from a "mystery" too great to face. What if Efraim, after Auschwitz, had assumed the role of hero-detective and investigated that crime in order to fix its guilt with moral and visual precision? An impossible project: there is no language for it. Efraim thinks he is writing to delay facing a painful ending but he is really writing against the terror and intractability of historical events which the mind cannot resolve or integrate. He chooses a substitute secret, the infidelity of his wife, to keep himself writing, and moving into ordinary life. *Efraim's Book* has no formal ending other than the decision of the writer to accept himself: to accept to survive, in spite of Auschwitz and the defiling reality of posthumous existence.

Most popular mysteries are devoted to solving rather than examining a problem. Their reasonings put reason to sleep, abolish darkness by elucidation, and bury the corpse for good. Few detective novels want the reader to exert his intelligence fully, to find gaps in the plot or the reasoning, to worry about the moral question of fixing the blame. They are exorcisms, stories with happy endings that could be classified with comedy because they settle the unsettling. As to the killer, he is often a bogeyman chosen by the "finger" of the writer after it has wavered suspensefully between this and that person for the right number of pages.

There exists, of course, a defense of the mystery story as art, whose principal document is Raymond Chandler's *The Simple Art of Murder*. In his moving last pages about the gritty life of the hero-detective, Chandler claims that mystery stories create a serious fictional world:

> It is not a fragrant world, but it is the world you live in, and certain writers with tough minds and a cool spirit of detachment can make very interesting and even amusing patterns out of it. . . . In everything that can be called art there is a quality of redemption. It may be pure tragedy, if it is high tragedy, and it may be pity and irony, and it may be the raucous laughter of the strong man. But down these mean streets a man must go who is not himself mean, who is neither tarnished nor afraid. . . . He is a common man or he would not go among common people. He has a sense of character, or he would not know his job. He will take no man's money dishonestly and no man's insolence without a due and dispassionate revenge. . . . He talks as the man of his age talks—that is, with rude wit, a lively sense for the grotesque, a disgust for sham, and a contempt for pettiness. The story is this man's adventure in search of hidden truth.

Ross Macdonald has also defended the social and psychological importance of the detective story and described it as rooted "in the popular and literary tradition of the American frontier." Neither writer puts much emphasis on problem solving, on finding out who killed Roger Ackroyd. But as the claims grow for the honesty, morality, and the authentic American qualities of the detective novel, one cannot overlook the ritual persistence of the problem-solving formula.

Only in France has the eye of the private eye been thoroughly questioned. I have mentioned Robbe-Grillet; his collaboration with Resnais on films like *Marienbad* is also significant in this respect. What is missing from *Marienbad*, yet endlessly suggested, is *tò pathos*. Nothing moves us so much as when the image on the screen tries to escape at certain points a voice that would pin it down to one room, one bed, one time, one identity. Yet the screen image cannot be "framed": by remaining a moving picture it defeats our wish to spot the flagrant act, or to have speech and spectacle coincide. The scene of pathos—call it "Hiroshima," "Marienbad," or "Auschwitz"—eludes the mind it haunts.

A danger, of course, is the closeness of all this not only to mobile dreaming but also to erotic fantasy. The inbuilt voyeurism of the camera eye makes love and death interchangeable subjects. It cannot distinguish between these "mysteries" because of the mind's hunger for reality, its restless need to spot, or give the lie to, one more secret. It seeks to arrest the eyes yet is never satisfied with the still or snapshot that reveals all.

After writers like Andersch and Robbe-Grillet, one turns with relief to Ross Macdonald and the naive reality-hunger of American detective fiction. In *The Underground Man* Macdonald keeps entirely within the problem-solving formula but broadens it by providing a great California fire as the background. This fire is an "ecological crisis" linked more than fortuitously to the cigarillo dropped by Stanley Broadhurst, the murdered son. Stanley belongs to a "generation whose elders had been poisoned, like the pelicans, with a kind of moral DDT that damaged the lives of their young." By combining ecological and moral contamination Macdonald creates a double plot that spreads the crime over the California landscape.

California becomes a kind of "open city" where everyone seems related to everyone else through, ironically, a breakdown in family relations that spawns adolescent gangs and other new groupings. The only personal detail we learn about the detective, Lew Archer, is that his wife has left him, which is what we might expect. Neither cynical nor eccentric, Archer resembles an ombudsman or public defender rather than a tough detective. He doesn't seem to have a private office, often being approached by his clients in public. One might say he doesn't have clients since anyone can engage his moral sympathy.

He is, then, as Chandler prescribed, a catalyst, not a Casanova, who sees more sharply than others do. It is curious how the detective, as a type, is at the same time an ingénue and a man of experience—his reasoning must take evil or criminal motives into account, but through his eyes we enjoy the colors of the familiar world. Like other realistic artists, the good crime writer makes the familiar new, but he can do so only under the pressure of extreme situations. It is as if crime alone could make us see again, or imaginatively enough, to enter someone else's life.

Archer is not better than what he sees but rather a knowing part of it. His observations (acute, overdefined, "Her eyes met me and blurred like cold windows") are those of an isolated, exposed man with a fragmented life. He finds just what he expects, people like himself, reluctantly free or on the run, and others equally lonely but still living within the shrinking embrace of an overprotective family. Yet just because Archer is so mobile and homeless he can bring estranged people together and evoke, as in *The Underground Man,* a consoling myth of community where there is none.

It is a myth only for the time being, perhaps only for the time of the book. Down these polluted freeways goes a man with undimmed vision, cutting through sentimental fog and fiery smog to speak face to face in motel or squalid rental or suburban ranch with Mr. and Mrs. and Young America! Superb in snapshot portraiture of California life, Macdonald gives us a sense of the wildlife flushed out by the smoke, the way people lean on one another when they fear crime and fire. They are neatly described by Archer, who moves among them as erratically as the fire itself.

This panoramic realism has its advantages. It is outward and visual rather than introspective, and so tends to simplify character and motive. There is a terrible urge—in Raymond Chandler even more than in Ross Macdonald—to make the most of gross visual impressions. Hence, Moose Malloy in Chandler's *Farewell, My Lovely,* "a big man but not more than six feet five inches tall and no wider than a beer truck" who "looked about as inconspicuous as a tarantula on a slice of angel food." The images flash all around us like guns, though we can't always tell to what end. Their overall aim is to make the world as deceptively conspicuous as Moose Malloy.

The detective (American style) tortures human nature until it reveals itself. People froth or lose their nerve or crumple up: the divine eye of the private eye fixes them until their bodies incriminate them. What can't be seen can't be judged; and even if what we get to see is a nasty array of protective maneuvers and defense mechanisms, the horror of the visible is clearly preferred to what is unknown or invisible.

There are, of course, differences of style among American mystery story writers. Macdonald's characters, for example, are more credible than Chandler's, because they are more ordinary, or less bizarre. Chandler is often on the verge of surrealism, of tragicomic slapstick: the first meeting between Marlowe and Carmen Sternwood in *The Big Sleep* goes immediately as far as a relation can go, short of complicity. The novels of Chandler and Macdonald have nevertheless the same basic flaw: the only person in them whose motives remain somewhat mysterious, or exempt from this relentless reduction to overt and vulnerable gestures, is the detective.

Yet Chandler's Marlowe is not really mysterious. Just as in his world punks are punks, old generals old generals, and the small guys remain small guys killed by small-time methods (liquor spiked with cyanide), so a detective is a detective:

> "The first time we met I told you I was a detective. Get it through your lovely head. I work at it, lady. I don't play at it."

When Marlowe is asked why he doesn't marry, he answers "I don't like policemen's wives." To marry Mr. Detective means becoming Mrs. Detective. Nothing here is immune from specializations: you can hire killers or peekers or produce sex or sell friendliness. Identities are roles changed from time to time yet as physically clear as warts or fingerprints. Your only hope is not being trapped by your *role* into an *identity*. Once you are marked, or the bite is on you, fun is over. It is consequently a clownish world: grotesque, manic, evasive, hilariously sad. Chandleresque is not far from Chaplinesque.

The one apparent superiority of the detective is that although he can be hired, he doesn't care for money (even if he respects its power). We really don't know whether the other characters care for it either, but they are placed in situations where they *must* have it—to make a getaway, for instance—or where it is the visible sign of grace, of their power to dominate and so to survive. What Marlowe says to a beautiful woman who offers him money is puzzlingly accurate: "You don't owe me anything. I'm paid off." Puzzling because it is unclear where his real satisfaction comes from. He seems under no compulsion to dominate others and rarely gets pleasure from taking gambles. What is there in it for him? The money is only expense money. We don't ever learn who is paying off the inner Marlowe or Archer. Their motives are virtually the only things in these stories that are not visible.

We are forced to assume that the detective is in the service of no one—or of a higher power. Perhaps there is an idealism in these tough tales stronger than the idealisms they are out to destroy.

> I sat down on a pink chair and hoped I wouldn't leave a mark on it. I lit a Camel, blew smoke through my nose, and looked at a piece of black shiny metal on a stand. It showed a full, smooth curve with a small fold in it and two protuberances on the curve. I stared at it. Marriott saw me staring at it. "An interesting bit," he said negligently. "I picked it up the other day. Asta Dial's *Spirit of Dawn.*" "I thought it was Klopstein's *Two Warts on a Fanny,*" I said.

This is merely a sideshow, but behind other and comparable scenes big questions are being raised: of reality, justice, mercy, and loyalty. When Lew Archer says, "I think it started before Nick was born, and that his part is fairly innocent," he begins to sound theological, especially when he continues, "I can't promise to get him off the hook entirely. But I hope to prove he's a victim, a patsy" *(The Goodbye Look).*

The moral issues, however, are no more genuinely explored than the murders. They, too, are corpses—or ghosts that haunt us in the face of intractable situations. So in *The Goodbye Look,* a man picks up an eight-year-old boy and makes a pass at him. Boy shoots man. But the man is the boy's estranged father and the seduction was only an act of sentiment and boozy affection. Grim mistakes of this kind belong to folklore or to high tragedy. The detective story, however, forces them into a strict moralistic pattern or, as in Ross Macdonald, into a psychoanalytic parable with complicated yet resolvable turns.

Since man does not live on tragedy alone, and since the crime story could be considered a folk genre, this may seem no condemnation.

There is, however, an exploitative element in all this: our eyes ache to read more, to see more, to know that the one just man (the detective) will succeed—yet when all is finished, nothing is rereadable. Instead of a Jamesian reticence that, at best, chastens the detective urge—our urge to know or penetrate intimately another person's world—the crime novel incites it artificially by a continuous, self-canceling series of overstatements, drawing us into one false hypothesis or flashy scene after another.

Thus, the trouble with the detective novel is not that it is moral but that it is moralistic; not that it is popular but that it is stylized; not that it lacks realism but that it picks up the latest realism and exploits it. A voracious formalism dooms it to seem unreal, however "real" the world it describes. In fact, as in a B movie, we value less the driving plot than moments of lyricism and grotesquerie that creep into it: moments that detach themselves from the machined narrative. Macdonald's California fire affects us less because of its damage to the ecology than because it brings characters into the open. It has no necessary relation to the plot, and assumes a life of its own. The fire mocks the ambitions of this kind of novel: it seems to defy manipulation.

Crime fiction today seems to be trying to change its skin and transform itself (on the Chandler pattern) into picaresque American morality tales. But its second skin is like the first. It cannot get over its love–hate for the mechanical and the manipulative. Even mysteries that do not have a Frankensteinian monster or superintelligent criminal radiate a pretechnological chill. The form trusts too much in reason; its very success opens to us the glimpse of a mechanized world, whether controlled by God or Dr. No or the Angel of the Odd.

When we read a popular crimi we do not think of it as great art but rather as "interesting" art. And our interest, especially in the hard-boiled tale of American vintage, has to do more with its social, or sociological, than with its realistic implications. I don't believe for a moment that Chandler and Macdonald tell it like it is, but perhaps they reveal in an important way why they can't tell it like it is. The American "realist in murder," says Chandler, has purged the guilty vicarage, exiled the amateurs, thrown out Lord Peter Wimsey cum chicken-wing-gnawing debutantes. We therefore go to the American tale expecting a naked realism. What do we find, however? A vision that remains as before, a mixture of sophisticated and puerile elements.

The American hero-detective is not what Chandler claims he is, "a complete man." He starts with death, it is true; he seems to stand beyond desire and regret. Yet the one thing the hard-boiled detective fears, with a gamblerlike fascination, is being played for a *sucker*. In Hammett's *Maltese Falcon* the murder of Miles, who trusted Miss Wonderly, begins the action; Spade's rejection of Brigid O'Shaughnessy completes it. To gamble on Brigid is like gambling that love exists, or that there is, somewhere, a genuine Falcon. Spade draws back: "I won't play the sap for you."

No wonder this type of story is full of tough baby talk. So Archer in *The Chill:*

"No more guns for you," I said.
No more anything, Letitia.

Taking the gun from Letitia, at the end of *The Chill,* is like denying a baby its candy. It seems a "castration" of the woman, which turns her into a child once more.

In Ross Macdonald's novels the chief victim is usually a child who needs protection from the father or society and gets it from Momma as overprotection—which is equally fatal. Enter the dick who tries to save the child and purge the Momma. Children are always shown as so imprisoned by the grown-up world that they can't deal with things as they are; and so the child remains a "sucker." There is often little difference between family and police in this respect. The psychiatrist is another overprotector. "They brought me to Dr. Smitheram," Nick says bitterly in *The Goodbye Look,* "and . . . I've been with him ever since. I wish I'd gone to the police in the first place." The detective alone is exempt from ties of blood or vested interest, and so can expose what must be exposed.

Both the arrested development of the detective story and its popularity seem to me related to its image of the way people live in "civilized" society—a just image on the whole. For we all know something is badly wrong with the way society or the family protects people. The world of the detective novel is full of vulnerable characters on the one hand, and of overprotected ones on the other. Macdonald complicates the issue by emphasizing the wrong done to children, and especially to their psyches. Dolly in *The Chill,* Nick Chalmers in *The Goodbye Look,* and Susan Crandall in *The Underground Man* are as much victims of what Freud calls family romance (that is, family nightmare) as of society. We don't know what to protest, and sympathize with the adolescents in *The Underground Man* who kidnap a young boy to prevent him from being sacrificed to the grown-up world.

Yet "protective custody" doesn't work. In *The Chill,* relations between Roy and Letitia Bradshaw are a classic and terrible instance of the man being forced to remain a man-boy as the price of making it. Roy, the social climber, marries a rich woman who can send him to Harvard and free him from class bondage. But the woman is old enough to be his mother and they live together officially as mother and son while she kills off younger women to whom her "child" is attracted.

Protection, such novels seem to imply, is always bought; and much of the price one pays for it is hidden. Macdonald tends to give a psychological and Chandler a sociological interpretation of this. Chandler is strongly concerned with the need for a just system of protection and the inadequacy of modern institutions to provide it. He indulges, like so many other crime writers, in conventional woman hating, but suggests at the same time that women become bitches because they are overprotected. Helen Grayle, in *Farewell, My Lovely,* is the exemplary victim who (like the Sternwood sisters in *The Big Sleep*) is allowed to get some revenge on her "protectors" before she is caught. Yet Chandler often lets his women criminals escape, knowing sadly or bitterly that they'll be trapped by the system in the end.

To avoid being a sucker and to expose a crisis in the protective institutions of society are psychological and social themes that are not peculiar to the American detective novel. They have prevailed since chivalric romance invented the distressed damsel and her wandering knight. But the precise kinds of family breakup, together with new and menacing groups (similar to crime syndicates) which the detective is pitted against, give crime novels a modern American tone. That the detective is a *private* sleuth defines, moreover, his character as well as his profession, and makes him the heir to a popular American myth —he is the latest of the uncooptable heroes.

Yet detective stories remain schizophrenic. Their rhythm of surprising reversals—from casual to crucial or from laconic detail to essential clue—is a factor. The deepest reversals involve, of course, feelings about the blood tie. As in Greek tragedy *pathos* is strongest when there is death in the family. The thrill of a "thriller" is surely akin to the fear that the murderer will prove to be not an outsider but someone there all the time, someone we know only too well—perhaps a blood relation.[12]

In Macdonald's fiction human relations tend to polarize: they are either quasi-incestuous (Roy and Letitia Bradshaw in *The Chill*) or markedly exogamous, exhibiting that inclination to strangers so characteristic of the hero-detective. It is as if our kinship system had suffered a crazy split. There seems to be no mean between the oppressive family ("I felt . . . as if everything in the room was still going on, using up space and air. I was struck by the thought that Chalmers, with family history breathing down his neck, may have felt smothered and cramped most of the time") and the freewheeling detective. Nothing lies between the family and the loner but a no man's land of dangerous communes: virile fraternities, like criminal mobs or the police, which are literally based on blood.

It is, then, an exceptional moment when we find Lew Archer lingering with Stanley Broadhurst's widow and her young son, at the end of *The Underground Man*. For one moment the family exists and the detective is the father. The woman touches him lightly, intimately. It ends there, on that caress, which already has distance and regret in it. We must soon return, like the detective, to a world of false fathers and disabled mothers, to children as exposed as Oedipus or Billy Budd, and to a continuing search for manifest justice. "O city, city!" *(Oedipus Rex).*

NOTES

1. S. H. Butcher, ed. and trans., *Aristotle's Theory of Poetry and Fine Art*, 4th ed., XI.6 (1452b 9–13). There is a second brief mention at XIV.4 (1453b 17–22).
2. See Gerald Else, *Aristotle's Poetics* (Cambridge, Mass., 1967), pp. 356–58.
3. See Jacques Barzun, "The Novel Turns Tale," *Mosaic* 4 (1971): 33–40.
4. The elliptical "cuts" of Eliot's *The Wasteland* often produce a similar

effect. Ellipsis joined to the technical principle of montage (in Eisenstein's conception) consolidate the international style we are describing.

5. *Maidstone* is a blatantly eclectic script-tease: it flirts with crime, sexploitation, politics, and film about film. Its plot consists of a wager by Norman T. Kingsley that the actors in the film will invent that scene of passion, he, the director, cannot or will not invent—that they will kill the King, that is, the director, that is, Norman.

6. For a straight psychoanalytic interpretation, see Marie Bonaparte, "The Murders in the Rue Morgue," *Psychoanalytic Quarterly* 4 (1935): 259–293; G. Pederson-Krag, "Detective Stories and the Primal Scene," *Psychoanalytic Quarterly* 18 (1949): 207–214 [reprinted in this volume—Eds.]; and, especially, Charles Rycroft, "The Analysis of a Detective Story" (1957) reprinted in his *Imagination and Reality* (London, 1968). I emphasize in what follows the eye rather than the cry; but, as in Wordsworth's ballad, there is often something ejaculative or quasi-inarticulate (a "tongue-tie," to use Melville's phrase in *Billy Budd*) accompanying.

7. See Freud's "The 'Uncanny' " (1919). His analysis of repetition, in relation to (ambivalent) reanimation may prove essential to any psychoesthetic theory of narrative. This may also be the point to introduce thematics, especially the thematics of the genius loci: animism, ghosts, ancestor consciousness, quasi-supernatural hauntings of particular places. Freud connects them either with memories of an intrauterine (oceanic) state or with the later illusion of "omnipotence of consciousness." In Poe, one might speculate, the mystery story is intrauterine Gothic while the detective story is omnipotence-of-consciousness modern. See also note 8.

8. This almost inverts the sense of the Gothic novel which Poe transformed into a modern tale of detection by dividing its mystery part from its rationalizing part. The mystery story, as he develops it, deals mainly with *vestiges* that intimate someone's *life-in-death*, and he exploits the horror of that thought. His detective stories tend to sublimate this theme of the "living dead" by demystifying vestiges as clues: signs of (and for) a persistent or mad or "omnipotent" consciousness. Frederic Jameson's "On Raymond Chandler," *Southern Review* 6 (1970): 624–650, gives an interesting account of how the "formal distraction" of the detective quest leads into genuine revelations of death-in-life. [Jameson's essay is reprinted in this volume.—Eds.]

9. Sterne's *Tristram Shandy* may be the original of this comic anamnesis which cannot begin (find the true starting point) and so cannot end.

10. See my "The Voice of the Shuttle" in *Beyond Formalism* (New Haven, 1970).

11. Andersch is a distinguished German journalist and man of letters who has written several novels and was one of the original members of the famous postwar association of writers called "Group '47."

12. Charles Brockden Brown's *Wieland* (1797) remains the classic instance of a pattern which recalls Freud's understanding of family ambivalences.

ALBERT D. HUTTER

Dreams, Transformations, and Literature: The Implications of Detective Fiction

For Hutter, detective fiction, like dream interpretation, "involves the transformation of a fragmented and incomplete set of events into a more ordered and complete understanding." He believes that in the best detective fiction this "understanding" is never merely a solution based on the uncovering of hidden facts but rather a deeper comprehension of some aspect of human nature. To illustrate his position, he shows how Wilkie Collins's The Moonstone, *despite its clear affinities with standard detective puzzle-narratives and with psychoanalytic dream-allegories, cannot be reduced to either. To discover hidden facts of infantile wish-fulfillment fantasies is never fully to explain the meaning or the function of a dream or a first-rate detective novel. What the two have in common, Hutter argues, is a latent structure based on confrontation and the active resolution of conflicts. What this structure reveals is the dynamic nature of human relations and the human personality.*

Hutter's essay builds on Pederson-Krag's and complements Hartman's. Albert D. Hutter teaches English at UCLA. This article first appeared in Victorian Studies *in 1975.*

Freud characterizes the dream as the fulfillment of a wish. . . . If you would . . . propose to chart this field by offering better terms, by all means do so. But better terms are the only kind of refutation here that is worth the trouble.[1]

Dreams have always provided the standard psychoanalytic analogy to the work of art: as we interpret the dream or analyze the dreamer, so we interpret literature or make deductions about the psyche of the artist. But the psychoanalytic theory of dreaming has undergone a radical revision in the past twenty years—perhaps the most dramatic alteration of any Freudian model in current psychoanalytic thought. The literary model needs to be changed accordingly, particularly because it continues to be attacked for a reductionism which is mistakenly, or belatedly, ascribed to psychoanalysis as a whole. . . .[a]

II

Detective fiction involves the transformation of a fragmented and incomplete set of events into a more ordered and complete understanding. As such it seems to bridge a private psychological experience, like dreaming, and literary experience in general. And like a psychoanalysis, the detective story reorders our perception of the past through language. Although psychoanalysis and detective fiction are so different in conscious design and intent, they share a significant structural relationship, just as they share a close historical relationship: *The Moonstone*[b] (1868) was the first full-length English detective novel, and it preceded Freud's first work on hysteria by less than twenty-five years.

The Moonstone is the prototypical detective novel. It combines a narrative structure that is thoroughly subjective and unreliable with the characteristic action of all detective fiction: the restatement and restructuring in the present of a past event. Thus, the detective stories of Edgar Allan Poe and Arthur Conan Doyle begin with the recent impact of a crime and work backward to restructure the incomplete fragments of present knowledge into a more intelligible whole and

---

[1] Kenneth Burke, *The Philosophy of Literary Form*, 3rd ed. (Berkeley: University of California Press, 1973), p. 272.
[a] In the original essay there followed a long first section outlining Freud's theory of the dream as the disguised fulfillment of a wish and tracing the many ways in which this theory has been modified since Freud's time. Because of space limitations, we have regretfully omitted this section as not directly related to the subject of this anthology. Readers especially interested in dream theory will find these pages valuable and should consult them in the original essay.—Eds.
[b] By Wilkie Collins.—Eds.

consequently to explain the past. A total reliance on intellectual restatement fostered, in the early part of this century, a series of sterile subgenres, like the stories of pure puzzle or the tales from the badly misnamed "Golden Age of Detection." What saves Poe and Conan Doyle from sterility is not that, like Collins, they came first, but that the relentlessly logical process of ratiocination is thrown into question by a deeper irrationality. Dupin seeks the dominance of pure intellect, but, as with Holmes, there is always the presence of some profound personal disturbance which impinges on the apparently objective vision of the detective; Dupin, "enamored of the Night for her own sake,"[2] loathe to interact with others except at a distance and through a distancing mind, anticipates Holmes and his need for seclusion, his addictions and depressions.

Not only are the objective and the rational called into question by the subjective and intuitive vision of the detective, but they are made to appear as two faces of the same coin. This duality is essential in Poe's "Purloined Letter": the ingenuity of the police blocks their discovery of the truth, whereas Dupin provides instead a combination of poetic imagination and "mathematical" reasoning. Stories of pure puzzle fail to sustain a tension in the reader between mystery and solution. When we read such stories we are driven to anticipate the plot and deduce, in advance, the solution to the crime; but if we succeed, the work is a failure. In Poe, the essential interest is not so much in solution as it is in recognition, testing the limits of rational deduction in a world of subjectivity and deceit, a world ultimately irrational. Just as the reader is meant to identify with the relentless logic of Dupin, he is also forced to recognize another part of his own personality which is uncivilized and instinctual, like the ape of the Rue Morgue.[3] Collins connected the elements of rational detection

[2]James A. Harrison, "The Murders in the Rue Morgue," in *The Complete Works of Edgar Allan Poe*, edited by James A. Harrison (New York: Crowell, 1902), III, 151.
[3]Marie Bonaparte was one of the first to point to the connection between the orangutan and man's instinctual life: *The Life and Works of Edgar Allan Poe*, translated by John Rodker (London: Imago Press, 1949), p. 445. Also see: Richard Wilbur, "The Poe Mystery Case," The New York Review of Books, 13 July 1967, p. 25; Daniel Hoffman. *Poe Poe Poe Poe Poe Poe Poe* (Garden City, N.Y.: Doubleday, 1972), pp. 112–115; and David Halliburton, *Edgar Allan Poe: A Phenomenological View* (Princeton, N.J.: Princeton University Press, 1973), pp. 237–245. Halliburton offers an excellent phenomenological account of Poe and the detective genre. For a more general study of the genre see A. E. Murch. *The Development of the Detective Novel* (London: Peter Owen, 1958).

with subjective distortion in *The Moonstone's* narrative structure itself, forcing us to build a rational solution from the distorted and fragmented visions of his individual narrators. The novel begins with the tale of a priceless Indian diamond, "passed . . . from one lawless . . . hand to another,"⁴ and the possession of the diamond leads again to theft and murder when it is taken by Colonel John Herncastle at the seige of Seringapatam. The colonel maliciously wills the gem to his niece, Rachel Verinder, on her eighteenth birthday, knowing that it carries a curse with it, a curse materially aided by three ruthless Brahmans who have devoted their lives to returning the diamond, at any cost, to their moon-god. Rachel's cousin, Franklin Blake, brings her the moonstone and then, it seems, steals it during the night of her birthday celebration. Rachel, we learn much later, has seen him do so and is even more outraged by Franklin's hypocritical attempt to catch the thief, for it is Franklin who thinks to call in Inspector Cuff from London. Several romances are twisted into these events: Rachel and Franklin fall in love with each other; Rosanna Spearman, a misshapen servant girl with a criminal past, falls hopelessly in love with Franklin and behaves mysteriously in what seems to be an effort to help him cover his crime; Godfrey Ablewhite, a too-charming philanthropist, pursues the reluctant Rachel and almost succeeds in the aftermath of her disappointment in Franklin. The Hindus appear and disappear, along with servants, clairvoyants, pawnbrokers, lady philanthropists, and lawyers, in a setting that ranges from India through London to the Brontë-like Yorkshire coast where Rosanna kills herself. Collins makes use of his own intimate knowledge of opium to provide a suitable final twist. A local doctor, Ezra Jennings, helps Franklin to reconstruct the crime. He discovers that Franklin did indeed take the stone, unknowingly, out of his anxiety over its safety and while under the influence of opium. He reproduces Frank-

⁴Wilkie Collins, *The Moonstone*, 3 vols. (London: Tinsley Brothers, 1868), prologue, pt. III. All future references are to this edition. For an analysis of Collins and detective fiction see Dorothy Sayers's "Introduction" to *The Moonstone* (London: J. M. Dent, 1944); J. I. M. Stewart's "Introduction" to *The Moonstone* (Middlesex: Penguin Books, 1966); and Robert P. Ashley, "Wilkie Collins and the Detective Story," *Nineteenth-Century Fiction*, VI (1951), 47–60. Ashley's article is a good summary of the detective elements in all of Collins's fiction, although I believe he misreads *The Moonstone* by insisting on its formalaic adherence to the sensation novel. The most complete and balanced current appraisal of Collins is William H. Marshall, *Wilkie Collins* (New York: Twayne, 1970).

lin's original state on the night of the theft and succeeds in solving part of the mystery. With the discovery of a murdered Ablewhite, the real thief who had seen Franklin pick up the stone and had relieved Franklin of it while he slept, the solution is completed. The novel ends where it began, in India, with the stone restored to its rightful place.

This intricate tale is further complicated by a prologue that describes the theft of the jewel at the seige of Seringapatam, a three-part epilogue that traces the jewel back from England to India where it is restored, and the nine-part narration itself, in which each narrator tells his tale for different reasons and with different information—or misinformation. Old Betteredge, the Verinder family steward, contributes twice to the narrative, as does Franklin Blake: Betteredge because he is asked, Franklin because he wants to clarify further his own innocence and to bring together all the threads of the story. Miss Clack, a family retainer, writes because she is paid to do so, and others —like Dr. Candy—contribute unknowingly. Collins achieves verisimilitude by this method, and he is legitimately able to withhold important information from the reader, delaying the solution while increasing the story's suspense. But the most important function of this complex narration is its involvement of the reader in a wealth— or morass—of contradictory detail. We must experience the confusion of observation and of report until we can decipher the language of the text, probe its ambiguities and contradictions and symbolism in order fully to understand the crime itself. Detective fiction is the peculiarly modern distillation of a general literary experience that makes central the subtle interaction with, and interpretation of, language.

Detective fiction is generally conceived of as an offshoot of the Gothic or some combination of Gothic romance and the detailed realism associated with the rise of the novel. But this purely literary genealogy ignores the historical rise of the detective police and their relationship to a form of fiction that is essentially urban. England needed the New Police only when the older forms of self-policing in a rural or restricted urban area were obviously inadequate. City slums provided a safe warren for what eventually became a popular and elaborately organized system of lower-class employment—as Mayhew eloquently testifies—and the middle classes required protection to deal with the increasingly puzzling and anonymous face of crime as it rapidly evolved into that "organized crime" which now reflects the modern corporate state. Crime, like the Victorian city, was growing, diffuse, confusing, materialistic, and violent largely in proportion to material deprivation and exclusion. The first function of the new detective police was the preservation of property and the protection of the middle-class consumer; the police were needed to "read" a city which had grown far beyond the easy knowledge of its inhabitants. They were part of that elaborately constructed social system which developed in response to a bewildering jump in technology, and it is no accident that railway timetables and telegraphic communication were almost instantly absorbed into the fictional representation of detection.

The first fictional detectives were amateur scientists. They were also first-rate actors (Dupin's bluffing the minister, Holmes's impersonations, Bucket's disguises). The ability to impersonate, to identify with, and to reproduce the idiosyncratic behavior of the criminal, characterizes the way in which Dickens portrayed Bucket's original, Inspector Field. Like Bucket, Field uses his knowledge to pierce to the very heart of a labyrinthine city and identify that larger disease which affects all levels of society.[5] Detectives are thus inevitably concerned with the problem of knowledge, a problem only intensified by the urban upheaval of the world in which they move, by the disorder, the multiplicity of detail, the constant impinging presence of other people, other accounts, other viewpoints.

A confusion of subjective and objective knowledge is present everywhere in *The Moonstone*. It shows itself, for example, as the central conflict in the hero's personality, epitomized by his foreign education:

> ... he had come back with so many different sides to his character, all more or less jarring with each other, that he seemed to pass his life in a state of perpetual contradiction with himself.... He had his French side, and his German side, and his Italian side—the original English foundation showing through, every now and then ...
>
> (first period, chap. 6)

[5] See particularly "On Duty with Inspector Field," *The Nonesuch Dickens: Reprinted Pieces* (Bloomsbury: The Nonesuch Press, 1938), pp. 177–189. See also Elliot L. Gilbert, "The Detective as Metaphor in the Nineteenth Century," in Francis M. Nevins, ed., *The Mystery Writer's Art* (Bowling Green, Ohio: Bowling Green University Popular Press, 1970), pp. 285–293.

When Franklin is left with time to himself, "it let out all the foreign sides of his character, one on the top of another, like rats out of a bag" (first period, chap. 22). And Franklin, in despair over Rachel's treatment of him, mocks his own confusion as he argues that Rachel is not really Rachel but someone else:

> "Now, being in a state of nervous excitement, how are we to expect that she should behave as she might otherwise have behaved to any of the people about her? Arguing in this way, from within-outwards, what do we reach? We reach the Subjective view. I defy you to controvert the Subjective view. Very well then—what follows? Good Heavens! the Objective-Subjective explanation follows, of course! Rachel, properly speaking, is *not* Rachel, but Somebody Else. Do I mind being cruelly treated by Somebody Else? You are unreasonable enough, Betteredge; but you can hardly accuse me of that. Then how does it end? It ends, in spite of your confounded English narrowness and prejudice, in my being perfectly happy and comfortable. Where's the sherry?"
> (first period, chap. 22)

Here, the comedy reminds us that it is the very failure of the characters to know not only the motivation of others, but even their own minds, which has led to the central crime of the novel: Franklin's "theft," itself an unconscious act. The more we learn about the mystery, the more we are ourselves confused, in much the same way that Betteredge is confused by Franklin's sophistry: "My head was by this time in such a condition, that I was not quite sure whether it was my own head, or Mr. Franklin's" (first period, chap. 22). Rachel cannot decide on the basic moral nature of the hero or the villain, and her confusion adds to our own. Rosanna Spearman also deceives us, and so, in his way, does Cuff, who suspects Rachel. Even Miss Clack, if she can still amuse a modern audience, does so because of her perverse refusal to understand anyone's real motives, especially her own.

Collins contributes significantly to a changing fictional esthetic: verisimilitude is combined with intentional contradiction and subjective inconsistency; opposing viewpoints are the very basis for *The Moonstone*'s artistic integration. Collins had already experimented with multiple narration, and he was undoubtedly influenced by the double narrative of Dickens's *Bleak House*, which was also directly linked to *The Moonstone* because it was the first British novel to introduce a detective. But *The Moonstone,* and the rise of detective fiction generally, signal a more pervasive literary change. William Marshall writes that in *The Moonstone* "in the dramatic and ironic manipulation of character, in the exploration of the reality of the self lying beneath the personality, Collins reflected some of the serious intellectual concerns of his age" (Marshall, p. 82). In 1868 Robert Browning wrote *The Ring and the Book,* and like Collins, Browning builds carefully from fact, the true gold of the ring,[6] which is then shaped by a variety of subjective truths that add further meaning to the factual surface. Browning was more deliberate and self-conscious in his intentions than Collins, and art in his poem "shows the truth twice in that it shows the physical facts and the metaphysical meaning behind them"; art plays off detailed observation against imagination (Langbaum, p. 110).

The broader cultural shift which led to changes in narrative fiction reflects the nineteenth-century Englishman's fundamentally new perspective of himself, both politically and psychologically.[7] Collins's sensitivity to British colonial exploitation is apparent in the political moral of *The Moonstone,* which closes when the gem is restored to its proper and original shrine. In Collins's narrative everyone suffers who possesses the moonstone's wealth without a full right to such possession. As Dickens was to do two years later in *The Mystery of Edwin Drood,* Collins also exploits the racial prejudice of his characters—and readers. He creates a false solution to the mystery and

[6]Robert Langbaum, *The Poetry of Experience* (New York: Norton, 1963), p. 109.
[7]Sir Leslie Stephen is most interesting here as a representative Victorian—self-conscious and conscience-stricken—and his attitude is a product of battles like Seringapatam. Initially, Seringapatam seemed indicative of England's total domination of India. One nineteenth-century historian describes the battle and its importance for English colonization with obvious relish: "Seringapatam . . . was invested and reduced to extremities, and Tippoo Sahib was obliged to sign a peace, surrendering half his dominions to the allies, paying a sum of more than four million sterling in compensation for the war, releasing all his prisoners of war, and giving up two of his three sons as hostages to the English." (W. E. H. Lecky, *A History of England in the Eighteenth Century* [London: Longmans, 1887], p. 210.) But before the end of the nineteenth century Seringapatam, which had been ceded to the British, was restored to Mysore. For a detailed account of other connections between English colonization of India and *The Moonstone,* see John R. Reed, "English Imperialism and the Unacknowledged Crime of *The Moonstone," CLIO,* II (1973), 281–290. Reed oversimplifies the novel in arguing that "the Moonstone becomes the sign of England's imperial depredations—the symbol of a national rather than a personal crime" (p. 286), but he does convincingly connect Collins's novel with an English policy of exploitation.

attributes the crime to the Indians; Jennings is at first discredited by his strange appearance and "his complexion . . . of a gypsy darkness" (second period, chap. 4); even Ablewhite's final disguise, with black hair and a "swarthy" complexion, encourages our misperception and prejudice until the very end of the tale. And the mystery, fear, and prejudice associated with the Indians is built into the very structure of a novel, which is itself founded on prejudicial testimony, misunderstanding, and exploitation. The conflicting motives of disinterestedness and greed, love and exploitation, are made to coexist in the way the characters see themselves and, until the final solution, in the way the reader must regard the characters, as he regards them in virtually every detective story—with suspicion. The novel does end with a solution; but the reader's experience throughout *The Moonstone* is weighted the other way: it encourages us to distrust closure. This particular mystery may be solved, but the mystery of the characters and the shadowy space between their actions, their observations, and their intentions are meant to puzzle. The novelist himself has come to distrust his own fictional world.

New psychological theories, like the changing political attitudes of the mid-nineteenth century, are significant in Collins's solution to *The Moonstone*. Collins relies particularly on two medical authorities, Dr. William Benjamin Carpenter and Dr. John Elliotson, to introduce into his dialogue descriptions of preconscious thought, memory, and the related effects of drugs and hypnosis that authenticate "the physiological experiment which occupies a prominent place in the closing scenes of *The Moonstone*":

> Having first ascertained not only from books, but from living authorities as well, what the result of that experiment would really have been, I have declined to avail myself of the novelist's privilege of supposing something which might have happened, and have so shaped the story as to make it grow out of what actually would have happened—which, I beg to inform my readers, is also what actually does happen in these pages.
>
> (preface)

An admirable piece of reasoning, in which the final proof of the reality of an event is fictional. What Collins never reveals—although it is something his original readers would have known—is that Elliotson, in spite of a number of valuable contributions to physiology, had been regarded by many as a quack. He was eccentric in his dress and appearance, had an early reputation for prescribing large quantities of dangerous drugs, was founder and first president of the Phrenological Society, and was forced to resign his professorship at University College, London, because of his espousal of mesmerism. Carpenter, on the other hand, with a reputation for a careful and conservative approach to new scientific claims, was an eminent biologist and physiologist very much a part of the medical and scientific establishment, and a strong critic of mesmerism and phrenology. The basis for Collins's apparently factual authority is itself, then, contradictory—like the testimony of his characters or the confused evidence of the crime. Ezra Jennings resembles Elliotson, not only in his intelligence and imagination, but also in his role as outcast and quack. Bruff, for example, finds his experiment "like a piece of trickery, akin to the trickery of mesmerism, clairvoyance, and the like" (second period, fourth narrative). Like Cuff, he is an eccentric. It was as important for Collins to introduce the element of quackery in the method of the novel's solution as it was first to assert, in the prologue, the scientific basis of the solution: he deepens, simultaneously, our belief and our distrust.

Historically, the line between scientific investigation of the mind and the rash claims of the mesmerists or phrenologists was blurred; modern psychoanalysis owes its origins to an interest in the same phenomena of hypnotic trance, free association, and sleepwalking described by Collins, and so important to nineteenth-century studies of the occult. Clairvoyance is described as the highest state of mesmerism: it connects the forgotten past and even the unknown future with the present; it overcomes space and time.[8] And in *The Moonstone* we are confronted with apparent clairvoyance in the performance of the Hindu's medium, the English boy who looks at the ink they pour onto his hand, goes into a trance, and foretells the future. Murthwaite assures the reader that this is nonsense, " 'simply a development of the romantic side of the Indian character.' " He connects such behavior to the child's being " 'a sensitive subject to the mesmeric influence' " (second period, chap. 3) and assures us it is simply a trick of

[8] John Elliotson, *Human Physiology*, 5th ed. (London: Longman, 1835), pp. 662, 674. See also Robert Darnton, *Mesmerism* (New York: Schocken, 1970).

the imagination—all of which seems to be quite true. There is a great deal the Indians do not know, and Murthwaite analyzes the issue of clairvoyance with admirable scientific rationality. But the action of the novel, and in particular Jennings's solution, will prove him wrong, as, for example, when Murthwaite asserts that " 'we have nothing whatever to do with clairvoyance, or with mesmerism, or with anything else that is hard of belief to a practical man, in the inquiry that we are now pursuing. My object . . . is to trace results back, by rational means, to natural causes' " (second period, chap. 3). Here again we have that tension between rational deduction and the presence of the irrational which is so crucial to this novel and to detective fiction generally. Such contradictions cannot be overcome by pure logic but require the force of the imagination.

The very title of the novel recalls Coleridge's romantic concept of the imagination, which gives new shape to familiar landscapes by accidents of light or shade, moonlight or sunset.[9] Betteredge discovers "under the light of the moon" (first period, chap. 8) the inky substance used in the boy's palm reading; Herncastle, who steals the diamond, was the only one among the British who had had the imagination to believe the tales of the precious stone and to seek it—his "love of the marvellous induced him to believe," writes Collins (prologue, pt. III). And Cuff lectures Seegrave for failure of imagination, using an example that must remind us of the clairvoyant boy "reading" ink: " 'I made a private inquiry last week. . . . At one end of the inquiry there was a murder, and at the other end there was a spot of ink on a tablecloth that nobody could account for. In all my experience along the dirtiest ways of this dirty little world, I have never met with such a thing as a trifle yet' " (first period, chap. 12). He anticipates Sherlock Holmes's famous dictum from "A Study in Scarlet": "From a drop of water, a logician could infer the possibility of an Atlantic or a Niagara." However, we require Poe's particular kind of logician, combining imagination and reason; even Cuff is unable to reconstruct the crime because it exceeds the range of his imagination.

Ezra Jennings is the ultimate detective of the novel who succeeds precisely because he is able to see both the significance of the most trivial details and to allow his mind to wander past the boundaries of

---

[9] Samuel Taylor Coleridge, *Biographia Literaria* (London: Rest Fenner, 1817), chap. 14.

rational thought. Even more than Cuff, he is able to adopt the perspective of others and thus use their subjective experience. When he discovers, for example, the significance of Dr. Candy's fevered ravings, he has hit upon the quintessential method of the modern detective and also on something which sounds remarkably like psychoanalytic free association:

> "I reproduced my short-hand notes in the ordinary form of writing —leaving large spaces between the broken phrases, and even the single words, as they had fallen disconnectedly from Mr. Candy's lips. I then treated the result thus obtained, on something like the principle which one adopts in putting together a child's 'puzzle.' It is all confusion to begin with; but it may be all brought into order and shape.... I filled in each blank space on the paper, with what the words or phrases on either side of it suggested to me as the speaker's meaning; altering over and over again, until my additions followed naturally on the spoken words which came before them.
> ... I found the superior faculty of thinking going on, more or less connectedly, in my patient's mind, while the inferior faculty of expression was in a state of almost complete incapacity and confusion."
>
> (second period, chap. 9)

Here is the reconstructive core of detective fiction, that restatement of the past in the language of the present which transforms the shape of a personal or collective history, which provides it with new meaning and coherence. The reconstructive act is essential to both form and content in detective stories, and it is most gripping when it is in opposition to an equally powerful sense of mystery—not merely the mystery of the crime but of human experience more generally. Psychoanalysis undertakes a similar and broader reconstruction, and it, too, attempts to shape a personal history into its most complete and most convincing form. Reductionism occurs, as it occurs in the sterile forms of detective fiction, with an insistence on total explanation.

There have been several psychoanalytic readings of both *The Moonstone* and detective fiction; but all of these articles suffer from the limitations of an earlier and reductive model of wish fullfillment.[10]

---

[10]See particularly Leopold Bellak, "On the Psychology of Detective Stories and Related Problems," *Psychoanalytic Review,* XXXII (1945), 403–407; Edmund Bergler, "Mystery Fans and the Problem of 'Potential Murderers,'" *American Journal of*

Sexual symbolism is unquestionably important in any full reading of *The Moonstone,* and the title image, like all gems, may be linked with women and sexuality (beauty, great value); the association to the moon further identifies the diamond with women. Collins's description of " 'a defect, in the shape of a flaw, in the very heart of the stone' " (first period, chap. 6) even suggests some of the sexual prejudice so strongly attached to women in the nineteenth century. And these sexual symbols help to integrate the various love stories with the theft of the jewel; they also explain some of those elements of the story which still puzzle its critics.

What is stolen from Rachel is both the actual gem and her symbolic virginity. Rachel finds herself attracted to Franklin as she is coming of age. She is in the process of deciding between suitors and sorting out, as well, the nature of her own desire. Franklin's questionable conduct on the continent ("some imprudence . . . with a woman or a debt at the bottom of it" [first period, chap. 8], thinks Betteredge) greatly disturbs her, and she in turn persuades Franklin to give up cigars. As a result, Franklin is thrown into a state of nervous tension until he enters Rachel's room in the middle of the night and steals her most valued possession. If we see the taking of the jewel only in its most literal meaning, then we cannot understand Rachel's behavior. The *Spectator*'s review in 1868, for example, describes her as "an impulsive girl, generally slanging somebody, whose single speciality seems to be that, believing her lover had stolen her diamond, she hates

---

Orthopsychiatry, XV (1945), 309–317; Geraldine Pederson-Krag, "Detective Stories and the Primal Scene," *Psychoanalytic Quarterly,* XVIII (1949), 207–214 [reprinted in this volume.—Eds.]; Charles Rycroft, "A Detective Story: Psychoanalytic Observations," *Psychoanalytic Quarterly,* XXVI (1957), 229–245; and Lewis A. Lawson, "Wilkie Collins and *The Moonstone,*" *American Imago,* XX (1963), 61–79. It is also instructive to look at the clinical uses of detective fiction, particularly Edith Buxbaum, "The Role of Detective Stories in a Child Analysis," *Psychoanalytic Quarterly,* X (1941), 373–381 and Rudolf Ekstein and Seymour W. Friedman, "The Function of Acting Out, Play Action and Play Acting in the Psychotherapeutic Process," *Journal of the American Psychoanalytic Association,* VII (1959), 581–629. Buxbaum sees only the neurotic use of detective stories in her young patient, and her case study is used in turn as further evidence for those psychoanalytic critics writing about adult detective fiction. Ekstein and Friedman perceive a very different function for an adolescent patient's fictionalized identifications with criminals and detectives: here the patient's fantasies allow him to break the repeated neurotic patterns of his earlier childhood, to adapt and change. The detective fantasies are malleable and become, like literature, a vehicle for growth.

him and loves him both at once, but neither taxes him with the offense nor pardons him for committing it."[11] And Rachel does seem to behave in a most irrational way: she watches Franklin take the jewel but makes no attempt to stop him. Later she will claim that she continued to hope for some explanation, although all of her actions contradict such a hope. In fact, her behavior is so ambiguous and so incriminating that Sergeant Cuff finds *her* guilty of the crime. She is unable to confront Franklin, unable to forgive him, unable to help in finding another solution, and unable not to love him after what he has done (she does later find the strength to call him a " 'mean, miserable, heartless coward!' ") (second period, chap. 7). Her sudden reversal, in response to the theory of an unknown doctor, is equally puzzling: "She tells me," writes Jennings, "in the prettiest manner, that my letter has satisfied her of Mr. Blake's innocence, without the slightest need (so far as she is concerned) of putting my assertion to the proof" (second period, fourth narrative).

All of these contradictions are resolved when we regard Franklin's action both as a literal theft and as a symbolic seduction which leads to confusion, ambivalence, and finally, to marriage and a child. Seduction is implicit in the very clues, like his stained nightshirt, which help connect Franklin to the first taking of the stone. And Rosanna Spearman does, in fact, see one link between the paint-smeared nightshirt and the supposed seduction of Rachel by Franklin:

"I saw the stain of the paint from Miss Rachel's door!

"I was so startled by the discovery that I ran out, with the nightgown in my hand, and made for the back stairs and locked myself into my own room, to look at it in a place where nobody could intrude and interrupt me.

"As soon as I got my breath again, I called to mind my talk with Penelope, and I said to myself, 'Here's the proof that he was in Miss Rachel's sitting-room between twelve last night, and three this morning!'

"I shall not tell you in plain words what was the first suspicion that crossed my mind, when I had made that discovery. You would only be angry—"

(second period, chap. 4)

---

[11] Reprinted in Norman Page, ed., *Wilkie Collins: The Critical Heritage* (London: Routledge and Kegan Paul, 1974), p. 172.

However, Rosanna is regarded by the other characters as either criminal or lunatic, and Collins encourages the reader to dismiss her thinking because she is blinded by her own passion—another example of the way in which we must learn to accept and use the distorted visions of individual characters if we are to arrive at the fullest comprehension of the novel's action. Rosanna's suspicion of Franklin and Rachel is both a false clue to the solution of the mystery and a correct reading of the sexual implications of their relationship.

To some extent Collins used his wit to stretch the accepted limits of sexual discussion in the Victorian novel. Betteredge amuses the very proper Lady Verinder with his unintended double entendres and a naive linking of women and money: " 'I have been turning Selina Goby over in my mind . . . and I think, my lady, it will be cheaper to marry her than to keep her' " (first period, chap. 13); and Ablewhite is urbanely described as "a man of pleasure, with a villa in the suburbs which was not taken in his own name, and with a lady in the villa, who was not taken in his own name, either" (second period, sixth narrative). Within the conventions of melodrama, Collins could also allude to a sordid past (and, at the same time, connect theft and sexual exploitation): " 'I was put in the prison,' " writes Rosanna Spearman, " 'because I was a thief. I was a thief, because my mother went on the streets when I was quite a little girl' " (second period, chap. 4). Collins, however, could not make this connection between his hero and heroine. Instead, he adopts, consciously or intuitively, the device so common to the Victorian novel of splitting hero and villain and giving one the crime and punishment so that the other may be free to enjoy his rewards without guilt. Dickens, for example, linked his heroes with a convenient and ultimately expendable alter ego, like Steerforth or Uriah Heep in *David Copperfield* or Orlick in *Great Expectations*. Thus, Franklin steals the jewel and appears to be guilty and despised by the heroine; but, conveniently, Ablewhite will finally be exposed as the true thief just as he is exposed as a consummate betrayer of women. The sexual implications of the theft make a clearer connection between the stealing of the jewel and the various love stories of the novel while they also explain some of the apparent contradictions of the text.

Most psychoanalytic studies, however, identify a more deeply buried content in *The Moonstone* and in all detective fiction, and they reduce adult conflicts to their presumed sources in infancy. Oedipus, like the inevitable butler, always proves to be the true villain, the original perpetrator of the crime:

> ... for all the diversity, only a few repressed wish fantasy types are the force behind all art. The sexual force is responsible for much of the wish phantasy that accounts for art. The usual expression of the sexual wish-fulfillment phantasy is through some form of the Oedipus situation, the sexual desire of the child for his parent of the opposite sex.
> Now, to return to *The Moonstone,* what do the characters symbolize to their creator?
>
> (Lawson, p. 72)

With such a limited and relentlessly one-directional set of assumptions, the question hardly requires an answer. The wish-fulfillment model commits us to oversimplification and distortion. And the larger the subject the more sweeping the distortion:

> Mystery fans . . . are, criminologically speaking, harmless people with an unsolved unconscious hysteric-passive tension, stemming in man from the "negative" Oedipus complex, in women, from the "positive" Oedipus. These people get temporary release of their tension vicariously.
>
> (Bergler, p. 317)

"Of course," we are quickly assured, "the whole process is unconscious." Even when it is not pushed so absurdly, such criticism invariably confuses affective and biographical issues: it moves too glibly from "what do the characters symbolize for their author" to the unresolved oedipal tensions of mystery readers. In the process, form is virtually ignored.

Another application of the wish-fulfillment model uses a specific early memory connected to the oedipal complex. It reads detective fiction as an expression of primal scene fears and wishes, that is, as an expression of the conflicts of the child who witnesses parental intercourse. Charles Rycroft takes an earlier article by Pederson-Krag on "Detective Stories and the Primal Scene" and applies it to *The Moonstone.*[12] Pederson-Krag's original assumption is badly oversimplified:

---

[12] Rycroft, "A Detective Story: Psychoanalytic Observations." This article suffers from some of the same reductionistic assumptions which Rycroft attacks in his recent articles

> The reader addicted to mystery stories tries actively to relive and master traumatic infantile experiences he once had to endure passively. Becoming the detective, he gratifies his infantile curiosity with impunity, redressing completely the helpless inadequacy and anxious guilt unconsciously remembered from childhood.
>
> (Pederson-Krag, p. 214)

Yet the specific application of this theory to *The Moonstone* may help our critical understanding of the novel because so much of the formal structure of the text is built around a visual tension—seeing and not seeing, the characters watching a crime committed in a bedroom at night, not understanding it, and suffering because they are forced into a new view of a loved object.

The fear of intercourse expressed by the primal scene is most strikingly presented in *The Moonstone* through the image of The Shivering Sand, "the most horrible quicksand on the shores of Yorkshire" (first period, chap. 4). Like the title image, the sands are connected to the phases of the moon, here through the movement of the tide: "At the turn of the tide, something goes on in the unknown deeps below, which sets the whole face of the quicksand shivering and trembling in a manner most remarkable to see" (first period, chap. 4). And the tide itself behaves like some grotesque coquette: "The broad brown face of it heaved slowly, and then dimpled and quivered all over" (first period, chap. 4). Several of the women in the novel are seen as strong-willed and hurtful, like Rachel; violent, like Limping Lucy; even deadly, like the symbolic tide or the moonstone itself. Rosanna Spearman is most clearly identified as a mankiller by her explicit last name, and she identifies herself in turn with the sands that suffocate hundreds of people, " 'all sinking lower and lower in the dreadful deeps! Throw a stone in, Mr. Betteredge! Throw a stone in, and let's see the sand suck it down!' " (first period, chap. 4). She finally merges with the quicksand in death, strengthening the symbolic connection between the deadly sands and unrequited passion. When Franklin later probes the sands with a stick to find a chest left by Rosanna, the

---

for *The New York Review of Books*. However, he has provided the most sensitive psychoanalytic reading of *The Moonstone*, both because he includes a wider range of evidence from Collins's fiction and because he seems to recognize the clear formal limitations of his analysis.

combination of sexual excitement and sexual fear seems to permeate Collins's language:

> In this position, my face was within a few feet of the surface of the quicksand. The sight of it so near me, still disturbed at intervals by its hideous shivering fit, shook my nerves for the moment. A horrible fancy that the dead woman might appear on the scene of her suicide, to assist my search—an unutterable dread of seeing her rise through the heavy surface of the sand, and point to the place—forced itself into my mind, and turned me cold in the warm sunlight. I own I closed my eyes at the moment when the point of the stick first entered the quicksand.
>
> The instant afterwards, before the stick could have been submerged more than a few inches, I was free from the hold of my own superstitious terror, and was throbbing with excitement from head to foot.
>
> (second period, chap. 3)

Collins's images connect one "superstitious terror" with another, and the implicit sexual fantasies of this passage intensify the excitement and terror of the mystery. We can see at once that this reading also tells us something of Collins's deeper fears and desires, and something as well about what a reader might be responding to as he is thrilled, or fearful, or even bored by *The Moonstone*. But an identification of the novel's hypothetical first cause, or an important component of a reader's response, unconscious or not, still does not "explain" the novel; it cannot even offer a full psychological explanation without being placed in that larger structural context I have described.

Take, for example, Miss Clack. This frustrated spinster adopts the most sanctimonious tone and bludgeons her way through the world with religion. She is continually prying and eavesdropping, and when she spies on her beloved Godfrey Ablewhite, she transforms mere looking into a comically voyeuristic nightmare. Obviously jealous of Godfrey's attentions to Rachel, Miss Clack is also excited vicariously, although she tries to hide this by her religious fervor. Godfrey and Rachel think they have escaped Drusilla by retreating from library to drawing room, but she is there, "inadvertently" secreted in a neighboring closet: "A martyrdom was before me. In justice to myself, I noiselessly arranged the curtains so that I could both see and hear.

And then I met my martyrdom, with the spirit of a primitive Christian" (second period, chap. 5). It becomes more primitive than she knows as she suffers the extremes of "a burning fever" and shivering cold very similar to Franklin "turned . . . cold in the warm sunlight" by the Shivering Sand. She watches Godfrey confess his love: "Alas! the most rigid propriety could hardly have failed to discover that he was doing it now" (second period, chap. 5). Her prudery exaggerates every gesture. She tells us that Rachel sat

> without even making an effort to put his arms back where his arms ought to have been. As for me, my sense of propriety was completely bewildered. I was so painfully uncertain whether it was my first duty to close my eyes, or to stop my ears, that I did neither. I attribute my being still able to hold the curtain in the right position for looking and listening, entirely to suppressed hysterics. In suppressed hysterics, it is admitted, even by the doctors, that one must hold something.
> . . . He had another burst—a burst of unholy rapture this time. He drew her nearer and nearer to him till her face touched his; and then—No! I really cannot prevail upon myself to carry this shocking disclosure any farther. Let me only say, that I tried to close my eyes before it happened, and that I was just one moment too late. I had calculated, you see, on her resisting. She submitted. To every right-feeling person of my own sex, volumes could say no more."
> (second period, chap. 5)

Miss Clack's account reproduces the most essential features of the primal scene: the vision of lovemaking which is both attractive and repellent to the viewer and which is accompanied by excitement and guilt particularly focused on looking and hearing. It connects a comic subplot with the fantasies generated by the central mystery. The parody of Drusilla also parodies that very hypocrisy which prevents a frank description of adult relationships and which Collins fought both in his fiction and in his personal life.[13] Drusilla comically provokes and tantalizes the reader by seeing too much and telling too little, as Collins more subtly manipulates the reader through the puzzling theft of the moonstone, making him fear the worst while

---

[13]Marshall describes Collins's contempt for "the shams of the Victorian middle class" from *Basil* on (p. 25). See also Kenneth Robinson, *Wilkie Collins: A Biography* (New York: Macmillan, 1952) and Nuel Pharr Davis, *The Life of Wilkie Collins* (Urbana: University of Illinois Press, 1956).

revealing only half-truths until the close. And partially perceived truth is most essential to Drusilla's account: her attempt to explain an action she cannot comprehend because of her own bias and the reader's need to combine her observation and her bias to arrive at the truth. Even her obsession with seeing and not seeing, hearing and not hearing, reproduces that "detective fever" which has gripped us from Collins's time to our own. The content of Drusilla's thought seems to be sexual, but the form of her behavior reproduces that larger process of looking, interpreting, and reinterpreting which goes on throughout the novel. Miss Clack, of course, cannot reinterpret, but she teaches the reader to distrust all eyewitness accounts until he can make from them his own more complete version of the truth. The specific early psychological configuration called "primal scene" does *contribute* here to the novel's dominant concerns with looking and with the problem of knowledge; but it does not *determine* those concerns, nor is it the central focus of a full psychological reading of the text. Latent structure, not latent content, is the critical interpretive issue.

III

Dreaming and detective fiction are connected by a common latent structure; and in order to perceive that structure, we require that literary criticism—like current analytic dream interpretation—subordinate an earlier libido theory into a model of conflict resolution, a model no longer exclusively aimed at wish fulfillment or the most primitive conflicts of childhood. Freud provides a clear final illustration for us in his most famous literary analysis, which first appeared in *The Interpretation of Dreams:*

> The action of the play consists in nothing other than the process of revealing, with cunning delays and ever-mounting excitement—a process that can be likened to the work of a psychoanalysis—that Oedipus himself is the murderer of Laius, but further that he is the son of the murdered man and of Jocasta. Appalled at the abomination which he has unwittingly perpetrated, Oedipus blinds himself and forsakes his home. The oracle has been fulfilled.
> (Freud, IV, 261–262)

Freud's full account stresses an "oedipal" subject matter as the essential ingredient of the play, whereas here the key seems to be the repeated word "process" and the comparison of the play to the clinical technique of psychoanalysis. The process of *Oedipus Rex* is an insistent movement toward self-discovery by a reconstitution of the past through language. Oedipus' "complex" is less central than his behavior, that repeated, even obsessive, probing of his own history. He behaves as the dreamer does, or the good detective: confronted with a present conflict, he forms a series of new patterns, reordering the present and integrating into it wishes and conflicts from the past, always aiming toward the resolution of contradiction. The infantile sexual subject matter of *Oedipus Rex* is of unquestionable importance, and it must touch, in turn, the most archaic and universal conflicts of its audience. But the powerful unconscious fantasies the play stirs in us are brought into the service of process, of formal movement: past to present, conflict to resolution, ignorance or partial knowledge to a more integrated truth. Parricide and incest form part of a larger psychological structure, akin to the therapeutic pattern of psychoanalysis itself and to the broadest pattern of mythical thought which "always progresses from the awareness of oppositions toward their resolution."[14]

Detective fiction, as we have seen, sustains a tension between subjective mystery and objective solution. Although it often uses rational thought in the service of solution, it need not allow that rationality to dominate; instead, the intellect may destroy absolute predictability and determinism, as it does more generally in play: "play only becomes possible, thinkable, and understandable when an influx of *mind* breaks down the absolute determinism of the cosmos."[15] Detective fiction intensifies a quality present in dreaming, in literary experience, and indeed in all those activities our culture defines as "play" by taking as both its form and its subject a conflict between mystery and unifying solution. Put another way, the tension between mystery and solution is so essential to every detective story that it superimposes itself onto any subject matter or plot and thus becomes a second story. Tzvetan Todorov has claimed that there must always be two stories in a single detective tale—the story of the crime and the story

[14]Claude Lévi-Strauss, "The Structural Study of Myth," in *European Literary Theory and Practice*, edited by Vernon W. Gras (New York: Dell, 1973), p. 307.
[15]Johan Huizinga, *Homo Ludens: A Study of the Play Element in Culture* (Boston: Beacon Press, 1955), p. 3.

of the investigation.[16] It is precisely because *Oedipus* is built around this same duality that it is most usefully compared to detective fiction:

> While many a hero finds himself, Oedipus is unique in being the only one who, when he finds himself, is looking for himself. In other words, this is the only play in which the finding of the self is the whole process, not a product of the action but the whole of it.[17]

The ultimate conflict of *The Moonstone* is not within the novel but within the reader who must distrust the story's various narratives in order to create his own more authentic story. The resolution of the mystery is never as important as the process itself of connecting and disconnecting, building a more complete account from an incomplete vision or fragment. And as in a dream, it is precisely this tension between the reordering imagination and the facts on which it works that formally defines the genre. The dream, like all fiction, projects into the shape of a story the changing responses to our own changing conflicts, the "creative and esthetic experiences that depict . . . the present state of our connections and disconnections with the world about us."[18] Literary process and dreaming share a pattern of conflict resolution, and psychoanalytic textual analyses need to subordinate the search for infantile wish-fulfilling fantasies, and their defenses, to such a pattern. This should bring us closer to an appreciation of the unique style of individual works because the literary work is in this sense identical with the dream: a freshly created attempt at integration and solution which becomes final only with the death of the dreamer.

---

[16] Tzvetan Todorov, "Typologie du roman policier," in *Poetique de la prose* (Paris: Editions du Seuil, 1971), p. 57.
[17] Alister Cameron, *The Identity of Oedipus the King* (New York: New York University Press, 1968), p. 51.
[18] Ullman, "The Transformation Process in Dreams," *The Academy*, XIX (1975), 9.

DAVID I. GROSSVOGEL

Agatha Christie: Containment of the Unknown

Oedipus the King *asserts the persistence of mystery; classic detective stories assert its solubility. The former shows us the real abysses yawning beneath our smug everyday respectability; the latter fabricate phony disturbances in the social order in order to demonstrate how easily they can be remedied. At the end of* The Mysterious Affair at Styles, *"the lovers are reunited, the upper-middle-class ritual is once again resumed. Law, order, and property are secure, and, in a universe that is forever threatening to escape from our rational grasp, a single little man with a maniacal penchant for neatness leaves us the gift of a tidy world, a closed book in which all questions have been answered." Grossvogel's critique of the detective story makes an interesting comparison with Kaemmel's and Hartman's.*

David I. Grossvogel is Professor of Comparative Literature and Romance Studies at Cornell. The piece reprinted here is a chapter from his book Mystery and Its Fictions: From Oedipus to Agatha Christie, *published in 1979.*

●*edipus the King* is a sample, not a solution, of the perdurable mystery. The spectator knows what will happen before the fictional event unfolds, but that knowledge and the confirming resolutions do not allay the spectator's sense of mystery. After Oedipus has been led away at last, there remains within each spectator an intimate sphinx who continues to ask him fateful and unanswerable questions. The experience of Oedipus was meant only to reinforce his awareness that no man can compose with the gods: the spectator could not be in ignorance before the start of the tragedy. If there are benefits to be derived from this type of rehearsal over and above the Freudian pleasure in repetition and the masochistic reexperiencing of primal frustrations, it is in the kind of grandeur that the awareness of an original condemnation confers on the victim who confronts his knowledge: Oedipus' quandary is the spectator's as well, and the latter shares in his dignity; far beyond the fiction, the part of *Oedipus* that its spectator lives out in his own experience is *real*.

The "reality" of Oedipus is in its metaphysical discretion: it assumes as an inalienable given that there are dark regions that can be alluded to only, not broached. The awesomeness of the oedipal myth is that of a remarkable mechanism intended to instance and comment upon the assertion of those limits. For Oedipus as well as the spectator, there is no possible transgression: when the truth so doggedly sought is finally understood in the fullness of its perfect circularity, there remain just as many oracles to decipher as before. Oedipus learns to displace limits in order to learn about the permanency of limits.

The detective story does not propose to be "real": it proposes only, and as a game, that the mystery is located on *this side* of the unknown. It replaces the awesomeness of limits by a false beard—a mask that is only superficially menacing and can be removed in due time. It redefines mystery by counterstating it; by assuming that mystery can be overcome, it allows the reader to play at being a god with no resonance, a little as a child might be given a plastic stethoscope to play doctor. Judging by the large number of its participants, this kind of elevation game is sufficient for the greatest part of the fiction-reading public.

Agatha Christie wrote her first detective story, *The Mysterious Affair at Styles,* in 1920. Thereafter, and for over half a century, she was the most popular purveyor of the genre.[1] During that time she

---

[1] At least in the aggregate. Even if one excludes the handful of Agatha Christie's works that were not detective stories, a total sales of well over 400 million by 1975, translated into 103 languages, is undeniable proof of her huge readership. Her play *The Mousetrap* (an adaptation of her short story "Three Blind Mice" that first appeared in 1950) opened in London in 1952 and set a record for the longest uninterrupted run in theater history. (See Nancy Blue Wynne: *An Agatha Christie Chronology* [New York: Ace Books, 1976].)

wrote works that would not fit quite as well within the narrowest definition of the genre. But detective fiction is a form that loses definition in proportion as it extends beyond its intentional narrowness—a truism confirmed by the lasting appeal of even as rudimentary a work as *The Mysterious Affair at Styles:* after the book had gone through many printings by Lane, in England, by Dodd, Mead and Company, by Grosset and Dunlap, Bantam Books was able to issue ten printings of the novel between 1961 and 1969. In 1970 there followed another edition by Bantam, which has reached so far eleven printings. The publicity on the cover of the eleventh capitalizes on other Christie successes—the well-known and final *Curtain*[2] and the extended run of the film *Murder on the Orient Express* (from her 1934 *Murder on the Calais Coach*). The detective story requires characters only in sufficient numbers, and sufficiently fleshed out, to give its puzzle an anthropomorphic semblance and to preserve the reader from boredom for as long as the veil of its "mystery" is drawn. When it restricts itself to this kind of functional stylization, it exposes little to the dangers of age: how many novels written at the end of the First World War could find such a ready, face-value acceptance today?

To say that the detective story proposes a puzzle is not quite accurate either: one must assume that only an infinitesimally small number of Agatha Christie's half-billion readers ever undertook or expected to solve her stories in advance of Jane Marple or Hercule Poirot. What the detective story proposes instead is the *expectation* of a solution. The detective story offers confirmation and continuity at the price of a minor and spurious disruption. The continuity that it insures includes, ultimately, that of the genre itself: nearly every part of the world within which *The Mysterious Affair at Styles* is set must surely be dead and gone by now (if it ever actually existed), and yet thousands of readers who have never known that world still accept it as real, with little or no suggestion of "camp."

That world was the one possibly enjoyed for yet awhile by the English upper class after 1918.[3] Styles is a manor scarcely ever de-

---

[2]Agatha Christie, *Curtain* (New York, Dodd, Mead, 1975). *Curtain* was meant to be published posthumously, but was written in the early part of the 1940s.
[3]Agatha Christie was among those who perceived most shrewdly the disappearance of that world. In one of the best of her later stories, *At Bertram's Hotel* (London: Collins, 1965), the mystery became clear to Miss Marple when she realized that an antebellum

scribed—"a fine old house,"[4] and little more: like nearly every other part of this world, it is a functional cliché. It has many rooms (whose communicating doors can be mysteriously bolted, and, even more mysteriously, unbolted) available to house a large, landowning family, several summer guests, and a full complement of servants (all these people are, of course, equally valid suspects). Among so many people, love has adequate means to bloom, or hit a rocky course, for the sake of a secondary plot that keeps the action from slowing down. The mood out of which Styles Court is built cannot fail to include "a broad staircase" (p. 9) down which you descend after you have "dressed" ("Supper is at half-past seven"—"We have given up late dinners for some time," pp. 8–9); an "open French window near at hand," with, just beyond it, "the shade of a large sycamore tree" (p. 5) where tea is punctually spread out in July; and a tennis court for after tea. Styles Court exists only in our expectation of what it might be if it were a part of our imaginings. It comes into being through a process of diluted logic that assumes, since mystery is given as an unfortunate condition that can, and should be, eliminated, that life without such unpleasantness must perforce be agreeable and desirable. In a place like Styles, the plumbing is never erratic (unless for the limited purpose of serving the plot), personal sorrow is as evanescent and inconsequential as a summer shower, age and decay cannot inform the exemplary and unyielding mien of its people: the young know that they will be young forever, the professionals are admirably suited to their faces ("Mr. Wells was a pleasant man of middle-age, with keen eyes, and the typical lawyer's mouth," p. 54), and the good-natured fool (the one character who is only seldom a suspect) will neither mature nor learn, however many of life's grimmer vicissitudes he is exposed to. In such a garden of delightfully fulfilled expectations, there rarely occurs anything worse than murder.

Where the corpse of Laius was a scandal that affronted even the

---

place like Bertram's simply could not exist in postwar England. And in *Curtain,* when Poirot and Hastings return for the last time to Styles, it is no longer a private estate but a hotel.

[4]Agatha Christie, *The Mysterious Affair at Styles* (1920; New York: Bantam Books, 1970), p. 4. This, the seventh printing of this edition, announces, with pride and all caps, that "NOT ONE WORD HAS BEEN OMITTED." All subsequent quotations refer to this edition.

gods, the poisoning of Emily Inglethorp at Styles is an event that is just barely sufficient to disrupt the tea and tennis routine. "The mater" (as John Cavendish calls her, not being any more than the others one to derogate from his own cliché—even though she is not quite his mater, but rather his stepmater) cannot be, after all, "a day less than seventy" (p. 1), has already been left by her first husband "the larger part of his income; an arrangement that was distinctly unfair to his two sons" (p. 2), and, as if that didn't clinch it, she has recently married again, a younger man this time, who "wears very peculiar clothes" (p. 72)—a certain Alfred Inglethorp, described by John Cavendish as a "rotten little bounder" (p. 2). If one adds to the list of the dispossessed spunky and cute little Cynthia Murdoch with "something in her manner [reminding one] that her position was a dependent one, and that Mrs. Inglethorp, kind as she might be in the main, did not allow her to forget it" (p. 8; though presumably forgetting herself that sweet Cynthia does volunteer work in a dispensary that is a veritable arsenal of violent poisons); Evelyn Howard, the blunt and sensible friend with whom Mrs. Inglethorp has quarreled; John's wife, "that enigmatical woman, Mary Cavendish" (p. 9), who keeps disappearing with the mysterious Dr. Bauerstein, by no coincidence "one of the greatest living experts on poisons" (p. 11), it begins to look as if not doing away with Mrs. Inglethorp would be the height of irresponsibility, so clearly must her disappearance signify, instead of murder, the righting of an order she has grievously upset.

It is not the act of murder that casts a pall over this idyllic landscape. The pity of murder is that, as slugs ruin lettuce beds (something that would be unheard of at Styles, of course), murder spoils what was otherwise good. Styles St. Mary (or Jane Marple's identical St. Mary Mead) is not the world of high romance: it is the bucolic dream of England, with its decent pub for food, half-timbered lodging and ruddy fellowship, its fine old homes belonging to the landed gentry and the moderately well-to-do (that is to say, nearly everyone), and the quaint (but immaculate) homes of the less than well-to-do. Those who dwell in this land by right are good, or at the very worst, lovably eccentric: the immorality of murder is patent in the way it injects them with a tincture of suspicion and, for a while (for no longer than will tax the tolerance of the reader, who is never to be completely cast adrift but must remain in sight of the sound land soon to be recovered), darkens the vision of a pristine Devonshire belonging to two English girls who recalled their "childhood and young girlhood as a pleasant time of infinite leisure with ample time for thinking, imagining and reading."[5]

The people in that landscape are as tautological as the landscape itself: an adjective or two are sufficient to call their identity to mind. There is "Miss Howard. She is an excellent specimen of well-balanced English beef and brawn. She is sanity itself" (p. 103). The reader's store of familiar images conjures her out of seven words when he first encounters her: "A lady in a stout tweed skirt" (p. 4), the moral qualities of stoutness combining with the British virtue of tweed to convey the instant vision of a hearty, hardy, and honest soul. Thereafter, Evelyn Howard turns into the manifest emblem of her inner nature: "She was a pleasant-looking woman of about forty, with a deep voice, almost manly in its stentorian tones, and had a large sensible square body, with feet to match—these encased in good thick boots" (p. 4). Agelessness, together with an utter lack of gender or esthetic qualities, confer on her the quintessential merit visually attributed to John Bull.

In another part of this predictable landscape, there is a "parlour maid" with no apparent duties but to confirm our expectation of finding her there. She is simply and suitably named Dorcas, with neither a family nor a face. Like lawyer Wells and Evelyn Howard, she is a pleonasm: "Dorcas was standing in the boudoir, her hands folded in front of her, and her grey hair rose in stiff waves under her white cap. She was the very model and picture of a good old-fashioned servant" (p. 39).

But once murder has been committed, the tautological evidence can no longer be trusted: even Evelyn Howard or Dorcas may actually have done it. And so might Cynthia Murdoch, though she is "a freshlooking young creature, full of life and vigour" (p. 8): however clearly she may stand for innocence and the simplicity of first love, once there has been the nastiness of Mrs. Inglethorp's poisoning, even her very selflessness in the wartime dispensary must become as suspect as Lucrezia Borgia's efforts to entertain. Or again, the finger might point

---

[5]Wynne, *Agatha Christie Chronology*, p. 262. It is said that Agatha Christie wrote *The Mysterious Affair at Styles*, when still quite young, on a bet with her sister that she could do a detective story.

at the stepsons: under more normal conditions, they would be, as befits their station, the respectable and tenanted failures of the manor (John, the barrister without a practice; Lawrence, the doctor who never made it). But now, even John's justifiable indignation at an interloper is subject to scrutiny (" 'Rotten little bounder too!' he said savagely. 'I can tell you, Hastings, it's making life jolly difficult for us,' " p. 2). And as for Lawrence, he must suffer something like character in what might otherwise be an acceptably innocuous face: "He looked about forty, very dark with a melancholy clean-shaven face. Some violent emotion seemed to be mastering him" (p. 9).

At least Lawrence is clean-shaven: even under stressful conditions he preserves certain unmistakably British characteristics. But there are also those with beards; and when beards are out of style, they give the impression of disguising something that is unsavory (or, in the paradox of the mystery story, of proclaiming an unsavoriness that might not necessarily be there).[6] At Styles St. Mary, there are three outlandish beards; the real ones (belonging to Dr. Bauerstein and Alfred Inglethorp) and the false one thanks to which the criminal's accomplice is able to disguise an otherwise noticeable identity. When Hastings first catches sight of Inglethorp's beard, he confides, "He certainly struck a rather alien note. I did not wonder at John objecting to his beard. It was one of the longest and blackest I have ever seen" (p. 6)—even though John Cavendish, however outraged he might have been, has limited his tonsorial comments to the following words: "He's got a great black beard" (p. 3). Hastings is speaking about an objection that does not need to be voiced in order to be evident: there is something unnatural about Alfred's beard, even though it is quite real; in Styles St. Mary, it proclaims itself as being alien. It is unfamiliar, repugnant, adverse, and may well signal danger. The antifashion becomes a form of the anti*physis*. "It struck me," muses Hastings, "that he might look natural on a stage, but was strangely out of place in real life" (p. 6): it is this being out of place, this strangeness that contradicts "real life," that is the most evident consequence of the crime that has been committed.

[6]The trend had been towards the clean-shaven since the Anglo-Saxon 1880s. In cities beards were still worn, but mainly by older and professional men. The eleventh edition of the *Encyclopaedia Britannica* (1909) suggests that by the decade in which *The Mysterious Affair at Styles* is set, the upper classes showed an inclination to shave clean.

If one can equate in a beard degrees of evil with the depth of its roots, Dr. Bauerstein's is even more threatening. Since Bauerstein is required merely to trigger a sense of revulsion that awaits his coming, there is little for Agatha Christie to do once she has named him. Her only portrait of the bad doctor proclaims him "a tall bearded man" (p. 11). But this is sufficient to plunge the good (and deeply intuitive) Hastings into an agony of metaphysical forebodings: "The sinister face of Dr. Bauerstein recurred to me unpleasantly. A vague suspicion of every one and everything filled my mind. Just for a moment I had a premonition of approaching evil" (p. 12). This is because Dr. Bauerstein comes by his beard even more naturally than Alfred Inglethorp: in the words of John Cavendish, "He's a Polish Jew, anyway" (p. 118). As far as Hastings and Cavendish are concerned, Bauerstein would wear a black beard even if he were clean-shaven: his beard, like his name, is a stigma that classifies him in the reader's mind regardless of the role that he might be called on to play in the story.

Alongside these aliens whose difference shows in their person like a plain and unmistakable curse, there are the ones in whom strangeness is better concealed. Like that of the others, its source is in the reader's prejudices, but it is allowed to show as only a flickering of danger. The sphinxlike Mary Cavendish turns out to be Russian on her mother's side (" 'Ah,' " says Hastings, " 'now I understand.' 'Understand what?' " asks Mary Cavendish. " 'A hint of something foreign—different—that there has always been about you' " p. 133). Or there is farmer Raikes's wife, believed to be dallying with a number of the men, who is understandably a "young woman of gypsy type" (p. 12). Besides such naturally endowed women, transparent little Cynthia Murdoch has only her poison dispensary, and Evelyn Howard her gruffness, to justify the suspicion the death of Mrs. Inglethorp has cast upon them all.

These characters lay no claim to being people: they are dyspeptic evidence of a déjà vu. Out of such reminders of minor unpleasantness within the world, the detective story creates the temporary annoyance to which it reduces an otherwise all-enclosing mystery. The suggestion of the foreigner, the gypsy, the Jew, echoes such fleeting moments of dyspepsia. Alfred Inglethorp and Dr. Bauerstein do not exist any more than does Dorcas—they are only shadows upon which have been hung the ostentatious beards that activate our minor qualms.[7] They are our prescience of evil, as they are Hastings's—and with as little warrant: if we cease to believe in beards, the trigger mechanism fails to operate and with it the sense of mild discomfort induced by the detective story in order to create the gap, within which it is situated, between two contrastive moments of imagined control. Even though today's sales figures would seem to show that the small phobias depicted in *The Mysterious Affair at Styles* are still much a part of our lives, it should be pointed out that they are not exclusive; there are others: their only requirement is that they be relatively mild but recognized by a large number of readers. Over the years this kind of precise dosing has become increasingly difficult to maintain. Since 1920 the world has continued to shrink, and the idea of the "alien" as represented by someone who is not quite like us has had to be modified. Lately, Ian Fleming was still recruiting his cast of villains rather exclusively from among the ranks of those whom his English hero would recognize as distinctly non-British (primarily central Europeans and Asiatics), but the minor annoyance that once was their nearly reflex consequence now required their sinister part to be bolstered. One was more likely to rub elbows with them, and the world had become increasingly tense (perhaps, in part, because of such elbow-rubbing?): in a universe that had lost, along with its green areas, its bucolic problems, the minor annoyance of such "alien" presences, already tempered through familiarity, would be the more likely to pass unnoticed. James Bond was thus required to confront, instead of village poisoners or even large-scale embezzlers, foreigners intent on nothing less than taking over the whole planet. With Ian Fleming, the detective story, as it often does, becomes something else.

But in 1920 Agatha Christie could still rely on her world and the responses of her people. The canniest person in *The Mysterious Affair at Styles* is neither the criminal (doomed to defeat within the expecta-

---

[7] And by them hang some of the illogicalities that crowd upon one when he attempts to see the shadows for more than what they are. Dr. Bauerstein turns out to be a red herring, in this case a German spy—that is to say, someone who presumably works under cover. Yet his function in the novel is to draw attention to himself *through* his cover (his beard). As for Alfred Inglethorp, the simple-minded but eminently British Hastings sees through him from the start ("A wave of revulsion swept over me. What a consummate hypocrite the man was," p. 29); but the intelligent Poirot, who sees Inglethorp as a mechanism rather than as an emblem, unfailingly finds him (and his schemes) to be "clever" and "astute" (pp. 172ff.).

tions of the genre) nor, obviously, the singularly inept narrator, Hastings. But it is not Hercule Poirot either: it is Agatha Christie herself. She moves in a world she knows so well she can pretend not to be a part of it, counting on the reader's prejudice that associates him with her characters, while she herself avoids contamination. Her mode allows her to show the guilty and the innocent in what appears to be the same light by dissociating herself ostensibly from the convention on which she relies, while in reality she knows that she is casting suspicion on those who should not be suspect. Farmer Raikes's wife is a gypsy, but pretty enough to turn the appreciative (if empty) head of Hastings: the narrator seems quite ready to become a part of the immorality that appears to radiate from her, but the author has done no more than provide us with factual evidence about her origins and her encounters. That Hastings (and the reader) should fall sway, with the rest, to a belief suggested by the word "gypsy" is a consequence that Agatha Christie will not reject but that she has done nothing to encourage.

Again with Hastings, we sense that the mysterious and dangerous part of Mary Cavendish is Russian. However, danger and mystery (when kept within bounds) are also part of the attractiveness of someone who is more than just a pretty face. If we allow our Slavophobia to suggest that Mary might be one of the suspects, the author has no objections, but that Russian ancestry is certainly not given as a valid clue to assist us in solving the riddle. As for Dr. Bauerstein, with whom Mary increases the chances of her possible guilt through association, he is rewarded with the backhanded compliment that Jews are in the habit of receiving from anti-Semites: he is (like that other beard, Alfred Inglethorp) "A very clever man—a Jew, of course" (p. 129). Poirot's words echo those of Mary Cavendish, whose semialienism is spurred by a fit of pique at husband John: " 'A tinge of Jewish blood is not a bad thing. It leavens the'—she looked at him—'stolid stupidity of the ordinary Englishman' " (p. 118). And on this note of worldly dismissal, the author (her seeds sown as she intended them to be) turns her back on such petty squabbling among foolish mortals.

In the detective story world of a mystery made portable, the initiate is the detective who benefits, unlike the initiate in the real world, from the reduction of the mystery. He enters his realm with the full intention of becoming, in due time, an unequivocal discloser of something that, for once, can be disclosed. The assurance of the detective's infallibility results in structural difficulties that are further evidence of the skillful dosing required by the genre. Too manifest an expectation of the detective's success will weaken fatally the delicate tension that must be maintained during the time of subtle unpleasantness that extends between the crime and its resolution. However infallible the detective (and, in the traditional genre, all are equally infallible), he cannot be so percipient as to reveal instantly the sham for what it is. In proportion as Poirot's foes were relatively easy to dispose of at the time of his first introduction to the world, Poirot himself was proportionally the more flawed. Other than the remarkable activity of "the little gray cells" of his brain (for the publicity of whose performance he is the main impresario), Poirot has little to recommend him to us or to denizens of Styles Court. From the first he is marred by the same imperfection as the other aliens—his conspicuous foreignness: nowhere is it more evident than in the fact that he is *short*. Even before he appears, he has been patronizingly dismissed by most of the Britishers in the cast. To Hastings, he is "a marvelous little fellow" (p. 7); to Cynthia, "a dear little man" (p. 17). Dorcas is immediately on her guard: "in her attitude towards Poirot, she was inclined to be suspicious" (p. 39). Even Manning, the gardener, casts "sharp and intelligent" eyes at Poirot that are filled "with faint contempt" (p. 58). Of course, this is meant to be a joke on Manning, Dorcas, and all the rest, but it is a double-edged joke nevertheless; though it confirms Poirot in the end, it helps to blend him a little better with the "alien" quality of murder until the final and brief moment of his triumph.

Starting with his insufferable shortness, everything about Poirot confirms the others' opinions of him:

> Poirot was an extraordinary looking little man. He was hardly more than five feet, four inches, but carried himself with great dignity. His head was exactly the shape of an egg, and he always perched it a little on one side. His moustache was very stiff and military. The neatness of his attire was almost incredible. I believe a speck of dust would have caused him more pain than a bullet wound. Yet this quaint dandyfied little man who, I was sorry to see, now limped badly, had been in his time one of the most celebrated members of the Belgian police. (pp. 16–17)

The author was aware of the faintly ridiculous figure cut by Poirot when she baptized him. She named him after a vegetable—the leek (*poireau*, which also means a wart, in French)—to which she apposed the (barely) Christian name Hercule, in such a way that each name would cast ridicule on the other. Virtues that might have been British in someone of normal stature were undercut by Poirot's height—five feet four inches. His moustache, characteristic enough of the military class at a time when the razor was making its presence felt among most other classes of British society, lacked an adequate body for virile support. The elegance one would have expected of an Englishman could only "dandify" a body that was not up to standard requirements. And the last resort of dignity was reserved, traditionally, for men of tolerable size.

Such indignities were visited on Poirot by virtue of his birth; but in the parts of his personality over which he might have been expected to exercise some self-control, he showed a deplorable tendency to indulge his foreignness. His English was unaccountably Gallicized ("The mind is confused? Is it not so?" p. 30; "Ah! Triple pig!" p. 64; "Mesdames and messieurs! I speak! Listen!" p. 97; "enchanted, Madame," p. 140), with altogether too many exclamation marks, too much boastfulness (frequently voiced by the redundant "I, Hercule Poirot," after which, to compound everyone's embarrassment, "he tapped himself proudly on the breast," p. 137), and an excess of continental posturing ("He made an extravagant gesture with his hand. 'It is significant! It is tremendous!' " p. 30—a trait that distressed even the plain folk at Styles St. Mary: "A little chap? As waves his hands when he talks? One of them Belgies from the village?" p. 74). Even Poirot's single greatest asset—his brain—is ostentatiously displayed in a head exactly like an egg.[8] But perhaps the most serious injury inflicted by Poirot's shameless exuberance is the extent of the overstatement into which he forces those who must describe him, starting with the hapless Hastings.

However, these imperfections notwithstanding, Poirot is not entirely dismissible, either. Part of the artificial surprise of the detective

[8] In a manner reminiscent of our own mildly contemptuous "egghead," which demonstrated what Colin Watson terms the public's inclination "to be in awe of knowledge but to distrust intelligence" (*Snobbery with Violence* [London: Eyre and Spottiswoode, 1971], p. 168).

story is contained within the detective who triumphs, as he brings the action to a close, over even his own shortcomings. (A layer of the genre's optimism derives from the individualism it champions: threats to law, order, and ethnic purity, with which the amorphous aggregate of the police cannot cope, are within the power of a single individual to master.) Agatha Christie is faithful to her method in distancing herself from the aspersions cast at her detective. Not only is his intelligence the brighter for having to shine through his mannerisms, but he has been endowed by his maker with a saving grace of no mean consequence: gallicized as he might be, Poirot is still not quite French. Rather, he is as Nordic as can possibly be someone using the French language—he is Belgian. And he is Belgian at a time (World War I) when "gallant little Belgium" (the smallness of the country perhaps atoning in part for Poirot's own diminutiveness) is overrun by Germany.[9] The good Dorcas sums it all up with the perspicacity of rural Devonshire: "I don't hold with foreigners as a rule, but from what the newspapers say I make out as how these brave Belges isn't the ordinary run of foreigners, and certainly he's a most polite spoken gentleman" (p. 107).

Lastly, Poirot is conferred a kind of honorary citizenship in being awarded a sacrificial, native goat—Hastings—used for purposes of contrast and to ask Poirot questions, the withholding of whose answers is necessary for suspense within the story (very properly, the predetermined time during which disclosure of what was known all along is *suspended,* held up). Hastings is wholly functional: until the arrival of Poirot, that is to say, before the story can devolve from a dialectical process, Hastings is the sole reliance of the reader. He is considerably more urbane than John Cavendish (and far less cliché-ridden); he appraises Lawrence shrewdly; he is suavely avuncular with Cynthia. But once Poirot enters the scene, Hastings becomes no more than a bumbling foil: he sounds for all the world like John Cavendish, he becomes the ludicrous suitor at whom Cynthia Murdoch simply laughs, and he spends most of his time with Poirot being insulted. Just as the unsatisfactory Watson is positioned between the

---

[9]Part of whose evil lies in the fact that an Anglo-Saxon can never be quite sure of exactly what races have gone into its making. Colin Watson notes the privileged status of Belgium at the time, in that by 1918, "the British [had] unaccountably neglected to coin a derogatory epithet for the inhabitants of Belgium" (*Snobbery,* p. 166).

reader and Sherlock Holmes, Hastings acts as the reader's intercessor to the intercessor—though he is manifestly the most obtuse of the characters. Presumed to be the spyglass through which the reader is able to "follow" Poirot, he in fact prevents the reader from seeing much; Poirot is clear on that score, if on few others: "As you know, it is not my habit to explain until the end is reached" (p. 32), or: "Do as I ask you. Afterwards you shall question as much as you please" (p. 57). The reader, tainted by the identity of his own ignorance with that of dumb Hastings, is subsequently disposed to accept the kind of praise that straight men have bestowed on their betters since the Anytus of the Socratic dialogues (" 'Dear me, Poirot,' I said with a sigh, 'I think you have explained everything,' " p. 180): according to his temperament, he will be prepared to admire either Poirot or the author.

And so, the trivial unpleasantness that was contrived for the pleasure of ending it is brought to a close. A spoilsport old lady has been eliminated, foreigners (or those who act like them) have either been justly punished or made to disappear. Those who were only half-foreigners, but actually good, emerge as their better halves. The lovers are reunited, the upper-middle-class ritual is once again resumed. Law, order, and property are secure, and, in a universe that is forever threatening to escape from our rational grasp, a single little man with a maniacal penchant for neatness leaves us the gift of a tidy world, a closed book in which all questions have been answered.

The detective story treats the reader's expectations and prejudices with gentle solicitude. Alongside its disposable annoyances, the planetary triumphs of James Bond are unsettling: the evil he overcomes is of such magnitude that, even when undone, it leaves a menacing trace. We are left wondering whether the secret agent with license to kill is not, in his apotheosis, a reincarnation of what he has eliminated. In a novel by Ian Fleming, an anxiety caused by the awareness that such a tale could be told seeps through the closed covers within which that anxiety was meant to be contained. The anxiety we feel is, of course, more than its fiction intended, and its seepage is an accident. But that seepage makes the world that writes Bond into being much like ours: both are one. Agatha Christie's world, on the other hand, was never more than nostalgia and illusion. Her continued success suggests only that the illusion has not yet receded completely beyond our ken.

STEPHEN KNIGHT

". . . some men come up" – the Detective appears

In this chapter, Knight traces the development of crime fiction from the popular eighteenth-century English tales known collectively as the Newgate Calendar *through Godwin's* Caleb Williams *(1794) to the* Memoirs *(1828–1829) of the great Parisian criminal and police official, Vidocq, surveying in the process the social, ideological, historical, and literary ground from which the modern, individualistic detective has sprung. For Knight, the* Newgate Calendar *tales represent a nostalgic look back at some golden time when crime was a local, communal, or even familial matter and criminals were brought to justice by a combination of community solidarity and their own Christian guilt.* Caleb Williams, *in turn, represents an uneasy transition from the authority of the community to the authority of the individual, something Godwin himself seems to have foreseen without approving. Williams is no "Great Detective," but he is the central figure in a narrative more unified than the Newgate tales. Despite Godwin's idealistic communitarianism, the novel points toward the investigator as romantic hero. This trend reaches an early bloom in the* Memoirs of Vidocq, *the autobiography (overly melodramatized by a series of rewriters and collaborators) of a Parisian master criminal turned police commissioner. Vidocq is not the alienated romantic reasoner embodied by Poe's Auguste Dupin and slightly domesticated in Sherlock Holmes: he combines hard, down-to-earth police work and an authentic sense of identity with the Parisian masses with his own heroic style and "genius." Knight's account of the rise of the detective novel nicely complements those by Ernst Kaemmel and Richard Alewyn.*

"... *some men come up*"—*the Detective appears*

Stephen Knight is a member of the Department of English at the University of Sydney. The selection that follows makes up the first chapter of his book, Form and Ideology in Crime Fiction, *published in 1980.*

At the center of modern crime fiction stands an investigating agent —an amateur detective, a professional but private investigator, a single policeman, a police force acting together. Specially skilled people discover the cause of a crime, restore order, and bring the criminal to account. This function has been so important in recent crime stories that two well-known analysts sought the history of the genre in detection from the past. Régis Messac goes back to the classics and the Bible for his earlier examples in his enormous book *Le "Detective Novel" et l'influence de la pensée scientifique.*[a] Dorothy Sayers does the same in her first *Great Short Stories of Detection, Mystery and Horror.* Both writers take detective fiction to be the same as crime fiction. But before the detective appeared there were stories that suggested how crime could be controlled. Most would have been oral, and many of those that were written down were evanescent, in pamphlet form. Yet enough material has survived to establish the nature and ideology of crime fiction without detectives. *The Newgate Calendar* is a convenient source for such a study. This will make it possible to see clearly the patterns of meaning established through the persona of the detective. These begin to emerge in *The Adventures of Caleb Williams* and *Les Mémoires de Vidocq,* which will also be examined in this chapter. The full, confident deployment of the detective in recognizably modern ways takes place in the texts discussed in later chapters.

I The Newgate Calendar

Stories about criminals survive in reasonable numbers from the late sixteenth century. Robert Greene's "cony-catching" pamphlets are good examples. In them smart criminals trick the innocent "conies" (or "bunnies" in a more modern version of the same metaphor) out

---

[a]See notes at the end of this article for all bibliographical information.—Eds.

of money and property, but come to an inevitably bad end. The narrative always has a moral framework: there is a striking resemblance to the sensational and sententious stories and confessions we still find in magazines and newspapers. The "true confessions" of criminals in pamphlet form have survived from the seventeenth and eighteenth centuries, and this material was sometimes organized into books of memoirs like Richard Head's *The English Rogue*, or more obviously fictional accounts like Daniel Defoe's *Moll Flanders*. But to recognize that these narrative forms still exist can obscure the fact that this material was based on and recreated ideas about crime and society no longer current, as becomes clear in examining a very successful collection of crime stories, *The Newgate Calendar*.

There is no one book with this title. The first large collection of crime stories called *The Newgate Calendar* appeared in 1773. The title had been used before, but then a shrewd publisher saw a market for a reasonably expensive and well-produced set of volumes which brought together accounts of the crimes and punishments of major criminals. Some of the material came from official records, but much was gathered from contemporary accounts hurriedly published as the criminal was punished—usually by execution. By no means all of the criminals had been kept in Newgate, but the famous prison provided a useful catch-all title. The collection was reprinted, expanded, and altered many times. Knapp and Baldwin's edition of 1809 was a particularly well-known and successful one, and versions kept appearing until the late nineteenth century; abridged editions still find a publisher from time to time.

A short moral preface offered the stories as dreadful warnings; an early version recommended the collection for the educational purposes of parents and also—presumably as a diversion—for those going on long voyages. The intended audience is clearly not the huge numbers of poorer people who bought pamphlets. In the 1830s James Catnach was printing up to a million copies of the confession of a particularly thrilling murder, and many people might read or listen to a single pamphlet. They could not afford access to the bound collection we can now study. But the difference of price and format does not disqualify *The Newgate Calendar* as a means of access to widely held ideas about crime and society. The collection's only new feature is its moralizing preface, and the tone of this is invariably present at the end of separately published stories, however flimsy the pamphlets they appeared in. Although this is a collection, there is no special organized structure—indeed the accounts change their order from edition to edition. The meaning of form is to be a major topic in this book, but the difference in form between the widespread pamphlets and the collected *Newgate Calendar* has no special significance, and the collected version can be examined for evidence of a view of crime and society that was widely spread through different classes.

The details of setting and action, and particularly the way criminals are caught, are the best initial guides to the implicit meaning of *The Newgate Calendar* stories. With these in mind, it is both necessary and fairly easy to see how the form in which the stories are presented gives this material convincing life as a credible way of maintaining social order and personal security. A typical *Newgate Calendar* tale of crime and punishment will show the important and recurrent content details.

Matthew Clarke was born in 1697, the son of a "poor honest farmer." Unlike his family, Matthew was "idle"—no fuller explanation is given for his dislike of work. To support himself he "lurked" about the country, committing small crimes. The verb used suggests that already he is in hiding, a threatening outcast. He was unwilling to marry as his family wanted; his refusal to play his part in normal social activity is stressed as a publican sees him wandering at harvest time, when everybody is engaged in productive labor. Matthew accepts the haymaking job that is pressed on him, not from any residual conscience or wish to earn honest money, but because "employment might prevent his being suspected." His motives rise solely from his antisocial state, which he will not abandon. A maid in the publican's inn is a former girlfriend; while kissing her in the kitchen he cuts her throat, then robs her and the house.

At once he is struck by the awful nature of his action and runs away. As he is on the road "some men come up," see that he looks frightened, and notice blood on his clothes. They take the "terrified" man to a justice, and he confesses at once. Before long he is executed and hung in chains where the murder was committed. A brief moral points out how he harmed his fellows and gained nothing: the girl would have given him, for affection, more than he stole by murder. The concluding comments rise above this secular pragmatism to state that, apart from the honest profit involved, a life of integrity, virtue, and piety lets us hope for the blessing of God.

These components are typical of *The Newgate Calendar* stories. The criminals are ordinary people who reject the roles society and their families offer them. Even when a hardened villain appears, the story gives a brief sketch of how he or she fell into that state. Sometimes the criminal is led astray by another renegade from a life of integrated industry. Those who commit crimes are not innately, incurably evil. They have turned aside from normal patterns, and fail to take their chances to resume a life of common morality. The setting of the stories also creates a basis of ordinary life. Farms, towns, shops, inns, and roads in everyday Britain are the places where crimes appear: here are no foreign settings for fantastic horrors. In the same way the crimes are generally simple and direct ones. Robbery and murder in the act of robbery are most common, though murder as a crime of passion is fairly frequent. Forgery and rather small-scale treason occur from time to time, but elaborate accounts of major treason and unusual crimes like piracy are normally associated with well-known figures like Lord Lovat and Captain Kidd. There are not many foreign criminals, and those who do appear are residents in Britain, have no specific alien villainy, and are hard to distinguish from the native-born except by name.

The general effect of these content details is that crime is not seen as some foreign, exotic plague visited on the British public, but as a simple disease that can, by some aberration, grow from inside that society. The heart of the social body is the family. The criminal turns away from family ties and duties, and is finally so outrageous that the family stops trying to help or amend its straying sheep. The family mirrors not only the corporate peace but the social order: static, hierarchical, and male dominated. Wife murder is a capital offense, but husband murder is punished by burning, and in some cases the story tells with relish that the executioner failed to throttle the woman before the flames took hold. This particular crime is called petty treason: attacking a husband is a little version of high treason, attacking the head of the national family.

The way in which the criminals are caught is a crucial feature in crime stories of all kinds, and here it confirms this sense of an organic model of society. There is no special agent of detection at all. The stories imply that just as society can sometimes suffer from disorderly elements, so it can deal with them by its own integral means. Some of these evildoers, mostly murderers, are transfixed by guilt in the process of their crime. More often the sense of guilt makes them act rashly afterwards, so drawing attention to themselves and to crucial evidence, such as bloodstains or stolen property. The idea behind this is that the Christian conscience is suddenly awakened, the objective Christian pattern reasserts itself against the subjective criminal rejection of those values. The criminals go to their inevitable execution as penitents, making (by courtesy of the pamphleteers, no doubt) short prayers on the scaffold, warning others to learn by their fates. One of the main ideological features of these stories is the basic notion, and hope, that the all-pervasive, inescapable Christian reality provides a protection against crime.

The other, more common explanation of how criminals are caught asserts that society itself is so tightly knit that escape will not be possible. The murderer is seen in the act and caught at once, or seen, described by the witness and soon recognized. Sometimes the criminal's identity is obvious from the crime, and the fugitive is gathered in. Similarly, a known robber is recognized from a physical description, by meeting an acquaintance, or having identifiable property on his person. A highwayman may be taken through some accident of recognition or given away by some friend or accomplice who has, in his turn, been a victim of conscience or pursuit. The striking thing is the imprecise, unspecific, scarcely explained or motivated way in which these things happen. Pure chance is very often the mechanism by which a criminal is recognized. The generality and arbitrariness extends to the people involved in the recognition and the arrest. They are imprecisely characterized, or not described at all. In Matthew Clarke's case "some men" ride up to him, and that is a very common turn of phrase in *The Newgate Calendar*. If there has been a murder "some gentlemen" will come along and take the criminal to a magistrate, or hurriedly raise the "Hue and Cry," a formalized general hunt where everyone is on the lookout for the proclaimed criminal.

The vague generality and unconcerned use of chance in the stories does to some extent arise because the capture is regarded as inevitable; the methods themselves are of little interest since the ideology insists that they must succeed. But there is more to it; the events, given in appropriately unindividualized terms, imply that the very community the criminal shunned can muster its forces and throw up the hostile body. Because of the "bloody code" in force at the time, identification almost always leads to death—the only alternative is nearly as absolute an exclusion from society, transportation. A few stories tell how criminals have tried to rejoin society by returning illegally. They are given no second chance: execution is the mandatory penalty for this crime.

Throughout all this material runs a belief in the unity of society, and organic metaphors are very often used—"crimes injurious to their country," "acts harmful to the body of the state." Society, the stories imply, can deal with its own aberrances without mediation, without specialists. The watch will arrest an identified criminal and the courts will pass sentence, but no skilled agent is needed to detect the criminal. The processes of the law are in the background and its officers serve society only in established, invariable ways; they are not independent agents acting upon society. This whole "organic" view emerges strikingly in the common feature where a criminal is executed or hung in chains near the scene of the crime. In many ways the stories are shaped to give a model of unmediated social control of crime.

It is easy enough to see that these two systems of detecting crime, personal guilt and social observation, could only develop in a deeply Christian world, with small social units where everybody is known, where hiding is hard and socialization tends to be public. That had been the general situation in medieval England—though the notorious difficulty of finding and convicting medieval criminals suggests that the crime-control system implicit in *The Newgate Calendar* was never more than a brave hope. But in the period when the stories were printed, the implied social model was disappearing. Not everybody was devotedly Christian, many people lived in large and increasing conurbations, and there was a hardened and relatively successful criminal class, hostile to the "normal" society, which had, in London at least, its own fortresses, later known as the "rookeries" of central London. In fact, *The Newgate Calendar* is not offering a real account of crime control: it is ideological in that it offers hope and comfort to people, and in that it is itself based on ideologies, the twin beliefs that we are all Christian at heart and that our society is integral and at root a single healthy body. This would be what is normally called a "strain ideology," that is, an optimistic account selecting and ordering material to provide a consoling fable in the face of disturbing reality.

The constant patterns of detail and plot that have been described are one way of seeing such an ideology at work: anything that would contradict its validity is excluded. Pierre Macherey has recently argued, in the book translated into English as *Theory of Literary Production,* that the silences in a text are crucial to its ideological force. But he, like Roland Barthes, has also drawn attention to "fissures" in the text. These are not so much large-scale omissions of material but moments where the text shows itself unable to gloss over tensions inherent in even the material that is presented. Both critics see these signs of strain as crucial to the overall force of the text; Macherey interprets them in a more consistently political way, while Barthes' reading, though aware of the social implications, is more directed towards semantic, even esthetic understanding of the effect. In *The Newgate Calendar* there are some examples of these fissures, specific moments where the strain ideology is most tenuously stretched to deal with contradictions that cannot be fully ignored.

The case of Mary Edmondson tells how one evening she called for help from the door of her aunt's house; "some gentlemen" came from a nearby inn to find her aunt murdered and a cut on Mary's arm. One of the men, a Mr. Holloway, makes careful inquiries. Mary says that burglars did the damage, but she is arrested and executed for the crime. Yet she never confesses, and insists to the very end that she is innocent. The story admits that only circumstantial proof is ever brought, and finally says: "Nothing has ever yet transpired to overthrow the proofs of her guilt; and until that happens, we must look upon her as one who was willing to rush into eternity with a lie in her mouth." The guilt system has failed, and the evidence from social observation is stretched very thin. The narrator finds material in the Christian principle to assuage his doubts, but there is clear lack of a system of close investigation to arrive at proof. As if to compensate for this lack, we are for once given the name of the "gentleman" who satisfied himself of Mary's guilt, and we are assured that his inquiries were minute—but they are not described at all.

This "crack" in the text shows the weakness of Christian guilt as a defense against crime; the account of the murder of Mrs. King in 1761 reveals, as a complement, the inadequacy of the notion that society is fully and defensively integrated. Again the contradiction is explained away from inside the ideological system. Mrs. King was murdered by Theodore Gardelle, her Dutch lodger. He hid her body in pieces all round the house, and said she had gone away. A fortnight later a servant came across some of her, and the lodger confessed readily enough. The problem is that nobody knew she was dead. The narrator resolves this challenge to the notionally organic society by excluding Mrs. King, without any evidence other than the problem, from respectable society. She must herself have been a shady isolate: "But who is there, of honest reputation, however poor, that could be missing a day, without becoming the subject of many important enquiries? without occasioning such fears, that no rest could have been had till the truth was discovered, and the injury revenged?"

One other contradiction is passed over in silence—and often still is by our modern ideology. These stories frequently claim that the laws of England fall on all who cause harm to the corporate social body, whatever their station in life. But we actually find that the nobility elude the severity of the law, unless they are traitors and so faithless to their own real class. A Mr. Balfour kills the man his former sweetheart chose to marry. He escapes overseas, becomes penitent, is eventually pardoned, and inherits the family title. Lord Balfour has the chance to become a reconstructed member of society, not given to those ordinary criminals who cannot arrange or afford escape overseas, and so die. In another story Lord Baltimore shows no sign of repentance at all. He has a girl kidnapped, tortures and rapes her, and then manages to get off by legal trickery. Here, where the law is obviously a mediator because it can be manipulated, the unusual feature of a detailed court scene occurs. The plotting recognizes reality, but this does not impinge on the ideology, as the next story follows on with no sign of the law's fragility or its mediation to maintain class hierarchy. What was for the bulk of the people a strain ideology, revealed clearly in these contradictory instances, was, of course, an "interest" ideology for the propertied classes who benefited from the deeply conservative social structure and from the corresponding ideology that is dramatized in these stories, as in so much of the culture of the period.

The patterns of meaning that can be seen in the preceding description of the content of *The Newgate Calendar* are brought to life within a specific theory of knowledge and view of the world by the form of the stories: the form validates, makes real and convincing, the ideology present in the selected material. To a modern eye the formal pattern seems very simple, but analysis shows it to have quite far-reaching implications. To start with the prose style, the bulk of each story is told in a straightforward narrative prose, easy for unskilled readers to follow—particularly when it is read aloud. Its syntax and vocabulary do not need to be scrutinized closely before surrendering their meaning. The suggestion in the prose is that we look straight at our world and know it. But for all its simplicity, this is by no means a value-free narrative. It frequently uses words that directly involve values: "this miserable wretch," "this damnable villain," "with fiendish cruelty." It is, then, a world the reader can observe, but he continually judges his observations by assumed and shared moral values. These standards are called up by key terms, which do not need demonstration and definition in each new story. Towards the end of each account the prose style changes, and confirms these shared values in a final Christian exhortation, suitably shaped in its own form. The more elaborate and slightly archaic tones of the preacher and the Authorized Version are the medium of the conclusion, setting the secular lessons we have learned in the light of eternity with a less demotic, less world-oriented prose style.

There is a formal element that comes between the detailed verbal selection and the large overall structure of a story. I shall call this "presentation." It is the aspect most studied by Erich Auerbach in his book *Mimesis*, and this is basically what he means by "mimesis" itself, the detailed presentation of reality in the scene. In *The Newgate Calendar* the presentation is in part very specific. Geography, tools of trade and of crime, names and ages of criminals and victims are all given in crisp, factual detail. This does not extend to a clear view of the individual and the causes of action. Like the shared moral values that guide our feelings about the events, the motivation tends to be general—fear, greed, lust are the explanations often given. Sometimes —as in the case of Matthew Clarke—we do have a more detailed individualistic account of causes. But even this greater precision of motive does not explain the basic attitude, only the specific development of the generally described states of mind. We know why Matthew accepted the job of haymaking, but not in any detail why he was "idle." And this restricted type of detailed motive is only found in the cases of criminals: it reflects the fact that the criminal has turned away from the general collective values into individualistic action, and so now specific motivation may be relevant, as the great generalized truths of collective society have been abandoned. The same process occurs in medieval romance: the audience knows the hero only in general ethical terms, but knows the detailed physical appearance of his enemy, because this ogre has abandoned the world of ethics. So even when the text offers a specific motivation of an act, this does not actually change the generalizing nature of the narrative's presentation of character.

In the same way, the narrative does not articulate the plot details in a subjectively perceived, or a rational, detailed way. Major events are explained by general objective evaluations, stating whether these acts are sinful or morally right. If the plot needs to bridge a gap in events, sheer coincidence is convincing enough. This is not clumsy or crude: the random events of chance fit comfortably into a world view which does not aspire to explain the intricacies of behavior but assumes that events occur beyond human control. Indeed, chance has positive aspects, for the plots show it to be one of the weapons of normalcy, one of the ways in which the global society restores its healthy order, controls individualistic disturbances without any specific and subjective comprehension of them. The general, shared value judgments and uncomprehended ordering of human events both cohere and derive in a divine, not a human, realm of thought and order.

In accordance with this world view the narrator is not omniscient. The all-knowing hero-narrator, so important to the nineteenth-century novel, was already a feature of eighteenth-century fiction, and this revealed the growing force of bourgeois individualism. In *The Newgate Calendar* the narrator can do no more than watch, listen, record reports, and apply "normal," shared evaluative reactions. This gives the impression of an unmediated, direct form of narration which responds to the underlying idea that society needs no special mediation to restore itself. The narrator is himself a member of the social body, not the specially gifted subjective voice that the rational novel was to lean on for its account of human action, and for the structural unity that replicated the creative and resolving power of a single mind.

The presentation found in *The Newgate Calendar* has its structural corollary in the episodic nature of the stories. Many of them are no more than one narrative event; the longer ones have a structure which does not move steadily through each sequence by cause and effect to a climax, but rather is a series of episodes, the last of which gives the capture and punishment of the criminal. The stories relate to each other by mere juxtaposition and by having the same underlying principles—*The Newgate Calendar* is no more than the sum of its parts: stories can be easily added or removed, their order can be changed, and the whole is not in any real way different. This sort of structure has been fully discussed in the context of medieval literature, and it clearly responds to a particular view of the world.

The system of values in an episodic story is outside the text, assumed by the society and readily applied: the artist does not need to give a detailed justification of the value system. Nor does he need to create within the text an esthetic effect of single unity, an enclosed system of development and pattern: the sense of coherence and integrity, like the sense of values, is generalized through the culture, and neither needs to be recreated in the work of art. Episodic structure, medievalists have said, is vertical: it looks up to objective heavenly verities for its truth; these are also the base of the organization, with no need to create subjective artistic models of human order. The ideology of a Christian world, socially integrated, is behind the apparent "bittiness" of *The Newgate Calendar* stories as a collection and behind the "bittiness" of the longer stories in themselves. This structure and the readiness to rely on chance, on generalized human action and on shared values are all formal aspects of that same faith—or hope, or delusion—that society is one here in the world and has its resolution and ultimate guidance in heaven. The popularity and the effectiveness of the stories lie to a large extent in this successful formal realization of the implicit beliefs revealed in the selection and direction of the content.

The image that *The Newgate Calendar* presents, a world of integrated Christian society, was still credible through the nineteenth century, though the real world was increasingly unlike the one assumed and implied in these stories, and though other versions of society and the control of crime were being dramatized in fiction. Any thorough cultural analysis reveals how patterns overlap in many confusing ways; there is rarely a simple linear progress to be found and one society can sustain quite contradictory views of the world at one time, many of them quite outdated. Even while the calendar was in its early editions, professional thief-catchers, such as the Bow Street Runners, were at work. They were not a salaried force, though, often little more than paid informers—and they made little impact in crime fiction. Dickens uses two Runners in *Oliver Twist,* but they play no crucial part in the plot or the implicit meaning of the novel. In fact, its final sequences are fully in tune with the ideology of *The Newgate Calendar,* and show finely how a great artist's imagination can bring into dramatic clarity the essence of ideas elsewhere found in fragmentary and muffled form. As Sikes is pursued by the people of London, the Hue and Cry of the whole city is seen as a great river. This organic symbol of London itself realizes integrated, objective, and remorseless nuances of society's imagined power against crime. And Sikes is also tormented by conscience. In the grand climax, as he is about to lower himself on a rope to safety he screams "The Eyes": Nancy's dying eyes haunt his conscience. He slips, the rope catches around his throat, and Sikes hangs himself. This public, autonomously generated execution is a vivid and precise symbolic statement of the ideas about society and crime behind *The Newgate Calendar* stories.

Oliver Twist has been called a Newgate Novel; many of them appeared through the nineteenth century. The name indicates the force of *The Newgate Calendar* tradition; the collection of stories was a widely accepted representation of a particular world view and its attitude to crime. The title of the collection itself reveals a good deal, and so do the names carried by similar publications. *The Malefactor's Bloody Register* is the subtitle of the 1773 edition, and other titles and subtitles include *Chronicles of Crime, The Tyburn Chronicle, Chronology of Crime, The Criminal Recorder, Annals of Crime.* Each title refers to a system of classifying events or objects. That in itself is interesting enough—in keeping with the view that crime was an aberration, the vocabulary of social organization embraces it, crime is not an evil world elsewhere, but is just the other side of our orderly, classified world. The calendar is a Newgate one, the annals are those of perverted deeds. But the titles do not only imply crime is a negative aspect of an integrated whole; the classifying involved in the titles responds to the understanding of the world basic to the Calendar's ideology. The words used all refer to unsorted collections of data: lists, registers, chronicles, annals do not analyze and conceptualize their material, but merely record the objective phenomena of life. A conceptual, standing-off—and therefore subjective and ultimately alienated—intelligence is not represented in the titles. They reflect the limits and the ideology of the stories: the world implied is one where people have names and locations, and so can be categorized, but where order lies in the continuing process of social life, and the only synthesis needed lies in the assumed Christian values. Human intelligence is limited to repeating and applying that system: it is in literary terms episodic, that is clerical rather than analytic.

This clerical activity in itself was part of a developing world that made the organic model of the Calendar increasingly unrealistic; reading, publishing, selling books were all aspects of the wider bourgeois and capitalist forces that the ideology of the Calendar works to conceal. In crime fiction an increasing number of writers and readers would need new models through which to contemplate the nature of society, the criminal threat in particular. The detective was to be a central part of those new patterns, but he did not spring into life as we know him overnight; some surprising and revealing versions of crime prevention preceded the figure who has come to dominate our own crime fiction.

II *The Adventures of Caleb Williams*

William Godwin's novel, published in 1794, deals with a crime, but appears to have little else in common with *The Newgate Calendar*, though the author knew it well. Caleb Williams is a single, intelligent detecting hero. His story has much of the unified structure of a novel, with a conceptual, probing, and subjective presentation. This may suggest the modern detective novel came into being at once. But Godwin's novel is less than, and more than, the modern detective novel: it is both a preliminary to and a comment on the crime novel as we know it. Godwin does not believe in the absolute value of the individual hero's intelligence as a bulwark against crime. His search for a different central value shows that subjectivism, rationalism, and individualism did not immediately appear in crime fiction as imagined guardians of life and property. As Steven Lukes shows in his book *Individualism*, both before and after the French Revolution many thinkers, including radicals like Godwin, did not see the individual consciousness as a viable basis for a successful social structure. A specific set of proindividualist attitudes and a world view supporting the power of such a figure was necessary before the hero-detectives we know could be presented with confidence and fictional success.

Godwin's novel indicates that the comforting and old-fashioned fables of *The Newgate Calendar* would not satisfy a questioning intellectual of the period. But the internal contradictions and overall sense of gloom in his novel make it clear no ready alternative fictional system of crime control, no compelling new ideological comfort was available. The unexamined "organic society" theories implicit to *The Newgate Calendar* are inadequate to keep society ordered properly, in Godwin's eyes, but he is by no means satisfied that a subjective questing intellect will do either. Later writers were content with such an individualist authority against crime. Godwin's sense of the weakness of the solitary thoughtful enquirer as a basis for general hope is one that crime fiction has only recently come to share. . . .

The plot of the novel alone exposes the basis of Godwin's theme. Caleb Williams, an intelligent lower-class youth, is befriended and educated by Mr. Falkland, a local squire. Caleb becomes his secretary: he is not only indebted to Falkland but a part of his household. Falkland is essentially a good man, very conscious of his honor and the outward respect he must maintain for his own peace of mind and authority. His qualities lead him to disapprove strongly of Tyrrel, a neighbor whose bullying and cruel nature degrades the rank and ignores the responsibility of a squire. In a climactic argument Tyrrel, who is sharp tongued as well as physically brutal, disgraces and beats Falkland in public. Falkland murders him in secret immediately afterwards—though the novel does not reveal this at once. Falkland has ignored the advice of John Clare, a poet who represents the absolute value of the novel; he warns Falkland to control his temper and use his authority in charities that amount to a program of slow reform.

The facts about the murder are established by Caleb; an uncontrollable curiosity makes him study Falkland and reveal his crime. Once Falkland realizes Caleb knows what has happened, he persecutes him. Caleb is pursued across Britain, imprisoned, and, largely because of Falkland's prestige, steadily discredited and humiliated. After a long series of painful experiences, in prison, among outlaws, and in hiding,

Caleb confronts Falkland, who is now physically and mentally a much reduced man: guilt and the fear of exposure have both worked upon him. In the original ending of the novel Caleb fails again: Falkland once more outfaces him, and he ends his story as a raving madman with little time to live. A few days later a less emotionally involved Godwin wrote a less stark ending that finds room for some positive feeling. Here the confrontation kills Falkland, but Caleb realizes he, too, is at fault: he feels that the debts he owed Falkland should have made him speak openly about the matter long ago, when Falkland's better self would have led him to acknowledge the crime and make amends.

Godwin's view is finally stated through Caleb: while much is wrong with the existing patterns of society, the flaw is structural and cannot be put right by one-to-one conflicts between men. The individual attack on Falkland which Caleb pursues has isolated and destroyed them both; obsessive subjective inquiry is a misuse of Caleb's personal and intellectual strength. Godwin presents the recommendations for a better society that he had given in theoretical form in his recently finished book *An Enquiry Concerning Political Justice*. A small, mutually honest and affectionate society is the model he believes will work. It is essentially a system where the individual is subsumed, supported, and protected; but unlike that of *The Newgate Calendar* it is not a static, conservative system that is assumed to work of its own inertia. Godwin's emphasis on love and truth telling reveals his early years as a nonconformist minister but, more importantly, it emphasizes his conviction that a successful society demands constant mutual effort.

Godwin's belief that only a new corporate society can heal the injuries created by the existing corporate one indicates that for him individualism had not become a valid view of the world: his rejection of a one-to-one conflict shows, by contrast, how deeply individualist, how fully subjective in basis, are the later crime stories which rely so heavily on single conflicts to realize a fictional idea of crime control. Yet Godwin is not only interesting for this negative revelation of the ideological base of later crime fiction. The forces that shaped the bourgeois and romantic faith in individualism were already at work, and operated against Godwin's conscious will. The book's title is an obvious example. Originally it was *Things As They Are: The Adventures of Caleb Williams;* but the personal, subjective subtitle appealed much more than the general objective main title, and by the 1831 edition Godwin himself sanctioned a reversal of order. The external attitudes that induced this change are present within the novel. Godwin's first ending was a deeply felt, subjectively presented account of the destruction of an individual. It was only cooler reflection that enabled him to change this emphasis and bring the novel finally back to the theoretical, superpersonal argument implied by the original title. This rewriting did not only go against Godwin's feelings as he finished his story; as he worked backwards to bring his narrative to that climactic point (a technique crime fiction was to make its own), his basic collective ideas came inevitably into conflict with the implicit individualism embedded in the structure of the novel form itself.

To speak generally, the shape of a novel has certain implications. The idea that someone has written all this down and that others will read it carefully in itself indicates that writing and reading are worthwhile ways of spending time. They are not merely techniques involved in social and economic activity, but are ends in themselves. The idea that someone has invented a story, that it has a named author and a named individual hero or heroine all add the implications of individualism to the intellectualism the form itself ratifies. The whole asserts that one person can create, in the context of a single character, experiences and thoughts that we will find useful—whether for entertainment or instruction. The value of individualized experience is strengthened particularly when, like *Caleb Williams,* the novel is told in the first person. Many critics have argued the novel responds to a bourgeois social formation that has time, education, money; one product of fully divided labor is conceptualized analysis alienated into books, outside normal activity, and there is a corollary emphasis on the subjective value of the individual.

The climax of the novel form is in the work of Austen, Eliot, and James: the subtly developed, perfectly controlled response of one pair of authorial eyes and ears fictionally creates the myth, so important for our period, that a single individual, if clever and patient enough, can unravel the world of experience. The system of knowledge (an epistemology)—watching, listening, and thinking—reveals subjective, humanly controlled motives for events, and so validates an idea of being (an ontology), in which the individual can believe that he or she is truly "real," and can exist alone. The self is known against society, not in it. The structure of the plot—carefully linked, leading up to a climax of action which is also a crucial revelation of the gathered meaning of the novel—provides the model of order, esthetic and moral, which the individualist consciousness feels it can derive from the raw material of experience. This structure is opposite to the effect and the implicit meaning of the episodic pattern discussed in the case of *The Newgate Calendar*, where the belief in an organic society, divinely controlled, is the gathering point, and no overt artistic or moral organization is therefore required in art.

To some degree then, *Caleb Williams* responds to the individualistic and artistic pressure of the novel form. Caleb is intelligent and to a degree perceptive and analytic; writing his own story is a last effort to communicate and establish his own good intentions and explain his errors. To that extent a subjective world view is present. But, more revealingly, there are some telling fissures, moments of contradiction, where Godwin's collectivist intention works against the meaningful control of the rational, organically structured novel. At the beginning of volume II, Caleb says: "I do not pretend to warrant the authenticity of any part of these memoirs except so much as fall under my own knowledge," and this theme is recapitulated at the beginning of the third chapter of the same volume: "It will also most probably happen, while I am thus employed in collecting together the scattered ingredients of my history, that I shall upon some occasions annex to appearances an explanation, which I was far from possessing at the time, and was only suggested to me through the medium of subsequent events."

The omniscience of the narrator (which can even include a first person narrator) is a crucial part of the illusion by which the classic novel asserts the world is comprehensible to a gifted single intelligence. Caleb does want to move from "appearances" to "an explanation," but he recognizes his limitations and the sheer difficulty of making the world explicable through one brain. Elsewhere Godwin makes it clear how Caleb actively errs in his intentions and his explanations. His confidence will rise, then sag as new events contradict him. His attempted escape from prison is a good example, and a convenient contrast with the many successful escapes of later detectives. Caleb's misjudgments and blunders are communicated through his detailed presentation and mishaps as well as by the overarching design of the novel.

If Caleb is shown to be unreliable, there remains the author; Godwin's own voice, like that of Henry James, could still realize through the uncertain characters the power of an individual authorial intelligence. But even at this level, uncertainty shows through. The two endings are a crucial piece of evidence, of course, but there are so many changes of feeling in the novel, so many prevarications about the value of people and the nature of events that Godwin does not have, and is not seeking, a single authoritative version. A particularly sharp example of this breach of individualistic control comes in the curious sequence where Tyrrel is briefly seen as a man who might be redeemable; truth lies in social interaction, not in single summaries.

In its large structure *Caleb Williams* is continuous and has a meaningful climax like the classic nineteenth-century novel, but the material is not totally subdued to rational development and orderly control. Caleb's experiences are often lengthy and random; they do not give the sense of a controlled, climactic development, that crucial pattern by which the "organic" novel expresses its mastery of events (as Terry Eagleton argues in *Criticism and Ideology*). In *Caleb Williams* there is a general sense of Caleb's increasing delusion and his multiplying errors, but the incidents could be reordered to a certain extent without destroying this impression.

The novel also finds room for themes outside the persona's consciousness and development. Godwin includes material on the disgusting and damaging state of prisons at the time; there are passages arguing that the revolutionary views held by the outlaws are not a proper response to contemporary injustice. These sequences, like Caleb's errant adventures, pull against the organic structure of the fully individualist novel; they press home formally Godwin's distrust of the single intelligence and so enact the idea that some form of collective security is necessary.

The use of coincidence in the story has a similar anti-individualist effect. Coincidence is, of course, the bugbear of the rational novel, because a world view that holds human beings can, and so should, control their actions in a comprehensible way, must reject sheer accident as a cause of events. Literary critics, dependent for their organized livelihood on the rational explanation of rational novels, have come down very heavily against coincidence. *The Newgate Calendar* used sheer chance as one of the functions by which divine order confounds the aberrant; Godwin employs several chance meetings, especially between Caleb and Falkland. In a rationalist context this is bad plotting, but the effect (and, in my view, the cause) is to suggest that human beings do not control everything about them. At best they respond to their often random experience, and by mutual support this is made easier.

Caleb's own prose style is another formal feature which hints at his limitations. He is often wordy and ineffective. He says of himself early on: "I delighted to read of feats of activity, and was particularly interested by tales in which corporeal ingenuity or strength are the means resorted to for supplying resources and conquering difficulties. I inured myself to mechanical pursuits, and devoted much of my time to an endeavor after mechanical invention." The intellectual, stilted frailty of the style seems clear enough to a modern reader, especially in its contrast with its content. However, it might be dangerous to assume that Godwin has consciously created a voice which implies Caleb is too involved in cerebration for his own—and others'—good. Godwin's own style in *An Enquiry Concerning Political Justice* is often ponderous, and Angus Wilson has suggested it is a natural eighteenth-century voice. This may be so; but Caleb's prose certainly does not bespeak a consciously confident control of the world, as does Jane Austen's voice. Godwin may well have had at least some sense of dramatizing Caleb's persona in language: even at his most philosophical he is rarely as pompous and self-indulgently wordy as Caleb at his most introspective.

The central thematic analysis of the novel, like its formal patterns, basically rejects an individualistic view of the world. Although the story tells of a single crime, Godwin's analysis of its origin is sociopolitical as well as moral, and so, in its own conceptual way, his work has a social base as broad as the one intuited through *The Newgate Calendar* descriptions. Of course, conceptualization is in itself a form of alienation from real processes of living. But Godwin was acute enough to see the failure of contemporary society in structural and ideological terms, not saying in merely idealistic and moral terms that certain people were "evil." His analysis remains an impressive one, and is more historically and politically important, because more far-reaching, than the elements of historical allegory suggested by Gary Kelly in his recent book on the Jacobin novel.

Anthropologists and sociologists since Godwin wrote have distinguished between two value systems, often called shame-oriented and guilt oriented. In a shame-oriented society values are public and shared, and anyone who acts contrary to them is disgraced, losing status in society as a result. Honor is crucial to the individual; acts, clothes, bearing, and speeches all reflect a knowledge of what honor requires for its continued possession—and its corollary display. Shame is greatly feared since it is an exclusion from the valued and ultimately mutually protective group. The Celtic notion that a poet may satirize a man to death arises from this system. In a guilt-oriented society, on the other hand, the individual creates his or her own ideas of rectitude, and misbehavior is felt personally as guilt even if it is not publicly criticized or even recognized as wrong. Morality is private, and public displays of virtue and honor are seen as hollow shams.

We are now in general thought to be guilt-oriented, though there are strong strains of shame-orientation running through our culture —but to recognize them would contradict the prevailing individualist ideology. The fascinating thing about *Caleb Williams* is that Godwin clearly grasped the socially functional importance of the honor-shame system. He sees Falkland's obsession with honor as his major fault, the direct cause of his crime, and Caleb articulates this judgment. Honor is in the novel the living structure of what in the *Enquiry* Godwin called "government." By this he did not mean just the Westminster-based organization of the country but the system that ratified authority at all levels, the set of instrumental values which governed private as well as public life.

Although Caleb can identify and criticize this system through the sharp intelligence Godwin gives him, neither he nor the novel espouses a system based on guilt. Caleb finally sees his great disaster as having lost his reputation, that central totem of the shame-oriented society. He is writing the story "with the idea of vindicating my character"—"character" here is used in the old sense of a testimonial, a public knowledge of a person's value. And Godwin himself offers in the revised ending a new version of a corporate society where Christian affection has replaced honor as a central mechanism of value and mutual support. But as the novel has not been able to dramatize this process in action, and as the chosen novel form requires an internal demonstration of the values finally espoused, Godwin's offered system is hardly convincing. The effective weight of the novel lies in the attack on the existing system and the telling exposition of the isolated state of the intellectual individual. Indeed, just as later writers have theorized the account Godwin gives of Falkland's system of values, so Caleb's own career has since been shown to be an archetypal one for the alienated intellectual. Godwin's imagination works very accurately as he shows Caleb, at last free from prison, disguising himself as various types of contemporary outcast—a beggar, an Irishman, a wandering rustic, and finally a Jew. When Caleb looks for work he takes up jobs that later sociologists would describe as classically those of alienated skilled workers—freelance writer, jobbing watch-mender, teacher. And finally, the best touch of all, Caleb becomes an etymologist, a man who works in the world of isolated words themselves.

When Godwin rejects the authoritarian ideology of the honor-based society he does not adopt the ideology that was largely to replace it, but offers instead a corporate substitute. His world view remains a collective, Christian one, though one arrived at by the rational mechanisms that were to destroy such a world view—and such a world. In the *Enquiry* he recommends education for all, believing that all would then see the need to be mutually loving and supportive. He does not conceive that education and intellectualism could become of themselves a profession and a life style, and a theoretical defense against the disorders of ordinary existence—and (in fiction at least) against threats to life and property. In his amateur detective Godwin makes essential weaknesses out of just those qualities which would dominate the armories of the great fictional detectives—curiosity, subjectivism, individualism, arrogance, lonely endurance. After a crucial change of viewpoint in the context of romantic theory and the full development of bourgeois ideology, that lonely questing figure would become a hero, an absolute value. When author and audience could believe in the subjective individual as a basis of real experience and could see collectivity as a threat, when rationalism was more than a tool of inquiry and had become a way of dominating the whole world, when professionalism, specialization, and rigorous inquiry replaced the values of affection and mutual understanding as means of controlling deviance, then the figure that Godwin presents as misguided and destructive would emerge as a culture-hero bringing comfort and a sense of security to millions of individuals.

III The Memoirs of Vidocq

The "autobiography" of Eugène François Vidocq presents the first professional detective in literature, and so has considerable historical importance. But if the misleading positivist simplicities of literary history are set aside and the text examined for its own ideological function, the *Memoirs of Vidocq*, like *Caleb Williams* and unlike *The Newgate Calendar,* has a curiously ambiguous effect. To a degree the *Memoirs* are surprisingly realistic, yet they are also exaggerated and melodramatic. These two strands partly derive from two levels of authorship, Vidocq's own experiences and the imagination of his rewriters and translators. The literary professionals who remodeled Vidocq's experiences directed them towards a shape like that of the novel and a world view like that of later crime fiction. But Vidocq himself had a world view and an idea of its suitable literary realization; both were more like *The Newgate Calendar* than the ideology and literary form that are emergent in the *Memoirs.* Vidocq was a criminal who turned police informer with such success that in 1811 he became a full-time inquiry agent in the newly formed Sûreté, the plainclothes detective arm of the recently founded national police. When he retired in 1827 he arranged for the publication of his memoirs; two volumes appeared in 1828, another two in 1829. After a lengthy account of how he worked his way through the prison system into the police force, the *Memoirs* tell a series of fairly brief encounters with criminals. Typically, Vidocq is given a particularly difficult case, to catch and bring proof against some hardened criminal and, usually, his accomplices. He gains information or infiltrates the gang with disguise, patience, and cunning as his major methods. He displays courage and swift judgment when his lowlier police colleagues come to make the arrest. The crimes are usually robbery with violence and the action is mostly set in the seamy quarters of Paris, though sometimes Vidocq will pursue his man to a country inn or a provincial town. The criminals are seen as a hostile and powerful enemy, not as aberrant members of normal society; Vidocq is supremely skillful against them, frequently taking care to humiliate the most powerful and feared villains by showing how easily and completely he outwits them.

This makes Vidocq quite a hero, but he was apparently annoyed by aspects of his characterization. According to his own preface to volume I of the memoirs, his publisher forced a rewriter on him, probably a literary hack called Emile Morice. Vidocq was disgusted with his handling of the material and had him sacked. The preface claims that from the last chapter of volume II the work is Vidocq's own. In fact, it is generally agreed that it stemmed from a new rewriter, L. F. L. L'Héritier. The obviously fictional elements, stock melodramatic situations, and the theatrical climaxes are more common in the last volumes than the first, and volume IV actually includes a short novel about Adèle d'Escars which L'Héritier had previously published. The stylish and formal nature of Vidocq's preface suggests that even this was part of the new rewriter's work.

Whoever wrote it, the preface disagrees with what had been done, and the complaints are revealing. The hero has been falsely represented. The "teinturier," the "dyer" of the material, has coarsened Vidocq's language and has in any case written badly—there is a "multitude de locutions vicieueses, de tournures fatigantes, de phrases prolixes."[b] The charge that his character was not respectable enough sounds credible from a retired detective, though it has other implications to be considered later. The stylistic criticism may well reveal a new rewriter taking a professional potshot at his predecessor. As the complaints go on, they lead us into the wider meaning of the stories.

The character Vidocq wishes for is not only decently spoken: he is also to be lively. The preface regrets the changes of "les saillies, la vivacité et l'énergie de mon caractère"[c] into a figure "tout-à-fait dépourvue de vie, de couleur et de rapidité."[d] This seems obscure, since the character, even in the first volume, is vigorous enough, but the preface gives an important clue when it criticizes the plotting of the rewritten version. Vidocq complains that "les faits étaient bien les mêmes, moins tout ce qu'il y avait de fortuit, d'involontaire, de spontané dans les vicissitudes d'une carrière orageuse, ne s'y présentait plus que comme une longue préméditation de mal."[e]

[b]"multitude of incorrect locutions, tiring turns of phrase, and prolix sentences."—Eds.
[c]"the leaps, the vivacity, and the energy of my character."—Eds.
[d]"completely bereft of life, of color, and of swiftness."—Eds.
[e]"The facts were the same, except that everything fortuitous, involuntary, and spontaneous in the vicissitudes of a stormy career was presented there as nothing but a long premeditation of evil."—Eds.

Vidocq feels his character is diminished because the action is too planned and too many rational links have been made between events; he is not able to show himself nimble enough, spontaneously reacting to sudden threats, bad turns of luck, troublesome surprises. What we might regard as a sophistication of plot, according to this preface both falsifies reality and reduces the heroic human character who faced and defeated the potentially baffling vicissitudes of life among criminals. Although a mediating, heroic detective agent is the means of restoring order, the view of reality the *Memoirs* present is essentially like that of *The Newgate Calendar*. The world is not analyzable in unified conceptual terms, but given to sudden starts and threatening abnormalities. The hero gains status (and honor is important) by demonstrating his power to respond successfully to sudden disturbance and to restore order again. But he is not involved in a systematic explanation of events, a comprehended chain of cause and effect. The rewriter, on the other hand, has begun to create his own idea of reality, a world that can be explained, by pulling together the incidents into a more fully motivated and unified plot.

This process continued in the work of the second French rewriter. In the third and fourth volumes more and more of the chapters connect. An arrest in one chapter brings information that leads to another arrest in the next. These details all indicate that the form of the memoirs is moving away from episodic structure towards a unified organic narrative. The English translator confirmed this development strongly. The direct, racy effect of the original is slowed and given a more thoughtful, pausing, analytic tone, partly by the frequent use of an often balanced, judgment-implying syntax and partly by a more conceptual, analytic and polysyllabic vocabulary.

That tone itself meshes with the added passages that explain a sudden and amazing event in the original. In chapter XXVII Vidocq tries to trap Constantin Gueuvive and his men. He has become a member of the gang, active as lookout during a robbery. When the criminals are dividing the spoils Vidocq's colleagues, tipped off by him, arrive to make the arrests. But he does not want them to reveal who he is as there are more accomplices to gather in. In French, the police beat on the door and:

> Soudain, je me lève et me glisse sous un lit: les coups redoublent, on est forcé d'ouvrir.

> Au même instant, un essaim d'inspecteurs envahit la chambre.[f]
> (vol. II, p. 348)

This is driving, dramatic narrative. But the English is more interested in telling us how it was that Vidocq could hide:

> Amidst the confusion occasioned by these words, and the increased knocking at the gate, I contrived, unobserved, to crawl under a bed, where I had scarcely concealed myself when the door was burst open, and a swarm of inspectors and other officers of the police entered the room. (p. 200)

The lack of spontaneity that Vidocq's preface complained of is much more evident in the English, and the translation is plainly more conceptual and rationally connected.

These patterns have their large structural analogue in the fact that the editor of the 1859 English edition consciously streamlines the shape of the *Memoirs*. In his preface he says he has "thought it needful to suppress all such matter as appeared to us to be foreign to the Work as an Autobiography, or in any way so to act as to interrupt the continuous thread of its history." He leaves out stories he judges digressive, some of the longer dramatized conversations which are a feature of the French, and some informative but, to him, rambling discussions of Vidocq's world. He cannot, though, bear to exclude the moving humanitarian digression about Adèle d'Escars, and so prints it—a finely quasi-organic compromise—as an appendix. He feels the *Memoirs* need a continuous explanatory thread, the orderly developing structure that validates a subjective control of experience. In reworking Vidocq's material (which may have been in note form originally) first French then English literary intellectuals dramatized their own ideology through language, presentation and structure. The detective hero is still a rugged and unintellectual man, but his exploits are presented in terms that increasingly respond to the bourgeois individualism which permeates the classic novel.

In spite of these changes, much that relates to an earlier world view, one that Vidocq himself would apparently support, has survived in the *Memoirs*. A series of literary conventions is used which tends towards heightening the excitement, conveying tension in a scene. The pres-

---

[f]"Suddenly I get up and slip under the bed. The knocks increase, and they are forced to open. Immediately, a swarm of inspectors invades the room."—Eds.

ence of excitement does not automatically mean rationalism is excluded, of course: the romantic poets in England and Rousseau in France indicate emotion and rationalism were not yet seen to be at odds with each other in high culture, and John Clare in *Caleb Williams* represents that authority figure of romanticism, the poet-philosopher. However, such a resolution of feeling and thought is not supported by Vidocq or the basic structure of the text. The preface asserts that vitality, wit, and direct feeling are not consistent with an organized rational unity of plot, and in this particular text sensational feeling, exciting crises are at odds with organized thought. This spontaneous excitement arises from an old-established, integrated view of society. Where Godwin and his alienated hero invented a new corporate social model that might work well, Vidocq, uncerebral and unalienated, has a sense of being deeply involved in the flow of ordinary life. As I have argued, organic structure, conceptual analysis, and ordering are absent from texts which see an integrated ongoing social process as reality—albeit one that now needs specialized heroes to defend it and is not satisfied by the old pattern of heroes who exemplified widespread qualities. The exciting crises present a hero who can respond successfully to sudden unexpected threats in a world not considered to be fully comprehensible to humans but which can be hostile in random ways. This is a pattern familiar from myth and folklore: the quick-wittedness, courage, and speed of reaction that Vidocq displays on behalf of his society relates him to heroes from the past, not to the rational detectives of our period.

A typical set of crises (with an obvious heritage in folklore and popular story) shows Vidocq in disguise. The villain boasts that if Vidocq were present, he would destroy him utterly. Vidocq answers, on one notable occasion, no, Vidocq is so clever that even if he were here you would give him a drink—and as he says this our hero holds out his glass for a refill. To jaded rational palates this may seem contrived: but the incident creates in finely melodramatic and spontaneous terms the cunning and élan of the character—so important, the preface insists, to the real Vidocq himself. The enemy is not only defeated but made to seem foolish beside the spirited, life-restoring hero. This itself relates to the shame-oriented consciousness, for to make a fool of the enemy is to deprive him of status and power. Although Vidocq is in disguise, the assertive power of his "name" recreates the honor he attaches to it. This is just the triumph Vidocq means by his "saillies."

Spontaneous cunning does not prevent Vidocq from reflecting at times. But when he ponders a problem he does not methodically plan a way through it. He thinks about its difficulty, shrugs, and trusts in his "bon génie"[g] to resolve matters—and gets on with the action to find an answer as sudden and complete as the problem is random and difficult. Later detective fiction will place great stress on the methodology of the detective, and the translation, as has been shown above, does introduce some aspects of this. It also usually omits reference to Vidocq's "bon génie": so irrational an explanation of success is discordant with the translator's notion of the meaning the events should dramatize. But in what we can establish of the original spirit of the memoirs, the scientific method is not yet a viable or emotionally real approach: to detail the cerebral technique, to intellectualize would diminish the authentic "caractère" of the hero.

Although Vidocq boasts of his "génie" and has high moments of melodramatic cunning, the basis of his success is still realistic, plodding police work. Indeed, this is where we find the central illusion of the Vidocq *Memoirs*. Hard work, information, bribery, undercover activity are the means to arrive at a climax, the moment where the hero's brilliance emerges. A figure of Herculean courage and endurance, of Odyssean cunning, is built on an infrastructure of solid French police activity. The audience is offered the convincing background and minutiae of action and the consoling resolutions that locate a specially gifted figure on their side. *The Newgate Calendar* provided the familiar English background and the illusion that social observation and Christian guilt would somehow identify the criminal. *Caleb Williams* gave the final illusion that if Caleb had encountered Falkland honestly and lovingly, all would have been amended. A central illusion, a way of shaping an optimistic ideology which is attractive and viable in terms of a culture group's expectations and beliefs is a major feature of popular, successful crime fiction. Vidocq's memoirs recognize real crime in a real setting, and resolve its pressure through the hero's agency; but even his special ability is socially integrated. Vidocq's talents are normal ones raised in power.

---

[g]"guardian spirit."—Eds.

In one exemplary case, Vidocq is looking for a female hunchback who lives near a market and has yellow curtains. He ponders the problem, decides he can rely on his "bon génie" and plods round Paris to discover more than 150 possible locations. He then reasons that hunchbacked women tend to be gossips and tend to be keen cooks (they have no other ways of catching a husband), so he watches the food shops—with eventual success. The unalienated hero uses just the collective wisdom of the people he defends. In the same way his crucial feats are often only exaggerated versions of the ordinary—he arrests a man bravely, he hides under nothing more unusual than a bed, he can stand on watch for long hours. It is his speed of reaction, his instinct to do these rather ordinary things at the right time that gives him his special status.

Even in his moments of extreme success and melodrama, Vidocq is not an isolated hero as the later detectives are to be. He works for the police, he is in intimate contact with the people of Paris, protecting their money and avenging damage to them and their property. He is not really one of the crowd, of course: he is much better than the average policemen and is often in conflict with them because of that; and he is not an ordinary Parisian at all. But when he is on the job he disguises himself as one of them, becomes one of them, as it were. He is a hero who operates for and through the people, not a hero distinguished in manner and method by isolation and alienated intelligence. Vidocq fills a need in *The Newgate Calendar* pattern that occurs when the criminal is no longer seen as an aberrant member of society but as a member of a hostile class. Against hardened criminals, impervious to guilt and able to hide successfully, the special skills of Vidocq are necessary to make crime control convincing in story, just as they were in reality.

As a result of this need for an agent of detection, we frequently find Vidocq engaged in one-to-one conflicts with a criminal. In later crime fiction the personalization of good in the detective and of evil in the villain is an important way of obscuring the social and historical basis of crime and conflict, in keeping with the individualist mystifications of bourgeois ideology. But this limited personalization of conflict does not yet occur in Vidocq's memoirs, though there is a tendency in that direction. One restraining force is seeing criminals as an enemy class: they have areas, language, and relationships that bind them as a common enemy. This class sense is based on moral, not social or economic, criteria, and assumes there is no other classification of people other than good or evil. It does not, however, limit crime as dramatically and simplistically as the later presentation.

The other important pressure against an individualistic, one-to-one drama in the memoirs comes from their structure. Vidocq fights many battles against the members of the criminal class, but no single one is made central, asserted to be the climactic release of criminal pressure. So Vidocq acts like the knight of romance or the hero of folklore, repeating his victories in a reassuring series. His complaint that too much plot linking damages his "caractère" implicitly recognizes it is in episodic action that the figure of the socially integrated agent gains its true force, has formal authority to dramatize its meaning. The episodic structure, as has already been argued in the case of *The Newgate Calendar*, replicates a society that believes itself integral but not comprehensible in analytic terms. And where the constant change of places and characters in *The Newgate Calendar* created the idea that the crucial protective values were pervasive through society as a whole, here, where evil is seen as a hostile force, the agent needed to protect society must himself be the constant feature, the personification of the values of morality and quick-responding defense. Vidocq's irritation at the vulgarity of the language given him indicates his awareness of his special dignity as this defensive figure. He needs a language which will pass among the people, but still distinguish him from them, just because he is, by his work, among them all the time and disguised like one of them.

In simpler, intentional terms, Vidocq was no doubt anxious to put his own unrespectable criminal life behind him, but this past in itself also links his literary figure with the pattern of a hero who acts episodically to help his people. The criminal past of the detective or at least his intimate knowledge of criminal life is a common feature in detective stories, and the *Memoirs* show this strongly. Ian Ousby has discussed the phenomenon in some detail in *Bloodhounds of Heaven*. The absence of a lone enquirer in *The Newgate Calendar* excludes such possibilities, but an intimate knowledge of evil is a familiar pattern in heroic stories of the past—a journey to hell, temptation, and partial sin are elements of the archetypal hero's life as Lord Raglan and Joseph Campbell have outlined it.

One basic explanation of the hero's criminal contacts is that as detectives still know (sometimes to their cost) successful crime solving demands intimate contact with the underworld. Or, a little more elaborately, it may be that an audience both ignorant and fearful of crime and criminals needs to feel its hero is equipped with greater experience and knowledge to justify his success. Freudians like Charles Rycroft go further still, arguing that the detective represents the superego, the criminal the id. When the detective and the criminal are close or identical, this represents our own internal struggles between selfish antisocial behavior and the acceptance of social sanctions. In Vidocq all three forces may well operate: his knowledge is functional, it makes him credible, and the disguise feature in particular seems good support for the Freudian analysis. In this respect, too, Vidocq is more integrated with society than later detectives: he really has been a criminal, where later detectives, while often retaining some criminal contact, were to be much more distanced from criminal reality, just as they were to be alienated from the society on whose behalf they were to operate.

In general, we can see the memoirs of Vidocq as a more up-to-date system of imaginary crime control than the one offered in *The Newgate Calendar*. In response to Vidocq's real experience against crime, the detective has emerged, and the contemporary view of the criminal threat found the figure consoling. But this detective is not a rational and conceptual operator, and is by no means an alienated figure, however far his "teinturiers" and his translator wanted to move in that direction. The events, the setting and the character of Vidocq himself resisted that.

Godwin's approach, though not his conclusions, had shown the growing pressures that enshrined rational individualism, and Vidocq's rewriter and translator suggest how this world view was to affect crime fiction. It is no surprise, then, that the development of crime fiction in France followed their course rather than Vidocq's, stressing skill and individual authority in the figures who contained crime and finding suitable forms in organic literature rather than in episodic reality. The Leatherstocking novels of James Fenimore Cooper realized the figure of the lonely, skillful, determined hunter and Dumas' *Les Mohicans de Paris* is only the best known of many such stories. Here the pursuit is still physical, the special knowledge employed sense-available and natural, but in the figure of Prince Rodolphe in *Les Mystères de Paris* the weight of superior education, class, and morality all fall on the erring criminal. In his part of *The Holy Family*, the first criticism written about crime fiction, Marx identifies Rodolphe as an archetype of bourgeois, authoritarian consciousness, which feels that a little reformist kindness will solve the criminal problem, and pays no attention to the real origins of crime.

Marx would, of course, be equally critical of the organic Christian society envisaged in *The Newgate Calendar* and the *Memoirs* view that criminals are a naturally evil class. But he sharply identifies Sue's implicit movement away from an objective sense of society in action towards a subjective dream of order created by values that in reality were—and are—quite inappropriate in the face of social conflict and its manifestation as crime. Dumas and Sue merely indicate some of the passing trends in crime fiction as moral and literary stereotypes filled out the figure of the detective. A new pattern was to grip the imagination of readers and writers of crime fiction for a long time, because it would use the power of romanticism and intellectualism to validate the alienated individual detective. This would create a confident new illusion to console the anxiety caused by crime, and would dramatize powerfully a world view that is beginning to emerge in the last texts examined in this chapter. This development, the beginning of what we recognize clearly as detective fiction, was the work of Edgar Allan Poe.

REFERENCES

Texts
The Newgate Calendar or The Malefactor's Bloody Register, from 1700 to the Present Time, J. Cooke, London, 1773.
Caleb Williams, OUP, London, 1970.
An Enquiry Concerning Political Justice, Pelican, London, 1976.
Mémoires de Vidocq. 4 vols. Tenon, Paris, 1828–9.
Memoirs of Vidocq, 4 vols, Whittaker, Treacher and Arnot, London, 1829.
Memoirs of Vidocq, Bohn, London, 1859.

Criticism
Erich Auerbach, *Mimesis: The Representation of Reality in Western Literature*, Princeton University Press, Princeton, 1953.
Roland Barthes, *The Pleasure of the Text*, Cape, London, 1976.

Joseph Campbell, *The Hero with a Thousand Faces*, Pantheon, New York, 1949.
Terry Eagleton, *Criticism and Ideology*, New Left Books, London, 1976.
Garry Kelly, *The English Jacobin Novel, 1780–1805*, Clarendon Press, Oxford, 1976.
Steven Lukes, *Individualism*, Blackwell, Oxford, 1973.
Pierre Macherey, *Theory of Literary Production*, Routledge & Kegan Paul, London, 1978.
Karl Marx and Friedrich Engels, *The Holy Family or Critique of Critical Critique*, Foreign Languages Publishing House, Moscow, 1956.
Régis Messac, *Le "Detective Novel" et l'influence de la pensée scientifique*, Champion, Paris, 1929.
Ian Ousby, *Bloodhounds of Heaven: The Detective in English Fiction from Godwin to Doyle*, Harvard University Press, Cambridge, 1976.
Lord Raglan, *The Hero*, Watts, London, 1949.
Charles Rycroft, "A Detective Story: Psychoanalytic Observations," *Psychoanalytic Quarterly*, XXVI (1957) 229–45.
Dorothy Sayers, *Great Short Stories of Detection, Mystery and Horror*, Gollancz, London, 1928.
Angus Wilson, "The Novels of William Godwin," *World Review*, June 1951, 37–40.

D. A. MILLER

The Novel and the Police

André Gide called the novel "the most lawless... of all literary genres." D. A. Miller demonstrates the complicity of this traditionally antiauthoritarian form with society's efforts to control lawlessness; with social convention, middle-class morality, the police, and the law itself. He shows first how the nineteenth-century novel insists upon the importance of middle-class social control by restricting the activities of the police to a specifically criminal milieu. In Dickens's Oliver Twist *and Trollope's* The Eustace Diamonds, *Miller argues, middle- and upper-class characters and institutions perform the functions of detectives and policemen, effectively excluding these alien social forces from their midst without actually yielding to lawlessness. More important still, in these novels, and in the works of Zola, Stendhal, and Balzac, among others, the novel form itself asserts the power of authority, using the narrator's and hence the reader's superior knowledge and position to dominate, classify, and manage such characters as Nana and Vautrin. Borrowing an analogy from Foucault, Miller sums up his argument by comparing the knowledge and the power claimed by the novel to the link between knowledge and power asserted by "Jeremy Bentham's plan for the Panopticon, a circular prison disposed about a central watchtower" in which "surveillance" is exercised on fully visible prisoners by unseen guards. His article represents a sophisticated development from earlier analyses of the relations between a particular culture and its fictions and a modification of the concept of the role of the police in detective fiction as it had been sketched by such writers as Kaemmel, Alewyn, and Knight.*

D. A. Miller is a member of the English Department of the University of California at Berkeley. His article was first published in Glyph, *vol. 8 (1981).*

The frequent appearance of policemen in the works we call novels is too evident to need detecting. Yet oddly enough, the ostensive thematic of regulation thereby engendered has never impugned our belief that "of all literary genres, the novel remains the most free, the most *lawless*."[1] Though the phrase comes from Gide, the notion it expresses has dominated nearly every conception of the form. If a certain puritanical tradition, for instance, is profoundly suspicious of the novel, this is because the novel is felt to celebrate and encourage misconduct, rather than censure and repress it. A libertarian criticism may revalue this misconduct as human freedom, but it otherwise produces a remarkably similar version of the novel, which, in league with rebel forces, bespeaks and inspires various projects of insurrection. This evasive or escapist novel persists even in formalist accounts of the genre as constantly needing to subvert and make strange its inherited prescriptions. All these views commonly imply what Roger Caillois has called "the contradiction between the idea of the police and the nature of the novel."[2] For when the novel is conceived of as a successful act of truancy, no other role for the police is possible than that of a patrol which ineptly stands guard over a border fated to be transgressed. In what follows, I shall be considering what such views necessarily dismiss: the possibility of a radical *entanglement* between the nature of the novel and the practice of the police. In particular, I shall want to address two questions deriving from this entanglement. How do the police systematically function as a topic in the "world" of the novel? And how does the novel—as a set of representational techniques—systematically participate in a general economy of policing power? Registering the emergence of the modern police as well as modern disciplinary power in general, the novel of the nineteenth century seemed to me a good field in which these questions might first be posed. Practically, the "nineteenth-century novel" here will mean these names: Dickens, Collins, Eliot, Trollope, Balzac, Stendhal, Zola; and these traditions: Newgate fiction, sensation fiction, detective fiction, realist fiction. Theoretically, it will derive its ultimate coherence from the strategies of the "policing function" which my intention is to trace.

One reason for mistrusting the view that contraposes the notions of novel and police is that the novel itself does most to promote such a view. Crucially, the novel organizes its world in a way that already restricts the pertinence of the police. Regularly including the topic of the police, the novel no less regularly sets it against other topics of surpassing interest—so that the centrality of what it puts at the center is established by holding the police to their place on the periphery. At times, the limitations placed by the novel on the power of the police are coolly taken for granted, as in the long tradition of portraying the police as incompetent or powerless. At others, more tellingly, the marginality is dramatized as a gradual process of emargination in which police work becomes less and less relevant to what the novel is "really" about.

Even in the special case of detective fiction, where police detectives often hold center stage, the police never quite emerge from the ghetto in which the novel generally confines them. I don't simply refer to the fact that the work of detection is frequently transferred from the police to a private or amateur agent. Whether conducted by police or private detectives, the sheer intrusiveness of the investigation posits a world whose normality has been hitherto defined as a matter of *not needing* the police or policelike detectives. The investigation repairs this normality, not only by solving the crime, but also, far more importantly, by withdrawing from what had been, for an aberrant moment, its "scene." Along with the criminal, criminology itself is deported elsewhere.

In the economy of the "mainstream" novel, a more obviously circumscribed police apparatus functions somewhat analogously to define the field which exceeds its range. Its very limitations bear witness to the existence of other domains, formally lawless, outside and beyond its powers of supervision and detection. Characteristically locating its story in an everyday middle-class world, the novel takes frequent and explicit notice that this is an area which for the most part the law does not cover or supervise. Yet when the law falls short in the novel, the world is never reduced to anarchy as a result. It seems a general principle that where the law leaves a gap, there it is reinvented. In the same move whereby the police are contained in a marginal pocket of the representation, the work of the police is superseded elsewhere by the operations of another, informal and extralegal principle of organization and control.

Central among the ideological effects that such a pattern produces is the notion of *delinquency*. For the official police share their ghetto with an "official criminality": the population of petty, repeated offenders, whose conspicuousness qualifies it to enact, together with the police, a *normative* scenario of crime and punishment. To confine the actions of the police to a delinquent milieu has inevitably the result of consolidating the milieu itself, which not only stages a normative version of crime and punishment, but contains it as well in a world radically divorced from our own. Throughout the nineteenth-century novel, the confinement of the police allusively reinforces this ideology of delinquency. We may see it exemplarily surface in a novel like *Oliver Twist* (1838). Though the novel is plainly written as a humane attack on the institutions that help produce the delinquent milieu, the very terms of the attack strengthen the perception of delinquency that upholds the phenomenon.

A large part of the moral shock *Oliver Twist* seeks to induce has to do with the *coherence* of delinquency, as a structured milieu or network. The logic of Oliver's "career," for instance, establishes workhouse, apprenticeship, and membership in Fagin's gang as versions of a single experience of incarceration. Other delinquent careers are similarly full of superficial movement in which nothing really changes. The Artful Dodger's fate links Fagin's gang with prison and deportation, and Noah Claypole discards the uniform of a charity boy for Fagin's gang with as much ease as he later betrays the gang to become a police informer. Nor is it fortuitous that Fagin recruits his gang from institutions such as workhouses and groups such as apprentices, or that Mr. and Mrs. Bumble become paupers "in that very same workhouse in which they had once lorded it over others."[3] The world of delinquency encompasses not only the delinquents themselves, but also the persons and institutions supposed to reform them or prevent them from forming. The policemen in the novel—the Bow Street runners Duff and Blathers—belong to this world, too. The story they tell about a man named Chickweed *who robbed himself* nicely illustrates the unity of both sides of the law in the delinquent context, the same unity that has allowed cop Blathers to call robber Chickweed "one of the family" (p. 227). Police and offenders are conjoined in a single system for the formation and reformation of delinquents. More than an obvious phonetic linkage connects the Police Magistrate Mr.

Fang with Fagin himself, who avidly reads the Police Gazette and regularly delivers certain gang members to the police.

In proportion as Dickens stresses the coherence and systematic nature of delinquency, he makes it an *enclosed* world from which it is all but impossible to escape. Characters may move from more to less advantageous positions in the system, or vice versa, but they never depart from it altogether—what is worse, they apparently never want to. With the exception of Oliver, characters are either appallingly comfortable with their roles or pathetically resigned to them. An elsewhere or an otherwise cannot be conceived, much less desired and sought out. The closed-circuit character of delinquency, of course, is a sign of Dickens's progressive attitude, his willingness to see coercive system where it was traditional only to see bad morals. Yet one should recognize how closing the circuit results in an "outside" as well as an "inside," an "outside" precisely determined as *outside the circuit.* At the same time as the novel exposes the network that ties together the workhouse, Fagin's gang, and the police *within* the world of delinquency, it also draws a circle around it, and in that gesture, holds the line of a *cordon sanitaire.* Perhaps the novel offers its most literal image of holding the line in the gesture of *shrinking* that accompanies Nancy's contact with the "outside." "The poorest women fall back," as Nancy makes her way along the crowded pavement, and even Rose Maylie is shown "involuntarily falling from her strange companion" (p. 302). When Nancy herself, anticipating her meeting with Rose, "thought of the wide contrast which the small room would in another moment contain, she felt burdened with the sense of her own deep shame, and shrunk as though she could scarcely bear the presence of her with whom she had sought this interview" (p. 301). Much of the proof of Nancy's ultimate goodness lies in her awed recognition of the impermeable boundaries that separate her from Rose Maylie. It is this, as much as her love for Bill Sikes (the two things are not ultimately very different), that brings her to say to Rose's offers of help: "I wish to go back . . . I must go back" (p. 304). Righteously "exposed" in the novel, the world of delinquency is also actively *occulted:* made cryptic by virtue of its cryptlike isolation.

Outside and surrounding the world of delinquency, of course, lies the middle-class world of private life, presided over by Oliver's benefactors Mr. Brownlow, Mr. Losberne, and the Maylies. What repeatedly and rhapsodically characterizes this world is the contrast that opposes it to the world of delinquency. Thus, at Mr. Brownlow's, "everything was so quiet, and neat, and orderly; everybody was kind and gentle: that *after the noise and turbulence in the midst of which [Oliver] had always lived,* it seemed like Heaven itself"; and at the Maylies' country cottage, "Oliver, *whose days had been spent among squalid crowds, and in the midst of noise and brawling,* seemed to enter on a new existence" (pp. 94, 238, italics added). No doubt, the contrast serves the ends of Dickens's moral and political outrage: the middle-class standards in effect, say, at Mr. Brownlow's dramatically enhance our appreciation of the miseries of delinquency. However, the outrage is limited in the contrast, too, since these miseries, in turn, help secure a proper (relieved, grateful) appreciation of *the standards themselves.* It is systematically unclear which kind of appreciation *Oliver Twist* does most to foster. Much as delinquency is circumscribed by middle-class private life, the indignation to which delinquency gives rise is bounded by gratitude for the class habits and securities that make indignation possible.

The "alternative" character of the middle-class community depends significantly on the fact that it is kept free, not just from noise and squalor, but also from the police. When this freedom is momentarily violated by Duff and Blathers, who want to know Oliver's story, Mr. Losberne persuades Rose and Mrs. Maylie not to cooperate with them:

> "The more I think of it," said the doctor, "the more I see that it will occasion endless trouble and difficulty if we put these men in possession of the boy's real story. I am certain it will not be believed; and even if they can do nothing to him in the end, still the dragging it forward, and giving publicity to all the doubts that will be cast upon it, must interfere, materially, with your benevolent plan of rescuing him from misery." (p. 225)

The police are felt to obstruct an alternative power of regulation, such as the plan of rescue implies. Not to cooperate with the police, therefore, is part of a strategy of surreptitiously assuming and revising their functions. Losberne himself, for instance, soon forces his way into a suspect dwelling in the best policial manner. In a more central and extensive pattern, Oliver's diabolical half-brother Monks is subject to a replicated version of a whole legal and police apparatus. There is no wish to prosecute Monks legally because, as Mr. Brownlow says, "there must be circumstances in Oliver's little history which it would be painful to drag before the public eye" (p. 352). Instead, Brownlow proposes "to extort the secret" from Monks (p. 351). Accordingly, Monks is "kidnapped in the street" by two of Brownlow's men and submitted to a long cross-examination in which he is overwhelmed by the "accumulated charges" (pp. 372, 378). The Bumbles are brought in to testify against him, and the "trial" concludes with his agreement to render up Oliver's patrimony and sign a written admission that he stole it.

We would call this vigilantism, except that no ultimate conflict of purpose or interest divides it from the legal and police apparatus that it supplants. Such division as does surface between the law and its supplement seems to articulate a deeper congruency, as though the text were positing something like a doctrine of "separation of powers," whereby each in its own sphere rendered assistance to the other, in the coherence of a single policing action. Thus, while the law gets rid of Fagin and his gang, the amateur supplement gets rid of Monks. Monk's final fate is instructive in this light. Retired with his portion to the New World, "he once more fell into his old courses, and, after undergoing a long confinement for some fresh act of fraud and knavery, at length sunk under an attack of his old disorder, and died in prison" (p. 412). The two systems of regulation beautifully support one another. Only when the embarrassment that an initial appeal to the law would have created has been circumvented, does the law come to claim its own; and in so doing, it punishes *for* the vigilantes. A similar complicitousness obtains in the fate of the Bumbles. If the reason for dealing with Monks privately has been to keep the secret of Oliver's parentage, it is hard to know on what basis the Bumbles are "deprived of their position" at the end, since this would imply a disclosure of their involvement in Monks's scheme to the proper authorities. Even if the confusion is inadvertent, it attests to the tacit concurrence the text assumes between the law and its supplement.

If both come together, then, in the connivance of class rule, more is covered by the rule than outsiders such as Fagin or monsters such as Monks. Perhaps finally more interesting than the quasi-legal procedures that the amateur supplement applies to Monks are the disciplinary techniques that it imposes on Oliver himself. From his first moment at Mr. Brownlow's, Oliver is subject to incessant examination:

> "Oliver what? Oliver White, eh?"
> "No, sir, Twist, Oliver Twist."
> "Queer name!" said the old gentleman. "What made you tell the magistrate that your name was White?"
> "I never told him so, sir," returned Oliver in amazement.
> This sounded so like a falsehood, that the old gentleman looked somewhat sternly in Oliver's face. It was impossible to doubt him; there was truth in every one of its thin and sharpened lineaments.
> (p. 81)

However "impossible" Oliver is to doubt, Brownlow is capable of making "inquiries" to "confirm" his "statement" (p. 96). The object of both interrogation and inquiry is to produce and possess a *full account* of Oliver. "Let me hear your story," Brownlow demands of Oliver, "where you come from; who brought you up; and how you got into the company in which I found you" (p. 96). With a similar intent, when Oliver later disappears, he advertises for "such information as will lead to the discovery of the said Oliver Twist, or tend to throw any light upon his previous history" (p. 123). It is clear what kind of narrative Oliver's "story" is supposed to be: the continuous line of an evolution. Not unlike the novel itself, Brownlow is seeking to articulate an original "story" over the heterogeneous and lacunary data provided in the "plot." It is also clear what Oliver's story, so constructed, is going to do: it will entitle him to what his Standard English already anticipates, a full integration into middle-class respectability. Another side to this entitlement, however, is alluded to in Brownlow's advertisement, which concludes with "a full description of Oliver's dress, person, appearance, and disappearance" (p. 123). The "full description" allows Oliver to be identified and (what comes to the same thing here) *traced*. And if, as Brownlow thinks possible, Oliver has "absconded," then he will be traced *against his will*. To constitute Oliver as an object of knowledge is thus to assume power over him as well. One remembers that the police, too, wanted to know Oliver's story.

The same ideals of continuity and repleteness that determine the major articulations of this story govern the minor ones as well. The "new existence" Oliver enters into at the Maylies' cottage consists predominantly in a routine and a timetable:

> Every morning he went to a white-headed old gentleman, who lived near the little church: who taught him to read better, and to write: and who spoke so kindly, and took such pains, that Oliver could never try enough to please him. Then, he would walk with Mrs. Maylie and Rose, and hear them talk of books; or perhaps sit near them, in some shady place, and listen whilst the young lady read: which he could have done, until it grew too dark to see the letters. Then, he had his own lesson for the next day to prepare; and at this, he would work hard, in a little room which looked into the garden, till evening came slowly on, when the ladies would walk out again, and he with them: listening with such pleasure to all they said: and so happy if they wanted a flower that he could climb to reach, or had forgotten anything he could run to fetch: that he could never be quick enough about it. When it became quite dark, and they returned home, the young lady would sit down to the piano, and play some pleasant air, or sing, in a low and gentle voice, some old song which it pleased her aunt to hear. There would be no candles lighted at such times as these; and Oliver would sit by one of the windows, listening to the sweet music, in a perfect rapture. (p. 238)

This "iterative" tense continues to determine the presentation of the idyll, whose serenity depends crucially on its *legato:* on its not leaving a moment blank or out of consecutive order. "No wonder," the text concludes, that at the end of a very short time, "Oliver had become completely domesticated with the old lady and her niece" (p. 239). No wonder indeed, when the techniques that structure Oliver's time are precisely those of a domesticating pedagogy. Despite the half-lights and soft kindly tones, *as well as by means of them,* a technology of discipline constitutes this happy family as a field of power relations. Recalling that Blathers called Chickweed "one of the family," conjoining those who work the police apparatus and those whom it works, we might propose a sense—only discreetly broached by the text—in which the family itself is "one of the family" of disciplinary institutions.

Oliver Twist suggests that the story of the Novel is essentially the story of an active regulation. Such a story apparently requires a double plot: regulation is secured in a minor way along the lines of an official police force, and in a major way in the working through of an amateur supplement. As an example of high-realist fiction, Trollope's *The Eustace Diamonds* (1873) reverses the overt representational priorities of *Oliver Twist*. Trollope is much more concerned to explore his high bourgeois world than he is to portray delinquency, which he seems prepared to take for granted. Thus, by way of shorthand, the novel will illustrate both the generality and the continuity of the doubly regulatory enterprise I've been discussing in Dickens. What needs regulation in *The Eustace Diamonds*, of course, is Lizzie's initial appropriation of the diamonds. The very status of the "theft" as such is open to question. Lizzie cannot clearly be said to "steal" what is already in her possession, and her assertion that her late husband gave her the diamonds cannot be proven or disproven. Although the family lawyer Mr. Camperdown is sure that "Lizzie Eustace had stolen the diamonds, as a pickpocket steals a watch," his opinion is no more a legal one than that of the reader, who knows, Trollope says, that Mr. Camperdown is "right."[4] In fact, according to the formal legal opinion solicited from Mr. Dove, the Eustace family may not reclaim the diamonds as heirlooms, while there are some grounds on which Lizzie might claim them herself as "paraphernalia."

Part of what places Lizzie's theft in the interstices of the law is her position as Lady Eustace. It is not just that John Eustace refuses to prosecute on account of the consequent scandal or that Lizzie is invited and visited by the best society. The law does not cover a lady's action here for the same reason that Mr. Camperdown is ignorant of the claim for paraphernalia:

> Up to this moment, though he had been called upon to arrange great dealings in reference to widows, he had never as yet heard of a claim made by a widow for paraphernalia. But then the widows with whom he had been called upon to deal, had been ladies quite content to accept the good things settled upon them by the liberal prudence of their friends and husbands—not greedy, blood-sucking harpies such as this Lady Eustace. (1:254)

If, as Dove's opinion shows, the legal precedents about heirlooms do not clearly define the status of Lizzie's possession of the diamonds, it is because a similar question has not previously arisen. In the world Lizzie inhabits, the general trustworthiness of widows of peers has been such that it didn't need to arise. Nor—a fortiori—have the police been much accustomed to enter this world. As Scotland Yard itself acknowledges, at a later turn in the story, "had it been an affair simply of thieves, such as thieves ordinarily are, everything would have been discovered long since;—but when lords and ladies with titles come to be mixed up with such an affair—folk in whose house a policeman can't have his will at searching and browbeating—how is a detective to detect anything?" (2:155).

The property whose proper ownership is put in doubt is the novel's titular instance of the impropriety that comes to rule the conduct of Lizzie, characterize her parasitical friends (Lord George, Mrs. Carbuncle, Reverend Emilius), and contaminate the otherwise decent Frank Greystock. Significantly, Lizzie's legally ambiguous retention of the diamonds opens up a series of thefts which—in certain aspects at least—resemble and prolong the initial impropriety. First, the notoriety of the diamonds in her possession attracts the attentions of professional thieves, who attempt to steal the diamonds at Carlisle, but (Lizzie's affidavit to the contrary) fail to obtain them. Their failure in turn generates a later attempt in London, in which the diamonds are successfully abstracted. In part, Trollope is no doubt using the series to suggest the "dissemination" of lawlessness. But if one theft leads to another, this is finally so that theft itself can lead to *arrest* within the circuit of the law. Subsequent thefts do not simply repeat the initial impropriety, but revise it as well, recasting it into what are legally more legible terms. The plot of the novel "passes on," as it were, the initial offense until it reaches a place within the law's jurisdiction.

Thus, the last theft is very different from the first. It involves a breaking and entering by two professional thieves (Smiler and Cann), working in collaboration with Lizzie's maid (Patience Crabstick) and at the behest of a "Jew jeweler" (Mr. Benjamin) who exports the stolen diamonds and has them recut. In short, theft finally comes to lodge in the world of delinquency: within a practice of power that binds thieves and police together in the same degree as it isolates the economy they form from the rest of the world represented in the novel. In the circulation of this economy, nothing is less surprising than that Lizzie's maid should pass from a liaison with one of the thieves to a marriage with one of the thief-takers or that the other thief should be easily persuaded to turn Crown's evidence. Even in terms of the common idiom they speak, police and thieves are all closer to one another than they are to Frank Greystock and Lord Fawn. Yet if theft now has the transparent clarity of pickpocketing a watch, it also has some of the inconsequence. As it is moved down to a sphere where it can be legally named, investigated, and prosecuted, it becomes—in every respect but the magnitude of the stolen goods—a *petty theft:* committed by petty thieves and policed by petit-bourgeois detectives, all of whom are confined to the peripheral world of a subplot. The impropriety which gave rise to the narrative is arrested on so different a terrain from the novel's main ground that, even after the police investigation has solved its "pretty little mystery," the larger question of Lizzie herself must remain:

> Miss Crabstick and Mr. Cann were in comfortable quarters, and were prepared to tell all that they could tell. Mr. Smiler was in durance, and Mr. Benjamin was at Vienna, in the hands of the Austrian police, who were prepared to give him up to those who desired his society in England, on the completion of certain legal formalities. That Mr. Benjamin and Mr. Smiler would be prosecuted, the latter for the robbery and the former for conspiracy to rob, and for receiving stolen goods, was a matter of course. But what was to be done with Lady Eustace? That, at the present moment, was the prevailing trouble with the police. (2:261)

Ultimately, however, it is a trouble *only* with the police. Though Lizzie is never punished by the law, never even has to appear at Benjamin and Smiler's trial, she does not quite get off the hook. For the novel elaborates another far more extensive and imposing principle of social control in what Trollope calls the "world." The coercive force of the "world" shows up best in the case of Lord Fawn, who, if asked what was his prevailing motive in all he did or intended to do, "would have declared that it was above all things necessary that he should put himself right in the eye of the British public" (2:247). Under this principle, Fawn first tries to break off his engagement to Lizzie, when it looks as though the world will disapprove of her holding on to the Eustace diamonds. Later, when, in the person of Lady Glencora Palliser, the world takes up Lizzie and considers her a wronged woman, Fawn is once again willing to marry her. The coercion exercised by public opinion in the novel is purely mental, but that apparently suffices. The social order that prevents Frank Greystock from duelling with Fawn—"public opinion is now so much opposed to that kind of thing, that it is out of the question"—allows him to predict with confidence, "the world will punish him" (1:216). As Stendhal might say, society has moved from red to black: from the direct and quasi-instantaneous ceremonies of physical punishment to the prolonged mental mortifications of a diffuse social discipline. Trollope's obvious point in the novel about the instability of public opinion (taking up Lizzie to drop her in the end) should not obscure its role as a policing force. Lizzie may fear the legal consequences of her perjury at Carlisle, but what she actually suffers is the social humiliation of its being publicly known. It is enough to exile her to an untouchable *bohème* in which there is nothing to do but marry the disreputable Reverend Emilius. The Duke of Omnium, whose interest in Lizzie had extended to the thought of visiting her, is at the end quite fatigued with his fascination. "I am afraid, you know," he declares to Glencora "that your friend hasn't what I call a good time before her" (2:375).

The understatement is profoundly consistent with the nature of discipline. What most sharply differentiates the legal economy of policing power from the "amateur" economy of its supplement is precisely the latter's policy of *discretion*. It would be false to see Trollope or Dickens engaged in crudely "repressing" the policing function carried on in everyday life, since, as we have seen, the world they create exemplifies such a function. Yet it would be equally misleading to see *Oliver Twist* or *The Eustace Diamonds* advertising such a function. Though both novels draw abundant analogies between the official police apparatus and its supplementary discipline, they qualify the sameness that such analogies invite us to construe with an extreme sense of difference. When in *The Eustace Diamonds,* for example, Lizzie's gardener Andy Gowran is brought before Lord Fawn to attest her misbehavior with Frank Greystock, he sees this situation in the legal terms of a trial: "this was a lord of Parliament, and a government lord, and might probably have the power of hanging such a one as Andy Gowran were he to commit perjury, or say anything which the lord might choose to call perjury" (2:175). But the naive exaggeration of the perception ironically repudiates the metaphor it calls into play.

The metaphor is more tellingly repudiated a second time, when Fawn refuses to solicit what Gowran has to say. "He could not bring himself to inquire minutely as to poor Lizzie's flirting among the rocks. He was weak, and foolish, and, in many respects, ignorant—but he was a gentleman" (2:177). "Gentlemanliness" is thus promoted as a kind of social security, defending the privacy of private life from its invasion by policelike practices of surveillance. Yet there is a curious gratuitousness in Fawn's principled refusal to hear Gowran. Though Gowran never makes his full disclosure to Fawn, the latter can hardly be in any doubt about its content. That he already knows what Gowran has to tell is precisely the *reason* for his shamed unwillingness to hear it. Octave Mannoni, following Freud, would speak here of a mechanism of *disavowal (Verleugnung):* "Je sais bien . . . mais quand même"—"Of course I know . . . but still."[5] By means of disavowal, one can make an admission while remaining comfortably blind to the consequences of that admission. The mechanism allows Fawn to preserve his knowledge about Lizzie together with the fantasy of his distance from the process of securing it. In more general terms, the discretion of social discipline in the Novel seems to rely on a strategy of *disavowing the police:* acknowledging its affinity with police practices *by way of* insisting on the fantasy of its otherness. Rendered discreet by disavowal, discipline is also thereby rendered more effective—including among its effects that "freedom" or "lawlessness" for which critics of the novel (perpetuating the ruse) have often mistaken it. Inobtrusively supplying the place of the police in places where the police cannot be, the mechanisms of discipline seem to entail a relative *relaxation* of policing power. No doubt this manner of passing off the regulation of everyday life is the best manner of passing it on.

What has been standing at the back of my argument up to now, and what I hope will allow me to carry it some steps further, is the general history of the rise of disciplinary power, such as provided by Michel Foucault in *Surveiller et punir.*[6] There Foucault documents and describes the new type of power that begins to permeate Western societies from the end of the eighteenth century. This new type of power ("new" perhaps only in its newly dominant role) cannot be identified with an institution or a state apparatus, though these may certainly employ it or underwrite it. The efficacy of discipline lies precisely in the fact that it is only a *mode* of power, "comprising a whole set of instruments, techniques, procedures, levels of application, targets" (p. 215). The mobility it enjoys as a technology allows precisely for its wide diffusion, which extends from obviously disciplinary institutions (such as the prison) to institutions officially determined by "other" functions (such as the school) down to the tiniest practices of everyday social life. This mobile power is also a modest one. Maintained well below the level of emergence of "the great apparatuses and the great political struggles" (p. 223), its modalities are humble, its procedures minor. It is most characteristically exercised on "little things." While it thus harkens back to an earlier theology of the detail, the detail is now significant "not so much for the meaning that it conceals within it as for the hold it provides for the power that wishes to seize it" (p. 140). By the sheer pettiness of its coercions, discipline tends to keep them from scrutiny, and the diffusion of its operations precludes locating them in an attackable center. Disciplinary power constitutively mobilizes a tactic of tact: it is the power that never passes for such, either invisible or visible only under cover of other intentionalities. Traditional power founded its authority in the spectacle of its force, and those on whom this power was exercised could, conversely, remain in the shade. By contrast, disciplinary power tends to remain invisible, while imposing on those whom it subjects "a principle of compulsory visibility" (p. 187). As in Jeremy Bentham's plan for the Panopticon, a circular prison disposed about a central watchtower, surveillance is exercised on fully visible "prisoners" by unseen "guards." What the machinery of surveillance is set up to monitor is the elaborate regulation (timetables, exercises, and so forth) that discipline simultaneously deploys to occupy its subjects. The aim of such regulation is to enforce not so much a norm as the normality of normativeness itself. Rather than in rendering all its subjects uniformly "normal," discipline is more interested in putting in place a perceptual grid—a *dispositif*—in which a division between the normal and the deviant inherently imposes itself. Throughout the nineteenth century, discipline, with its principal mechanisms of hierarchical surveillance and the *dispositif de normalisation,* progressively "reforms" the major institutions of society: prison, school, factory, barracks, hospital.

And the novel? May we not pose the question of the novel—whose literary hegemony is achieved precisely in the nineteenth century—in the context of the age of discipline? I have been implying, of course, that discipline provides the novel with its essential "content." A case might be made, moreover, drawing on a more somber tradition than exemplified in the fundamentally "comic" novels thus far considered, that this content is by no means always discreet. The novel frequently places its protagonists under a social surveillance whose explicit coerciveness has nothing to do with the euphoria of Oliver Twist's holiday in the country or the genteel understatement of Trollope's "world." In Stendhal's *Le Rouge et le noir* (1830), for instance, the seminary Julien Sorel attends at Besançon is openly shown to encompass a full range of disciplinary practices. Constant supervision is secured either by Abbé Castanède's secret police or through Abbé Pirard's "moyens de surveillance."[7] [a] Exercises such as saying the rosary, singing canticles to the Sacred Heart, and so forth, and so on, are regulated according to a timetable punctuated by the monastic bell. Normalizing sanctions extend from examinations to the most trivial bodily movements, such as eating a hard-boiled egg. Part of what makes Julien's career so depressing is that he never really finds his way out of the seminary. The Hôtel de la Mole only reduplicates its machinery in less obvious ways: as Julien is obliged to note, "Tout se sait, ici comme au seminaire!"[b] (p. 465). And the notorious drawback of being in prison is that the prisoner may not close the door on the multilateral disciplinary attempts to interpret and appropriate his crime. One scarcely needs to put great pressure on the text to see all this. The mechanisms of discipline are as indiscreet in Stendhal's presentation as his disapproval of them is explicit.

Something like that disapproval is the hallmark of all the novels which, abandoning the strategy of treating discipline with discretion, make discipline a conspicuous practice. If such novels typically tell the story of how their heroes come to be destroyed by the forces of social regulation and standardization, they inevitably tell it *with regret*. Just as Stendhal's sympathies are with Julien rather than with the directors of the seminary or the bourgeois jury that condemns him, characters like Dorothea Brooke and Tertius Lydgate seem far more admirable to George Eliot than the citizens of *Mid-*

[a]"means of surveillance."—Eds.
[b]"Everything is known, here as in the seminary."—Eds.

dlemarch (1873) who enmesh them in their "petty mediums." It might seem as though, in the explicitly thematized *censure* of discipline, one had surer ground for retaining the opposition between the novel and the police that our readings of Dickens and Trollope put in question. The specific liabilities we have seen in that opposition when its terms were an official police and an amateur supplement cease to pertain when *both* modes of policing are opposed to the transcendent, censorious perspective taken by the novel. No longer arising from within the world of the novel, the opposition could now less vulnerably play between the world of the novel and the act of portraying it.

Yet we have already seen how the "disavowal" of the police by its disciplinary supplement allows the latter to exercise policing power at other, less visible levels and in other, more effective modes. Similarly, the novel's own repudiation of policing power can be seen not to depart from, but to extend the pattern of this discreet *Aufhebung*.[c] Whenever the novel censures policing power, it has already discreetly reinvented it, in *the very practice of novelistic representation*. A usefully broad example of this occurs in Zola's *Nana* (1880). The prostitutes in the novel, one recalls, are in mortal terror of the police. So great is their fear of the law and the prefecture that some remain paralyzed at the door of the cafés when a police raid sweeps the avenue they walk. Nana herself "avait toujours tremblé devant la loi, cette puissance inconnue, cette vengeance des hommes qui pouvaient la supprimer."[8] [d] Even amid her luxury, she "avait conservé une épouvante de la police, n'aimant pas à en entendre parler, pas plus que de la mort"[e] (p. 1374). The greatest anxiety is apparently inspired by the prospect of being "mise en carte": put on a police list entailing obligatory medical examination. Zola permits us no illusions about the policing of prostitution. When not seeking simply to terrorize, the *agents de moeurs* underhandedly trade their protection for sexual

---

[c] A term derived from the philosophy of G. W. F. Hegel (1770–1831). In the movement of the dialectic, a later stage negates earlier ones but does so by preserving them in some form and thereby transcends them. The English translation is usually "sublation."—Eds.

[d] "had always trembled before the law, that unknown power, that means men had of taking revenge that could wipe her out."—Eds.

[e] "had kept her terror of the police, not liking to hear people talk about them, any more than she liked to hear about death."—Eds.

favors, as the experience of Nana's friend Satin shows. Yet the police procedures that are censured in the story reappear less corruptibly in Zola's method of telling it. What is *Nana* but an extended *mise-en-carte* of a prostitute: an elaborately researched "examination" sustained at the highest level by the latest scientific notions of pathology and at the lowest by the numerous "fiches" on which data is accumulated? In a larger social dimension, and with a similar prophylactic intention, Zola wants to register the Parisian *fille* no less than the police. *Nana* is the title of a file, referring both to the prostitute who resists the record and to the novel whose representational practice has already overcome this resistance.

To the extent that the genre of the novel *belongs* to the disciplinary field that it portrays, our attention needs to go beyond the policing forces represented in the novel to focus on what Foucault might call the "micropolitics" of novelistic convention. By way of broaching this micropolitics, I would like to consider a crucial "episode" in its genealogy, where the police and the narrative devices that usurp their power are most in evidence: namely, the encounter between Fouché's secret police and Balzac's omniscient narration in *Une Ténébreuse Affaire* (1841). While it is an exaggeration to say that Fouché "invented" the modern police, the greater organization and extent of the police machine over which he presided were considerable enough to make it substantially new.[9] The increased importance of the *secret* police was a particularly significant aspect of this newness. Disguises and dissimulation began to encroach upon uniforms and naked force as dominant modes of police action. Alongside the "old" virtue of speed and the "old" routine of pursuit, the "new" methods of detective investigation arose into prominence. The contrast between old and new policial "styles" is precisely the burden of the comparison between Balzac's two agents, Peyrade and Corentin.

> Le premier pouvait couper lui-même une tête, mais le second était capable d'entortiller, dans les filets de la calomnie et de l'intrigue, l'innocence, la beauté, la vertu, de les noyer, ou de les empoisonner froidement. L'homme rubicond aurait consolé sa victime par des lazzis, l'autre n'aurait pas même souri. Le premier avait quarante-cinq ans, il devait aimer la bonne chère et les femmes. Ces sortes d'hommes ont tous des passions qui les rendent esclaves de leur métier. Mais le jeune homme était sans passions et sans vices. S'il

était espion, il appartenait à la diplomatie, et travaillait pour l'art pur. Il concevait, l'autre exécutait; il était l'idée, l'autre était la forme.[10] [f]

The differences announce the passage from a dominantly corporal and spectacular punishment to a hidden and devious discipline: from a police whose practice is best exemplified in the act of capital execution, occupying a single moment in time at a single point of space, to a police defined in terms of the spatial extension of its "filets"[g] and the temporal deployment of its "intrigues." Not unlike the novel, the new police has charge of a "world" and a "plot."

Both men, of course, are privileged seers. Like Balzac's doctors and lawyers, his *agents de police* are privy to what goes on behind the "scènes de la vie privée," and they thus resemble the novelist whose activity is also conceived as a penetration through social surfaces. Nonetheless, the text pointedly distinguishes the vision of each. Peyrade's eyes present a powerful image: "Ces deux yeux fureteurs et perspicaces, d'un bleu glacial et glacé, pouvaient être pris pour le modèle de ce fameux oeil, le redoutable emblème de la police, inventé pendant la Révolution"[h] (p. 36). But what is impressive as an emblem is less effective than what it emblematizes. Openly displaying their prying acuteness, Peyrade's eyes virtually constitute a warning against their own powers. Not surprisingly, the eyes of the more effective agent are simply "impénétrables": "leur regard était aussi discret que devait l'être sa bouche mince et serré"[i] (p. 37). Yet, of course, the "impenetrable" powers of vision ascribed to Corentin have already been penetrated by the narration that renders them. Much as the eyes

[f]"The first could cut off a head with his own hands, but the second was capable of entangling innocence, beauty, and virtue in nets of slander and intrigue, of drowning them, or of poisoning them in cold blood. The ruddy man would have consoled his victim with jests, but the other would not even have smiled. The first man was forty-five, and appeared to enjoy good food, and women. This kind of man has all the passions that make him a slave of his trade. The young man, on the other hand, was without passions or vices. If he was a spy he was also a diplomat, and did his work for the sake of his art. He thought things up, the other carried them out. He was the idea, the other was the form."—Eds.
[g]"nets."—Eds.
[h]"Those two prying, discerning eyes, of a glacial, icy blue, might have been used as the model for that famous eye, the redoubtable emblem of the police, that was invented during the Revolution."—Eds.
[i]"Their glance was as discreet as his thin pinched mouth seemed to be."—Eds.

of Peyrade advertise a power that is better served in the inscrutable Corentin, the eyes of both glance at the superiority of the narration that has improved upon the perspicacity of the one and the impenetrability of the other. On the side of perspicacity, Balzac's omniscient narration assumes a fully panoptic view of the world it places under surveillance. Nothing worthy of being known escapes its notation, and its complete knowledge includes the knowledge that it is always right. This infallible supervision is frequently dramatized in Balzac's descriptions as an irresistible process of detection. Thus, from the worn creases of Peyrade's breeches, the text infers that he has a desk job; from his manner of taking snuff, that he "must be" an official. One thing inevitably "indicates," "betrays," "conceals" a defining something else. On the side of impenetrability, this panoptic vision constitutes its own immunity from being seen in turn. For it intrinsically deprives us of the outside position from which it might be "placed." There is no other perspective on the world than its own, because the world entirely coincides with that perspective. We are always situated inside the narrator's viewpoint, and even to speak of a "narrator" at all is to misunderstand a technique that, never identified with a *person*, institutes a faceless and multilateral regard.

Flaubert famously declared that "l'auteur, dans son oeuvre, doit être comme Dieu dans l'univers, présent partout et visible nulle part."[11] j But God is not the only such unseen overseer. In an early detective novel, Monsieur Lecoq (1869), Emile Gaboriau calls the police "cette puissance mystérieuse . . . qu'on ne voit ni n'entend, et qui néanmoins entend et voit tout."[12] k It doesn't finally matter whether we gloss panoptical narration as a kind of providence or as a kind of police, since the police are only—as Gaboriau also called them—a "Providence au petit pied" (p. 234), a "little providence" fully analogous to the great. What matters is that the faceless gaze becomes an ideal of the power of regulation. Power, of course, might seem precisely what the convention of omniscient narration foregoes. Omniscient narration may typically know all, but it can hardly *do* all. "Poor Dorothea," "poor Lydgate," "poor Rosamond," the narrator

---

j"The author, in his work, must be like God in the Universe: everywhere present and nowhere visible."—Eds.

k"that mysterious power which one neither sees nor hears, but which itself sees and hears everything."—Eds.

of *Middlemarch* frequently exclaims, and the lament is credible only in an arrangement that keeps the function of narration separate from the causalities operating in the narrative. The *knowledge* commanded in omniscient narration is thus opposed to the *power* which inheres in the circumstances of the novelistic world. Yet by now the gesture of disowning power should seem to define the basic move of a familiar power play, in which the name of power is given over to one agency in order that the function of power may be less visibly retained by another. Impotent to intervene in the "facts," the narration nevertheless commands the discursive framework in which they are perceived as such. One thinks, for example, of the typologies to which novelists like Balzac or Zola subject their characters, or of the more general "normalizing function" which automatically divides characters into good and bad, normal and deviant. The panopticism of the novel thus coincides with what Mikhail Bakhtin has called its "monologism": the working of an implied master voice whose accents have always already unified the world in a single interpretative center. Accordingly, in the monological novel, "every struggle of two voices for possession of and dominance in the world in which they appear is decided in advance—it is a sham struggle."[13]

Yet to speak of sham struggles is also to imply the necessity for shamming them. The master voice of monologism never simply soliloquizes. It continually needs to confirm its authority by qualifying, canceling, endorsing, subsuming all the other voices it lets speak. No doubt the need stands behind the great prominence the nineteenth-century novel gives to *style indirect libre,* in which, respeaking a character's thoughts or speeches, the narration simultaneously subverts their authority and secures its own. The resistance that monologism requires to confirm itself, however, is most basically offered by the narrative itself. For the "birth of narrative" marks an apparent *gap* in the novel's system of knowledge. The thoroughness with which *Père Goriot* (1834) masters every inch of space belonging to the Pension Vauquer, for example, lapses abruptly when it comes to the pensioners themselves. Instead of making assertions, the narration now poses questions, and in place of exhaustive catalogues, it provides us with teasingly elliptical portraits. Exactly at the point of interrogation, the exposition ceases and the narrative proper—what Balzac calls the "drama"—begins. Yet the "origin" of narrative in a cognitive gap also indicates to what end narrative will be directed. Substituting a temporal mode of mastery for a spatial one, Balzac's "drama" will achieve the same full knowledge of character that has already been acquired of habitat.

The feat is possible because nineteenth-century narrative is generally conceived as a *genesis:* a linear, cumulative time of evolution. Such a genesis secures duration against the dispersive tendencies that are literally "brought into line" by it. Once on this line, character or event may be successively placed and coherently evaluated. It should be recalled that, in *Oliver Twist,* both the police and Mr. Brownlow sought to construct for Oliver a story organized in just this way. The ideal of genetic time prevails in nineteenth-century fiction even where it appears to be discredited. A novel like *Middlemarch* forcefully dismisses the notion of a "key" which would align "all the mythical systems and erratic mythical fragments in the world" with "a tradition originally revealed,"[14] but when it comes to its own will-to-power, the novel presents its characters in a similar genetic scheme. The moral lesson George Eliot seeks to impose depends on our ability to correlate the end of a character's career with what was there in germ at the beginning—in Lydgate's "spots of commonness," for instance, or in Bulstrode's past.

Structured as a genesis, the narrative that seems to resist a novel's control thereby becomes a technique for achieving it. So that, as it forwards a story of social discipline, the narrative simultaneously advances the novel's omniscient word. It is frequently hard to distinguish the omniscience from the social control it parallels, since the latter, too, is often a matter of "mere" knowledge. Lizzie Eustace poses a threat to Trollopian society precisely because she is unknown. Lord Fawn "knew nothing about her, and had not taken the slightest trouble to make inquiry" (1:78). "You don't know her, mama," Mrs. Hittaway tells Lady Fawn (1:81). "Of the manner in which the diamonds had been placed in [Lizzie's] hands, no one knew more than she chose to tell" (1:15). What mainly happens in *The Eustace Diamonds* is that the world comes to know Lizzie better. Paradoxically, what gives both the world and the narration that idealizes its powers a hold on Lizzie are her own undisciplined desires. These generate the narrative by which she is brought under control. Leo Bersani has argued that the realist novel exhibits a "fear" of desire, whose primal disruptiveness it anxiously represses.[15] Yet power can scarcely be exercised *except* on what resists it, and—shifting Bersani's emphasis somewhat—one might claim that the novel rather than fearing desire *solicits* it. Through the very intensity of the counterpressure it mounts, desire brings the desiring subject into a maximally close "fit" with the power he means to resist. Thus, Lizzie's desires are at once the effect of the power she withstands and the cause of its intensified operation.

Insistently, the novel shows disciplinary power to inhere in the very resistance to it. At the macroscopic level, the demonstration is carried in the attempt of the protagonist to break away from the social control which thereby reclaims him. At the microscopic level, it is carried in the trifling detail which is suddenly invested with immense significance. Based on an egregious disproportion between its assumed banality and the weight of revelation it comes to bear, the "significant trifle" is typically meant to surprise, even frighten. For in the same process as the detail is charged with meaning, it is invested by a power already capitalizing on that meaning. Power has taken hold where hold seemed least given: in the irrelevant. The process finds its most programmatic embodiment in detective fiction, where the detail literally incriminates. "I made a private inquiry last week," says Sergeant Cuff in *The Moonstone* (1868); "At one end of the inquiry there was a murder, and at the other end there was a spot of ink on a tablecloth that nobody could account for. In all my experience along the dirtiest ways of this dirty little world, I have never met with such a thing as a trifle yet."[16] The inquiries of Sherlock Holmes rely similarly upon trivia, as he repeatedly reminds us. "You know my method. It is based on the observation of trifles." "[T]here is nothing so important as trifles." "My suspicions depend on small points, which might seem trivial to another."[17]

If the mainstream novel proves ultimately to be another instance of such detection, this is because, both in its story and its method of rendering it, it dramatizes a power continually able to appropriate the most trivial detail. What makes Corentin a better agent than Peyrade in *Une Ténébreuse Affaire* is his ability to see such details and seize them as clues. While Peyrade, for instance, is fatuously "charmed" by Michu's wife Marthe, Corentin more acutely discerns "traces of anxiety" in her. "Ces deux natures se peignaient toutes entières dans cette petite chose si grande"[1] (p. 39). *Cette petite chose si grande:* if the incident that registers the contrast is thus *minor,* then the narration can cite Corentin's power only by sharing in it. We have already seen how Balzacian narration bases its interpretative mastery on minutiae (for example, Corentin's breeches) that it elaborates into "telling" details. A semiological criticism might be tempted to take the conspicuous legibility of these details for a "readerly" assurance.[18] But its effects seem more disturbing than that, if only because such legibility is generally thematized as the achievement of a sinister power like Corentin's. As in the detective story, meaningfulness may not always be comforting when what it appropriates are objects and events whose "natural" banality and irrelevance had been taken for granted. "[R]ien dans la vie n'exige plus d'attention que les choses qui paraissent naturelles."[19] [m] This remark from *La Rabouilleuse* (1842) defines exactly the unsettling *parti pris* of Balzacian narration: what had seemed natural and commonplace comes all at once under a malicious inspection, and what could be taken for granted now requires an explanation, even an alibi. Balzac's fiction characteristically inspires a sense that the world is thoroughly traversed by techniques of power to which everything, anything gives hold. This world is not so much totally intelligible as it is totally suspicious. Even private life partakes of that extreme state of affairs in *Les Chouans* (1829) when the war has begun: "Chaque champ était alors une forteresse, chaque arbre méditait un piège, chaque vieux tronc de saule creux gardait un stratagème. Le lieu du combat était partout ... [T]out dans le pays devenait-il dangereux: le bruit comme le silence, la grâce comme la terreur, le foyer domestique comme le grand chemin."[20] [n]

What we spoke of as the "genetic" organization of narrative allows the significant trifle to be elaborated *temporally:* in minute networks of causality that inexorably connect one such trifle to another. One thinks most immediately of the spectacularly intricate plotting of sensation novelists like Collins and Mrs. Braddon or *feuilletonistes*[o]

---

[l]"These two natures were perfectly depicted in this one very large little thing."—Eds.
[m]"Nothing in life demands more attention than what appears to be natural."—Eds.
[n]"Each field was then a fortress, each tree contemplated a trap, every hollow willow-trunk held a secret plan. The field of battle was everywhere ... Everything in the country became dangerous: noise as well as silence, grace as well as terror, the domestic hearth as well as the great high road."—Eds.
[o]Writer of popular fiction for newspapers.—Eds.

like Eugène Sue and Ponson du Terrail. But the "high" novel of the nineteenth century displays an analogous pride in the fineness of its causal connections. Maupassant argues in the Preface to *Pierre et Jean* (1887) that, whereas an earlier generation of novelists relied on a single "ficelle"[p] called the Plot, the *romancier moderne* deploys a whole network of thin, secret, almost invisible "fils."[21] [q] Inevitably, so threadlike a causal organization favors stories of entrapment, such as we are given in *Madame Bovary* (1857) or several times in *Middlemarch*. Lydgate unwittingly prophesies the disaster of his own career when he says that "it's uncommonly difficult to make the right thing work: there are so many strings pulling at once" (p. 536); and Bulstrode is undone because "the train of causes in which he had locked himself went on" (p. 665), to unforeseeable destinations. Much like Balzac's use of the significant trifle, George Eliot's insistence on causal ramification is meant to inspire wariness. "One fears to pull the wrong thread in the tangled scheme of things." Once a power of social control has been virtually raised to the status of an ontology, action becomes so intimidating that it is effectively discouraged.

Though power thus encompasses everything in the world of the novel, it is never embraced by the novel itself. On the contrary, the novel systematically gives power an unfavorable press. What more than power, for instance, serves to distinguish bad characters from good? Oliver Twist can represent "the principle of Good" (p. 33, Dickens's Preface) because he is uncontaminated by the aggression of his exploiters; and the supreme goodness of Lucy Morris in *The Eustace Diamonds* and Victorine Taillefer in *Père Goriot* depends similarly on their passivity vis-à-vis the power plays going on around them. Conversely, the characters who openly solicit power are regularly corrupted by it: the moral failings of a Rastignac or a Bulstrode are simply gradual, nuanced versions of the evil that arises more melodramatically in a Machiavellian like Corentin or a "poème infernal" like Vautrin. If they are to remain good, good characters may only assume power when—like Oliver's benefactors—they are seeking to neutralize the negative effects of a "prior" instance of it. The same "ideology of power" is implied by the form of the novel itself, which,

[p]"string."—Eds.
[q]"strands."—Eds.

as we have seen, fastidiously separates its "powerless" discourse from a fully empowered world. Yet to the extent that power is not simply made over to the world, but made over *into* the world, literally "secularized" as its ontology, the novel inspires less a distaste for power than a fear of it. What ultimate effects the fear is calculated to produce may be suggested if we turn to a master of fear, who, though not a novelist and living in the seventeenth century, articulated the vision of power which the nineteenth-century novel would so effectively renovate.

> Le moindre mouvement importe à toute la nature; la mer entière change pour une pierre. Ainsi, dans la grâce, la moindre action importe par ses suites à tout. Donc tout est important.
>
> En chaque action, il faut regarder, outre l'action, notre état présent, passé, futur, et des autres à qui elle importe, et voir les liaisons de toutes ces choses.[22][r]

In his first paragraph, Pascal evokes the world of significant trifles related to one another in a minute causal network: the world to which the nineteenth-century novel gives solidity of specification. In his second, he points to what it entails to act wisely in this world: the nineteenth-century virtues of caution and prudence. And finally, in his last sentence, which I have not yet given because it will also be my own, he discloses the natural consequences of thus living in a world thus constructed: "Et lors on sera bien retenu." The novelistic panopticon exists to remind us that we too inhabit it. "And then we shall indeed be put under restraint."[23]

NOTES

1. André Gide, *Les Faux-Monnayeurs,* in *Oeuvres complètes,* ed. L. Martin-Chauffier. 15 vols. (Paris: Nouvelle Revue Française, 1932–39), 12:268. "[D]e tous les genres littéraires . . . le roman reste le plus libre, le plus *lawless.*"

[r]"The smallest movement has meaning for all of nature; the whole sea changes for a rock. So it is with grace: the slightest action has meaning because of its consequences for everything. Therefore everything is important.

"In each action we must consider, besides the action itself, our present, past, and future states and those of others to whom it may be important, and see the links connecting all these things."—Eds.

2. Roger Caillois, *Puissances du roman* (Marseilles: Sagittaire, 1942), p. 140.
3. Charles Dickens, *Oliver Twist* (Oxford: Oxford University Press, 1949), p. 414. In the case of novels cited more than once, page references to the edition first noted will be thereafter given parenthetically in the text.
4. Anthony Trollope, *The Eustace Diamonds*, 2 vols. in 1 (Oxford: Oxford University Press, 1973), 1:252.
5. Cf. Octave Mannoni, "Je sais bien, mais quand même..." in his *Clefs pour l'imaginaire* (Paris: Seuil, 1969), pp. 9–33.
6. Michel Foucault, *Surveiller et punir* (Paris: Gallimard, 1975). For the sake of exposition, Foucault will be cited in the English translation of Alan Sheridan, *Discipline and Punish* (New York: Pantheon, 1977).
7. Stendhal, *Le Rouge et le Noir*, in *Romans et Nouvelles*, ed. Henri Martineau, 2 vols. (Paris: Bibliothèque de la Pléiade, 1952–55), 1:406.
8. Emile Zola, *Nana*, in *Les Rougon-Macquart*, ed. Armand Lanoux and Henri Mitterand, 5 vols. (Paris: Bibliothèque de la Plèiade, 1960–67), 2:1315.
9. Cf. Leon Radzinowicz, "Certain Political Aspects of the Police of France," in his *A History of English Criminal Law*, 4 vols. (London: Stevens and Sons, 1948–68), 3:539–574 (Appendix 8).
10. Honoré de Balzac, *Une Ténébreuse Affaire* (Paris: Collection Folio, 1973), p. 37.
11. Gustave Flaubert, in a letter to Louise Colet (December 9, 1852), *Extraits de la correspondance ou Préface à la vie d'écrivain*, ed. Geneviève Bollème (Paris: Seuil, 1963), p. 95.
12. Emile Gaboriau, *Monsieur Lecoq: L'Enquète* (Paris: Garnier, 1978), p. 18.
13. Mikhail Bakhtin, *Problems of Dostoevsky's Poetics*, trans. R. W. Rostel (Ann Arbor, Mich.: Ardis, 1973), p. 168.
14. George Eliot, *Middlemarch* (Baltimore: Penguin, 1965), p. 46.
15. Leo Bersani, *A Future for Astyanax* (Boston: Little, Brown and Co., 1976). Bersani's stimulating case is made in Chapter Two, entitled "Realism and the Fear of Desire."
16. Wilkie Collins, *The Moonstone* (Baltimore: Penguin, 1966), p. 136.
17. Arthur Conan Doyle, *The Complete Sherlock Holmes* (Garden City, N.Y.: Doubleday, 1930), pp. 214, 238, and 259. The quotations are respectively from "The Boscombe Valley Mystery," "The Man with the Twisted Lip," and "The Adventure of the Speckled Band."
18. Cf. Jonathan Culler, *Flaubert: The Uses of Uncertainty* (Ithaca, N.Y.: Cornell University Press, 1974), pp. 82–84 and pp. 94–100; and Roland Barthes, *S Z* (Paris: Seuil, 1970), pp. 79–80 ("La maîtrise du sens").
19. Honoré de Balzac, *La Rabouilleuse* (Paris: Garnier, 1959), p. 15. The passage suggestively continues: "on se défie toujours assez de l'extraordinaire: aussi voyez-vous les hommes de l'expérience: les avoués, les juges, les médecins, les prêtres, attachant une énorme importance aux affaires simples; on les trouve méticuleux."

20. Honoré de Balzac, *Les Chouans* (Paris: Garnier, 1957), pp. 26–27.
21. Guy de Maupassant, *"Préface à Pierre et Jean,"* collected in *Anthologie des préfaces de romans français du XIXe siècle,* ed. Herbert S. Gershman and Kerman B. Whitworth, Jr. (Paris: Union Générale d'Editions, 1971), p. 369.
22. Blaise Pascal, *Pensées,* in *Oeuvres complètes* (Paris: Bibliothèque de la Pléiade, 1969), p. 1296 [no. 656].
23. A version of this essay was presented during a symposium on "Rethinking the Novel," held in July, 1979 by the Summer Institute in Literature at the University of Texas at Austin. I am happy to thank the head of the Institute, J. Michael Holquist, for kindly inviting my contribution. I must also express my gratitude to Zelda Boyd and Jonathan Crewe for their help in matters of revision.

DENNIS PORTER

Backward Construction and the Art of Suspense

Porter discovers the source of detective fiction's popularity in its manipulation of standard narrative devices to produce suspense. Detective novels are structured, he believes, by two contradictory necessities, that of moving inexorably toward a conclusion and that of delaying the conclusion as long as possible to prolong the reader's pleasurable tension. In this excerpt, Porter shows how Raymond Chandler uses wit, irony, and attention to language as well as plot reversals and the traditional red herrings to produce this tension in The Big Sleep. *His incisive analysis not only helps explain the detective novel's popularity, it also demonstrates how the techniques of Parisian structuralism and Russian formalism can contribute to other kinds of critical discourse. It should be read in the context of Barthes' work, and Eco's.*

Dennis Porter is Professor of French and Italian at the University of Massachusetts in Amherst. What follows is an abridged version of the second chapter of his book, The Pursuit of Crime, *published in 1981.*

Apart from a type of heroic detective, what Doyle acquired above all from Poe was an art of narrative that promotes the reader's pleasure through the calculation of effects of suspense on the way to a surprise denouement. Moreover, the effects of suspense involved depend on the step-by-step process of rational inquiry. The traditional suspense of fear—either fear of threatened disaster, which characterizes tragedy or melodrama, or fear of love unfulfilled, which is central in romance or romantic comedy—is largely supplanted in "The Murders in the Rue Morgue" by the suspense of an unanswered question. Mysterious circumstances are adduced right at the beginning in order to trigger the reader's desire to know the cause. Except in the most cerebral and nonviolent works in the genre, however, there is some combination of the two forms of suspense; the desire to know "whodunit" is excited alongside the fear that whoever it was might repeat his crime.

All narrative, from the most popular to the most subtle, from Ian Fleming to Henry James, traditionally depends for its success with a reader to some extent on its power to generate suspense. Suspense involves, of course, the experience of suspension; it occurs wherever a perceived sequence is begun but remains unfinished. And it may be present in verbal forms at all levels, from a sentence to a full-length novel—something that accounts for the urge felt by listeners to complete other people's dangling sentences. Suspense, as we know from the example of a rhythmically dripping tap, is a state of anxiety dependent on a timing device. And the particular device employed in the detective story is related to its peculiarity of structure mentioned above. In the process of telling one tale a classic detective story uncovers another.[1] It purports to narrate the course of an investigation, but the "open" story of the investigation gradually unravels the "hidden" story of the crime. In other words, the initial crime on which the tale of detection is predicated is an end as well as a beginning. It concludes the "hidden" story of the events leading up to itself at the same time that it initiates the story of the process of detection.

Consequently, there is involved one of those displacements of chronological time which for the Russian formalists distinguished the art of plotting from the raw material of fable. The effect of the crime

---

[1] Raymond Chandler made the point in an essay first published in the *Saturday Evening Post* on March 11, 1939: "Yet, in its essence the crime story is simple. It consists of two stories. One is known only to the criminal and to the author himself. It is usually simple, consisting chiefly of the commission of a murder and the criminal's attempts to cover up after it.... The other story is the story which is told. It is capable of great elaboration and should, when finished, be complete in itself. It is necessary, however, to connect the two stories throughout the book. This is done by allowing a bit, here and there, of the hidden story to appear." Frank MacShane, ed., *The Notebooks of Raymond Chandler* (London: Weidenfeld and Nicolson, 1976), p. 42.

is revealed before the statement of its causes. This means that detective fiction is preoccupied with the closing of the logico-temporal gap that separates the present of the discovery of crime from the past that prepared it. It is a genre committed to an act of recovery, moving forward in order to move back. The detective encounters effects without apparent causes, events in a jumbled chronological order, significant clues hidden among the insignificant. And his role is to reestablish sequence and causality. Out of the *nouveau roman* of the offered evidence he constructs a traditional readable novel that ends up telling the story of the crime.

A classic detective novel may be defined, then, as a work of prose narrative founded on the effort to close a logico-temporal gap. Writing about the Gothic tradition, Macherey observes, "The movement of the novel is double, since it must first hide before it reveals its mysteries. Right until its end the secret must weigh on the imagination or the reason of its hero, and the whole course of the story concerns the description of this wait as well as its creation" (p. 40). The appeal of both Gothic and detective novels, on the other hand, depends on the fact that closure of the logico-temporal gap referred to does not occur right away but only after significant delay. That state of more or less pleasurable tension concerning an outcome, which we call suspense, depends on something not happening too fast. In other words, the detective story formula offers a remarkably clear example of the crucial narrative principle of "deliberately impeded form."[2]

The sharpness of the anxiety felt by the reader of a novel as a consequence of an unresolved and therefore suspenseful situation varies enormously. It depends on such factors as the length of time elapsed between the initial moves in a sequence and the approach to a conclusion, the sympathy evoked for the characters concerned, the nature of the threat represented by the obstacles, or the desirability of the goal. There is obvious suspense as long as imminent danger goes uncontained, but there is also suspense where an orphan is without parents, a lover without his loved one, or a problem without a solution. The need for the relief from tension which comes with a concluding term is felt in such situations just as much as in those that threaten violence or death.

---

[2]See Victor Erlich's discussion of this concept in *Russian Formalism*, p. 178.

If, of all the literary genres, detective fiction, along with melodrama in general, depends for its success primarily on the power to generate suspense, it is also clear that the key device employed in its production is a form of impediment. More obviously than most other fiction or drama, a detective novel is composed of two contradictory impulses. On the one hand, it is made up of verbal units that combine to close the logico-temporal gap between a crime and its solution. On the other hand, it also contains at least an equal number of units that impede progress toward a solution. Like all fiction, detective novels are constructed of progressive and digressive elements; they are at the same time concentrated and diffuse. There must be a journey but it must be circuitous and preferably strewn with obstacles: "The crooked road, the road on which the foot senses the stones, which turns back on itself—this is the road of art."[3] Without a journey you have *Tristram Shandy,* a riotous milling about among overlapping digressions, a tour de force of diffusion that has the form of a shaggy dog story. Yet with mere progression there is simply a rush to the pleasure of a denouement that turns out to offer no pleasure at all. Furthermore, the progression/digression dichotomy, which is as old as Laurence Sterne, has been revived by formalists and structuralists. Boris Tomashevsky distinguished between "bound motifs"—those units of plot which form themselves into indispensable logico-temporal sequences —and "free motifs"—"those which may be omitted without disturbing the whole causal-chronological course of events."[4] Umberto Eco, on the other hand, writes of "fundamental moves" and "incidental moves."[5]

That an appropriately rich emotional response to dramatic and narrative works alike depends on some combination of the two elements may be illustrated from no less a source than Aristotle's *Poetics.* If the chief articulatory moments out of which a detective novel is constructed may still be usefully defined by the critical concepts of

---

[3]Viktor Shklovsky, "The Connection between Devices of Syuzhet Construction and General Stylistic Devices (1919)," in *Russian Formalism: A Collection of Articles and Texts in Translation,* ed. Stephen Bann and John E. Bowet (Edinburgh: Scottish Academic Press, 1973), p. 48.

[4]"Thematics," in *Russian Formalist Criticism: Four Essays,* ed. Lee T. Lemon and Marion J. Reis (Lincoln: University of Nebraska Press, 1965), p. 68.

[5]"The Narrative Structure in Fleming," in *The Bond Affair,* ed. O. del Buono and Umberto Eco (London: Macdonald, 1966), pp. 53–56 [reprinted in this volume].

actively intervene in a variety of ways to prevent unmasking and capture. There are also other blocking figures, such as recalcitrant or confused witnesses, false detectives like Watson or Lestrade, who take time misrepresenting the evidence, and false criminals or suspects. These figures first have to be unmasked before they can be proved innocent and the real criminal can be concentrated on.

3. On the level of character types, there are typically the taciturn Great Detective—in the interest of suspense his thought processes are not disclosed until the recognition scene itself—the garrulous assistant, and the more or less large cast of "characters" or grotesques, whose very oddness makes them for a time impenetrable.

4. On the level of content, there are the episodes themselves, which, as in adventure novel or odyssey, intervene in greater or lesser numbers between a given point of departure and a fixed destination. And there are also the false clues, which mixed together with the true clues make unraveling more complex.

5. On the level of formal elements, finally, apart from plot, it seems that almost any device in a verbal artifact may be employed to perform at a given moment the delaying function, from the episodes themselves conceived as formal units to the employment of a "perpetual idiot" as a narrator, passages of description or dialogue, narrative commentary, and authorial interventions. . . .

The Big Sleep embodies the inherited detective formula because it narrates the story of a criminal investigation that fills a gap in time. It begins with the mystery of a blackmail and of a disappearance and proceeds with great deliberateness through a series of peripeteias to a reenacted scene of suffering and a recognition scene with the power to shock. . . . It opens and concludes with a scene situated on the Sternwood estate in order to reveal that Marlowe need have looked no further for his criminal than the first character he meets after the butler on entering the Sternwood mansion, namely, General Sternwood's psychopathic younger daughter, Carmen. The crooked path in this case turns out to double back on itself; the way out of the investigative maze proves to be right next to the way in. The important difference is that by the end the investigator's point of view on the scene he confronts has been profoundly modified. The journey may have been unnecessary as part of the effort to capture the criminal —Carmen even pretends to faint into Marlowe's arms in that first peripeteia, recognition scene, and scene of suffering, it is because these concepts are important examples of the contradictory impulses referred to. The first signifies, of course, a reversal, or the sudden taking off of the action in an unexpected direction; the second, the passage from ignorance to knowledge; and the third, "a destructive or painful action, such as death on the stage, bodily agony, wounds and the like."[6] The end of a traditional detective novel is the recognition scene in the form of an unmasking and, in a manner to be discussed in a later chapter, the scene of suffering. Together they constitute the desired goal or solution. Peripeteia, on the other hand, refers to what is, in effect, a device of retardation on the level of the action, as Viktor Shklovsky noted: "the fundamental law of peripeteia is that of retardation: of the braking of recognition" (p. 66).

In a detective story peripeteia implies the sudden and unexpected postponement of the apparent approach to a solution. The gap that seemed to be closing opens again. Yet without such an alternate approach to and retreat from a recognition scene there is no suspense. It is therefore a central paradox not only of detective fiction but also of dramatic and narrative literature in general that pleasure results to a large degree from the repeated postponement of a desired end.

Of the many devices of retardation employed in detective novels, some are also features of other narrative genres and others are peculiar to the process of criminal investigation. Among those occurring in the detective novel but not necessarily exclusive to it are the following:

1. On the level of plot, there is peripeteia itself. That is to say, a discovery or event involving a deflection or rebound from progress toward resolution. Examples of this are parallel intrigues, including rival investigations or love motifs that intermittently suspend the principal investigation, and false trials and false solutions, that is, solutions that apparently account for the data and are offered by a foil to the Great Detective or are assumed by him for a time to be accurate.

2. On the level of roles, there is the antidetective or criminal, who may remain passive and not impede the Great Detective's search or

---

[6]Quoted by Geoffrey Hartman, "Literature High and Low: The Case of the Mystery Story," in his *The Fate of Reading* (London and Chicago: University of Chicago Press, 1975), p. 203 [reprinted in this volume].

scene—but it is made indispensable for the moral education of the investigator and, even more importantly, for the appropriate esthetic experience of the reader.

After Dashiell Hammett, Chandler constructs a novel that has the obvious form of a hunt or chase insofar as it follows the trail of clues in an unbroken chain from person to person and from place to place through the urbanized landscape of Southern California. From its beginning in *The Red Harvest,* the form taken by the hard-boiled detective novel suggests the metaphor of the spreading stain. The initial crime often turns out to be a relatively superficial symptom of an evil whose magnitude and ubiquity are only progressively disclosed during the course of the investigation. An important formal consequence of this is apparent in a work such as *The Big Sleep,* which has a large cast of characters, rapidly shifting locations, and an intricately plotted but episodic narrative structure. Philip Marlowe is always on the move, always encountering fresh situations and new characters that hamper his progress toward the solution of crime. In other words, among the principal devices of retardation employed by Chandler are stunning peripeteias and the proliferating episodes themselves. And the agents of his plot are blocking figures of all kinds, from the professional criminals and their hit men to corrupt cops, siren women, and that most recalcitrant of witnesses, a dead man.

It is hardly a matter of hard-boiled realism, in fact, if there are no fewer than six murders in *The Big Sleep,* two of which at least are committed for the sake of thrilling peripeteias by characters who have the smallest of parts. From the point of view of the art of narrative, the functional value of the discovery of a corpse is that it often represents the most brutal of reversals—murder, in spite of its repetition in detective novels, is always produced as a surprise—and the deadest of dead ends. After a death the investigative task often has to begin again. And similar peripeteias are produced by the blow from behind or the drugged drink which delivers the detective into the hands of his adversaries. One of the reasons why Chandler's plots are so complicated, in fact, is that in order to refocus suspense, Philip Marlowe's search is often broken off and relies on an outstanding clue or the surfacing of a fresh face before it can be resumed.

In Chandler's hands, then, the detective novel is seen to break down more clearly than in the formal detective story into a succession of independent episodes linked by an investigative purpose and a point of view. And it is because of its fundamentally episodic structure that a novel like *The Big Sleep* illustrates the apparent paradox that the progressive and digressive units of a narrative sequence are often one and the same. Every action sequence that occurs in a detective novel between a crime and its solution delays for a time that solution even when it appears logically required by it. Down to the level of a sentence, all telling involves the postponing of an end simply because articulate speech is linear and expresses itself in the dimension of time. It is a situation that the most interesting authors of detective novels have knowingly exploited.

More obviously than other narrative genres, the detective novel promotes the myth of the necessary chain. It implies that the only path to the destination that is the solution of a mystery is the step-by-step path of logico-temporal reconstruction. But the only genuine necessity in a detective novel is that minimum of impediments required for the production of the thrills of suspense and for the experience of sudden insight after blindness. Along with *The Moonstone* and *The Hound of the Baskervilles, The Big Sleep* confirms how the best detective novels are constructed backward and in the knowledge of the paradox that the circuitous and even painful path in fiction—"a detour that might be avoided"[7]—is also the path of pleasure. Thus, in Chandler's novel the disclosure of Carmen Sternwood's guilt at the outset would short-circuit the whole reading experience designed by the author. Philip Marlowe is the necessary principle which joins all the intermediary links of the chain that brings the reader by a roundabout route back to the point of departure viewed now with new knowledge. For the novelist, to make his reader go the long way round is to make him feel something he would not otherwise feel. It is also, if more rarely, to make him learn something impossible to learn any other way, that is, by the experience of having lived through it.

Unlike the works of the two English authors, *The Big Sleep* appears to be in the mainstream of a twentieth-century American realism. It dispenses with the suggestion of the supernatural, situates criminal

---

[7]Pierre Macherey, *Pour une théorie de la production littéraire* (Paris: Maspero, 1970).

activity where it mostly occurs, in modern urban settings, points to the psychological and even socioeconomic causes of crime, and employs a tough-minded contemporary vernacular. In its technique, too, it shows a preference for dramatized scenes, dialogue, and description over narrative summary that is also characteristic of modern American realism. Yet what Chandler's example allows us to perceive is that even the familiar storytelling devices of realism are far from "natural" vehicles for the communication of meaning. The calculated narrative art of *The Big Sleep* makes clear how such apparently progressive features as description and dialogue are also digressive and manipulatory. That this is the case may be illustrated by a brief analysis of . . . [t]he short scene in Chapter 26 that narrates the poisoning of the small-time crook, Harry Jones, by the hired killer, Canino. . . . The scene is also a remarkable example of the apparent "naturalness" of Chandler's storytelling method.

In the first place, much of the scene's power derives from the adoption of the limited point of view of Philip Marlowe. As a result, the reader is put in the position of eavesdropping on a murder that takes place on the other side of a glass partition. The narrator is restricted to the reporting of effects perceived indirectly, leaving room for the play of the reader's fantasy and the drawing of appropriate inferences.

The scene opens slowly with the careful description of a run-down commercial building, the function of which is to connote squalor and charged menace.

> There was a tarnished and well-missed spittoon and a gnawed rubber mat. A case of false teeth hung on the mustard-colored wall like a fuse box in a screen porch. . . . The fire stairs hadn't been swept in a month. Bums had slept on them, left crusts and fragments of greasy newspaper, matches, a gutted imitation-leather pocketbook. In a shadowy angle against the scribbled wall a pouched ring of pale rubber had fallen and had not been disturbed. A very nice building.

There follows Marlowe's arrival outside an office and the overhearing of Harry Jones's voice:

> I froze. The other voice spoke. It had a heavy purr, like a small dynamo behind a brick wall. It said: "I thought you would." There was a vaguely sinister note in that voice.

A chair scraped on linoleum, steps sounded, the transom above me squeaked shut. A shadow melted behind the pebbled glass. (pp. 158-64)

The passage is in itself a notable example of the way in which Chandler promotes suspense out of a mosaic of narrative devices. In sentences marked by their rhythmic variety, he alternates spoken phrases with sharp descriptive detailing, narrator commentary ("There was a vaguely sinister note in that voice"), and a suggestive simile in order simultaneously to foreshadow and to retard a violent denouement that the reader is led to expect, although he is surprised and shocked by the form it finally takes. Involved is a type of action writing designed to arouse a disturbingly mixed response. Placed in the position of a voyeur at a murder, the reader is submitted to the characteristic form of Chandler's hard-boiled irony that is wit in a context of cruelty.

The idiom employed in the dialogue itself is a picturesque and alien vernacular—alien at least to any reader likely to read to the end such stylistically sophisticated fiction—of the marginal world of gangsters and petty hoodlums. Apart from the standard "punks," "dough," and "blonde broads," there are words of criminal period slang such as "gat," "shill," "twist," and "Chicago overcoat," and phrases like "tapping the peeper" and "dummying up to you." But the entertaining novelty of the language is largely effective in the dramatic context because it functions as euphemism. What is overheard implies something like the opposite of what actually happens.

Chandler's art consists primarily in taking the conventional devices of narrative realism and infusing them with a tension-producing ironic power by his mastery of pace, style, and tone. He is unusual among writers of detective novels because he is aware that the most satisfactory way of impeding the rush to the denouement is to force the reader to pay attention sentence by sentence by virtue of the precision and energy in the prose—that "lightning struck on every page" of which Billy Wilder spoke.[8] The closing lines of the poisoning of Harry Jones by Canino provide a characteristic example of the rich texture and careful shaping to be found in Chandler's writing.

[8] Miriam Gross, ed., *The World of Raymond Chandler* (London: Weidenfeld and Nicolson, 1977), p. 47.

Backward Construction and the Art of Suspense 337

The little man begins by responding to the killer's apparent effort at reconciliation:

> "No," Harry Jones said. "No hard feelings, Canino."
> "Fine. Let's dip the bill. Got a glass?" The purring voice was now as false as an usherette's eyelashes and as slippery as watermelon seed. A drawer was pulled open. Something jarred on wood. A chair squeaked. A scuffing sound on the floor. "This is bond stuff," the purring voice said.
> There was a gurgling sound. "Moths in your ermine, as the ladies say."
> Harry Jones said softly: "Success."
> I heard a sharp cough. Then a violent retching. There was a small thud on the floor, as if a thick glass had fallen. My fingers curled against my raincoat.
> The purring voice said gently: "You ain't sick from just one drink, are you, pal?"
> Harry Jones didn't answer. There was labored breathing for a short moment. Then thick silence folded down. Then a chair scraped.
> "So long, little man," said Canino. (p. 163)

The narrative elements of the passage are by now familiar. The actual dialogue largely consists of a few fixed phrases of Canino's normally employed to express conviviality but sadistically ironic in the context. The narrator's interventions, on the other hand, are limited to the precise notations of perceived phenomena, chiefly heard sounds, and to reminding the reader of his presence through the use of two ostentatious, hard-boiled similes that also confirm the approaching treachery. But for the most part the passage is constructed out of short declarative sentences ("A drawer was pulled open. Something jarred on wood.") that constitute a form of action commentary and that, as in a radio sportscast, give a blow-by-blow account of an event with a feared but long postponed outcome. The violent climax is made to appear all the more chilling because it is experienced only indirectly. Apart from the purring voice, the killer remains unknown and the killing itself is confirmed only when Marlowe examines the body and smells the cyanide.

The point of the whole scene is not what happens in it—the fate of Harry Jones, for example, is of no significance for the plot—but how

Chandler makes it happen for the reader. The significance is in obliging the reader to play the role of reluctant voyeur, forced to await a violent climax. The scene embodies a remarkable lesson of how not to make something happen too quickly, if you want to elicit the reader's involvement. The spareness of action writing that hides the cunning of its craft clearly derives from the tradition of Hemingway. Yet the terse wit that defines the evil and makes the waiting pleasurable as well as painful is pure Chandler.

The power of promoting the suspense of fear is common to all forms of popular literature, dramatic as well as narrative. It is, for instance, acknowledged to be one of the chief defining characteristics of stage and film melodrama from the genre's beginnings in the French revolutionary period down to James Bond. One of the crudest examples of a device of retardation is found in early film melodrama. It involved typically alternating images of a young woman lashed to a track, on the one hand, with those of an approaching locomotive and a galloping posse, on the other. However crude the technique, it does indicate the indispensable element of all suspense in film or literature, namely, that of witnessing an action evolve along a timeline toward a fixed point in the future that will signify salvation or rescue for the characters concerned.

One of the best-known applications of the cinematic technique of cutting to promote suspense is in *High Noon*. Fred Zinnemann's formal frame, reminiscent of Collins's broken courtship in *The Moonstone*, is provided by the motif of the interrupted wedding. Sexual consummation is made dependent on the successful resolution of an unequal combat in the street between gladiators, thus furnishing a double focus for suspense. But between the wedding ceremony and the postponed departure for the honeymoon, there occurs the relentless countdown to the shoot-out with the famous alternation of images of railroad station, hotel, sheriff's office, clock, and train. The rhythmic cutting that in this case was deliberately heightened by the music protracts the waiting and brings out into the open the patently erotic structure of melodrama.

Similarly, in the detective novels discussed in this chapter the various narrative devices have the primary function of preventing premature disclosure in the interest of suspense. Only a story that embodies an appropriate quantity of resistance in its telling is experienced as satisfactory; the longest kept secrets are the ones we most desire to know. It is a circumstance that probably explains why the short story has never achieved such widespread popularity as longer fiction or serial narrative; the reader's desire is gratified too quickly for the pleasure to be particularly intense.

Finally, what an analysis of detective novels also helps us realize is the centrality of suspense in novel reading generally. Reading fiction of all kinds is an activity which generates tension that can be relieved only through the experience of an end. All storytelling involves the raising of questions, the implied promise of an answer, and, in traditional narrative at least, the provision of that answer in time. When the proper time for the provision of an answer will be in a given story obviously depends on a number of factors among which the most crucial is probably the writer's capacity to sustain suspense while convincing the reader that his digressions are pleasurable and purposeful in themselves. The shortest version of *The Hound of the Baskervilles,* one wholly devoid of digression, would be no longer than a grammatically complete sentence—"The murder of Sir Charles Baskerville and the attempted murder of Sir Henry Baskerville by a relative seeking to inherit the family fortune were solved by the distinguished amateur detective, Mr. Sherlock Holmes, assisted by his friend, Dr. Watson." Whatever else Doyle puts into his novel adds nothing to the announcement of a crime and the naming of a criminal, although it does involve the reader in the experience of strange and chilling possibilities. In other words, a detective novel's length is determined less by a supposed organic necessity inherent in the material itself than by the need to promote in a reader the excitement of some combination of the suspense of fear and the suspense of an unanswered question. Consequently, whether or not the length of a book is felt to be appropriate will depend on such extraneous factors as reading habits and the prevailing conventions in book production as well as on an author's skill. The minimum appropriate length is that required to generate the experience of suspense; the maximum appropriate length is that which is compatible with the maintenance of a reader's concern about an outcome without loss of his interest on the way to it.

What emerges most clearly from an analysis of detective fiction as opposed to that of most other kinds of novels is, then, that the art of narrative is always the art of withholding as well as of giving information. It is an art of timing that because of the nature of the novel as book is an art of spacing. Everything in a satisfactory traditional novel is placed by the author at a certain point between covers usually containing somewhere between 50,000 to 100,000 words, in order to be discovered there by a reader at the appropriate moment. And in this connection, reading narrative fiction can be seen to involve a form of participation different from that of looking at a painting or even listening to music.

Reading a novel is an activity of decipherment and discovery that involves the physical task of following the printed sentence down the page with one's eyes and of turning over the successive pages. It is a painstaking search for revelations that may occur at any point on the way to a culminating revelation. Whatever a given work's subject matter, therefore, reading it always takes for its reader the form of the special kind of adventure that is a treasure hunt. With the turning of each fresh page, there is communicated the thrill of exposure to the unknown, to the possibility of danger or of reward. With each fresh paragraph, new clues may appear that lead on, however circuitously, to the buried treasure of the denouement. It is perhaps no more than a happy accident of Western technology that a novel in our culture has the physical form of a shallow box which opens from the side. A certain feeling for a book's buried treasure must have been felt by those who once arranged to have their own books equipped with clasps and keys. It is in any case the desire to discover the nature of a given novel's secrets that often drives us to complete it, frequently in the face of considerable odds.

GLENN W. MOST

The Hippocratic Smile: John le Carré and the Traditions of the Detective Novel

Most begins by locating the real mystery of the mystery novel not in its crime, which always admits of a solution, but in the irreducibly enigmatic figure of the detective, whom Most identifies as the emblem of the reader in the text. If the detective represents an ideal interpreter, then differences in modes of detection can be understood as differences in implicit theories of how to read. In this light, Most contrasts the English tradition of detective fiction, represented for example by Conan Doyle and Christie, with the American tradition of Hammett, Chandler, and Macdonald, and suggests that the former emphasizes the product of reading and the latter the process. Most concludes by using this framework to interpret the novels of John Le Carré, tracing the development of his career from the straightforward detective novellas he first wrote to his more recent use of traditional detective-novel plots and devices in the service of larger moral and political meditations. Despite Le Carré's emphasis in content on spies, his true precursors are in the American school of detective fiction, and his innovations within this tradition cast light on the strengths and limits of the genre as a whole.

Most's article, previously unpublished, can profitably be read in the context of Heissenbüttel's philosophical study reprinted here. Most, in addition to being one of the editors of this volume, is Assistant Professor of Classics at Princeton, and a fellow (1982–1983) of the American Academy in Rome.

> Under her left breast and tight against the flame-colored shirt lay the silver handle of a knife I had seen before. The handle was in the shape of a naked woman. The eyes of Miss Dolores Gonzales were half-open and on her lips there was the dim ghost of a provocative smile.
> "The Hippocrates smile," the ambulance intern said, and sighed. "On her it looks good."
>
> —Raymond Chandler, *The Little Sister*[1]

I

The true mystery in a mystery novel is not that of the crime committed near its beginning and solved near its end but instead that posed by the nature of the detective who solves it. To be sure, the crime is always puzzling, either because it is so bizarre or because it seems so simple, and the plot of the novel always moves from the absence of an answer for this puzzle, through a series of false answers, to a final and therefore presumably true one. But at the end, there always is that final answer, that solution which accounts both for the initial crime and for the various inadequate hypotheses to which it gave rise; and, at the end, the reader wonders why he had not seen the answer sooner. For the mystery of the crime is, in essence, simply a riddle, a question that seems obscure before it is answered but oddly simple afterwards, a puzzle for which there is always allegedly one and only one solution. Its difficulty derives from the fact that a truth has been *concealed,* its ease from the fact that a *truth* has been concealed. For no concealment can be flawless (the fruitlessness of the genre's eternal search for the perfect crime is enough to show this), and the very measures that are taken to disguise the crime are the ones that in the end will point unmistakably toward its perpetrator. If one reason for the mystery novel's conventional preference for the crime of murder is that murder is perhaps the only human action in which there are usually only two participants, one absolutely incapable of narrating it later and the other disinclined to do so, then we may be tempted to explain this as part of an effort to make the puzzle as hard to solve as possible; yet the victim's unwilling silence is always more than compensated for by the murderer's onerous knowledge. The certainty of the latter's correct awareness of what really happened is the fixed point around which the novel moves and to which it can and therefore must inevitably return. The victim may have been duped by the murderer; but in the end, it is always the murderer who is the greater dupe: for he had imagined that merely concealing an answer would suffice to make it irretrievable, and had not realized that any process of concealment can be reversed and become, step by step, a process of discovery. The victim, whose corpse abashed survivors surround, may seem lonely in his death—but the criminal, to whom finally all point their fingers and proclaim, "Thou art the man," is, in fact, in his utter nakedness, far more terrifyingly so.

But if the crime is, in essence, merely a puzzle, the detective who solves it is himself a figure of far deeper and more authentic mystery. All the other characters may be stereotypes and may turn out to have acted from the most banal of motives; but the detective fits into none of the categories with which the actions of all the others can be exhaustively explained, and his own motives are cloaked in an obscurity that is never finally lifted. He is fundamentally at odds with the society of which all the other characters are part; he is the bearer of true rationality, opposed to both the murderer (who degrades reason to the cleverness with which an irrational crime can never be adequately concealed) and the police (who represent a reason that is institutionalized, technocratic, and therefore quite futile); he is the figure of decency surrounded by selfishness and immorality, the sole searcher for truth in a world given over to delusion and duplicity. He is in every regard a marginal figure: his profession is not to have a profession but to investigate all those who do; he derives his income not from a steady and productive job but, case by case, from those who have such jobs but require his services; he alone can move, competently but never at home, through every stratum of society, from the mansions from which the poor are excluded to the slums that the wealthy abhor; he is almost always single or divorced (it is marriage that provides the most fertile soil for this genre's crimes); his parents are almost never mentioned, and he is invariably childless. It is his freedom from all such categories that permits him so clearly to see through their workings in all the other characters; but at the same time this dispensation from the rules that bind all others makes him an enigma without an answer, a mystery which is never solved. What does the detective do between cases?[2]

Poe, with his usual prescience, endowed the literary detective with this aura of mystery at his birth. The first sentence of the first mystery story, "The Murders in the Rue Morgue," points the paradox nicely: "The mental features discoursed of as the analytical, are, in themselves, but little susceptible of analysis."[3] What is this analytical power to whose description Poe devotes the first pages of the story? His analysis of it juggles paradoxes of appearance and reality, means and ends, method and intuition, without even pretending seriously to provide a satisfactory answer. We are told that the man who possesses this power "is fond of enigmas, of conundrums, hieroglyphics" (p. 141); but the power itself (which suffices to solve such trivial problems, though they may confound us) cannot be approached directly, but only through the detour of such examples as checkers and whist provide. Even Poe's final correlation of ingenuity with fancy and the analytical ability with imagination serves only to translate the dilemma into the terms of English romantic literary theory, not to resolve it. From the beginning, that is, Poe is at pains to show us that the mysteries that can be solved are not as mysterious as those posed by the power that solves them; and his method is to use answerable puzzles as a means of demonstrating the unanswerableness of the deeper puzzle of the power that can answer them. The celebrated anecdotes that follow this opening—Dupin guesses the narrator's thoughts and solves the double murder in the Rue Morgue—are introduced simply as being "somewhat in the light of a commentary upon the propositions just advanced" (p. 143), and even they do not answer the questions that opening raises. They provide further, more extended examples; they pretend to demonstrate by narrative rather than by analogy; but they multiply the enigma rather than resolve it. Hence, not the least of the red herrings in Poe's story is its very form: by its structure it seems to begin with a mystery (what is the analytical power?) and then to provide its solution (by the narrative of Dupin's exploits). But those exploits—by their bizarre mixture of reckless leaps to conclusions with scrupulously logical method, by their combination of erratic erudition and cheap theatricality, and above all by their wildly improbable success—serve only to deepen the mystery rather than to dispel it. We ought to have been warned by the very name Dupin (which does not quite conceal the French verb meaning "to dupe")—or by the epigraph from Sir Thomas Browne that Poe brazenly affixes to his story and that propounds the solubility of questions to which no answer could possibly be found: "What song the Syrens sang, or what name Achilles assumed when he hid himself among women, although puzzling questions, are not beyond *all* conjecture" (p. 141).

Hence, the mystery of who killed Madame l'Espanaye and her daughter is definitively, if oddly, resolved; but the mystery of Dupin never is. The details of his past are entirely obscure; of his income we learn only that it suffices to free him of any occupation other than reading, writing, and talking all night long; we do not even know what he looks like. Dupin is, of course, an extreme example; but in the way in which he penetrates all others' secrets while remaining opaque to us he provides the model for all his followers:

> He boasted to me, with a low chuckling laugh, that most men, in respect to himself, wore windows in their bosoms, and was wont to follow up such assertions by direct and very startling proofs of his intimate knowledge of my own. His manner at these moments was frigid and abstract; his eyes were vacant in expression; while his voice, usually a rich tenor, rose into a treble which would have sounded petulant but for the deliberateness and entire distinctness of the enunciation. (p. 144)

The vacancy of his eyes seals him against our inspection: as the oracle, filled with divine inspiration, of which this latter sentence is designed to remind us, he offers us troubling insights into the truths we conceal within us, but himself escapes our detection.

Such coyness is, of course, profoundly seductive; and, from Poe onwards, the mystery genre has fascinated its readers at least as much through the person of its detective as through the ingenuity of its puzzles or the exoticism of its crimes. Future historians of the genre could do worse than to point to the striking proximity, in place and time, of the rise of the detective story and of that of the modern biography: for detective stories are, for many readers, installments in the fragmentary biographies of their heroes, each displaying his familiar virtues under a new and surprising light. Every new case presents a challenge to the detective's skills: we know he will meet it, and are pleased to discover we had not foreseen how. The natural result is the cult of the literary detective, so familiar in our time, whether that cult is centered upon holy sites (like number

221B, Baker Street) or upon the gifted actor who has succeeded in incarnating the detective on film (like Bogart's Sam Spade or Philip Marlowe).

But if the detective's essential enigmatic quality has persisted now for almost a century and a half, the specific form it has assumed has undergone radical transformation during that time. For the sake of simplicity (and at the cost of a certain schematism), we may distinguish between two basic and largely successive traditions: one that may be called English (though it begins with Poe) because it is brought to its classic form by Arthur Conan Doyle and continued by other British authors like Agatha Christie; and another, primarily American tradition, founded by Dashiell Hammett, perfected by Raymond Chandler, and prolonged by Ross Macdonald.

In the English tradition, every effort is made to keep the detective free of any other participation in the case he is investigating than that necessarily involved in his solution of its perplexities. This is, indeed, one of the hallmarks of the early modern detective story that separates it decisively from such forerunners as *Oedipus the King* or *Hamlet*, in which the investigator is intimately bound up, by links at least familial and dynastic, with the case in question. The invention of the professional detective, who investigates not because anything is at stake for him (other than the discovery of the truth) but simply because that is his job, serves the purpose of keeping him free of any taint of complicity in the case.[4] In this way, investigation and event, thought, and object, are kept entirely distinct from one another. The separation between these two realms engenders a narrative that can begin with the widest possible distance between them and moves, more or less haltingly, toward their identification. The standard plot within this tradition begins with the discovery of the crime in its apparently absolute inexplicability. The detective is brought into the case either by the accidental circumstance of his proximity or by a client who has been unjustly accused and whose innocence he is required to establish. The detective then begins to investigate, by means of perception (the discovery of clues), discourse (the interviewing of various parties), and the logically self-consistent interpretation of the material he thereby acquires. His activity proceeds until the mental construct of the original crime he has been gradually refining finally coincides with that crime: at this point there is at last an exact correspondence between his thought and the real event that had occurred before his entrance onto the scene, the discrepancies that had provided the impetus to his revision of earlier hypotheses have been resolved, and the truth can be announced. The criminal confesses and the innocent suspect is redeemed; the police enter and the detective exits; justice is done. In such plots, two particularly noteworthy kinds of exclusions tend to operate. On the level of the individual characters, relations of sex or violence between the detective and the other figures tend to be prohibited: the detective neither experiences nor exerts sexual attraction, and he neither inflicts nor is seriously endangered by physical violence. On the level of society, the characters tend to be isolated during the investigation from forces that would otherwise interfere with it; the result is a certain unity of place, which, at the limit, secludes all the possible suspects in a train, a hotel, or an island.

In all these regards, the contrast posed by the American tradition could hardly be more striking. Consider the plot structure most frequently found among these latter authors. The novel begins, not with a murder, but with the client's hiring the detective in some far more minor matter: a painting has been stolen, a blackmailer must be foiled, a runaway teenager must be found. The detective begins to investigate: and only then do the murders begin. The detective relentlessly pursues his course on a path increasingly strewn with corpses until a truth is uncovered for which the original assignment represented at best a misunderstanding, at worst a ploy. It generally turns out at the end either that the client was himself the criminal and had attempted to lure the detective into becoming the unwitting accomplice of his designs or that the minor incident that had brought the detective onto the scene was merely a distant epiphenomenon of a deeply hidden, far more heinous crime, which cannot remain unsolved if that minor incident is to be adequately explained. Here the detective is not only the solution, he is also part of the problem, the catalyst who by his very introduction both provokes murders and solves them. In the figure of this investigator, the investigation and its object become inextricably intertwined. Correspondingly, the two exclusions we noted in the English tradition tend to be annulled. On the one hand, the detective's relations with other characters are free from neither sex nor violence: he feels acutely a disturbing erotic interest in the women of the case, which they are all too ready to exploit; and conversely, he can become the victim of considerable violence and be seriously threatened with death, just as he can employ methods of interrogation and coercion that the English novelists might dismiss as ungentlemanly. These features are not just sensationalistic but are designed to further implicate the detective in the case and to jeopardize his autonomy: a sexual involvement would abolish his status as outsider, whereas the scenes of violence turn him into a version of the victim or of the murderer. And on the other hand, the ever-widening circle of his investigation constantly draws in new characters and forces that might seem to hinder his initial task but, in fact, fulfill it by placing it in its full context: it is only by indirections that he finds directions out, and his travels through the extreme reaches of different social classes and different parts of the city, always in pursuit of a unified truth, link what might have seemed disparate and unconnected fragments into a complex and deeply corrupt social network.

It is tempting to accuse the English tradition of naiveté and its products of being sterile intellectual puzzles or to praise the American tradition for its sophistication and social realism. But this is shortsighted. Not only can the English authors produce plots of a deeply satisfying complexity and psychological richness; not only can the American novelists fall into the trap of identifying the bizarre or the sordid with the realistic and fail to recognize how stereotyped their own plots are. More importantly, both traditions provide valid, if competing, versions of the fundamental mystery of the detective without which the genre can scarcely be conceived. In both, the detective is, in fact, the figure for the reader within the text, the one character whose activities most closely parallel the reader's own, in object (both reader and detective seek to unravel the mystery of the crime), in duration (both are engaged in the story from the beginning, and when the detective reveals his solution the reader can no longer evade it himself and the novel can end), and in method (a tissue of guesswork and memory, of suspicion and logic). That is why the literary detective (as distinguished, one supposes, from the real-life one) tends so strongly to marginality, for he is quite literally the only character who resides at and thereby defines the margin between text and reader, facing inward to the other characters in the story and facing outward to the reader with whom only he is in contact; so, too, that is why he is so isolated, insulated from family, economy, and his own past, for all such factors as these tend to be suppressed as distractions by readers during the activity of reading any literary text. To be sure, in cases where the story is told not by the detective himself or by an omniscient narrator but instead by the detective's confidante, the reader's identification may be split between the Holmes figure and the Watson one: but here the Watson character provides one pole of convenient stupidity that the reader is proud to avoid (though he must exert himself to do so), whereas the Holmes one represents the ideal pole of perfect knowledge, of an entirely correct reading, toward which the reader aims and which he ought never quite to be able to attain. In other regards as well (the suspense of the delay that intervenes between desire and fulfillment or between question and answer and without which the temporality of any plot is impossible), the detective story takes certain features inherent in any narrative and concentrates its textual operations upon their deployment; here, too, it exaggerates the reader's natural wish to identify with the characters in a story and offers him one character in particular who fulfills the criteria of an ideal reader, but tends to deny him all others. The reader of the detective novel, entranced by the impenetrable enigma of the figure of the detective, thereby forgets that he himself is a Narcissus, staring in wonder at the beauty of a disturbingly familiar face.

From this perspective, the difference between the English and the American traditions resides only in the way in which they conceptualize the activity of reading: for if the detective is a figure for the reader, different modes of detection can be construed as different implicit theories of reading. The English insulation of the detective from his case is designed to create one privileged discourse within the text that is capable of determining the value of all its other parts but that is not itself dependent upon them: the locus of truth is incarnated within the text in such a way that it can legislate to the other parts, so that it is in the text but not of it. Hence the tendency to unworldliness in the English detective, which contributes to his mystery and sometimes makes it difficult to imagine his existing in the same society as the other characters. His wisdom is essentially timeless, and his final correct understanding of the case takes the form of a momentary vision in which all its parts cohere: the time of the narrative of his investigation may mimic the temporality of reading but has none of the genuinely dialectic quality of the latter, none of its belatedness, duplicity, self-delusion, and hope. Unlike the American tradition, the English one can include the very short story, for the temporal deferral that separates crime from solution contributes in itself nothing to the latter and can be expanded, rearranged, or elided at will. It is this temporality of reading to which the American tradition accords so much importance: here the sequence of events may seem arbitrary but is, in fact, unalterable. Human time, in its despotic irreversibility, rules the American novels: the minor incident for which the detective is summoned must precede and cannot follow the murders that his entrance provokes, and his final account of the case takes the form of a narrative, of a chain of causes and effects in which the criminal became fettered more ineluctably the more desperately he sought to free himself. Here the detective is not the bearer of a higher wisdom but himself, at least in part, an imperfect agent. The threat of sex, like the actuality of violence, binds him to crimes for which he himself is in some sense responsible, for they would not have occurred (at least not in this way) if he had not entered the scene. His identification of the criminal is intended also to exculpate himself, but he can never be entirely freed of the burden of responsibility for having catalyzed the criminal's actions: at the end of each of these novels, Spade, Marlowe, or Archer is terribly alone, for these detectives embody that aspect of reading in which it is a guilty and solitary pleasure. Part of their mystery is that they continue in their professions at all, despite the bitterness of their knowledge of their world and of themselves.

Hence, the American tradition focuses upon the pain of the process of interpretation and the English upon the joy of its result. The English novelists presuppose the certainty of a correct reading and project back from that end to an initial stage of ignorance from which the path to that goal of knowledge is in principle never in doubt. The Americans, on the other hand, are caught up in the uncertainties of the activity of interpretation itself, for which a final and valid result may be imagined but can never be confidently predicted. From the point of view of the activity, the result is a utopia we may never attain; from the point of view of the result, the activity was meaningful only insofar as it led step by step to that end. The miracle of reading, and the dilemma of the mystery story, is that both are right.

II

In his book on the tragic drama of the German Baroque (a period that will be of importance for George Smiley), Walter Benjamin describes the difference between symbol and allegory in a way that casts light upon this contrast between the English and American traditions:

> Within the decisive category of time . . . the relation of symbol and allegory can be defined with an incisive formula. Whereas in the symbol destruction is idealized and the transfigured countenance of nature fleetingly reveals itself in the light of redemption, in allegory the observer is confronted with the *facies hippocratica* of history as a petrified, primordial landscape. History, in every regard in which, from the very beginning, it has been untimely, sorrowful, unsuccessful, expresses itself in a countenance—or rather in a death's head. . . . This is the heart of the allegorical way of seeing, of the baroque, secular explanation of history as the Passion of the world; it attains significance only in the stations of its decline.[5]

Much of the conceptual framework Benjamin employs in this section of his book has striking affinities with the differences between the traditions of the detective novel outlined earlier: a literary theoretical distinction could easily be elaborated between the English authors' symbolic approach, with its nonhistorical and redemptively synthetic view, and the secular temporality of the Americans' allegory. Instead, I should like to call attention here to a new element this passage introduces, to the *facies hippocratica* Benjamin uses as a symbol for allegory. We may take Benjamin's hint and ask what kind of countenance the literary detective wears: more specifically, how he smiles.

The answer is only at first surprising. Within the English tradition, perhaps only Poe's Dupin almost never smiles: despite his chuckle in the passage quoted earlier, he is usually too much the romantic *poète maudit* to engage in levity, and the only people who laugh aloud in Poe's stories are fools who thereby betray their incomprehension.[6] Elsewhere in this tradition, from Holmes through Poirot and Nero Wolfe, the detective smiles frequently:

> "It may seem very foolish in your eyes," I added, "but really I don't know how you deduced it."
>
> Holmes chuckled to himself.

> "I have the advantage of knowing your habits, my dear Watson," said he.
>
> "What is this, Holmes?" I cried. "This is beyond anything which I could have imagined."
>
> He laughed heartily at my perplexity.
>
> "Well, well, MacKinnon is a good fellow," said Holmes with a tolerant smile. "You can file it in our archives, Watson. Some day the true story may be told."
>
> Our visitor sprang from the chair. "What!" he cried, "you know my name?"
>
> "If you wish to preserve your incognito," said Holmes, smiling, "I would suggest that you cease to write your name upon the lining of your hat, or else that you turn the crown towards the person whom you are addressing."[7]

This is the smile of wisdom, complacent in the superiority of its own power and tolerant of the weakness of mere humanity; the detective adopts it in the moment when he has understood something that no one else has, yet it signifies not only the incomparability of his skill but also the benevolence with which he will use it. Ultimately, this is the smile of the Greek gods in their epiphanies to mortals: the smile of Aphrodite asking Sappho what is bothering her now or the so-called "archaic smile" on countless early Greek statues. In terms of our earlier discussion, it is also the smile of the reader who can close the book with the mixture of delight and satisfaction that a full understanding of it brings.

This smile is never found on the faces of the detectives of Hammett, Chandler, or Macdonald: they lack the requisite benevolence no less than the necessary superiority. To be sure, they do smile upon occasion, but only in two ways. Rarely, they smile to deceive, to pretend to a man they do not trust that they trust him so that they can lure him into their clutches. But more commonly, their smile is wry, bitter, helpless in the face of the corruption of the world and of their own complicity in it; it is the sardonic smile of the reader who knows that his own life is no less ambiguous and stalemated than the novel he is now reading. In Raymond Chandler, the Hippocratic smile is a recurrent symbol: the rictus of death, it suggests a fullness of wisdom that only the dead can have and that therefore comes too late to be of any use to the living. Hippocrates should be able to heal; but the man who wears the Hippocratic smile is past healing. One time it is Marlowe himself who wears it. This happens at a crucial moment in *The Big Sleep*. Marlowe has just witnessed, helplessly from the next room, a gangster's callous murder of a fellow detective, Harry Jones. Marlowe is partly responsible for Jones's death: it was he, after all, who had told the gangster's boss that Jones was following him; and though Marlowe had certainly not intended this result, he will feel it necessary to expunge and compound his guilt for it, when the time comes, by gunning down the gangster without mercy in his turn. At the very end, in the eulogy to Rusty Regan, the only thoroughly decent man in the novel, whose corpse had already been decaying in a sump before the story had even begun, Marlowe will give voice to a deep envy for the dead, who have attained to a peace that the living seem foolish for so desperately deferring. But now the plot must go on: and it requires Marlowe to take over briefly the role of Jones, whose death was unnecessary and who in a sense died for him. Chandler writes:

> It was raining hard again. I walked into it with the heavy drops slapping my face. When one of them touched my tongue I knew that my mouth was open and the ache at the side of my jaws told me it was open wide and strained back, mimicking the rictus of death carved upon the face of Harry Jones.[8]

III

Despite his name, George Smiley is not given much to smiling. Even at the moment of his greatest triumph, the forced defection of Karla at the end of *Smiley's People*, he does not share in the jubilation of his colleagues. Most often he seems worried, tentative; he blushes often; people think him confused and shy. These appearances both are and are not deceptive. For his name is no less carefully chosen than are those of Dupin, Sam Spade (direct and disillusioned, with the gravediggers' humor), Philip Marlowe (literate and endangered), and Lew Archer (a straight shooter and good guesser, a modern Apollo), and of most other literary detectives. As George, le Carré's hero is the slayer of the dragon, like his pseudonymous creator a defender of the faith, the guardian of traditional values. No wonder he is worried: for in a fallen world these can only be preserved by recourse to methods those same values must condemn. But as Smiley, he is not only put into contrast with such competing models of the secret agent as James Bond (can one imagine Ian Fleming's hero with Smiley's name?), but also placed firmly in the tradition of the literary detective, who, as we have learned to expect, ought by profession to smile. Why doesn't Smiley?

It may at first seem odd to consider Smiley a detective: after all, Le Carré has attained celebrity as a writer of novels of espionage, and Smiley has entered the annals of world literature as a master spy. In fact, stories about spies and about detectives have much in common. As the two major subgenres of the thriller, they share many features: the interpretation of clues and the construction, revision, and eventual confirmation of hypotheses; an atmosphere of deceit, where treachery is the rule and trust a sometimes fatal mistake; a curious fascination with the many varieties of violent death. And historically, there have been many crossovers between the two modes: already Dupin's services were enlisted in affairs of state in "The Purloined Letter," as were Holmes's in "The Naval Treaty" and "His Last Bow"; and Nazi agents turn up in Chandler's *Lady in the Lake* and many other detective novels of the 1940s.

Yet considerable differences separate the modes of espionage and of mystery, and clarifying these will suggest the degree to which many of le Carré's novels, though full of spies, no less clearly belong to the tradition of detective fiction. These differences are not only thematic, in the sense in which we can say, for example, that mystery novels tend to center upon the destinies of individuals, whereas in spy novels the interests of nations are at stake.[9] They are also, and even more clearly, formal. The plot of a mystery is retrospective: it looks backward to an event that happened before, at or shortly after its beginning, and, knowing that it has already occurred, asks how it happened. The plots of spy stories, on the other hand, tend to be prospective: they are directed toward an event that has not yet occurred and that must be either prevented (the threat against England must be warded off) or performed (the enemy must be given false information); they ask not who did it but what will happen. Because the event in a mystery has already occurred, the progress of its narrative is essentially a process of understanding, toward which the detective's actions are subordinated; because the event in a spy story has not yet happened, its hero must engage primarily in certain actions (to thwart or permit that event), and his gradually deepening understanding of the situation is valuable only insofar as it enables him to perform the decisive actions at the right moment. In a mystery, the culprit is identified only at the very end; in a spy story, the enemy can be known from the very beginning and the hero can be aware of his fiendish plan from a very early stage of the plot. Hence, the delay that is necessary for a narrative must be generated in a mystery story by the successive creation and refutation of interpretative models, whereas that in a spy story tends to take the form of temporary obstructions to the hero's freedom of action: whether he is captured, pursued, or injured by the enemy, the crucial point is that he be made incapable of fulfilling his mission at once. Usually, the motives for at least the original murder in a mystery are separate from the hero's activity of investigation: the murderer acted, at least the first time, from greed or jealousy, anger or revenge. In the spy novel, on the other hand, the victims are those who know too much, who could prevent the enemy's fulfilling his plan, and the hero is in no less danger than they were. If the spy story belongs to the genre of the picaresque novel (where the end is known in advance and is delayed by episodes) and goes back ultimately to the *Odyssey* (in which Odysseus acts over and over again the role of a spy), the mystery might be correlated with the folk form of the riddle (which begins with a question and ends with its answer) and has its classical forerunner in *Oedipus the King* (in which Oedipus is not only detective and judge but also criminal and, ultimately, victim).

An example will help to make the differences clearer. In John Buchan's *The Thirty-Nine Steps,* Scudder recounts to the hero, Hannay, in the very first chapter the full details of the plot to murder Karolides in London on July 15.[10] This same chapter ends with the murder of Scudder, but Hannay's reaction is revealing:

> Somehow or other the sight of Scudder's dead face had made me a passionate believer in his scheme. He was gone, but he had taken me into his confidence, and I was pretty well bound to carry on his work. . . . I hate to see a good man downed, and that long knife would not be the end of Scudder if I could play the game in his place. (pp. 36–37)

There is not a hint here of a desire to find the culprits and to bring them to justice: we have a murder, but not a mystery. To be sure, at the very end Hannay will confront the foreign agents with a warrant for their arrest for the murder of Scudder (p. 219); but we know that his intention is to prevent them from leaving the country with the details of the disposition of the British home fleet on mobilization and that this warrant is simply the most effective means available. Hannay knows from the beginning the enemy's intention to murder Karolides: the plot consists largely of a sequence of episodes entitled "Adventure", of pursuits, captivities, and escapes, in which the Black Stone try to track Hannay down and prevent him from thwarting their plans while the police seek him in connection with Scudder's murder (this latter element is the only aspect of the novel in which it approaches a mystery, but it is narrated from the point of view of the putative murderer, is largely tangential, and is never treated with full seriousness). In the end, it turns out that Karolides cannot be saved; but we have already learned that his death is inevitable and that the real danger comes from the planned betrayal of the naval secrets (pp. 73ff). This is the danger toward which the plot as a whole is directed; and it is one that Hannay succeeds in averting at the last minute.

With this in mind, we can return to le Carré and see that his novels fall easily into three categories: spy stories, mysteries that often involve spies, and a third and most interesting group, in which the two modes are played off against one another. That some of his works are more or less straightforward tales of espionage no one will deny. The plot of *The Looking Glass War* (1965), for example, is directed to the question of whether the East Germans are building a secret missile launching site. It turns out in the end that the indications that had seemed to point to this possibility had, in fact, been planted by Control in order to discredit a rival Ministry, and hence that the Head of the Circus is himself ultimately responsible for the murder of Taylor in the first chapter; but there is no murder investigation and no character who plays the role of the detective, and the question of who actually killed Taylor is barely raised and never answered. Again, *The Honourable Schoolboy* (1977) and *Smiley's People* (1979) are both directed toward bringing a foreign agent over into the West; though there are some extremely nasty murders, especially in the latter novel, those who die do so mostly because they knew too much, and the plots are aimed not toward the identification and punishment of the culprits but toward the final compromising and securing of the foreign agent;

to this end the complex web of investigation, deception, and extortion is woven.

In the present context, more interest attaches to le Carré's mystery stories. It is often forgotten that le Carré began his literary career with two quite short novels, *Call for the Dead* (1961) and *A Murder of Quality* (1962): though both feature Smiley, only the former involves any other spies and both are, in fact, best understood as detective novels. In *Call for the Dead,* Smiley investigates the apparent suicide of a member of the Foreign Office and discovers a series of anomalous circumstances that point unmistakably to murder. For the rest of the novel, Smiley tracks the murderers until, in a climactic confrontation, he himself kills the man who had ordered the diplomat slain. That this man was a foreign agent and that the diplomat had been killed because he had come to suspect that his wife was a spy are of little or no consequence for the plot of the novel (though they no doubt contribute to its success in other regards). We have here, in essence, a straightforward detective novel in the American tradition. Smiley has features in this first novel that he will retain throughout his literary career and that mark him as a familiar member of the ranks of literary detectives in general—his enigmatic nature (the novel introduces Smiley by dwelling upon the inexplicability for English society of Lady Ann's marriage to him); his marginality in matters personal (symbolized by his predilection for German literature, especially for the much-neglected Baroque period), marital (Lady Ann's separation from him is announced on the first page), and professional (in this, his first novel, he already retires from the Service); his cooperation with the authorized institutions of investigation (embodied, not for the last time, in Inspector Mendel) and his aloofness from them (indicated by his refusal to accept the Service's offer to decline his letter of resignation). These features would suffice to stamp Smiley as a detective; but others point no less clearly to the heritage of Hammett and Chandler rather than to that of Conan Doyle and Christie. Thus, Smiley becomes the victim of a physical assault to which he almost succumbs; conversely, at the end he does not arrest the criminal but instead slays him. Again, his participation in the case involves him personally in other ways than those connected immediately with the investigation: the head of the foreign agents had been Smiley's pupil before the war, and, although this gives Smiley the knowledge that enables him to lay a successful trap, it also means that, when Smiley kills him, he will be overwhelmed by remorse and self-loathing:

> Dieter was dead, and he had killed him. The broken fingers of his right hand, the stiffness of his body and the sickening headache, the nausea of guilt, all testified to this. And Dieter had let him do it, had not fired the gun, had remembered their friendship when Smiley had not.... They had come from different hemispheres of the night, from different worlds of thought and conduct. Dieter, mercurial, absolute, had fought to build a civilization. Smiley, rationalistic, protective, had fought to prevent him. "Oh God," said Smiley aloud, "who was then the gentleman . . ."[11]

Such passages are characteristic of the American tradition, where in the end there may be little difference between detective and criminal beyond the fact that the former succeeds at the cost of the latter: is there any doubt at the end of a mystery by Christie or Sayers who the gentleman was? But the most telling evidence for assigning *Call for the Dead* to the American tradition of detective fiction derives from the structure of its plot. For Smiley is brought in, not after the murder, but before it, and the murder is a direct result of his introduction into the story. An anonymous letter had been received, denouncing the diplomat as a former communist, and Smiley had been ordered to interview him. One of the ironies of the plot is that the matter was thoroughly trivial, and Smiley saw no reason to pursue the investigation; but a foreign agent had observed the two walking in a park together, had concluded that the diplomat would betray them, and had decided he must be killed. Another irony becomes obvious at the end, when it turns out that the agent was right: the anonymous letter had been written by the diplomat himself, not in order to jeopardize his career but so as to establish a first contact with Smiley's Service.

To turn from *Call for the Dead* to *A Murder of Quality* is to move from the American to the English tradition of mystery stories. This is le Carré's purest detective novel: its plot could have come directly out of Agatha Christie. The case involves the murder of the wife of a faculty member at an exclusive boys' school; Smiley enters it only because she had written, expressing fears for her life, to a friend of his. The murder occurs before he arrives; he solves it with the help of the local police; at the end, the murderer is arrested. To be sure, le Carré uses the novel as a vehicle to explore the social and psychological tensions arising from contemporary changes in English life, and a kind of negative personal complicity on the part of Smiley in the case he is investigating is established by the repeated references to Lady Ann, who belongs to the social class of which the school is part in a way that Smiley never will; but, in terms of its plot, the novel is thoroughly conventional. It almost gives the impression that le Carré, at the beginning of his career, had deliberately chosen to apprentice himself first in the one tradition and then in the other before going on to more serious work.

The results are evident in le Carré's most interesting mystery novel, *Tinker, Tailor, Soldier, Spy* (1974). Here the plot has the form of a murder mystery, although the victim, Jim Prideaux, did not die but was (only) shot, captured, and tortured. There are four suspects, four highly placed officials in the Circus who could have been the Russian agent responsible for the betrayal of Prideaux's mission; and Smiley is brought out of retirement in order to determine which of the four is the guilty party by investigative procedures no different from those any traditional detective would use. Moreover, the clue that firmly establishes the guilt of Bill Haydon is of the most conventional sort:

> "Sam, listen. Bill was making love to Ann that night. No, listen. You phoned her, she told you Bill wasn't there. As soon as she'd rung off, she pushed Bill out of bed and he turned up at the Circus an hour later knowing that there had been a shooting in Czecho. If you were giving me the story from the shoulder—on a postcard—that's what you'd say?"
> "Broadly."
> "But you didn't tell Ann about Czecho when you phoned her—"
> "He stopped at his club on the way to the Circus."
> "If it was open. Very well: then why didn't he know that Jim Prideaux had been shot?"[12]

This is only the slightest of variations upon the traditional scene in which the criminal, told the victim has been murdered, blurts out, "My God, who shot him?" and the detective murmurs, "Who said anything of his being shot?"

But this passage occurs only two-thirds of the way through the novel. Why, then, is Haydon not arrested at once? The reason casts light upon the way le Carré has modified the conventions of the mystery novel to suit his purposes. It will be recalled that the American tradition permits the detective's personal complicity in the case to become an important factor in the plot: here le Carré develops this feature ingeniously by having Bill Haydon become notoriously adulterous with Lady Ann. It was no accident that Haydon had been in bed with Smiley's wife on the night Prideaux was shot. For if Smiley were to finger Haydon on the basis of the kind of evidence just cited, it would be thought he was acting out of jealousy: this had been part of Karla's design. Hence, Smiley must create a trap in which some new action of Haydon's will prove his guilt beyond any possible doubt; and the last part of the novel is devoted to his setting this trap.

Another problem remains, however. If *Tinker, Tailor, Soldier, Spy* is, in fact, formally a murder mystery, why was Jim Prideaux not murdered? Why is the victim permitted to survive? Le Carré's innovation in this regard moves the detective novel beyond the realm of ordinary crime and inserts it into a specifically political context. For what is to be done with Haydon once he has been identified as the foreign agent? In the traditional criminal novel, the murderer's death or arrest provides an entirely satisfactory conclusion; but here both alternatives are quite problematic. For the English Service to kill Haydon would taint Smiley in a way le Carré is elsewhere at pains to avoid.[13] On the other hand, political considerations would require Haydon to be imprisoned and eventually sent to the East in exchange for some captured Western spy; yet, given the enormity of Haydon's betrayal, such an ending would violate the reader's sense of justice and seem intolerably weak. The demands of justice can only be satisfied if Haydon can be appropriately punished; and Prideaux's murder of Haydon, in spite of all of Smiley's precautionary measures, cleverly provides a satisfactory conclusion to the novel without implicating Smiley.

The last three novels we have considered can all be adequately interpreted in terms of their use of traditional mystery plots; but already in the third one we have seen how certain features point beyond the limits of that genre. In conclusion, I should like to turn to two other novels by le Carré in which the central categories of the mystery tradition are employed only so that they can be radically put into question.

The Spy Who Came in from the Cold (1963) begins with the death of an agent in Berlin. When Alec Leamas, his contact, returns to England, Control proposes to him a plan whereby the man responsible for the murder can be punished. Leamas accepts the plan because of his desire to avenge the agent's death upon the man who ordered it, the East German agent Mundt:

> "That is, of course, if you're *sure you want* to . . . no mental fatigue or anything?"
> "If it's a question of killing Mundt, I'm game." (p. 17)
>
> "He said there was a job he'd got to do. Someone to pay off for something they'd done to a friend of his." (p. 99)

Leamas, like the reader, is convinced that he is involved in a typical mystery plot: the guilty will be brought to justice and the moral order will be restored. There is, to be sure, no detection (Mundt's guilt is clear from the beginning), and the plot is prospective insofar as it is directed toward the eventual compromising of the East German: yet reader and hero always look backward as they move forward and envision that ending as a satisfactory answer to the problem posed by the beginning. But, of course, it is revealed in the end that Leamas, and we with him, have been deceived: the object of Control's plot turns out to have been the death not of Mundt (who was, in fact, an English agent) but of his subordinate Fiedler (who had been on the point of discovering Mundt's treason and himself acts the role of the detective within Control's elaborate scheme). The conventions of the mystery story are used as a red herring to deceive the reader as well as the characters and they are exploded by the ending, in which the murderer is saved while the East German detective and the English avenger are killed. Le Carré takes considerable pains to establish Mundt's vile and vicious character—in contrast to him, not only Leamas but also Fiedler are thoroughly sympathetic figures—and the resulting jolt to the reader's sensibilities helps to make the novel's ending so fully and satisfactorily unsettling. But the contribution le Carré's inversion of the generic conventions of the mystery novel makes to achieving this effect ought not to be neglected: to discover that the search for truth and justice is not the real object but only a ruse to protect their opposites for reasons of national self-interest provides an ingenious surprise by purely formal means. To be sure, the traditional American mystery had allowed the possibility that society was so corrupt that the detective's uncovering of the truth could no longer save it: Marlowe's Southern California is in many ways irredeemable, and, at the end of *The Big Sleep,* the small fry can be punished but Eddy Mars retains his nefarious power, and the murder of Rusty Regan may be brought to light but is immediately hushed up. Yet, by turning those who believe in the ideals of detection into naive pawns in the hands of the cynical practitioners of *Realpolitik, The Spy Who Came in from the Cold* pushes Chandler's moral disillusionment an important step farther. Le Carré's novel implicitly asks the question whether English society has not reached the point at which the truth must be suppressed and justice thwarted if the society is to be preserved. In terms of literary genres, this can be translated into the question whether the mystery story is still possible in our time.

It is to this question that le Carré's *A Small Town in Germany* (1968) is most systematically addressed. The plot begins when Leo Harting, an employee at the British Embassy in Bonn, vanishes; he has taken sensitive files with him, and the suspicion of his defection is immediately invoked. Alan Turner is sent from England to track him down, and we seem to be confronted with a standard mystery in which the detective (Turner) pursues the criminal (Harting). But in the course of Turner's investigation a surprising truth emerges: Harting is evidently not a spy for the East but has himself been investigating the background of an important West German political figure, Karfeld. Eventually, it becomes clear that Karfeld had committed an atrocity during the Second World War and that Harting had come upon the traces of his crime. Instead of the detective (Turner) pursuing the criminal (Harting), we find one detective (Turner) pursuing another detective (Harting) who, in turn, is pursuing the real criminal (Karfeld). The differences between the two detectives are obvious. Harting, "the memory man,"[14] is obsessed with discovering the truth about the past and with seeing justice done; no consideration of policy or of self-interest can prevent him from bending every effort to investigating the traces of a crime and to seeing to it that the man who bears the guilt for it is appropriately punished. In his moral rigor, unswerving determination, and investigative ingenuity, Harting is the perfect type of the classic literary detective. Turner, on the other hand, is

The Hippocratic Smile

bound by considerations of national policy: for the English have formed a secret alliance with Karfeld, based on mutual self-interest, and are desperately concerned that the German politician not be discredited. Turner is himself too much a detective not to feel a powerful sympathy with Harting and to try his best not to obstruct him; but in the end he cannot prevent Harting from being killed and Karfeld from being saved. The war criminal can continue in his meteoric political career; the interests of England are protected; but the authentic detective is murdered and the inauthentic one is condemned to futility and self-hatred. Turner's last conversation with the diplomat Bradfield, who incarnates the cynicism of power in the novel, establishes its ultimate frame of reference:

> Turner searched frantically around him. "It's not true! You *can't* be so tied to the surface of things."
> "What else is there when the underneath is rotten? Break the surface and we sink. That's what Harting has done. I am a hypocrite," he continued simply. "I'm a great believer in hypocrisy. It's the nearest we ever get to virtue. It's a statement of what we ought to be. Like religion, like art, like the law, like marriage. I serve the appearance of things. . . . He *has* offended," he added casually, as if passing the topic once more in review. "Yes. He has. Not as much against myself as you might suppose. But against the order that results from chaos; against the built-in moderation of an aimless society. He had no business to hate Karfeld and none to . . . He had no business to remember. If you and I have a purpose at all anymore, it is to save the world from such presumptions."
> "Of all of you—listen!—of all of you he's the only one who's real, the only one who believed, and acted! For you it's a sterile, rotten game, a family word game, that's all—just play. But Leo's *involved!* He knows what he wants and he's gone to get it!"
> "Yes. That alone should be enough to condemn him." (pp. 361–362)

If modern society is directed solely to the future rather than to the past, if the necessary and sufficient goal of national policy is survival, if the appearances must be preserved because there is nothing else besides them, what place can remain for the detective who seeks to decipher the enigma of the past, whatever the cost for the present? At the end of Chandler's novels, Marlowe may be condemned to futility;

at the end of le Carré's novel, Harting is condemned to death. Marlowe may don the Hippocratic smile; Harting can no longer doff it. In the murder of Harting is figured the death of the traditional mystery novel. Authors may continue to write detective novels; le Carré himself has done so. But the insight to which le Carré has given voice in *A Small Town in Germany* may well anticipate the end of the genre. Future generations may no longer understand why the past century has been so obsessed with the discovery of truth and the punishment of crime. For them, the mystery novel may become mysterious in a way we would prefer not to envision.

NOTES

1. Raymond Chandler, *The Little Sister* (Hammondsworth, Middlesex: Penguin, 1977), p. 247.
2. What I have described in this paragraph are what seem to me the basic generic conventions of the literary detective. Of course, exceptions can be found for every one of these generalizations. There are mysteries without a murder (Chandler's *Playback*, an anomaly in many ways and evidently Chandler's farewell to the genre); mysteries in which the detective's love interest plays an important and constructive role (Sayers's *Gaudy Night*); mysteries in which the narrator is the murderer (Christie's *The Murder of Roger Ackroyd*) or the hero is (Highsmith's *The Talented Mr. Ripley*); mysteries that the detective does not solve (Bentley's *Trent's Last Case*) or that are solved without a detective (Christie's *And Then There Were None*). But all such cases are deformations of the expected conventions and must be understood as such; that is their point. Likewise, detective novels in which the detective is a member of the regular police force (such as those of McBain and Simenon) are not exceptions to the general outline sketched here: for in these novels the hero is always at odds with the police force as a whole and operates as an often insubordinate loner; the constitutive opposition between detective and police is simply transposed to the interior of the police, but is not thereby abolished.
3. Edgar Allan Poe, *The Complete Tales and Poems* (New York: Vintage, 1975), p. 141. Future references to this edition are indicated by page numbers in parentheses in the text.
4. Such tales as E. T. A. Hoffmann's "Das Fräulein von Scuderi" (and even Poe's "The Murders in the Rue Morgue") are transitional phenomena in this regard: here, although the crime itself does not directly concern the detective, his involvement in the case is due to his feeling of personal concern for an acquaintance who has been unjustly accused and to whom the detective feels obligations arising from an earlier connection. In both cases, this excuse for the detective's participation has a very artificial air.

5. Walter Benjamin, *The Origin of German Tragic Drama*, translated by John Osborne (London: NLB, 1977), p. 166. I have revised the translation in a number of points to make it closer in meaning to the original.
6. So particularly in "The Purloined Letter," where the laughter of the Prefect (p. 209) and of the narrator (p. 215) suffices to condemn them.
7. Sir Arthur Conan Doyle, *The Complete Sherlock Holmes* (Garden City, N.Y.: Garden City Books, n.d.), pp. 474, 488, 1323, 404.
8. Raymond Chandler, *The Big Sleep* (New York: Vintage, 1976), p. 168.
9. Even here, the contrast cannot be taken too strictly. A spy novel in which personal destinies were not at stake would be unreadable; and, in all mystery writers at some level and in certain ones (like Ross Macdonald) quite explicitly, the ultimate subject is the society in which such murders are performed.
10. John Buchan, *Adventures of Richard Hannay* (Boston: Houghton Mifflin, 1915), pp. 20, 31–32. Subsequent references are indicated in the text.
11. John le Carré, *Call for the Dead* (New York: Bantam, 1979), p. 137.
12. John le Carré, *Tinker, Tailor, Soldier, Spy* (New York: Bantam, 1975), p. 238.
13. Elsewhere, Smiley is generally kept free from association with the more sordid activities of British Intelligence. In Le Carré, the English tend (unrealistically perhaps) to torture and murder far less than their communist counterparts and to rely instead upon cunning and deception: what is more, Smiley in particular is usually spared direct involvement in those operations that would tend to cast doubt upon the morality of the Circus. The following exchange, from *The Spy Who Came in from the Cold* (New York: Bantam, 1975), 49, is revealing:

> "Why isn't Smiley here?" Leamas asked.
> "He doesn't like the operation," Control replied indifferently. "He finds it distasteful. He sees the necessity but he wants no part in it. His fever," Control added with a whimsical smile, "is recurrent."

Subsequent references are indicated in the text.
14. John le Carré, *A Small Town in Germany* (New York: Coward-McCann, 1968), p. 125. Subsequent references are indicated in the text.

WILLIAM W. STOWE

From Semiotics to Hermeneutics: Modes of Detection in Doyle and Chandler

This essay argues that classic detective stories rely on a simple model of interpretation, treating sensory data ("clues") as signs for hidden facts about events in the past and hidden truths about the characters' personalities. This model served Doyle very well, produced the "Golden Age" of detective fiction in the 1920s and 1930s, and continues to structure much popular crime fiction. It did not, however, satisfy the literary ambitions of Raymond Chandler, who moved to modes of interpretation based on reciprocal interaction between the detective and the people, places, events, and circumstances under investigation. The action of Chandler's Farewell, My Lovely, *for example, is as much the product as the subject of Philip Marlowe's investigations, and Marlowe is challenged intellectually and physically by the situations he has helped to create. Here the strict distinction between the detective on the one hand and the case on the other, between the interpreter and the object of interpretation, is broken down.*

Stowe's previously unpublished contribution is the third in this volume to deal with the work of Raymond Chandler, and should be read in conjunction with those of F. R. Jameson and Dennis Porter. It also offers an alternative version to Grossvogel's of the process of interpretation in the detective novel. Stowe is Assistant Professor of English at Wesleyan University and author of Balzac, James, and the Realistic Novel *(Princeton, 1983).*

"Here is my lens. You know my methods. What can you gather yourself as to the individuality of the man who has worn this article?" . . .

"I can see nothing," said I, handing it back to my friend.

"On the contrary, Watson, you can see everything. You fail, however, to reason from what you see. You are too timid in drawing your inferences."

"Then, pray tell me what it is that you can infer from this hat?"

He picked it up, and gazed at it in the peculiar introspective fashion which was characteristic of him. "It is perhaps less suggestive than it might have been," he remarked, "and yet there are a few inferences which are very distinct, and a few others which represent at least a strong balance of probability. That the man was highly intellectual is of course obvious upon the face of it, and also that he was fairly well-to-do within the last three years, although he has now fallen upon evil days. He had foresight, but has less now than formerly, pointing to a moral retrogression, which, when taken with the decline of his fortunes, seems to indicate some evil influence, probably drink, at work upon him. This may account also for the obvious fact that his wife has ceased to love him."

"My dear Holmes!"[1]

No one who has read even a single Sherlock Holmes story will be surprised by such a passage as this. They are part of the Holmes formula; for all their predictability, we would be disappointed not to find them and would feel cheated out of yet another example of our hero's astonishing method. The assertion that it *is* a method, and not some mysterious power of Holmes's, is part of the formula, too. The readers and their stand-in, Dr. Watson, must be made to feel that they, too, could do what Holmes does if they only noticed what he notices and shared his vast store of information.[2]

Holmes's inferences are so accessible to us because they are extraordinary in degree but not in kind. They resemble the common-sense inferences we make every day; furthermore, they reinforce our conventional, unexamined assumptions about the efficacy of simple interpretation in moving from sensory data or narrated "facts" to other, intentionally or circumstantially hidden facts, and from them to ultimate truths, factual and/or moral. His method is a practical semiotics: his goal is to consider data of all kinds as potential signifiers and to link them, however disparate and incoherent they seem, to a coherent set of signifieds, that is, to turn them into signs of the hidden *order* behind the manifest confusion, of the *solution* to the mystery, of the *truth*.[3] This may look at first glance like simple code reading, but it is, in fact, a little trickier than that. Consider this standard semiotic representation of the act of communication:

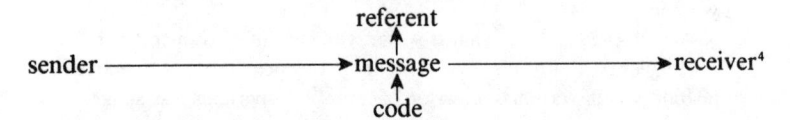

$$\text{sender} \longrightarrow \underset{\underset{\text{code}}{\uparrow}}{\overset{\overset{\text{referent}}{\uparrow}}{\text{message}}} \longrightarrow \text{receiver}$$[4]

According to this model, the message (understood not as the intended *content* but as the concrete *form* of the communication) moves between sender and receiver, refers to some content it intends to convey, and is constructed according to the rules of some conventional code, be it language, gesture, Morse, or whatever. Sherlock Holmes and the code reader both adopt the role of the receiver, they both treat certain data as parts of a message, and they both seek to determine the "truth" to which this message refers. Here, however, the similarity ends. The code reader assumes a clearly defined message—a given, limited, ordered number of signs—intentionally encoded by a conscious sender in some systematic way. For Holmes there is no single sender-encoder of the message he must decipher. The truth, so the theory goes, encodes its own message, to be decoded by the detective. This suggests that the message itself is not clearly defined but hidden in a mass of facts, all of which can be interpreted, but only a very few of which, taken together, can lead to a solution of the mystery. And as if this were not enough, the code in which this message is embodied is not unified, conventional, and efficient, like language, but multiform and diffuse, demanding not word-for-word translation by a single set of rules but sensitive interpretation of each element by an experienced interpreter who takes all possible readings of each clue into account, then sorts them, selects among them, and organizes them in such a way that they reveal hitherto obscure events in the past or aspects of the characters' personalities, which, in turn, suggest a solution to the mystery.

So Holmes must define the message and discover how it is encoded without the help even of an imaginary encoder. His difficulties do not end there, either, for whereas no one has planted clues attempting to convince Holmes of the truth, someone is often sending false messages designed to keep him or someone else from discovering it. His job therefore is not only to discover the truth by reading its signs but also to screen out those competing, misleading signs intentionally emitted by his adversaries. It is clearly more than simple cryptography, but just as clearly still a semiotic practice.

Take, for example, the third of the original *Adventures of Sherlock Holmes,* "A Case of Identity." Miss Mary Sutherland opens the case by appearing in Holmes's rooms in a dither: she has been left, it seems, pretty nearly at the altar by Mr. Hosmer Angel, who had gotten into a cab bound for St-Saviour's, King's-Cross, and somehow vanished before it reached its destination. The facts of the case all seem equally meaningless in Miss Sutherland's rambling narrative, but Holmes methodically sorts out the significant ones and shapes them into a message he can interpret. One cardinal fact sets the parameters of the investigation: Miss Sutherland has a small but tidy independent income, currently drawn by her mother and her stepfather, with whom she lives. Mr. Hosmer Angel therefore has much to gain from the marriage, whereas Miss Sutherland's mother and her young husband, Mr. Windibank, have a lot to lose.

This suggests to Holmes that the lamented Hosmer Angel did not disappear of his own accord. There is more, however: what Miss Sutherland reads as signs of her intended's gentle character, Holmes connects with the possible motive he has already detected:

> "He was a very shy man, Mr. Holmes. He would rather walk with me in the evening than in the daylight, for he said that he hated to be conspicuous. Very retiring and gentlemanly he was. Even his voice was gentle. He'd had the quinsy and swollen glands when he was young, he told me, and it had left him with a weak throat, and a hesitating, whispering fashion of speech. He was always well-dressed, very neat and plain, but his eyes were weak, just as mine are, and he wore tinted glasses against the glare." (p. 44)

Mr. Hosmer Angel in this case intentionally provides signs of his own character, and authorized interpretations of these signs: evening walks mean he is shy; hoarseness is a sign of an early illness; tinted glasses indicate weak eyes. Holmes, however, takes them all as signs that Angel has something to hide. He then notices two further facts, and takes them as signs for a third, which will explain the mystery. The two facts are these: Miss Sutherland has only seen Mr. Hosmer Angel when Mr. Windibank has been away on business; Mr. Hosmer Angel objects to his fiancée's typing her letters to him—" 'He said that when I wrote they seemed to come from me, but when they were typewritten he always felt that the machine had come between us' " (p. 44) —but he types his own to her, including the signature. Holmes's deduction is, of course, that Mr. Hosmer Angel and Mr. Windibank are one and the same. Holmes is certain that this is the case, but he provides himself with another bit of proof—and us with a neat example of his semiotic method—by writing Windibank at his office and requesting an interview. The reply comes back—typed—and Holmes has only to compare typescripts, to make letters into signs, not for sounds or words or referents, but for their own origin, to sew up his case. He has only, that is, to incorporate what look like ordinary, conventional signs—letters—into his own special ad hoc sign system to have them stand not for words and written messages but for a whole story he has pieced together independently. This story, of course, is a message in its own right, referring at last and pitifully to the Windibanks' greed. At the end of the story the faithful Watson inquires, " 'And Miss Sutherland?' " and the sexist detective replies:

> "If I tell her she will not believe me. You may remember the old Persian saying, 'There is danger for him who taketh the tiger cub, and danger also for whoso snatches a delusion from a woman." (p. 52)

Holmes's method has produced clear, if in this case ineffectual, results. He has uncovered facts and read them as signs, first of a general situation and then of a set of hidden events, a story that he easily interprets as a plot to keep Miss Sutherland's inheritance in the Windibank household for some time to come.

Like Holmes, Poe's Auguste Dupin is a semiotic interpreter who treats facts as signs of other facts, and eventually of "the truth."[5] The most exhaustive—and tedious—example of his method can be found in "The Mystery of Marie Roget," his transparently disguised treatment of a notorious New York disappearance of his day, a bravura attempt to solve a crime using conflicting newspaper reports as his only evidence. Here every reported "fact" is a sign of something, of

Marie's intentions (pp. 417–419), her abductor's sly attempts to muddy the trail behind him (pp. 424–426), or the reporters' own blindness (pp. 389, 391, 395–396). Dupin does sort all these signs and their putative referents into a credible story, but he has trouble imagining what this complex sign might mean, and leaves us in the end unimpressed with his efforts.[6]

Not surprisingly, Dupin's methods work better in fictions designed to demonstrate their efficacy rather than to test them against recalcitrant and distant facts. The classic example is, of course, "The Murders in the Rue Morgue."[7] In this tale Poe conceives of his hero as a romantic artist who uses true "analysis" as opposed to the inferior "ingenuity" of the police, and compares the two faculties to Coleridge's imagination and fancy, relating the first to analytic genius and the second to mere mechanical ingenuity (p. 126). The parallel is illuminating as far as it goes. The prefect of police does indeed exercise something like "fancy" in his systematic and indiscriminate collecting of facts: "The Fancy," writes Coleridge, "brings together images which have no connection, natural or moral, but are yoked together by the poet by means of some accidental coincidence."[8] The prefect yokes facts together by virtue of their spatial and temporal coincidence, but cannot articulate them into an intelligible whole. Dupin, for his part, is certainly imaginative in the ordinary sense of the word, and he does, like Coleridge's imaginative poet, give "unity to variety"[9] by reading apparently disparate facts as signs pointing toward a unified, hidden set of events and motivations rather than as separate "clues" with separate and, in this case, incompatible meanings. The prefect's methods and Dupin's have rather more in common, however, than Coleridge's fancy and imagination or than the work of the mechanic and the genius: both are semiotic interpreters; both read facts as signs. The difference is that while the prefect translates the signs separately, Dupin never stops looking for the message they convey as a whole. He proceeds, however, in a methodical fashion from facts to hypotheses, using his imagination, it is true, but no special genius or poetic inspiration. He reads the signs in "The Murders in the Rue Morgue" in two stages in order first to solve the closed-room mystery (how did the perpetrator escape?) and then to identify that perpetrator himself.

The first step involves a purely logical process of elimination. Having examined all other possible exits from the room, Dupin decides that the only way the culprit could have escaped and left the window locked behind him was if a certain nail were broken:

> "I had traced the secret to its ultimate result—and that result was *the nail.* It had, I say, in every respect, the appearance of its fellows in the other window, but this fact was an absolute nullity (conclusive as it might seem to be) when compared with the consideration that here, at this point, terminated the clue. 'There *must* be something wrong,' I said, 'about the nail.' I touched it; and the head, with about a quarter of an inch of the shank, came off in my fingers." (p. 146)

He has made the solid elements of the room into signs pointing the way to the one weak element, the broken nail.

The second step is methodical, too, but it brings Dupin's imagination and his prodigious store of information into play as well. Dupin determines by a process of elimination similar to the one he used to find the faulty nail that the murderer must have escaped from the room by swinging on a shutter to within reach of a lightning rod descending to the ground. The gap between shutter and rod is unfortunately too wide for an ordinary man to leap. Rather than be daunted by this simple fact, however, Dupin makes of it a sign which, taken with other fact-signs and a large measure of imagination and erudition, leads to the solution of the mystery. The width of the gap indicates that the criminal is either an extraordinarily agile man or no man at all. The greasy ribbon Dupin finds suggests the former, that is, that it is a question of a Maltese sailor accustomed to clambering in the rigging. The tuft of nonhuman hair in Madame L'Espanaye's hand and the widely spaced finger marks on her daughter's throat suggest the latter and, more precisely, that the perpetrator was an "Ourang-Outang." The witnesses' reports of hearing a strange "conversation" between one horror-stricken French voice and another, strange voice speaking a language all recognized as foreign but no foreigner recognized as his own confirm both hypotheses: the facts make sense together if and only if the murder was *committed* by an orangutan and *observed* by a Maltese sailor, presumably the escaped and uncontrollable beast's "master."

Dupin's investigations are not always so exhaustively logical as this

—the discovery of the "purloined letter," for example, involves an intuitive identification with the perpetrator's thought processes as well as the systematic elimination of all possibilities but the correct one. Still, they do move, by and large, from visible facts—signs—to invisible facts, facts that are revealed but never altered by their submission to analysis.

This sequence, as Poe and Doyle established it, has served since their times as a model for detective fiction, a model strictly followed by some practitioners of the genre and less strictly by others.[10] It has led such theorists of detection as David Grossvogel and Stephen Knight to describe the classic detective story as a kind of opium for the reading classes. "No presentation or analysis of the social causes of disorder is offered," Knight writes; "it is merely suggested that strange and terrible things can happen and a clever man will be able to explain them. . . . A comforting fable for skilled and dedicated readers is brilliantly fabricated."[11] And Grossvogel declares that, unlike more serious literature, "the mode of the detective story is to create a mystery for the sole purpose of effecting its effortless dissipation."[12]

Although these criticisms are valid for a large number of detective novels from police procedurals to the ratiocinative exploits of such eccentrics as Nero Wolfe, Lord Peter Wimsey, and Miss Jane Marple, they are not an inevitable feature of the genre. They are furthermore based on some widely held assumptions about man and the world that have been under attack for 100 years at least, without showing much sign of losing their influence. These are the assumptions that Hans-Georg Gadamer attributes to classical scientific thinking as it was developed by Descartes and his Enlightenment successors[13] and that are based on a radical distinction between subject and object and a belief that thought and language are best understood as neutral, transparent instruments that man uses to gain power over the world (pp. 210–213). They are the basis not only of traditional detective novels, but of a wide range of thinking about man's relation to the world, from ordinary and to some extent necessary common-sense assumptions about the instrumentality of language and thought to the neo-Enlightenment rhetorical and hermeneutic theories of E. D. Hirsch. Philosophers from Hegel to Gadamer and beyond, however, have argued that these assumptions are culturally and linguistically conditioned and that they can distort the way we think of ourselves and our relation to the world.

What Gadamer proposes is a new understanding of the interpretive act, based on a hermeneutic rather than a semiotic model. Interpretation is for him more closely related to philosophical introspection than it is to cryptography: it constantly questions the meaning and the value of the interpreter and his procedures, as well as the object of interpretation. His central thesis in *Truth and Method* is that we cannot discover truth (which he emphatically does not see as "hidden facts") by cultivating method. Gadamerian hermeneutics is an activity of mind in which subject, object, and mental process meet and act upon one another. None of these elements as it functions in the hermeneutical relationship is properly definable outside that relationship: the interpreting subject is affected by the object of interpretation, which is itself never the same for two interpreters.

So interpretation for Gadamer is never merely reproduction or revelation of the previously existing, but is always itself creative. "Not occasionally only, but always, the meaning of a text goes beyond its author" (p. 264). It is, in fact, recreated by every new interpreter, not because he intends to alter the "original" meaning to make it relevant to his own time, but because he cannot avoid seeing (interpreting) any text from his particular point of view. "To try to eliminate one's own concepts in interpretation is not only impossible, but manifestly absurd. To interpret means precisely to use one's own preconceptions so that the meaning of the text can really be made to speak for us" (p. 358). Interpretation is best defined, then, as a transaction with a "text," be that text a document, an array of historical facts, or a set of events. The ideal interpreter, like the ideal conversationalist, effaces neither himself nor his partner, but allows each fair time in the generation of an event whose meaning resides in the present, though it includes important elements from the past, among them, usually, the text itself, its traditions, and the traditions of the interpreter.

The detective resembles Gadamer's interpreter insofar as he responds to his "text"'s implicit challenges. Holmes and Dupin do listen harder and hear more of what the clues have to tell them than their fellow characters do. They do not, however, open themselves to questions from these clues, they do not allow the objects of their investigations to question their methods or the ideological assumptions that inform them, so they remain prisoners of method, brilliant technicians who can only go on repeating what they already do so well.

As we have seen, serious critics have deplored the consequences of this imprisonment for the twentieth-century detective novel. Some writers, however, have managed to avoid the semiotic trap while remaining within the vaguely defined borders of the detective novel, by creating detective-protagonists who understand their job as something more than puzzle solving. One such character is Chandler's Philip Marlowe.

Marlowe is a hard-boiled detective with a heart of gold, a private eye who sometimes begins his investigations for a fee but never ends them until he is satisfied—though rarely happy—with the solution he has reached or the crises he has provoked. In the framework of the client-directed search for facts, he invariably conducts another search, too, a search "not for a specific criminal, but for a *raison d'être*, a meaning in character and relationship, what the hell went on, rather than who done it."[14] In the process he opens himself to the questions—and the threats—his cases pose.

Farewell, My Lovely provides a good example of Marlowe's interpretive adventures: by the time he is actually hired to investigate the facts of the novel's central case, he is more thoroughly entangled in its complications than anyone suspects. The first few paragraphs put Marlowe's ordinary fee-for-service snooping in its proper place and give us some clues about his sensibility and his motivations.

> I had just come out of a three-chair barbershop where an agency thought a relief barber named Dimitrios Aleidis might be working. It was a small matter. His wife said she was willing to spend a little money to have him come home.
>
> I never found him, but Mrs. Aleidis never paid me any money, either.[15]

So much for step-and-fetch-it detecting. Marlowe's curiosity is piqued, however, and his interest aroused, by a very large man he discovers gazing at the windows of a "second-floor dine and dice emporium called Florian's ... with a sort of ecstatic fixity of expression, like a hunky immigrant catching his first sight of the Statue of Liberty" (p. 1). The large man means nothing, but his presence and his demeanor—"as inconspicuous as a tarantula on a piece of angel food" (p. 1)—ask questions: Who am I? Why am I here? Marlowe answers the first question in his description of the man as an archetypal American innocent, foolishly gaping at the symbol of his dreams and his desires. The figure mutely asks, Who am I? and Marlowe replies, You are a symbol of the dangerous American combination of ignorance and innocence. Neither Marlowe nor Chandler insists on this symbolic identification much further, but it does seem to explain and, in part, to justify Marlowe's interest in the man who turns out to be Moose Malloy, bank robber and ex-con: he is innocent and vulnerable in a way that appeals to Marlowe's imagination and his sympathies. The second question—Why am I here?—is, of course, harder to answer: most busy people, even those who might take the time to speculate on Malloy's meaning and his identity, would avoid it. Marlowe, however, opens himself to it with immediate, and astonishing, results:

> I walked along to the double doors and stood in front of them. They were motionless now. It wasn't any of my business. So I pushed them open and looked in.
> A hand I could have sat in came out of the dimness and took hold of my shoulder and squashed it to a pulp. Then the hand moved me through the doors and casually lifted me up a step. (p. 2)

The object of Marlowe's desultory interpretation has literally reached out and grabbed him: within two chapters Malloy will have killed a man and fled. The chase will be on.

Marlowe, then, is in on the Moose Malloy "case" before it involves a murder, but his presence has little effect on the first of the novel's crimes. This is not true for the other deaths in the book. Marlowe's interpretive activities produce something more than, and very different from, simple knowledge of previously existing facts; they produce murders.[16]

By following up on some remarks Moose made before his hasty flight, Marlowe upsets the balance of fear, money, knowledge, and power that keeps a lady's guilty secret hidden, and triggers a chain of events that leads to four otherwise perhaps avoidable deaths. The secret, briefly, is that the elegant and alluring young blonde, wife of elderly, ailing Mr. Lewin Lockridge Grayle, was once a cheap, redheaded saloon singer known as Velma Valento—Moose Malloy's "little Velma"—who got rid of her small-time crook boyfriend by informing on him to the police. One weak man knows the whole secret, and one drunken old woman knows part of it. When Marlowe starts poking around, the weak man must go. As Marlowe himself puts it to Mrs. Grayle in the book's final showdown,

> "And about that time a private dick starts nosing in also. So the weak link in the chain, Marriott, is no longer a luxury. He has become a menace. They'll get to him and they'll take him apart. He's that kind of lad. He melts under heat. So he was murdered before he could melt. With a blackjack. By you." (p. 239)

Mrs. Grayle is not alone with Marlowe at the showdown, however, and his exposition of "the facts" is more than the neat tying up of loose ends we expect at the end of a detective story. Out of motives that are never made clear, Marlowe has lured Malloy to his apartment, too, with predictable results.

> "I never thought," he said quietly. "It just came to me out of the blue. *You* turned me in to the cops. *You.* Little Velma."
> I threw a pillow, but it was too slow. She shot him five times in the stomach. The bullets made no more sound than fingers going into a glove. (p. 240)

Velma flees, only to be spotted by a detective in a Baltimore nightclub three months later. She kills him and then herself, bringing to four the number of deaths Marlowe's investigation has, at the very least, hastened.

And this is not all: since the beginning of his investigation Marlowe has been putting himself in mortal danger, both from those immediately involved in the Malloy–Velma story and from the other criminals—and cops—he crosses swords with. Velma saps him. Jules Amthor has him beaten up by a pair of Bay City cops. Sonderborg the drug doctor pumps him full of poison. Laird Brunette the mobster catches him snooping around his rusty tub of a gambling ship.

No stretch of the imagination, then, could allow us to call Marlowe's interpretation a neutral, simply instrumental act. It is, however, innocent, or at worst naive. Marlowe thinks he is motivated by simple curiosity,[17] but the moral aspects of the case pull him in to their complexities more slowly than, but just as surely as, Moose's large hand pulled him through the swinging doors of Florian's saloon.

Of course, Marlowe would scorn to label himself a "hermeneutical interpreter." It is nonetheless true that much of what distinguishes him and a few other "classic" detectives from their formalistic, potboiling confrères is his willingness to learn more than facts from his investigations and his vulnerability to the questions—and the dangers —they pose. Add to this Marlowe's ironic awareness of at least some of his own prejudices and his rudimentary sense of interpretation as a process of self-definition, and you have a rough sketch, at least, of a Gadamerian interpreter.

Marlowe's own interest in the case did not arise from hope for preferment or publicity. The facts take on meaning for him because he has already invested in them. " 'I liked the Moose,' " he says (p. 96), and he responds enough even to drunken Mrs. Florian to feel dirty after calling on her. As an alternative to the model of facts and exhibits brought together by a strictly professional investigator to form a coherent case, Marlowe, then, proposes by his own example a second model of interested interpretation. This version of detection includes two complementary actions, both of which have their counterpart in Gadamerian hermeneutics: listening—for and to—the "voice" of the case or text;[18] projecting one's assumptions about the case or text even as one listens for the voice and tries to make sense of the facts.

Marlowe listens intently for the voice of his case by opening himself to the challenges and the revelations it provides. So "open" is he, in fact, that he has been accused of passivity, of allowing his cases to solve themselves through coincidences and strokes of luck.[19] In Chandler, however, coincidences don't just happen. Marlowe puts himself in the right place at the right time and opens himself to them. Marlowe answers Marriott's call, listens to Anne Riordan's hypotheses, makes appointments with Mrs. Lewin Lockridge Grayle and Jules Amthor, always listening for some voice—not a set of facts but a human explanation, not a plot but a story—that will tell him how they fit together or show him that they don't.[20]

At the same time as Marlowe listens for a voice and a meaning, however, he also projects his preconceptions through his own distinctive voice and hears, in the end, a meaning that his beliefs predispose him to hear. Like Gadamer's reader of texts, Philip Marlowe cannot avoid prejudging everything he experiences, but like that reader, too, he is capable of adjusting his judgments the better to fit the text, the circumstances, the facts, or the voice that he hears. This is the process that Gadamer describes as the fusion of the "horizons" of the text and the interpreter.

We see Marlowe working toward this fusion most clearly in his language. Like all of us, Marlowe comes to terms with most of what happens to him through language, sometimes spoken, sometimes purely mental. His aggressively tough, "wise" language is more than a reflection of his world or his personality: it is a means of dominating that world by defining it in his own terms.

This is the language, in the first place, of a man who knows how things are and assumes—even insists—that his reader-interlocutors see them as he does: "It was one of the mixed blocks over on Central Avenue, the blocks that are not yet all Negro" (p. 1). "Ah, one of *those* blocks," the ideal reader nods in recognition as he[21] transports himself to an imaginary Los Angeles in which he knows just as well what things are like "over on Central Avenue" as Marlowe does. This is the language of authority, too, the language of an acute, informed observer:

> He had a battered face that looked as if it had been hit by everything but the bucket of a dragline. It was scarred, flattened, thickened, checkered, and welted. It was a face that had nothing to fear. Everything had been done to it that anybody could think of.
> The short crinkled hair had a touch of gray. One ear had lost the lobe.
> The Negro was heavy and wide. He had big heavy legs and they looked a little bowed, which is unusual in a Negro. (p. 4)

From observing the beaten bouncer to speculating about his past to issuing a general statement on his race's skeletal features, this description asserts that it knows its subject well.

Marlowe's language also distances the observer from everything he observes: its turns of phrase express admiration, perhaps, or amusement, but always distance, too, a distance Marlowe creates for himself and shares with his reader:

> He was a big man but not more than six feet five inches tall and not wider than a beer truck. (p. 1)

> The house itself was not so much. It was smaller than Buckingham Palace, rather gray for California, and probably had fewer windows than the Chrysler Building. (p. 103)

"She's a nice girl. Not my type [," I said.]
"You don't like them nice?" He had another cigarette going. The smoke was being fanned away from his face by his hand.
"I like smooth shiny girls, hardboiled and loaded with sin."
"They take you to the cleaners," Randall said indifferently.
"Sure. Where else have I ever been?" (pp. 166–167)

Like Dupin, Marlowe derives his authority, in part, from his practical knowledge and his power of observation. In addition, Marlowe regularly risks his life and his reputation in the service of what he believes is the truth. Finally, as a first-person narrator, Marlowe can establish and maintain an ironic distance from everyone and everything he encounters. Through his language, he projects the kind of world that his kinds of skills and talents are best suited to interpret, a hollow, hypocritical world, full of people whose pretenses are ripe for deflating with a well-aimed wisecrack, and/or whose hidden virtues (fidelity and love in Moose; final self-sacrifice in Velma) can be perceived by the cynical, worldly-wise private eye.

But this world talks back to Marlowe, too, and whereas the often sentimental content of the backtalk is perhaps the single weakest element of Chandler's novels, the fact that there is any room at all for backtalk in the story of Marlowe's investigations makes them all the more seductive to the reader. It creates the clear and appealing impression that Philip Marlowe, for all his hard-boiled toughness and savvy, is fallible and even vulnerable, and it helps us to see his interpretive process as a dialogic investigation rather than the application of a method.

The clearest bit of sentimental backtalk occurs at the end of the novel when hard-boiled Velma sacrifices herself—perhaps—for her pitiful husband. Marlowe greets the event by retreating far enough from his habitual hard-boiled wisecracks to quote, of all things, *Othello:*

"I'm not saying she was a saint or even a halfway nice girl. Not ever. She wouldn't kill herself until she was cornered. But what she did and the way she did it, kept her from coming back here for trial. Think that over. And who would that trial hurt most? Who would be the least able to bear it? And win, lose, or draw, who would pay the biggest price for the show? An old man who had loved not wisely, but too well." (p. 249)

From Semiotics to Hermeneutics

Randall demurs—"'That's just sentimental'"—and Marlowe retreats—"'Sure. It sounded like that when I said it'"—but the possibility of a different kind of world from the one Marlowe has been projecting is at least raised.

Marlowe's encounter with Red raises a similar possibility. It begins with a typical round of tough-guy linguistic one-upmanship, which gradually modulates into the language of mutual trust between two little opponents of big-time corruption:

> The light was dim and mostly behind him. "What's the matter, pardner?" he drawled. "No soap on the hell ship?"
> "Go darn your shirt," I told him. "Your belly is sticking out."
> "Could be worse," he said. "The gat's kind of bulgy under the light suit at that."
> "What pulls your nose into it?"
> "Jesus, nothing at all. Just curiosity. No offense, pal."
> "Well, get the hell out of my way then."
> "Sure. I'm just resting here."
> He smiled a slow tired smile. His voice was soft, dreamy, so delicate for a big man that it was startling. It made me think of another soft-voiced big man I had strangely liked.
> "You got the wrong approach," he said sadly. "Just call me Red."
> "Step aside, Red. The best people make mistakes. I feel one crawling up my back." (pp. 208–209)

Marlowe here insists on being hostile while Red alternates between responding in kind and offering his help. By the end of their furtive trip out to Laird Brunette's gambling ship, however, they are comrades in arms, seedy ex-cops united against the world:

> "Good-by," I said.
> "Maybe you need a little help."
> I shook myself like a wet dog. "I need a company of marines. But either I do it alone or I don't do it. So long."
> "How long will you be?" His voice still sounded worried.
> "An hour or less."
> He stared at me and chewed his lip. Then he nodded. "Sometimes a guy has to," he said. "Drop by that bingo parlor, if you get time."
> (p. 250)

The sentimentality may ring a little false here, but the pattern of the challenge to Marlowe's preconceptions is clear enough.

One of Raymond Chandler's great ambitions was to raise the detective novel to the level of literature by focusing its readers' attention on language and character and on "what the hell happened" rather than on the simple question of who done it. He achieved his ambition by moving away from semiotics toward hermeneutics, away from the methodical *solution* of "mysteries" toward the philosophical understanding of mystery. Holmes or Dupin could have discovered that Little Velma and Mrs. Grayle were one and the same in far less time than it takes Philip Marlowe. They would have dissipated a mystery by discovering a fact. Marlowe also discovers a fact, but he leaves the mystery of Velma's character and her motivations, as well as the much more vexed and vexing mystery of the sources of evil in the world, explored but unsolved. Doyle's readers and the readers of "The Murders in the Rue Morgue" are given reassuring examples of the power of human reason to make sense of the world. Chandler shows his readers just how little they learn from the results of such neat interpretation and what depths of mystery the process of interpretation can reveal.

NOTES

1. Arthur Conan Doyle, *The Original Illustrated Sherlock Holmes* (Secaucus, N.J.: Castle Books, 1981), p. 97; hereafter cited in the text.
2. Cf., e.g., " 'When I hear you give your reasons,' I remarked, 'the thing always appears to me so ridiculously simple that I could easily do it myself, though at each successive instance of your reasoning I am baffled, until you explain your process' " from "A Scandal in Bohemia," p. 12, or "Mr. Jabez Wilson laughed heavily. 'Well, I never!' said he. 'I thought at first that you had done something clever, but I see that there was nothing in it after all.' 'I begin to think, Watson,' said Holmes, 'that I make a mistake in explaining' " from "The Red-Headed League," p. 27.
3. The similarities between this method and Freudian dream interpretation are striking and have been widely noted. See, for example, the pieces by Hartman and Hutter in this volume.
4. This is a slightly simplified version of a diagram used by Roman Jakobson in "Linguistics and Poetics," in *Style in Language,* edited by T. Sebeok (Cambridge, Mass.: MIT Press, 1960), p. 353.
5. See for example his description of a card game in "The Murders in the Rue Morgue," *The Portable Poe,* edited by Philip Van Doren Stern (New York: Penguin, 1945), pp. 334–336. Subsequent references to Poe will be to this edition and will be cited in the text.

6. John Walsh examines the story and its sources in detail in his *Poe the Detective* (New Brunswick, N.J.: Rutgers University Press, 1968). See also William K. Wimsatt, Jr., "Poe and the Mystery of Mary Rogers," *PMLA* 56 (1941), pp. 230–248.
7. "The Purloined Letter" would be the only other choice. In his "Seminar on 'The Purloined Letter,' " reprinted in this volume, Jacques Lacan shows how Poe cheats in this story.
8. Samuel Taylor Coleridge, in *Specimens of the Table Talk of the late Samuel Taylor Coleridge* (New York: Harper and Bros., 1853), p. 518 (entry for June 23, 1834).
9. *Ibid.*, p. 518.
10. For a systematic description of the variations within the mode, see Tzvetan Todorov, "Typologie du roman policier" in *Poétique de la prose* (Paris: Seuil, 1971).
11. Stephen Knight, *Form and Ideology in Crime Fiction* (Bloomington: Indiana University Press, 1980), p. 44.
12. David I. Grossvogel, *Mystery and its Fictions: From Oedipus to Agatha Christie* (Baltimore: Johns Hopkins University Press, 1979), p. 14.
13. Hans-Georg Gadamer, *Truth and Method* (New York: Continuum, 1975), p. 411; hereafter cited in the text.
14. Dorothy Gardiner and Kathrine Sorley Walker, *Raymond Chandler Speaking* (Boston: Houghton Mifflin, 1977), p. 57. For critical corroboration see Peter J. Rabinowitz, "Rats Behind the Wainscoting: Politics, Convention, and Chandler's The Big Sleep," *TSLL*, 22 (1980), pp. 224–245, and Fredric Jameson, "On Raymond Chandler," reprinted in this volume.
15. Raymond Chandler, *Farewell, My Lovely* (New York: Ballantine, 1971), p. 1; hereafter cited in the text.
16. Cf. Jameson, p. 143: "In fact, Chandler's stories are first and foremost descriptions of searches, in which murder is involved, and which sometimes end with the murder of the person sought for. The immediate result of this formal change is that the detective no longer inhabits the atmosphere of pure thought, of puzzle solving and the resolution of a set of given elements."
17. "Nothing made it my business except curiosity" (p. 15).
18. "It is more than a metaphor to describe the work of hermeneutics as a conversation with the text." *Truth and Method*, p. 331.
19. See Knight, *Form and Ideology*, p. 151.
20. That he also listens, in a maudlin, self-pitying way, to the voice of despair in his own life and the tawdry world he moves in may make him less appealing as a character, but can only support our definition of him as a listener. See *Farewell*, p. 201.
21. Chandler seems to assume a male reader. See Knight on Chandler's female characters, pp. 157ff.

SOURCE REFERENCES

Roger Callois, Part II, "Le roman policier: jeu," from Chapter IV, "Puissances du roman," *Approches de l'Imaginaire* (Paris: Editions Gallimard, 1974). Originally published as "Le Roman Policier. II: Jeu," *Puissances du roman* (Buenos Aires: Sur, 1941).

Geraldine Pederson-Krag, "Detective Stories and the Primal Scene," *The Psychoanalytic Quarterly* 18 (1949), pp. 207–214.

Jacques Lacan, "Seminar on 'The Purloined Letter,'" *Yale French Studies* 48 *(French Freud. Structural Studies in Psychoanalysis)* (1973), pp. 39–72. Originally published in Lacan's *Écrits* (Paris: Seuil, 1966).

Ernst Kaemmel, "Literatur unterm Tisch. Der Detektivroman und sein gesellschaftlicher Auftrag," *Neue Deutsche Literatur* 10 (1962), pp. 152–156.

Richard Alewyn, "Der Ursprung des Detektivromans," *Probleme und Gestalten* (Frankfurt/Main: Insel, 1974).

Helmut Heissenbüttel, "Spielregeln des Kriminalromans," *Aufsätze zur Literatur* (Stuttgart: Ernst Klett Verlag).

Umberto Eco, "Narrative Structures in Fleming," *The Role of the Reader: Explorations in the Semiotics of Texts,* translated by R. A. Downie (Bloomington and London: Indiana University Press, 1979), pp. 144–163. Originally published as "Le strutture narrative in Fleming," *Il caso Bond,* ed. O. Del Buono and U. Eco (Milan: Bompiani, 1965).

Roland Barthes, *S/Z,* sections XXXII and XXXVII, translated by Richard Miller (New York: Hill and Wang, 1974). Originally published as *S/Z* (Paris: Seuil, 1970).

F. R. Jameson, "On Raymond Chandler," *Southern Review* 6 (1970), pp. 624–650.

Michael Holquist, "Whodunit and Other Questions: Metaphysical Detective Stories in Post-War Fiction," *New Literary History* 3 (1971–1972), pp. 135–156.

Frank Kermode, "Novel and Narrative," *Theory of the Novel: New Essays,* ed. John Halperin (New York: Oxford University Press, 1974), pp. 155–174.

Steven Marcus, "Introduction" to *The Continental Op* by Dashiell Hammett (New York: Random House, 1974), pp. xv–xxix.

Geoffrey H. Hartman, "Literature High and Low: The Case of the Mystery Story," *The Fate of Reading and Other Essays* (Chicago and London: University of Chicago Press, 1975), pp. 203–222.

Albert D. Hutter, "Dreams, Transformations and Literature: The Implications of Detective Fiction," *Victorian Studies* 19 (1975), pp. 181–209.

David I. Grossvogel, "Agatha Christie: Containment of the Unknown," *Mystery and its Fictions: From Oedipus to Agatha Christie* (Baltimore: John Hopkins University Press, 1979), pp. 39–52.

Stephen Knight, "'. . . some men come up'—the Detective appears," *Form and Ideology in Crime Fiction* (Bloomington: Indiana University Press, 1980), pp. 8–37. (Also London: Macmillan, 1980)

D. A. Miller, "The Novel and the Police," *Glyph* 8, ed. by Walter Benn Michaels (Baltimore: Johns Hopkins University Press, 1981), pp. 127–147.

Dennis Porter, "Backward Construction and the Art of Suspense," *The Pursuit of Crime* (New Haven: Yale University Press, 1981), pp. 47–52.

SUGGESTIONS FOR FURTHER READING

Three recently published bibliographies have facilitated the task of locating secondary material on detective fiction. Rather than printing a necessarily brief selection from them, we here merely suggest a few starting places, and urge interested readers to consult the bibliographies themselves if they need more material. One is *Crime Fiction Criticism: An Annotated Bibliography,* edited by Timothy W. Johnson and Julia Johnson (New York: Garland, 1981); it is sensibly annotated and especially useful for finding discussions of particular authors and works. The second, *Crime, Detective, Espionage, Mystery, and Thriller Fiction and Film: A Comprehensive Bibliography of Critical Writing Through 1979,* edited by David Skene Melvin and Ann Skene Melvin (Westport, Conn.: Greenwood, 1980) is more exhaustive, especially for foreign studies, but not at all informative about the content of individual pieces. The third is *What About Murder: A Guide to Mystery and Detective Fiction,* edited by Jon L. Breen (Metuchen, N.J., 1981).

Most of the classic essays in the field have been conveniently collected by Robin Winks in his *Detective Fiction: A Collection of Critical Essays* (Englewood Cliffs, N.J.: Prentice-Hall, 1980). Here the reader will find the basic studies by W. H. Auden, Edmund Wilson, Dorothy Sayers, Jacques Barzun, and Julian Symons, as well as more recent important work by such critics as Gavin Lambert, George Grella, and John Cawelti. Another collection of essays, which could serve as a transition between the classic period and our own, was published in a special issue of the magazine *Chimera* (vol. 5, no. 4, Summer 1947). For those who read French, the Parisian journal *Littérature* has announced a forthcoming special issue devoted to previously unpublished essays on detective fiction and edited by Uri Eisenzweig.

Readers interested in the history of detective fiction will enjoy Julian Symons' *Mortal Consequences: A History—From the Detective Story to the Crime Novel* (New York: Harper and Row, 1972) as well as Howard Haycraft's classic *Murder for Pleasure: The Life and Times of the Detective Story* (New York: D. Appleton Century, 1941).

A good general reference book is *A Catalogue of Crime*, by Jacques Barzun and Wendell Hertig Taylor (New York: Harper and Row, 1971), and a useful compendium of critical and biographical essays can be found in *Twentieth Century Crime and Mystery Writers*, edited by John M. Reilly (New York, 1980).

Many of the pieces reprinted in the present anthology are parts of longer works, which we urge our readers to read in full. Others are representative essays by writers who have more to say about the genre elsewhere. Three recent works which we have not excerpted but which bear looking into are Robert Champigny's *What Will Have Happened* (Bloomington: Indiana University Press, 1977), an extended formal analysis of the mystery novel; Jerry Palmer's *Thrillers* (New York: St. Martin's, 1979), a sometimes illuminating, sometimes opaque study of the relations between a popular genre and the society that produces it; and Robin Winks's *Modus Operandi* (Boston: Godine, 1982), a quirky personal essay that many readers will find charming.

INDEX

Alewyn, Richard, 55, 79, 149, 197, 211, 266, 299
Allingham, Margery, 67, 90
Amis, Kingsley, 98
Anders, Gunther, 152
Andersch, Alfred, 219, 221
Antonioni, Michelangelo, 213, 215
Aristotle, 211–12, 330–31
Auden, W. H., xi, 160
Auerbach, Erich, 275
Austen, Jane, 282–83
Austin, Hugh, 10

Bakhtin, Mikhail, 319
Balzac, Honoré de, 75; *Les Chouans (The Chouans)*, 322; *La Peau de Chagrin (The Wild Ass's Skin)*, 216; *Le Père Goriot (Old Goriot)*, 319–20, 323; *La Rabouilleuse (The Bachelor's House)*, 322; *Sarrasine*, 190–92, 195; *Une Ténébreuse Affaire (Murky Business)*, 316–18, 321–22
Barthes, Roland, 122, 171, 175, 186, 188, 189–92, 195, 273, 327
Barzun, Jacques, 154
Baudelaire, Charles, 41, 46
Bellak, Leopold, 14
Benjamin, Walter, 85–87, 152, 351
Benson, Ben, 90

Bentham, Jeremy, 313
Bentley, A. C., 180–85
Bergler, Edmund, 14, 15, 19, 245
Bergman, Ingmar, 215
Berkeley, Anthony, 86
Bierce, Ambrose, 81
Blake, Nicholas. *See* Lewis, C. Day
Bloch, Ernst, 66, 83–84, 85
Bogart, Humphrey, 140, 198, 346
Bonaparte, Marie, 17
Borges, Jorge Luis, 165, 171–73, 213
Braddon, Mary Elizabeth, 322
Brentano, Clemens, 74
Breton, André, 216
Brooks, Cleanth, 179
Brown, Carter, 80
Browne, Sir Thomas, 344–45
Browning, Robert, 237
Buchan, John, 355–56
Butor, Michel, 186–88
Buxbaum, Edith, 15

Caillois, Roger, 79, 300
Campbell, Joseph, 295
Camus, Albert, 214
Carr, John Dickson, 86, 162
Catnach, James, 268
Chadwick, Mary, 19
Chandler, Raymond, 67, 81, 86, 122–48, 163, 222–28, 346, 357, 363–64; *The Big Sleep*, 140,

Chandler (cont.)
147, 223, 227, 332–38, 352–53, 362; *Farewell, My Lovely,* 222, 227, 375–82; *The Lady in the Lake,* 354; *The Little Sister,* 342; *The Long Goodbye,* 131; "The Simple Art of Murder," 220
Chase, James Hadley, 81, 163
Chesterton, G. K., 67, 80, 86, 87–88, 172
Cheyney, Peter, 80
Chrétien de Troyes, 178, 179, 189, 192, 195
Christie, Agatha, 57, 60, 67, 86, 89, 159, 162, 164, 165, 171, 252–65, 346, 357; *The ABC Murders,* 7; *Murder in Mesopotamia,* 84–85; *The Murder of Roger Ackroyd,* 8; *Murder on the Orient Express,* 84–85, 88; *The Mysterious Affair at Styles,* 253–65
Coleridge, Samuel Taylor, 371
Collingford, Guy, 90
Collins, Wilkie, 162, 231–51, 321, 322, 334, 338
Conrad, Joseph, 193–94
Cooper, James Fenimore, 296
Crofts, Freeman Wills, 67

Defoe, Daniel, 268
Dekker, Thomas, 154
Dickens, Charles, 75, 155; *Bleak House,* 58, 235, 236; *David Copperfield,* 244; *Great Expectations,* 244; *The Mystery of Edwin Drood,* 58, 237;

Oliver Twist, 278, 302–08, 320, 323
Doderer, Heimito von, 145
Dorfles, Gillo, 151
Doyle, Sir Arthur Conan, 14, 19, 58, 60, 63, 67, 70, 77, 80, 86, 231–32, 327, 346, 351–52, 357, 367–70, 382; "The Adventure of the Naval Treaty," 354; "The Adventure of the Speckled Band," 4; "A Case of Identity," 369–70; "His Last Bow," 354; *The Hound of the Baskervilles,* 158–59, 334, 339; *A Study in Scarlet,* 240
Dumas, Alexandre, 296
Du Maurier, Daphne, 57

Eagleton, Terry, 284
Eco, Umberto, 1, 79, 327, 330
Eichendorff, Joseph von, 74
Eliot, George, 282–83, 314–15, 318–19, 320, 323
Eliot, T. S., 161, 178
Ellin, Stanley, 91
Elvestad, Sven, 81
Erikson, Erik, 205
Euripides, 212

Faulkner, William, 133, 214
Fenichel, Otto, 15–16, 17
Flaubert, Gustave, 318, 323
Fleming, Ian, 93–117, 353; *Casino Royale,* 94–96, 99, 102, 105; *Diamonds Are Forever,* 99–100, 104, 109–12; *Dr. No,* 98, 100–101, 103, 109; *From Russia With Love,* 100, 103,

115; *Goldfinger,* 101, 103, 105, 109; *Live and Let Die,* 99, 102; *The Man with the Golden Gun,* 95, 98; *Moonraker,* 100, 102–103, 105, 108; *On Her Majesty's Secret Service,* 100–102, 104, 109; "Risico," 100; *Thunderball,* 98, 101, 104; *You Only Live Twice,* 100, 101, 104, 107
Flora, Fletscher, 91
Fontane, Theodor, 57
Foucault, Michel, 312–14
Frazer, Sir James, 161
Freud, Sigmund, xiv, 16, 18–19, 21–54 *passim,* 161, 214–15, 230–31, 249–51, 312

Gaboriau, Emile, 318–19
Gadamer, Hans-Georg, xv, 373–75, 378–79
Gardner, Erle Stanley, 57, 67, 82, 86, 89
Gide, André, 214, 300
Godwin, William, 267, 279–88, 292, 293
Gould, Chester, 153
Greenberg, Clement, 150
Greene, Graham, 163
Greene, Robert, 267–68
Grossvogel, David, 1, 62, 211, 367, 373

Hambledon, Phyllis, 90
Hamilton, Donald, 163
Hammett, Dashiell, 81, 86, 163, 197–209, 346, 352, 357; *The Continental Op,* 201–209; *The Dain Curse,* 203; *The Maltese Falcon,* 203, 226; *Red Harvest,* 333; *The Thin Man,* 87
Harte, Bret, 81
Hartman, Geoffrey, 13, 230, 252
Haworth, Peter, 153–54
Head, Richard, 268
Heissenbüttel, Helmut, 1
Hemingway, Ernest, 61, 133, 138–39, 140, 338
Himes, Chester, 81
Hirsch, E. D., 373
Hoffmann, E. T. A., 71–78
Hottinger, Mary, 82
Huston, John, 198
Hutter, Albert D., 13

Innes, Michael. *see* Stewart, J. I. M.

James, Henry, 192–93, 213, 214, 225, 282–83, 284
Jameson, F. R., 79, 197, 366
Johnson, Barbara, 21
Joyce, James, 161, 164

Kaemmel, Ernst, 62, 252, 266, 299
Kaul, Friedrich Karl, 61
Kelly, Gary, 285
Ker, W. P., 177–78, 179
Kerényi, Karoly, 161
Kermode, Frank, 118
Kirkman, Francis, 155
Knight, Stephen, 56, 62, 79, 122, 197, 299, 373

Lacan, Jacques, 13, 122, 211
Lawrence, D. H., 184, 194–95

Lawson, Lewis A., 245
Leblanc, Maurice, 8
le Carré, John, 95, 163, 353–64; *Call for the Dead*, 357–58; *The Honourable Schoolboy*, 356; *The Looking-Glass War*, 356; *A Murder of Quality*, 357–59; *A Small Town in Germany*, 362–64; *Smiley's People*, 353, 356; *The Spy Who Came In from the Cold*, 361–62; *Tinker, Tailor, Soldier, Spy*, 359–60
Leroux, Gaston, 4, 8
Lewis, C. Day (pseud. Nicholas Blake), 159, 160–61
Links, J. G., 10, 166–67
Lockridge, Frances and Richard, 86, 90
Löwenthal, Heinrich, 57
Lukes, Steven, 279–80

MacDonald, John D., 163
Macdonald, Ross, 163, 220, 223–28, 346, 352; *The Chill*, 212, 216, 226–28; *The Goodbye Look*, 224, 226–27; *The Underground Man*, 216–17, 221–22, 227–28
Macherey, Pierre, 273, 329
Mahler, Margaret S., 17
Mailer, Norman, 215, 218
Mann, Thomas, 57, 161, 163, 172
Mannoni, Octave, 312
Manolescu, Georgiu Mercadente, 57
Marc, Marcel, 2
Marcus, Steven, 79, 122
Marx, Karl, 205–6, 297

Maupassant, Guy de, 323
Mehlman, Jeffrey, 21–23
Melville, Herman, 213, 228
Merivale, Patricia, 171
Merrill, P. J., 90, 91
Messac, Régis, 154, 267
Millar, Margaret, 91
Miller, D. A., 62, 79, 122, 197
Muir, Thomas, 90
Murch, A. E., 154

Nabokov, Vladimir, 124, 139, 171
Neville, Margot, 86, 90
Newgate Calendar, The, 267–81, 285, 288, 290, 293–97
Nielsen, Helen, 90–91
Nietzsche, Friedrich, 208
Novalis (Friedrich von Hardenberg), 74

O'Neill, Eugene, 134
Oppenheim, E. Phillips, 153
Ousby, Ian, 295

Pascal, Blaise, 324
Patrick, Quentin, 8
Pederson-Krag, Geraldine, 211, 230, 245–46
Pitaval, François Gayot de, 73
Poe, Edgar Allan, 19, 67, 75, 77, 155–57, 172, 231–32, 297, 327–28, 346, 351, 382; "The Murders in the Rue Morgue," 4, 58, 63, 69, 73, 78, 80, 232, 328, 343–45, 371–73; "The Mystery of Marie Roget," 78, 370–71; "The Purloined

Letter," 21–54 *passim,* 78, 232, 354, 373; "Thou Art the Man," 78
Poggioli, Renato, 151
Porter, Dennis, 118, 366
Proust, Marcel, 125
Pynchon, Thomas, 215, 218–19

Queen, Ellery, 7, 10, 56, 67, 80, 171
Queneau, Raymond, 185, 191

Radcliffe, Ann, 216
Radtke, Günter, 61
Raglan, Lord Fitz Roy R. S., 295
Resnais, Alain, 214, 221
Robbe-Grillet, Alain, 87, 164–66, 173, 178, 191, 193, 195, 212; *L'Année Dernière à Marienbad (Last Year at Marienbad),* 221; *Dans le labyrinthe (In the Labyrinth),* 124; *Les Gommes (The Erasers),* 124, 145, 172, 185–86, 214–15; *La Maison de Rendez-vous (La Maison de Rendez-vous),* 124; *Le Voyeur (The Voyeur),* 124, 167–71
Rodell, Marie F., 59
Ross, Ivan T., 90, 91
Rousseau, Jean-Jacques, 292
Rycroft, Charles, 245

Sarraute, Nathalie, 164–65
Sayers, Dorothy, 60, 66, 67, 86, 87–88, 159, 162, 163, 267
Scherf, Margaret, 86, 90
Schreyer, Wolfgang, 61
Settle, Elkanah, 155

Shklovsky, Viktor, 331
Simenon, Georges, 67, 80, 89–90
Sophocles, 154, 211–12, 216, 228, 250, 252–53
Spillane, Mickey, 57, 80
Sproul, Kathleen, 10
Steeman, Stanislas-André, 2, 10
Stein, Gertrude, 125–26
Stendhal (Henri Beyle), 314
Sterne, Laurence, 330
Stevens, Wallace, 174
Stevenson, Robert Louis, 57
Stewart, J. I. M., 159, 162
Stout, Rex, 67, 159
Sue, Eugene, 57, 75, 297, 323

Taylor, W. H., 154
Terrail, Ponson du, 323
Tieck, Ludwig, 74
Todorov, Tzvetan, 250–51
Tomashevsky, Boris, 330
Trollope, Anthony, 308–312, 320–21, 323
Twain, Mark, 81

Upfield, Arthur W., 86

Van Dine, S. S., 2, 6
Véry, Pierre, 5
Vidocq, Eugène François, 154–55, 267, 288–97
Vinaver, Eugène, 178–79

Wallace, Edgar, 4, 80
Walpole, Horace, 217
Weber, Max, 207
Weston, Jessie L., 161, 178
Wheatley, Dennis, 10, 166–67

Wilden, Anthony, 21
Wilson, Angus, 285
Wilson, Edmund, xi, 217
Wordsworth, William, 213–14

Zinneman, Fred, 338
Zola, Emile, 127, 315–16
Zulliger, Hans, 14